re.EVOLUTION

Mr. Guido Baechler

Copyright © 2018 Mr. Guido Baechler
All rights reserved.

ISBN: 1986499903
ISBN 13: 9781986499903
Library of Congress Control Number: **XXXXX (If applicable)**
LCCN Imprint Name: **City and State (If applicable)**

Guido wishes to thank many contributors to this book:

A special thanks to Christian Boeving who is an actor and body building professional. Thank you Christian for whipping my butt into shape more than 2 decades ago, changing my life forever and making a huge impact. Thank you for bringing the movie script R(e)Volution / R(e)Evolution to me and letting completely reinvent the early zombie film idea to a very evolved book. While this story has virtually nothing in common with the original idea, it was R(e)Evolution which jump started this 12-year-long project. For that I thank you.

I wish to also thank Andy Attenhofer (Gian Andrea Attenhofer), my dear friend and movie director for working with me on the "Cause & Effect" movie script, creating essential story plots and turning points. Thanks also to Peter Bean, a Hollywood script writer, who refined "Cause & Effect" into R(e)Evolution film script version 5.2. (yes... there have been many film script versions).

My love goes out to my wife Monika for being married to me 25 years and putting up with my many exciting storytelling and plot line-outs. In the past 3 years she has contributed much to certain essential ideas in the book, which I can't reveal without spoiler alerts. I can truly say this was a family project. When I wrote the character Tim, I pictured my older son Pierce Nathan-Calvin as Tim and in the storyline's flashbacks, my younger son Sebastian Ethan-Lucas as younger Tim. This is a special thanks to my family for waiting patiently to read the book until this story was released. I love you all!

I can't forget to mention Joel Mark Harris. A friendship has grown through the process of creating this book. I met Joel through a movie project called "Neutral Territory" on which he was the producer. Writing countless books and novels, Joel has received several awards for his story telling. I lived in Canada during the time I was looking for a ghost writer.

Joel who is born in Canada and resides on the West Coast embraced the idea of writing a new version of R(e)Evolution / Cause & Effect.

But more started happening and I realized I could tap into the huge imagination pot Joel has. Instead of hiring him as my ghost writer I decided to make him my full partner in this story. It was quit scary at the beginning, because I was worried he would take the story and miss the point, butcher it or deviate too much from all my ideas. But I was wrong. After many awesome brain storming hours together, over great food and wine, Joel incorporated all my story ideas and wrote the story better than I ever could have. Once version xxx-something-something was written we massaged the story line, the plots and details together to make sure you get a very entertaining read. Not only did I get an awesome book but I gained a friend for life. Thank you very much for believing in me and my story.

I wish to thank Jenny Paris for the exciting book cover and Maik van Epple for the amazing illustration inside the book. My love goes out to my wife Monika Baechler, lic. nutritionist for the "medical" fact based input during the story line. Alex Jones, Ken Jebsen and Dr. Daniele Ganser are all activists and plot lines have been inspired through them. Gilles Tschudi (Dr. Albert Winkler), Swiss actor, for his early work on a teaser trailer and countless support. Also Ewan McGregor for being the lead character's inspiration.

My mother Maria and my father Leo for giving me a great childhood and bond for life.

Joel wishes to thank:

Although I came late to the party, I have had a lot of fun playing in Guido's world. What drew me to this story was the characters and especially the bond between Ewan and Tim. I would like to thank Guido for this opportunity and for always believing in me.

I would also like to thank my family, my parents especially, for always being there, even when they thought I was crazy. Having a loving and supporting family makes all the difference in the world.

We are working hard on the second book while you are reading the first book and start of this book trilogy.

Stay tuned for the television mini series produced by Jeridoo Universe.

Book One: The Humans

The Museum

Ewan Walder woke up with a start. He opened his eyes, waiting for his sight to adjust to the darkness but no shapes came. The black void seemed to stretch on and on and on.

He shifted his weight slightly, listening to the sounds of the museum. He was always stunned by how buildings could groan and grunt despite being deserted. The different wind patterns and the rain played musically on the glass and brick. Soon the snow would come and bring the biting cold.

What was the month? September? October? Judging by the trees splattered in colourful pastel reds, browns and yellows, it was autumn but winter was hurling, tirelessly towards them and like an angry freight train would soon overtake them.

Ewan could sense the body beside him. He could tell his son, Tim, was also awake from his shallow breathing.

Ewan lay there, not moving, staring up at the dark ceiling. He could hear the soft patter of footsteps. Did he actually hear something or was it just his imagination? His nightmare?

"Dad, did you hear that?" Tim asked. His voice echoed across the cavernous room.

Ewan slowly sat up, rubbing his forehead. He felt groggy, lightheaded. He heard a sound again, a soft scuttle, like tiny feet crossing a pipe. He was sure it was real this time. No, not exactly a scuttle. It was heavier.

"Damn it. They're in," Ewan said. He reached his hand out to the left of his mattress, groping for the matches. He finally enclosed his hands on a small box and fumbled to get a match out. His hands were shaking now.

No need to be afraid, he told himself. *I'm fine. I'm fine.*

Ewan finally managed to strike a match illuminating the room in a pale light.

"I'm going to go check it out," Tim said, standing up quickly, much too quickly.

Ewan examined his son. Sometimes he reminded Ewan of a beaten dog. He had lost a lot of weight, loose skin hung around his cheeks and neck. His scraggily hair fell across his caramel-coloured forehead. Yet something in his young, wide eyes still held the promise of tomorrow. His body had grown old; his eyes had not.

"No, no, you stay here," Ewan said.

But Tim had already managed to find the flashlight and turn it on. He pointed the light, searching the room. Against the wall were eerie mannequins standing in a row like centurions.

Guarding what? Ewan wondered. They certainly didn't offer any protection, just a constant reminder that time was marching forward, slowly without haste.

Tim's flashlight moved to the right where there was a woolly mammoth standing in the corner, its mouth gapping as if it was being attacked by some unseen predator.

"We need to move right now," Ewan said, finally finding his backpack. "Right now."

"Nah," Tim said. "Don't worry. If it was one of them we'd be dead by now. It's probably just a stray dog."

"Timmy, you know there aren't any stray dogs left."

But Tim had already moved unhurriedly towards the exit.

"Tim, don't" Ewan pleaded. His voice sounded hollow and shaky even to his own ears.

"Chill Dad. I've got ol' Bessy here to protect me." Tim showed Ewan the old revolver they had found on a corpse several years ago.

"That's what I'm afraid of," Ewan replied, getting up.

Ewan wondered in what type of world a twelve-year-old needed to carry a revolver. But the answer quickly came to him: in this crazy, God-forsaken one.

Tim rolled his eyes at his father and put the revolver back in his pocket. He headed towards the door.

"Timmy, get back this moment," Ewan whispered.

Tim just turned and stared at him with his large child-like eyes. "Lighten up. Don't be such a party pooper."

Ewan took a step towards Tim, intending to stop him, but Tim ran ahead, into the darkness.

"Damn it," Ewan said to himself.

Ewan followed Tim through the doorway. He was in a long, wide hallway. He couldn't see more than several feet in front of him. Ewan lit another match. Once priceless paintings hung on either side of the walls but now they truly had no price. There was no one left to buy them.

Ewan walked down the corridor. His match slowly burned and then extinguished, forcing him back into darkness.

Was Tim right? If it was one of those Creatures then would they be dead already? They seemed to have an uncanny ability to sense when a person was close.

Ewan reached a large room but it was completely black. Where was Tim's light? Had the battery died?

"Timmy?" Ewan yelled out into the darkness. His voice reverberated off the ceiling and walls. If the Creatures were inside then they would surely come for him now. And he was defenceless.

"Tim?" Ewan yelled again, edging his way through the darkness. "Timmy? Where are you?"

No, I can't lose you too, he thought. *I can't. If there is a God, please...*

Ewan felt for the wall with his left hand. Should he light another match? Could the Creatures see in the dark? He didn't know. He didn't know a lot about them. He only had a few matches to spare therefore decided to save them. They were hard to come by.

Suddenly a Creature moved from within the darkness. Ewan's first thought was to turn and run but he needed to protect Tim.

Protect the kids, Amy had told him.

"Okay, Amy. Okay," Ewan said.

The large shadow shifted and Ewan ran towards the Creature, ready to pounce but as he got closer, Creature turned into the familiar outline of Tim.

"Boo," Tim said, giggling.

Ewan stopped and frowned, trying to calm his racing heart.

Tim flipped on his flashlight. The glow hurt Ewan's eyes.

"I scared you," Tim said.

Ewan faltered. "Jesus, Timmy. Why'd you do that?"

"Come on, admit it. You were scared shitless."

"Watch your language."

"You just swore. Why can't I swear?"

Ewan frowned. He needed to be careful around Tim but when he was the only one to talk to it was hard to remember he still needed to teach him about growing up. "Because I'm an adult," Ewan said.

"It was a rat," Tim said, explicitly.

"You sure?"

"Of course."

Ewan suddenly became angry. "Give me the gun."

Tim shook his head. "No."

Ewan put out his hand. "Just give it to me."

Tim just rolled his eyes again and took out the gun and gave it to Ewan.

"I'm tired of this John Wayne stuff," Ewan said. "You think you're going to kill them all?"

"Who's John Wayne?"

"Never mind."

Ewan sighed. He couldn't remain mad at Tim. That was part of the problem. He knew why evolution had given humans two parents. He couldn't be all things to Tim.

"Never mind," he muttered again.

Ewan walked further into the room.

"Point the flashlight straight ahead," Ewan said.

For once, Tim did as he was told and pointed the flashlight towards the end of the room.

"What are you doing?" Tim asked.

"We're going to find your rat. Call me paranoid."

The tangy light from the flashlight cast strange and ominous shadows across the room.

Ewan checked the safety and pulled the hammer back on the gun. The gun made a loud click, like the sound of somebody's tongue touching the roof of their mouth.

Ewan tried to organize the shades and light before him. He took several cautious steps forward, feeling slightly ridiculous.

Ewan was reminded of when he was a kid and his friends had dared him to go into a haunted house. Ewan had refused, telling them there was no such thing as ghosts. His friends had taunted him but eventually they had just left him all alone.

"There's no such thing as ghosts," Ewan had said.

A large mouse scuttled across the floor and disappeared into a gap in the floorboards. Ewan pointed the gun and almost shot it out of reflex.

Ewan sighed heavily, releasing the stress he felt in his neck and shoulders.

"That's not a rat, it was just a mouse," he told Tim, releasing the hammer and putting the gun into his pocket.

"No, it's not," Tim protested. "Did you see the thick tail? It was a rat."

Ewan frowned. "Who taught you about rats?"

"Can I have Bessy back?" Tim asked.

Ewan sighed. He seemed to be doing a lot of sighing in the past few weeks. He took the revolver out of his pocket.

"You promise not to go charging off into the darkness again? You've got to protect your dear old dad."

"I promise."

Ewan gave the gun back to Tim who took it eagerly. He knew the revolver would be useless if Creatures surrounded them but it made him feel safe and that was all that mattered.

"Come on," Ewan said. "We have to go get the power back on."

"You know rats actually kill and eat mice?"

Ewan glanced at Tim. "I don't think so, Timmy."

"They do. I saw a documentary on it once."

Ewan stopped and stared at Tim. The reference to the other world made them both pause. They rarely talked about things before the outbreak.

"Rats are scavengers, Timmy."

"Don't talk to me like that."

"Like what?"

"Like I'm a kid."

Ewan, feeling more relaxed, walked through another hallway and past a couple of empty rooms. They made their way to the basement where the generator was. Ewan took the stairs down, followed by Tim. Ewan pushed the door open and found himself in a musty, cold room. The generator was in the corner of the room. It was a box about the size of a fridge and had a metallic shine to it.

Ewan pressed a small button on the top right-hand corner of the generator and a tray slid out to reveal four neon purple-orange coils and a fifth that was burnt out.

"Just another blown coil," Ewan said. He turned to Tim. "Make yourself useful and fetch me a new one from the box."

Tim nodded and went over to a large metal bench on the far side of the room. Ewan watched as Tim opened a box and took out a new coil.

Ewan removed the burnt coil and took the new coil Tim had given him.

"It's the last one," Tim said, softly.

Ewan nodded at his son but didn't say anything. He didn't want to worry Tim. He didn't want to think of where they would get more coils.

Tim turned to look up at the generator. "You would think it wouldn't be so hard to maintain."

Ewan shrugged. "It's an older model."

Ewan pushed the shelf back and the generator hummed back to life and the lights flickered once and came back on. There was a hum and a glowing white digital display appeared, hovering in the air slightly in front of the generator. It showed energy and temperature readings and other measurements Ewan didn't understand.

Ewan smiled. It felt like the first time he had smiled in decades. It was something about the white light . . . the feeling of safety. Ewan listened to the hum of the generator and watched the numbers on the digital display change ever so slightly. He put his hand on the front of the generator, passing through the hovering display. Strangely it was cool to the touch.

Ewan turned to Tim. "Come on, let's get a couple more hours of sleep before we find breakfast."

Ewan pulled the door open and let Tim out first but even so the smell of decay and rot hit Ewan's nostrils. He felt like he had stepped into another country, another world maybe. Perhaps they had. He remembered the smell of flowers, the smell of vegetation and diesel.

Ewan glanced at Tim, to see if he would notice the smell but he had long stopped commenting on it.

Was this the life they would have? Would Tim be able to grow old? And even if he was, would he ever know the smell of a garden?

The entire metropolis was unnervingly silent. For a long time Ewan expected the sound of car engines, breaks, and squeaky wheels. The chatter of voices, children yelling but there was none of that. Nothing. Everything everywhere was permanently and eerily silent.

Ewan looked at the sun, was high in the sky, reflecting off the vacant, rusting skyscrapers all worn and disintegrated with time. Ewan shielded his eyes and looked towards the cracked streets, overgrown with moss and small plants.

Ewan and Tim walked around to the side of the Royal Ontario Museum to where they kept a small patch of dirt where they grew tomato plants with various degrees of success.

"I want to read," Tim said, suddenly.

Ewan looked at Tim surprised. "Are you trying to get out of working?"

"No," Tim said, shaking his head.

Ewan didn't really mind. They had more than enough time to get breakfast and do all the necessary chores before sundown. Ewan just wondered where Tim had gotten his habit for reading. Neither Amy nor Ewan had been big readers growing up. Perhaps it was just another way to stay connected to the world they had once known and had suddenly lost.

Ewan unzipped the backpack and took Tim's book and gave it to him. It was called *Phobias*. Ewan wondered where Tim had gotten it. He had probably found it somewhere in the museum. The gift shop perhaps?

Ewan watched as Tim found a spot in the sun, crossed his legs and started to read.

Ewan collected a few of his gardening tools from the side of the museum and started to rake an area of the garden that had been trampled by the Creatures the previous night.

"This morning you were talking about Mother," Tim said, without looking up from his book.

"I was?" Ewan asked.

"You said something like 'okay, Amy'."

"I don't remember saying that," Ewan said, his breathing became laboured as the rake cut into the dirt. Was he really that weak?

"Entomophobia. Fear of insects," Tim said.

Ewan smiled and shook his head. *Definitely his mother's doing*, he thought. He paused and wiped his brow, deciding it was the sun that was making him so tired. Had it grown hotter since the outbreak? He had no conceivable way of measuring such a thing but it sure felt like it.

"When did you become such a wise guy?" Ewan asked, looking up at the top of the museum where a replica Wright Brothers' Plane sat.

"Aerophobia. Fear of flying," Tim said, as if reading Ewan's thoughts.

"You know," Ewan said. "You might be interested to know that years ago there was a baby girl that didn't age. Only her hair and fingernails grew normally. Remember the movie Benjamin Button? Well, it is sort of like that. It's called Syndrome X. None of the scientists understood why or how some babies got Syndrome X. Could be as a result of an infection from a virus, or the child's DNA got scrambled in the womb somehow, or could be genetic . . . Could you imagine never growing up? Staying the same height and weight your whole life?"

Ewan knew he was rambling and looked towards Tim for some sort of piqued interest but Tim had returned to his book and was ignoring his dad. Ewan stubbornly continued.

"There is also a small fresh-water creature named Hydra that process radial symmetry that don't appear to die or grow older. Can you imagine an animal that lives forever?"

Tim gave a bored grunt, but didn't look up.

"It's interesting, isn't it?" Ewan asked. He knew Tim found such facts fascinating but Tim could be so stubborn sometimes.

Ewan returned to raking. He moved to a corner that had been completely ruined by the Creatures during the night. Ewan didn't know how smart the Creatures were or whether they were intentionally ruining the garden. Ewan sunk to his knees to examine the seeds. Everything would have to be replanted and if they were lucky the tomatoes would grow but more likely not.

Ewan took his shovel and started to overturn the soil. He dug into the ground, applying pressure with his foot. Despite his weakness, Ewan enjoyed the little bit of exercise he got. The third time he dug into the ground he hit something. It sounded too soft and squishy to be a rock. Perhaps it was a branch but just as he thought of that he knew it was wishful thinking.

Ewan squatted and examined the soil. With his hands he scooped away the topsoil and the dirt underneath. He reached in the small hole and pulled out the object and almost fell backwards.

"Shit," Ewan said, a little too loudly.

"What?" Tim asked.

"Nothing."

Tim stood up and peered into the hole and stared at what remained of a human hand. He didn't seem particularly disturbed by the hand. If anything he seemed more fascinated. The hand was pale blue and missing several fingers. A golden ring was still on one of the remaining fingers.

He had probably been married and had kids, Ewan thought. He knew he shouldn't think such depressing things but sometimes he couldn't help it.

"Don't look," Ewan said to Tim.

But Tim stayed planted where he was. "Necrophobia. Fear of dead bodies."

Tim took a pair of gardening gloves from the corner and started to pull on the hand.

"Tim, just leave it," Ewan said.

But Tim didn't seem to hear. He pulled harder and gradually pulled away the rest of the arm. It was broken off at the shoulder joint. The stub was a maroon colour and looked like it had been gnawed off by a savage animal.

"They got to him," Ewan said, needlessly.

"Must have been a midnight snack," Tim said, smiling grimly.

Ewan frowned. "Don't be so morbid."

Tim had moved one of the stuffed deer from the inside of the museum to the overgrown shrubbery just outside of the Royal Ontario Museum. Ewan watched Tim at the doorway of the museum. Tim walked with his arms stiff against his side and his shoulders rigid until he was about twenty paces away from the stuffed deer.

Ewan wondered what Tim was doing. It looked like he was acting out an eighteenth century duel, maybe something he had seen on television.

Tim turned and took out the revolver from his pocket and pointed it at the deer. Steadying his hand, Tim closed his right eye and fired a shot. A loud bang exploded from the pistol and the dear's stomach ripped open and the stuffing poured out onto the lawn.

Tim turned and smiled at his father.

What sort of parent am I? Ewan wondered. *What sort of parent allows his son to play with a revolver?*

Somewhere, something in his mind replied to his question: *one that wants his son to survive.*

"Come on," Ewan yelled. "Let's go inside."

"Don't you wanna take some practice? You need it, Dad."

"You're probably going to get yourself killed."

"Hoplophobic, agoraphobe."

Ewan frowned and looked down at the ground.

"It means fear of guns and outdoors," Tim explained.

"I know what it means," Ewan said, a little too quickly. One day he would take Tim's book and read it when he wasn't looking.

Tim turned and aimed his revolver at the deer again. He pulled the trigger and hit the deer in the neck this time.

He's getting good, Ewan thought. Then the same inner voice said, *Yes, but when those Creatures come at you will you be so calm?*

Tim looked back at Ewan. "It's easy. Just aim, take a deep breath and fire. I've been reading up on it."

"I know how."

"Yeah? Then show me."

Ewan could see the challenge in Tim's eyes.

Tim walked over and offered the gun to Ewan but Ewan didn't take it. He just looked at the old rusty handle and the dull silver case wondering how much longer Ol' Bessy would be functioning. And then what would they do?

Ewan imagined killing Tim and then taking the gun, biting down on it and blowing his brains out. He longed to do it with each passing day. To feel nothing. To be free of the world they were living in, this never ending nightmare. The Creatures would eventually get them. It was almost inevitable. He thought of the half-eaten arm in the garden. He didn't want to end up like that.

But then he looked down at the tiny brown eyes of his son and his thoughts were overwhelmed with love. How could he kill him? Maybe he could turn the gun on himself but he could never kill Tim. But then how could he leave Tim alone to fend for himself?

"It's getting late," Ewan observed. "Time to go inside."

"Stop treating me like a kid," Tim put the revolver into his pocket.

Ewan smiled. "You are a kid — last time I checked. Now get inside Timmy."

"Stop calling me Timmy. In case you haven't noticed, I'm twelve."

So old? Ewan thought. *When had he turned twelve?*

"Yeah, I see all that chest hair growing and look at all that peach fuzz on your chin. What a man we have here."

"Stop making fun of me."

Tim dropped his head and Ewan felt a deep sense of shame but he didn't let it show.

"Timmy . . . Tim. When you have to watch over a family like I do, then you can call yourself an adult."

"Yeah, that worked out real well," Tim muttered.

Ewan stepped towards Tim, his body tensed. He could feel the anger swell up inside of him. "What did you just say?"

"Nothin'."

Tim slipped by Ewan and scurried into the museum.

Ewan watched him walk down the hallway, past the ticket counter, his tiny body making tiny shadows against the wall. Despite everything, he couldn't stay mad at his son. Ewan turned and looked up at the sky. The sky was a beautiful clear aqua blue, more bright and sheen than usual.

Ewan remembered as a kid looking up at the sky and seeing a go from industrial progress, but the power plants had stopped, the cars had ceased and the oil drills had terminated. The world was empty as when it first began.

The gas cars were the first to stop working when gas stopped flowing. The popular electrical cars lasted a bit longer, but when the electrical grid was attacked by Creatures and the military were

17

unable to hold it, the electrical cars were unable to recharge so they too stopped working.

"He gets that rebellious nature from you," Ewan said to the sky, before turning and following Tim indoors.

Ewan made a dinner that consisted of tomatoes and carrots from the garden and a mouse they had managed to catch on the third floor. Whether it was the same mouse or it was the 'rat' Tim had seen earlier, Ewan didn't know.

Ewan used to tell Tim how anybody could go into a restaurant and order anything from a menu and somebody would bring the food to you.

Tim could hardly believe it. "You mean you could choose what to eat?"

"Yes."

"What if they didn't have something on the menu?"

"Well, you could choose a restaurant that had something you felt like eating."

Tim laughed. "Why didn't you ever take me?"

"You and Sophie were too young at the time to take anywhere, but I used to take your mother. We used to go to these veggie, gluten-free restaurants. She was such a hippie at heart."

"What's a hippie?"

Ewan sighed. "Never mind. Doesn't matter anymore."

Ewan had found a small wooden table in storage and had set it up in the Fossil and Evolution section. Behind Ewan was a large skeleton of a Brontosaurus cast in gloomy spotlights. It seemed to look down on them ruefully with large hollow eyes.

You're not too far behind us, the Brontosaurus seemed to say.

Ewan put the plates on the table. Tim had flipped open his book and didn't look up at Ewan.

"Finally some meat," Ewan said. "All those veggies were making me crazy."

"Lachanophobia. Fear of vegetables."

"Would you please put that book away?"

"But it's the only interesting one in the entire museum."

"Come on, can you just eat?"

Tim kept reading, ignoring Ewan.

"You know, I think you've got a nice-a-phobia," Ewan said.

Tim looked up at his father, a confused look on his face. "Fear of being nice?"

"Duh!"

"Come on Dad, that's not even a real thing," Tim said, distractedly scratching at his arm.

"Are you putting lotion on it like I said?"

"Of course," Tim said, finally putting down the book. He picked up his half of the mouse and took a small bite. Ewan did the same. They ate in silence, each lost in their own thoughts. Ewan remembered when Tim had been born and how it had been the happiest day in his life. He remembered the doctor placing Tim in his arms. How small Tim had been. So small and vulnerable. Nothing had seemed to change, yet everything had.

Everything was a new threat. Tim could have been run over by cars, or eaten a food he was allergic to, or fallen off a ledge of a balcony. Ewan, who had never given much thought to the city around him, saw danger everywhere.

Ewan wondered if it would have been better if Tim had never been born, if he had never had a family. He felt guilty every time he thought about it, but it still tortured him. If he had never met Amy, if they had never gotten married . . .

"They finished the meal and Tim pulled Ewan to his feet.

"Come on Dad, I want to show you something."

Ewan followed Tim into the next room where there were five mannequins showing the evolution of humans: the monkey, the Homo habilis, the Homo erectus, the Neanderthal and the modern day Homo sapien.

"I think we may have taken a step back in evolution," Tim said, sounding older than his twelve years.

Ewan grabbed Tim under his armpits and picked him up and placed him by the monkey. "Yes, I definitely see a resemblance."

"Stop it," Tim said, laughing.

Ewan smiled and squeezed Tim's armpits, making him laugh even harder.

"Dad, don't."

Tim tried to escape but Ewan caught him in his large arms and wrapped him up tightly. Tim's laughter turned into high-pitch shrieks. Ewan never wanted to let him go. Never. But he knew one day Tim would want to get out of the museum and explore the large empty world and perhaps he would meet somebody else and perhaps he would find something he wasn't meant to find.

Outside

Ewan had been lying on the cold, hard floor for hours before he decided to get up. He stumbled to the bathroom. He made his way down the wide hallway, past the exhibit of prehistoric animals and pushed the door open.

Tim was standing in front of the mirror, his shirt crumpled up in his hands. When he saw his father standing in the doorway he quickly slid his shirt back on.

"How's the rash?" Ewan asked. He tried to sound casual.

"Just fine."

"Let me see it."

"No, I'm fine. Really."

Ewan stared at Tim, trying to gage him.

He really was too much like his mother, Ewan thought.

"I just want to make sure it isn't . . ."

"It's not."

"Well if it is. . ."

"Then it'll kill me."

Ewan felt a knot deep in his stomach. The outbreak had started with a rash. A few of his students had shown him theirs. He had told them to go see a doctor but he doubted any of them did. They looked innocent enough: small discoloured blotches but had quickly turned deadly. He doubted even if his students had gone to a doctor they would have survived.

They ate breakfast in silence. Ewan tried to find something to talk about but Tim seemed to be pouting. What was there to talk about anyways? The past was too painful and the future too bleak. That just left the present, which was like the last frames of a roll of film.

After breakfast they got ready to go shopping — at least Ewan liked to call it shopping. It allowed for some normalcy in their life although there were no cashiers, no other shoppers and no money exchanged.

Tim and Ewan put their jackets on. Tim put the revolver in his pocket and Ewan took a baseball bat from behind the ticket counter.

They stepped out into the open air. Tim, as usual, took the lead, through the garden and along Queens Park Road. Ewan walked quickly to catch up to him. They usually turned left on Charles Street but this time Tim strode straight ahead towards Queens Park. Tim's head was completely still, his gaze fixed on the trees ahead.

"Where are you going?" Ewan asked.

"It's quicker through the park."

"You know we can't go in there."

"Why not?" Tim asked, not slowing his pace. He seemed like a man on a mission.

"You don't want to see what's in there."

"Then let's drive."

Ewan stopped but Tim kept walking.

"How many times?" Ewan asked. "We can't spare the gas."

"But we used to drive everywhere. I remember."

"Yes, that was before . . . it's different."

Tim stopped about fifteen yards ahead of Ewan. He turned to face his father. His body was rigid. He looked like he was about to pull the gun and fire, just as he had done with the stuffed deer.

Then all of a sudden, Tim's energy seemed to sap from him. He started to bite his bottom lip and he looked like he wanted to cry. He had tried to be tough for so long but it seemed like he just couldn't do it anymore.

It took every ounce of energy for Ewan not to run to him, to take him in his arms and hug him like he had done yesterday night but he knew if he did it now Tim would resent him.

"I want to go to the park."

"The Creatures will be there. You want to end up a corpse like the one in the garden?"

Tim didn't answer. He just stood there, his small hands clutched together.

Ewan turned and walked back to Charles Street. He knew he couldn't stop Tim from going into the park and even if they both went in they wouldn't be able to fend off the Creatures.

Ewan kept walking; eventually he looked back and was relieved to see Tim slowly following behind him.

They passed several large skyscrapers and flipped cars. When the wind picked up, it blew dark ash into their faces. Some skeletons were still in the driver's seats. Ewan tried not to look. Tim barely seemed to notice any more. Broken glass was everywhere. Garbage scattered across the sidewalk, blowing in the wind. Ewan wished they had time to clean it up a bit, at least put the garbage in some sort of pile, bury the dead, but they had to get back to the museum before nightfall.

They turned right on Bay Street. Bay Street. It used to be the financial capital of the city. The bankers' street, the stock brokers' street, the CEO's street. The street where everything happened. The street that had created a metropolis. But now it was just as empty and forlorn as any other street.

Ewan looked behind again and saw that Tim had slowed even more, his head down, his feet dragging across the dirt and grime.

"Come on Timmy."

"Tim."

"Your mother would be sick to hear that, you know. To her you were always Timmy."

"Well that was before they gutted her and everything went to shit."

Ewan tried not to cringe. How could his son, his very son, be so heartless sometimes? He definitely didn't get that from Amy. Had Ewan given him that trait?

"Please don't swear," Ewan said.

"Why not?"

"Because it's rude."

"Who's going to hear me? I mean really?"

"What about me? I don't count all of a sudden?"

Tim stared down at the ground. "I still say we should have driven."

They suddenly heard something behind them. Tim turned, drawing his gun out like he had practiced a thousand times.

Ewan looked down the street and saw a shadow move behind a car. A Creature.

"Let's go," Ewan said, taking hold of Tim's shoulder but Tim violently shrugged it off.

"No," Tim said. "I don't want to run."

The shadow streaked across the open road and Ewan saw the furry body and long tail. It was a racoon.

Ewan and Tim both started to laugh. How had a racoon managed to survive? It was quite miraculous really.

"You want to see if we can catch it?" Tim asked. "We could have it for dinner."

"I don't know. We need to keep going."

"Come on," Tim said, running down the street towards the racoon.

Ewan ran after him. "Be careful."

Tim stopped and fired the revolver. The bullet ricocheted off the walls, nowhere close to the racoon.

The racoon slinked down an alleyway and Tim followed it.

"No, not the alleyway," Ewan yelled, but Tim wasn't listening.

He heard another gunshot echo between the buildings.

Ewan followed Tim through the dark alley, crushing broken glass as he went. He raised his bat and wondered if a Creature was lurking somewhere above them but they got through without any sight of one.

On the opposite side, they found themselves on another wide street. He had lost his sense of direction and didn't know which one.

Tim was standing in the middle, his body posed. Ewan started to walk towards him but Tim waved him away. "You'll scare him away!"

"Come on, Tim. He's smarter than that."

Eventually Tim admitted defeat and they walked back the way they came. They didn't say anything until they found the grocery store. The front doors were smashed and the overhead halogens had long gone out.

"Be careful," Ewan said as they stepped into the store.

They quickly made their way through the empty isles looking for what they needed. Almost everything was gutted, taken long ago. Ewan stepped across a dried puddle of blood. He wondered what had happened to the corpse.

Tim wandered over to the toy section while Ewan looked for supplies they could use. He turned down isle nine, suddenly stopping. At his feet was a single bottle of Liberty Perfume. Ewan

24

bent over to pick it up. He turned it over in his hand. His heart started to pound in his chest and his hands started to shake violently. He unscrewed the top, closed his eyes and inhaled.

There she was, the smell of his wife lingering vividly in his senses.

Ewan opened his eyes and he was back with his family, transported into some memory of long ago. The shelves were full. People were chatting on their digital mobiles. People were excusing themselves as they maneuvered large shopping carts filled with soaps, magazines, tampons, pens and other household items.

Ewan watched as Amy put items in the cart.

"Honey?" Amy said. Her voice was soft and sweet but somehow carried a tone of authority. She had long shiny hair the colour of a glistening forest. She always wore it tied back in a ponytail. Her eyes were dark and lively and always seemed to be part of some ongoing joke. She was small in stature but somehow everybody noticed her presence when they were in the same room with Amy.

"Yes?" Ewan said.

"Forget something, babe?"

She held up her shopping list and Ewan took it.

"Remember, only things on the list," Amy said.

"Why don't we get the same thing every time? Then-"

"Then we would be boring," Amy said, smiling.

"That's because he is," Tim said, appearing from the toy isle holding a toy helicopter in his hand. At first Ewan thought it was the real Tim walking towards him but then he remembered he was still in his daydream.

How young he looks, Ewan thought. *He couldn't be more than six or seven.*

Ewan could feel himself laugh. "Come on, put that copter back."

Ewan thought the imaginary Tim would protest but he simply nodded and ran back to the toy isle. Apparently the imaginary Tim was better behaved than the real Tim.

Ewan looked down at the shopping list and followed Amy to the vegetable isle. They went to the very back where there was a sign that read "GMO FREE. ALL ORGANIC."

Ewan looked at the prices above the items. "Jesus, Amy. I don't see why we have to buy this stuff."

"Honey, we've been over this."

"I know, but look at the prices. We can't afford it."

Amy frowned. "You want cancer then eat whatever you want but I'm making sure the kids eat healthy."

Ewan held up his hand, conceding as he always did. "I'm sorry. Okay?"

"Tim! Stop it!" Sophie cried. Ewan turned to Sophie. Tim was dipping his fingers into his sister's vanilla ice cream.

Amy took hold of Tim's hand. "Be good to your sister, Timmy."

"But Mom, I didn't do anything," Tim claimed.

Ewan couldn't help but laugh at the obviousness of Tim's lie. Amy shot Ewan a dirty look.

"You're not helping," Amy scolded.

"I'm sorry . . . " Ewan protested, trying to think of a reasonable defence but came up empty.

"I don't want it anymore," Sophie said, trying to give the ice cream to Amy.

Sophie was two years older than Tim and had the same sandy-coloured hair as Tim. Her cheeks were bright rosy-red. She wore a light-pink dress and small white shoes; even at her young age, she kept them impeccable, free of dirt.

Tim had returned with a water gun and placed it in the shopping cart.

"Timmy, what did I say about guns?"

"Come on, Brian's got one."

"No, you know how I feel. Even pretend ones."

"You're no fun," Tim said.

Amy who had been placing fruit in the shopping cart put a hand on Ewan's elbow. "Let's just get him this one. It's not like it looks real or anything."

"I said no, Amy."

Ewan took the water gun from the shopping cart and noticed a small wooden heart-shaped pendant at the bottom of the cart.

"What's this?" Ewan asked Amy.

"Sophie wanted it. She saved up her allowance to buy it on her own."

26

Ewan picked up the wooden pendant, holding it up to the light. He smiled at Sophie. "It's pretty."

"It's stupid," Tim said, crossing his arms. "Doesn't even sparkle."

"Just because it doesn't sparkle doesn't mean it's not special," Sophie said, hiding her face in Amy's pants.

Ewan sighed. Girls were so much easier to handle than boys.

He bent down and placed the pendant around Sophie's neck, right above the birthmark on her upper chest which she was only recently becoming self-conscious about. Sophie blushed and hid her face in Amy's pants again.

"Come on, it's time to go," Amy said to the kids.

Ewan watched as Amy pushed her shopping cart up to the front where a robot arm unloaded her cart and placed all her items in a recycled bag.

"Thank you, have a nice day," the robot arm told Amy.

Ewan stood silently as Amy juggled the bags and took Sophie and Tim out of the store.

"Dad?" Ewan heard Tim say and suddenly he was back to the present, to the empty grocery store.

"Yes?"

"What's taking so long?"

"Nothing," Ewan replied.

Ewan put the perfume bottle back on the shelf where it had probably once belonged. He stared at it for a moment, debating whether he should take it or not. But what good was perfume in a world that reeked of decay and death already? Perfume wouldn't keep anything at bay.

Ewan moved to the end of the isle where he found the lotion for Tim's rash. It was the last bottle and he wondered where he would find some more once this bottle ran out. Ewan searched through the shelves and eventually he found a can of tomato sauce behind a box of envelopes.

He went in search of Tim and found him in the electronics section looking at the boxes of video games.

"Remember when we used to play these?" Tim asked, picking up a box.

"Look what I found," Ewan said, holding up the can of tomato sauce.

Tim took it, smiling up at Ewan. "Wow! Where did you get this?"

"It was behind a box of envelopes. Hidden."

"We are going to have a feast tonight!"

"Come on, it's time to move on," Ewan said.

The next stop was a building on Bay and Edwards Street. They walked outside and continued on their journey. In the next block the glass windows on either side were smashed and computer monitors and furniture lay scattered on the street. They walked past a rusted-out tank covered in ash. An upended green army helmet lay nearby.

The building they wanted wasn't hard to spot. It was eighty stories high and the second tallest structure in Toronto after the CN tower. A large sign hung above. "PERPETUUM INDUSTRIES: The Future is Now!"

Perpetuum Industries had been a multinational company that had aggressively corned the market on vibration energy by protecting its technology pattern, taking on large energy companies like Exxon-Mobil, Gazprom and Saudi Aramco. Before the outbreak, Perpetuum Industries had over a trillion dollars in network, but now its headquarters stood vacant and rusting in the harsh Toronto elements.

Ewan and Tim stood and stared up at the building. Even though it was cool, Ewan felt a damp sweat on his temples.

"Are we going in there?" Tim asked.

"I am. You're staying here.'

"You can't stop Bessy and I."

"You will stay out here and keep watch," Ewan said. "Give me the gun."

"No, I'm coming with you."

Tim looked up at his father with an intense glare. Ewan held Tim's glare for one moment but then let out a heavy sigh. He could use an extra pair of eyes if nothing else.

"Okay if you insist," Ewan said. "But remember the rules."

"I know Dad. Keep the light on, walk softly and stay near windows."

"And?"

"Uh . . . If I smell rotten eggs back away slowly."

"And if you see one?"

Tim pointed Ol' Bessy at an imaginary target by the doorway. "Blow its mother fucking head off!"

Ewan clamped Tim down on the shoulder. "Don't ever say that."

"Why not?"

"You even know what that means?"

"Brian taught me."

Ewan sighed and bit down on his bottom lip. "You run like hell, Timmy."

Tim nodded eagerly. At that moment he probably would have agreed to anything.

The Future is Now

Ewan went first, pushing the revolving door open and together they stepped in the large dark building. Their footsteps echoed off the linoleum floor. The sunlight from the tall windows gleamed down into the hallway. Ewan went first, his bat raised. He knew the bat wouldn't do anything against one of the Creatures but he felt braver carrying it.

"Come on. We better hurry up. The sun will be going down soon," Tim said.

Ewan nodded, but he couldn't make his limbs move any faster. Tim took several quick steps and walked in front of Ewan.

"Timmy wait!"

"Dad, if we go at your pace it'll take forever."

"I have a bad feeling about this," Ewan worried, looking around, trying to adjust to the darkness.

Tim didn't answer and walked towards the elevator. Tim pressed the elevator button which wasn't working and pretended to look at an imaginary watch on his wrists while tapping his feet.

"What are you doing?"

"Come on, it's funny."

Ewan shook his head and pushed the door to the stairs. They walked up three flights, every so often Ewan made Tim stop as they listened for any movement.

When the building had first opened, Ewan and Amy took a tour so Ewan was able to find his way around without much trouble.

They walked along the hallway until they came to a door that said "Repair Department."

Ewan slowly opened the door. The room was dark and airless.

"Now be careful," Ewan whispered.

"I've got it," Tim said, slipping past Ewan and disappearing into the darkness. Tim flickered on the flashlight and quickly looked around the room. "It's all clear," he said.

"Tim, what did I say?"

"Chill, Dad. Everything is fine."

Ewan stepped into the room, the bat still held high in his hand. As he did so he heard a small groan coming from overhead. Ewan swung his bat upwards towards the sound but didn't connect with anything.

"Timmy, I need your light," Ewan said, but when he didn't get a reply he looked around and Tim was nowhere to be seen.

"Tim, where are you?" Ewan shouted.

The groan came again, louder this time. They sounded like heavy footsteps from the floor above.

"Tim, get back here," Ewan shouted again. There was no point in remaining quiet. The Creatures knew they were there.

Panicked, Ewan ran blindly into the darkness, the dull sound of his soles shifted echoed off the walls and ceiling.

"Tim come back to me, come back to me," Ewan repeated between heavy breaths. He came to the end of the room and stopped to listen. His heart was pumping wildly in his chest. He couldn't see anything and he couldn't hear anything.

Why did Tim have to run off like that? What made him do it?

Ewan heard something from the darkness. What was that? Ewan strained to see through the blackness. Did something move?

"Tim?" Ewan asked, raising his bat again. His hands were shaking. His instincts told him to run back into the sunlight but he knew he couldn't leave Tim behind. He couldn't let him die like the others, like Amy.

This thought propelled Ewan forward. He took off to his right at full speed, almost smashing into the wall. He felt for a door, finally finding the ridge of a frame. But then he heard a snarl behind him and heavy footsteps.

Ewan turned and swung his bat blindly. His third swing connected with something solid. There was a loud thwack and a Creature roared in pain. Ewan swung again and hit the Creature a second time. The vibration from the swing rattled down his fingers.

Ewan reached out to his left and found the knob to the door.

Please God, let it be unlocked, he thought, as he turned the handle. It twisted easily, and the door swung open. Ewan swung his bat blindly. He stepped back into the room. The Creatures tried to follow but Ewan lunged forward and connected again with a satisfactory crunch of flesh and bones.

The Creatures howled and backed off long enough for Evan to close the door and lock it. Ewan listened to the thumping of the door as the Creatures tried to break it down but it was strong and would hold them for a while.

Ewan gave a heavy sigh, releasing the tension from his shoulders. He had made it alive, at least temporarily.

What were the Creatures exactly? Ewan asked himself. It wasn't the first time he had pondered this question and it probably wasn't going to be the last. They weren't human, yet they weren't animals either. They were somewhere in between. He knew the virus had made them that way but what exactly caused it, he didn't know.

He had heard once on the news the virus attacked the brain stem, killing off nerve tissue but he wasn't sure he believed it.

Ewan looked around the room. He felt around like a blind beggar and found a desk. The room had probably once been someone's office. Ewan imagined somebody sitting at the desk for eight hours, typing out reports, sending emails, making phone calls and then going home to his family for dinner. Could he have guessed the fate of the human race? Where was he now? Outside the door?

As if the Creatures could read his thoughts, he heard a loud roar from outside. Ewan could hear the Creature take a running leap at the door, crashing into the wooden boards. The door rattled but did not break. Seemingly undaunted, the Creature threw itself against the door again. The door groaned and Ewan could tell it was beginning to bend under the pressure.

It won't be long, Ewan thought. *The Creatures were going to get through.*

Ewan took several deep breaths. He had to move. He had to find Timmy. He looked through the darkness. Perhaps there was another door leading away from the Creatures. Ewan forced himself to move, making his way around the desk, hitting his shin against a chair and almost losing his balance.

The door finally splintered and with surprising quickness the Creatures were on Ewan. Ewan half turned, trying to swing the bat but a Creature grabbed Ewan's arm. The pungent smell of the Creature was overpowering. A low growl resonated from the Creature's throat. Its face was lost in darkness but he could make out its large dark eyes and for a moment Ewan thought he could see his own scared reflection in them.

In that moment, Ewan thought of Amy and Tim and Sophie. *I'm so sorry, Amy. I'm sorry.*

Ewan dropped the bat, now useless and pushed against the Creature. It was his only chance of survival, but the Creature was strong and forced Ewan to the ground. Desperately, Ewan fought against it, flailing his arms.

Another Creature tore into his leg and Ewan bit down on his bottom lip to stop from screaming.

His vision went blurry for a moment and he struggled to remain conscious. He turned his head to the left and saw a curtain. He reached out with his hand, pushing the Creature with his right forearm and managed to grab the edge and pull. A flicker of sunlight hit the room and for a moment Ewan could see the Creature clearly. It had veiny white skin; its hair was almost all gone, only a few thin strands remained. Its nose was twisted and deformed.

The sun hit the Creature, causing it to clutch at its eyes and scream hideously. The Creature backed away and gave Ewan enough space to grab more of the curtain and he managed to yank it to the floor, flooding the ground with light, illuminating the room with a bright tangy glow.

The Creatures all screamed together and ran from the office.

Ewan collapsed back to the floor. His fingers felt icy cold and he couldn't feel his leg.

The sun beam fizzled out at the edge of the room and beyond that was darkness. He couldn't see the hallway beyond but knew Tim was still out there.

Ewan listened. He could hear soft, quick footsteps coming from the hallway. They didn't sound like a Creature's.

"Tim?" Ewan whispered.

Ewan held his breath and didn't move. He lifted his eyes to look out the window. The sun was slowly sinking behind the empty buildings. It wouldn't be long before the light was gone and there was no defence.

Ewan had to move fast. Tim was on the side of the building with the Creatures. Ewan knew it and so did the Creatures. Ewan picked up the bat, hunched his body over like a linebacker's and charged into the hallway, expecting the Creatures to be there, just beyond the sunlight but they had disappeared.

33

Where did they go? Ewan heard a sound from behind him. He turned just in time to see a Creature attack. Ewan pulled his bat back and swung at it, realizing it had been lying in wait for him. Ewan connected with the side of the Creature's head. There was a loud crunching sound of bone and wood reverberating through the hallway. The Creature fell backwards and Ewan took the short end of the bat and drove it through the Creature's eye. There was a soft squishing sound like that of a crushed grape and then the Creature lay still.

Ewan looked around. He could see the burnt out Exit sign several doors down. Ewan scanned the rest of the hallway, looking for Tim but couldn't find him. Several dark shapes were moving quickly towards him. He hoped Tim had made it out because he had little choice but to flee towards the escape exit.

Ewan ran, reaching the door but a Creature blocked him off. Ewan didn't stop and bowled the Creature over. Ewan crashed into the lever, opening the door and he sprawled down the stairs.

Somehow Ewan managed to climb to his feet and keep going down the stairs. He didn't know where the Creatures were; if they were ahead or behind him. He just kept going. His legs pumped up and down until they started to burn but he couldn't stop.

Ewan turned the corner and went down another flight.

Almost there, Ewan thought. *Just a couple more to go.*

Ewan used the railing to propel himself down. He could now hear the Creatures crashing behind him. Ewan turned the corner again and saw the bottom exit door. He ran down towards it and with great effort pushed the door open and into the lobby.

He could see the door to the street just about twenty yards ahead but in front of him was a Creature running towards him.

Ewan didn't have any strength to run. He was out of breath and he couldn't feel his injured leg. He knew he couldn't turn back. He could hear the Creatures behind him coming up fast.

Just then Ewan heard a loud crack resound through the lobby and the Creature's chest exploded. Then there was another loud crack. The second bullet hit the Creature in the mouth, which disintegrated in a flash of white and black matter. The Creature fell to the floor. Ewan turned and saw Tim standing by a booth to his right. The gun held straight in front of him.

"Timmy?" Ewan gasped, trying to stay upright.

"Dad?" Tim yelled, running towards Ewan. Ewan closed his eyes and wrapped his arms around his son. He could feel his own heart pounding against Tim's chest. His strength seemed to return.

"You okay?" Ewan asked.

Tim broke from Ewan's grasp and looked up at his father. "Better than you."

Ewan forced a pitiful laugh. "Yeah . . . Sorry. I couldn't find the coils."

"That's okay. I got two of them." Tim held up his left hand. Ewan had somehow not noticed Tim's slender fingers wrapped around two coils.

Ewan ruffled Tim's head and smiled. "That's my boy."

Tim smiled back.

You get that courage from your mother too, Ewan thought.

The Creatures broke from the stairwell and into the lobby. Tim spun and fired several shots, hitting several Creatures. They fell but others kept going.

Ewan and Tim turned and ran towards the entrance. Tim was faster and sprinted out ahead of Ewan. Ewan limped along behind.

"Come on, Dad!" Tim yelled. He turned again and fired at the closest Creature, hitting it in the shoulder. The Creature roared but kept going. Tim aimed higher and fired again right into the Creature's forehead. The Creature collapsed only a few yards behind Ewan.

"Keep going," Ewan yelled at Tim.

Tim turned and ran, throwing the door open. The light hit the floor, forming a three-foot square and Ewan leapt into it. The Creatures behind him stopped and started yelling and screaming, almost sounding human. Ewan lay on the ground, unable to get up.

He felt himself being dragged out into the open and he felt cement steps underneath him. He managed to look up and saw Tim pulling him by the shoulders. How he had managed, Ewan didn't know.

"I'm okay, Tim."

Tim stopped and Ewan forced himself to his feet.

"We've got to keep moving," Tim said.

Ewan could only nod as he looked up at the sinking sun and its harsh red light that cast long shadows against the tall skyscrapers.

Tim reloaded his gun with bullets from his pocket. He then cut diagonally across the street, down a narrow alleyway.

"Where are we going?" Ewan asked.

"We're going to cut through the park."

Ewan slowed down. Tim looked behind him. "Come on, Dad. No time to argue."

Tim grinned and sped up. They came out of the alley, crossed the street towards Queen's Park. Large, colourful Spruce trees stood in clusters on small hills between the pathways.

Ewan took a deep breath. Tim was right. If they didn't cut across the park he knew they wouldn't make it to see sunrise.

The Cage

Stu Baillie was sitting on his lawn chair enjoying Beethoven on the sound system between piercing screams. He felt Beethoven wasn't complete without the sound of somebody in pain. He liked coupling the most beautiful sounds on Earth with the worst. It was just Yin and Yang. In the past people would have called him insane or at least tell him his hardwiring was haywire.

"Why're you doing this?" the man asked. He was tied to the post with thick wires and zap straps out in the open. The man was frantically trying to get himself lose but Stu had tied him tight.

Stu just smiled at him through the tiger cage where he was sitting. He didn't expect the man to understand. He didn't expect anybody to understand. But now it hardly mattered who thought what of him. There weren't any police that would come kicking down his door. No judge to sentence him to life in prison. It was almost better this way. There were no rules. The weak were at the mercy of the strong and Stu was definitely the strong.

"Because there's no more telecasts on," Stu told the man.

"Please untie me. I'll do anything," the man pleaded.

Stu sighed and leaned back in his lawn chair. The pleading always got boring after awhile. He wished the sun would set a little faster, but still he loved to watch the pinkish light hit the zoo and the surrounding buildings. The zoo was now empty of all the wonderful animals that had once populated it. He didn't know what had happened to the hippos, the giraffes or, his favourite, the powerful, sleek tiger. They were long gone by the time Stu had gotten there but it was clear there had been a large blood path judging by the amount of corpses he had to dispose of – both human and Creatures alike.

Stu loved the anticipation and watching despair slowly seep into his victims. Half of the fun was watching a man's spirit crush as he realized there was no hope, no escape and only a very bloody, horrible death waited.

The man started to cry. This was always a stage Stu hated.

"I'll give you everything I have," the man said, between tears.

Stu laughed. He hadn't heard that one before. It was new. "What is there that I can't take for myself?"

"I have a secret stash. I was a doctor. I have medicine," the man said.

"I don't need medicine. I don't intend on getting sick," Stu said, a slight smile on his face. But still he started to think about it. There was probably something he could use to get high. He hadn't gotten high since before the outbreak and he did miss it. But what if the man was lying to him?

In his former life, Stu had been a paramedic. He loved working the graveyard shift where he got to see the ugly side of humanity. He remembered seeing his first person die. The man had been stabbed in the stomach during a convenience store robbery. Stu had held his hand as the man begged Stu to save him. Stu supposed he could have stopped the bleeding and stitched him up but instead he just knelt there and watched. Stu was not a religious man but it was the closest thing he could describe to a religious experience. He thought about the man's suffering for days. Every little tick, facial expression as life seeped out of his body. It was mesmerizing and he became forever hooked.

But nothing would prepare him for what he witnessed after the outbreak. Neighbours killing neighbours. Family killing family. Every person for themselves. Stu had gone around burning cars and killing police officers and then when the military arrived he had started killing them too. It was so easy to play the victim and then break the soldier's neck or use his own gun against him.

That seemed so long ago. Now his fun was spread further apart. Stu wondered if at some point he would be unable to find survivors at all. He shuddered at the possibility.

Stu studied his victim carefully. He was probably in his mid-forties with light-brown hair and a scraggily beard. He could have been a doctor but it was so hard to tell sometimes. The outbreak had changed everybody.

But no, Stu thought. *If the man had a stash of drugs then I can find it for myself.* It wasn't like he had anything better to do with his time.

The sun was setting and the man started to struggle more.

"You're not going to get away with this," the man told Stu. "You might kill me, but somebody will get you. Karma's a bitch."

Stu laughed. The things that came out of people's mouths could be so funny. 'Karma's a bitch?' No doctor would say 'Karma's a bitch'.

Stu could see the Creatures in the shadows now coming through the trees. They came slowly, knowing there was no need to rush. Their prey wasn't going anywhere.

Stu wondered if they remembered his other sacrifices and if the Creatures felt any sense of gratitude towards him. Did they feel anything?

The man tried to turn to see the Creatures coming from behind but the stake was preventing his mobility. With all his strength he tried to free himself. Stu watched as the man frantically twisted and struggled.

The sun sank completely now and the Creatures came out from the shadows.

Stu studied them from the safety of his cage. The Creatures had grey skin that blended into the dark sky and they wore some resemblance of tattered clothing. They looked like they had a flesh eating disease.

Perhaps that was what the virus was, Stu thought. Regardless of how much the Creatures looked like humans they certainly didn't move or act like any humans as they slowly surrounded the helpless man who was screaming at what was ahead of him.

Stu got up from his seat and went to the bars of the cage, wanting to get a better look.

One Creature bit into the man's shoulder, removing a large piece of flesh. Blood squirted from the wound. Stu didn't think it was possible but the man seemed to scream louder.

This seemed to be a signal for the other Creatures as they pounced on the man. One tore off the man's nose, the other ripped off a finger. The man was a bloody mess of pink flesh and blood.

Stu was always fascinated by how long it took people to die. In movies before the outbreak it seemed people just keeled over and died but in real life people seemed to hang onto whatever threads they could.

Still the man died like the rest and soon there was nothing left of him but a bit of blood on the stake and a couple of bones. The Creatures had picked every ounce of flesh clean.

The Creatures then turned their attention to Stu and walked up to the cage, Stu was no more than a yard from their vile smelling breath. He could still smell the remnants of the man and it almost made him vomit.

Stu picked up his Samurai sword and started stabbing the Creatures through the fence. After that, most of the Creatures quickly backed off into the woods.

But one Creature managed to climb up onto the roof of the cage. Stu eyed the Creature wearily but once up there it seemed unsure of how to proceed next.

Stu would have to lure it down otherwise he wouldn't get any sleep. His adrenaline was slowly seeping from his body and he knew fatigue would soon over take him. He had been hunting all day and it had zapped his energy. He had to do something now and so he took the key to the cage from his pocket and unlocked the large padlock. He stepped out into the open.

In an instant the Creature jumped at Stu who took a quick step forward and thrust the sword at the Creature, causing it to fall with its full momentum. Stu pulled his sword free and turned to see if there was any immediate danger. There wasn't. He was utterly alone in the zoo.

Stu wiped his bloody sword on the grass and walked back into the cage and locked himself in. With the fun over, he could now go to sleep but tomorrow he would hunt again.

Queen's Park

"Oh shit," Ewan said.

Suddenly it seemed as if the whole park came alive as the bushes and the trees started to move. Tim raised his revolver just as a Creature appeared from a bush. Tim held steady and fired. The bullet caught the Creature right in the throat and blood gushed from the wound.

"Yes," Tim said, pumping his fist in the air.

Another Creature appeared from behind a tree.

"Keep shooting," Ewan said.

He had to admit to himself that Tim had become a good shot.

Tim turned, aimed and fired. His bullets hit their target. The Creature fell but more appeared.

Was this the end? Ewan wondered. *Such a stupid way to die.*

Ewan suddenly though of Amy. Her perfume filled his nostrils, traveling up towards his brain. He could almost reach out and touch her. He remembered her last kiss. Her soft lips on his. How he longed for her. He wished she were there so he could hold her hand, feel her warmth. She could be brave enough for the three of them.

Tim's gun brought him back to reality. Since Ewan had lost his bat, he bent down and picked up a thick stick just in time to hit a Creature that had jumped out into the clearing. The stick landed on the Creature's head and Ewan had to beat it back.

"Let's get out of here," Ewan said, beating at another Creature.

Tim nodded and fired some more. He ran and dodged the Creatures like a football star. Ewan followed him through the woods. They ran along the path until they came to a clearance. To their left was an old rustic sandstone building that used to be the Legislative Assembly, the seat of a defunct government.

Ewan looked up at it. There was a dim light on one of the top floors. Was that possible?

Tim noticed it too and pointed up at it.

"Dad, look!"

41

"Keep running, Timmy."

"But Dad, there must be survivors."

"No. To the museum. It's safe there. We can still make it."

The Creatures were behind them now and Ewan had to make a decision. With some reserved strength Ewan didn't know he had, he pulled Tim along until they passed the building. Ewan glanced behind and saw the Creatures were close behind. Tim turned and fired twice but then ran out of bullets and the revolver made a dull thud as the firing pin hit metal.

"I'm out of bullets," Tim announced, his eyes gleamed with panic.

Ewan realized there was no way they could outrun the Creatures. If only they had kept some of the bullets for themselves. Everything would come to an end so quickly but now . . . he imagined the sharp teeth of the Creatures sinking into his flesh.

Suddenly something – it was too dark for Ewan to see clearly what exactly – seemed almost to fly out of the trees and attack the Creatures. To Ewan's astonishment, some of the Creatures actually turned and started to run the other way from their attacker. Whatever it was, it was small, about half the size of the Creatures yet vicious. It snarled and swiped at the Creatures.

Ewan turned and put his hand on Tim's shoulder.

"What is that?" Tim asked, mesmerized by the dark attacking shape. Tim raised his flashlight but Ewan grabbed his hand.

"No, don't," he said. "Let's just get out of here."

Whatever it was, it was helping them and Ewan didn't want to scare it away or jinx it.

They made one last dash, breaking out of the park and across the street and. Ewan's foot felt like it was on fire but he ignored the pain.

Ewan looked back. The Creatures reminded Ewan of a pack of wild dogs, foaming at the mouth.

Ewan wondered if the Creatures were waiting for them at the entrance of the museum. What if the Creatures had cut them off? Ewan pushed the thought out of his mind. There was no use thinking about it.

Ewan and Tim reached Bloor Street and turned left. They could see the entrance in front of him now and there were no

Creatures there. Ewan had a renewed burst of energy and he caught up to Tim.

As they got closer, Ewan realized something was wrong. The power had blown again and the lights were off.

They made it to the entrance and opened the door. They stepped inside and Ewan put all his weight into the door. One of the Creatures reached out and stuck his hand into the door, preventing it from closing. Ewan took a deep breath and pushed with all his might but outside the Creatures were pushing back and there were too many of them.

"I can't hold it," Ewan said, through a clenched jaw.

Tim took the bat from Ewan and swung it at the Creature's arm until they heard the sound of bone snapping. The Creature didn't seem to feel it, however.

"Go down to the genny," Ewan told Tim.

"I don't know how to . . ."

"You've seen me do it a million times. Hurry."

Tim stood a moment terrified but then turned and ran towards the basement. When Tim was out of sight, Ewan let go of the door.

He turned and tried to run but he was so exhausted he only managed to get a couple of steps before he collapsed on the floor. He turned and watched as the Creatures poured in.

"Amy, please help us," Ewan said, looking up towards the ceiling of the museum.

He tried to gather his energy again and get to his feet but he knew it was useless. He just hoped it would be over quickly and Tim would be able to turn on the generator.

He closed his eyes and waited for his fate but it didn't come. There was a loud eruption behind him and he heard the Creatures scream. He opened his eyes and saw a Creature explode in front of him and collapse. There was another explosion and another Creature went down. The Creatures hesitated now as if they were unsure of how to proceed.

A figure appeared next to Ewan holding something. A gun? At first he thought it might be Timmy but if so, where had he gotten the weapon? The figure was dressed in dark clothes and was several inches taller than Timmy. No, it couldn't be Timmy. But then who was it? His vision was blurry and he had no energy to concentrate on the figure as it shifted its weight.

The figure dropped his weapon and brought out a pistol from his waistband and started to fire. His aim was excellent as he hit each Creature in the head.

Bet you didn't expect that, Ewan thought just as the lights turned on.

The Creatures let out a hideous scream and turned to run but it was too late. The light hit their greyish-white skin and as if on fire, they started to disintegrate. Their skulls collapsed as if made of plastic. They withered on the floor as if in great pain until there were only ugly streaks of dust and ash left.

After that, Ewan lapsed into darkness.

Ewan dreamed he was in bed and Amy was kissing him on the neck but Ewan was distracted. He was thinking about Tim's first day of school tomorrow. He was starting kindergarten and would have to adapt to a new group of kids. Ewan wondered what Tim was thinking, if he was lying in bed awake.

"I'm worried about Timmy," Ewan said to Amy.

The bedside lamp was on and let off a warm tranquil glow. Amy was wearing a white dressing gown and was kissing Ewan's ear playfully.

"He'll be fine," Amy said, putting a hand on Ewan's chest.

Ewan smiled and kissed Amy. "Can't we just keep him home forever?" Ewan asked, only half joking. As a biology teacher, Ewan saw firsthand how cruel kids could be to each other. He knew Tim wasn't a big kid and wouldn't be able to stand up for himself. If the kids bullied Timmy there was nothing he or Amy could do about it.

Amy laughed. "He wants to go. He's excited. He'll hate us forever if we keep him home."

"I suppose so," Ewan said, unconvinced.

Ewan woke up with a groan. He looked up. The light was casting a neon glow through the small office. That was a good sign. He was on a mattress stretched out on the floor. A photograph of the pyramids was still hanging on the wall and Ewan wondered who it had once belonged to.

A thin-faced woman was leaning over him. There was something about her presence, her delegate but firm touch that was reassuring. She was wearing a tattered white t-shirt stained with mud and blood and jeans with the knees frayed. Her skin was smooth and miraculously unblemished. She had dark, mature eyes and a small thoughtful mouth. Ewan judged her to be no more than thirty.

"You gave me quite the scare," the woman said, her voice seemed to echo in Ewan's head. "Are you thirsty? You should drink some water."

"Who are you?" Ewan asked. His lips and mouth were dry.

The woman tipped a bit of water down Ewan's throat. He coughed but it felt good running down his throat.

"Who's Amy?" the woman asked.

Ewan tried to take account of his body. His head was pounding and he had trouble thinking. He looked down at his injured leg. It was bandaged up with a cloth. "She's my wife," Ewan said. "Where's Timmy?"

"He's outside, in the garden I think."

Ewan tried to prop himself up on an elbow but a head rush made him lie back down. "You let him outside?"

"Yeah, he'll be fine. He couldn't stay cooped up in here all day."

"I'm Ewan Walder."

"Ashley Vulfriezer. Pleased to meet you."

Ewan remembered the Creatures coming after him. "What happened? You saved my life."

"It was nothing," Ashley answered, glancing away embarrassed.

"Where did you come from?"

"My family has been living in the park for a couple of weeks now."

"Your family is alive?"

"Well . . . they aren't my real family. Sort of adopted family I suppose. We've been watching you for awhile."

"Watching us? Why?"

"To make sure you were safe."

Ewan was confused. "What do you mean?"

"Well you never know. People may take advantage of . . . our situation."

Ewan tried to smile but it hurt. It seemed strange that anybody would think of Tim and himself as a threat but he supposed after the outbreak many bad things happened and he couldn't blame someone for not trusting anybody else. "It seems like you could take care of yourself."

Ashley shrugged. "There are twins, two boys about your son's age. Justin and Anthony. I would never let anything happen to them so I'm cautious. But I knew you were in trouble when you didn't return and you had no light so I went investigating."

"And that's when you found us."

"Exactly. Good thing I did too."

Ewan nodded. She was beautiful and seemed self-assured, as if she had been saving random strangers from death her entire life.

"Where's your wife?"

"She died."

"Oh," Ashley said, covering her mouth. "The way you spoke . . ." her voice trailed off into nothingness, leaving awkwardness.

"You said you were living in the park. How do you survive?"

"Well nothing as fancy as your generator – which is very impressive by the way. We just huddle by a fireplace. We take turns making sure the flame doesn't go down."

"And that works?"

Ashley shrugged. "More or less. Luckily the Creatures aren't too smart."

"Do you think you could go get Timmy?"

"Sure," Ashley agreed, standing up and for the first time Ewan got a good look at her. She was petite and thin hipped with round features. Her hair was braided and reached to the small of her back. She looked like no more than a child herself.

Or am I just getting old? Ewan thought. He never thought he would get old in this world.

I never thought I would see such a beautiful woman either, Ewan thought. He immediately felt regret for his thought.

"I'm sorry, Amy," he said. "Please forgive me."

A couple of minutes later, Timmy burst in and wrapped his small arms around Ewan.

"Dad, I thought you were dead."

This made Ewan burst into tears. Ashley hovered by the doorway but seemed to grow embarrassed by the outpouring of emotions and turned to go.

"No please stay, Ley-ley," Tim said.

"Ley-ley?" Ewan looked at his son questionably.

Tim smiled shyly. "That's my nickname for her."

Ewan rolled his eyes and everybody laughed. Ewan looked at Ashley. "Did you ask her if it's okay to give her a nickname? Some people don't like nicknames."

"No it's okay," Ashley said quickly.

"Alright then," Ewan said. "Where are you from?"

"You mean before . . ."

Ewan nodded.

"I grew up in Mississauga but my parents immigrated here from Sweden."

"Sweden?" Ewan said, surprised.

"I know what you're thinking but not everybody from Sweden has blonde hair and blue eyes."

Ewan laughed. "You're going to bring your family over here? It would be much safer than that building."

Ashley smiled and Ewan realized that was probably what they had been hoping for all along.

"That would be great," Ashley said. "If it's alright I'm going to go get them."

"Can I go with you, Ley-ley?" Tim said.

Ashley hesitated. "I think you should stay with your father. He might need you."

"No, it's okay," Ewan said. "I think I'll try and sleep some more."

But when Ashley and Tim were gone, Ewan couldn't sleep. He lay there staring up at the ceiling. His head had cleared but his ankle was burning.

After a while, Tim came back in and sat opposite Ewan. His small, round face was a mask of fear and concern.

The pain in Ewan's ankle started to throb almost unbearably.

"Do we have any painkillers left?" Ewan asked.

"I don't know but I think I know where to get some."

Tim rose but Ewan reached out and caught his arm. "No, just stay with me awhile," he requested, so Tim sat back down.

Tim was uncharacteristically quiet. It was times like these that Ewan didn't know what to say to his son. He wished Amy were alive. She always knew what to say to their children.

"You probably don't remember but there used to be times when you could go into almost any store and buy some painkillers."

Tim raised his eyebrows. "So nobody ever felt bad?"

"No, they didn't really work like that."

"How did they work?" Tim asked.

"I don't know . . . it's hard to explain."

They elapsed back into silence. Tim crossed his hands and his feet and looked around the room. In the distance Ewan could hear Justin and Anthony running around and the hum of the generator as it slowly worked away.

"Dad?"

"Yes."

"What was it that saved us back in the woods?"

"I don't know," Ewan said, softly. They had been saved twice in one night. The first time hadn't been Ashley. He knew that. Whatever it was had been small and quick, some kind of animal perhaps.

"Was it a person?"

"I don't know, maybe," Ewan said, and then adding, "Maybe it was a guardian angel."

"They don't exist."

"You were always so practical, Timmy. Even as a kid. Could never get you to believe in Santa either," Ewan reminisced, his eyes turning to the dark ceiling.

"The problem is you're a bad liar, Dad."

Ewan laughed. "Timmy, I need to get some rest."

Tim nodded and left the room. Ewan couldn't even hear Justin or Anthony anymore even though he strained to listen, just the low hum of the generator that seemed to pierce Ewan's eardrums and vibrate through his entire body.

Ewan tried to sleep but the pain in his ankle prevented him from getting any rest. After awhile he decided he would try and stand up but every time he lifted his head brought a wave of nausea and so he sat back.

Time went slower than usual, not that it mattered. He had no way of measuring whether he had been there a minute or an hour. He had no place to be and nothing to do. His thoughts drifted back, as they often did, to Amy.

He remembered when he used to sit in his Queen-sized bed marking papers. He could almost feel the softness of the mattress and the covers pulled up over his legs. Ewan had been the biology teacher at Vaughn Road Academy. Although he had enjoyed his job, he despaired at the lack of learning that went on within the classroom. The kids just weren't interested in biology —or any subjects for that matter.

Ewan soon got bored with the student's lackluster papers and he shifted his gaze to Amy who was snoring beside him. She could sleep through anything. He loved watching her slow breathing. She wore pink pajamas with flowers on them. And she seemed perfectly content. Her chest expanded and contracted with each breath. Her head sunk into the pillow, her thick hair sprawled across the pillow.

Then there was a thud from upstairs that was so loud it woke Amy. She turned and stared sleepily at Ewan.

"What was that?" she murmured.

"Probably just the kids goofing around. Go back to sleep."

Amy glanced at the digital clock on the bedside table. It read seven past eleven.

"Ewan, they're going to be cranky tomorrow."

Ewan put a hand on Amy's shoulder. "Go back to sleep. They need to learn."

"Please just go tell them to be quiet.

"It's fine."

Amy let out a sigh of exasperation and started to get out of bed.

"Okay, okay, I'll do it," Ewan said.

"It's too late now. I'm up."

Ewan just shook his head and returned to his students' exam. It was just as well. He had to get through a lot of papers. But as he heard Amy climb the creaky old steps he felt a pang of guilt and he closed his eyes. She shouldn't be the only one to discipline the kids all the time.

Ewan swung his feet around and touched the cold floor intending to give Amy some backup or at least moral support. The kids could be hard to manage sometimes. He got to the hallway when he heard another loud thud from upstairs, as if something heavy had been thrown to the floor.

"Honey?" Ewan called.

There was no response. What was going on?

Ewan walked quickly to the stairs. He was about halfway up when he heard Amy scream. For a moment Ewan was paralysed with fear. He could hear the beating of his heart in his ears and he felt his brain will his body to climb the stairs. He decided to quickly retreat back to their bedroom where he pulled a shoebox from underneath the bed. He opened the lid. Inside was a silver revolver. He took the gun, which was heavy and awkward in his hand, and started to climb the stairs. He felt like his body was going in slow motion, pushing the door open to the kids' bedroom.

"Ewan, help!" Amy screamed from somewhere in the blackness. Ewan groped for the light switch but when he flicked it nothing happened. What was wrong with the circuit?

Ewan pointed the gun and gradually his eyes adjusted to the darkness and he could make out a large shape of a burglar on the bed. He pointed his gun but was unsure of whether to fire. What if he hit Amy? What if he hit one of the kids?

As his eyes adjusted some more, he saw that the burglar had a large hunchback and lanky arms that were wrapped around Amy's neck. The burglar wasn't human, Ewan realized. It snarled with animal fierceness but it wasn't an animal either. It was something completely different.

Ewan took a deep breath and felt the blood drain from his body. He aimed his gun feeling faint. He closed one eye and tried to steady his hand.

For the first time he could see the kids. Tim was lying in the corner unconscious and Sophie was under the bed, her hands pressed against her mouth in an impression of Munch's famous scream.

"Protect the kids," Amy gasped and that seemed to knock Ewan out of his trance. He took one large step closer and raised his gun again, but before he could get off a shot another Creature appeared in the window. It was backlit against the street lamps and Ewan could see it clearly. Its flesh was a greenish brown colour, like that of a dirty puddle. Its neck was long and its features were sunken and deformed. Terrified, Ewan pointed the gun and squeezed the trigger twice. The gun kicked back and upwards, making a deafening crack that seemed to ricochet off the walls. The bullets missed the Creature and lodged into the wall.

The Creature in the window jumped into the room and charged Ewan, moving incredibly quickly. Ewan stood there unable to fire the gun again.

Ewan wanted to shout but his mouth was dry and so he stood there dumbly until the Creature hit Ewan full force, knocking him backwards against the doorframe. He felt the gun fall from his hand. The Creature tried to sink its teeth into Ewan but he clawed at its face, gouging its eyes.

Amy let out a high piercing scream and Ewan turned just in time to see the Creature on the bed bury its teeth into Amy's neck. Dark red blood squirted onto the sheets and pillow.

"Amy!" Ewan shouted, pushing against his attacker with all his force. The Creature was incredibly strong and wouldn't move. The Creature slashed at Ewan with its claws but Ewan managed to dodge its swipes. Ewan gave one last push and then dove for the gun. He landed awkwardly on it but managed to turn and pick it up. He fired at the Creature, which was bearing down on him. The Creature looked stunned as it clutched its chest. Ewan fired again but the Creature had already turned and retreated. With incredible speed it grabbed Sophie from under the bed and tucked her under its arm like a football and jumped out the window. Sophie barely had time to scream as she disappeared into the darkness.

Sophie! No! Ewan thought, but he had no chance to process what had happened as Amy moaned loudly.

Ewan turned and fired at the Creature on top of Amy. The bullet grazed the Creature, which roared and jumped off the bed towards Ewan.

With unsteady hands, Ewan aimed the gun again and pressed the trigger. The gun erupted in a quick flash of light but again he missed the Creature. But this time the gun seemed to scare the Creature and it quickly retreated back through the window.

Ewan dropped the gun and ran to Amy. She was pale, blood quickly draining from her body. She shivered as if she was cold. Ewan stood there, unsure of what to do. Only moments ago she was lying against him, happy and content. Now her life was leaving.

He took her arm and squeezed it tightly. With the other hand he pressed it against it against the deep gash in her neck but it was useless. Blood seeped through his fingers and down onto the sheets.

No . . . no . . . no . . . this can't be happening. I'm going to wake up, Ewan thought.

Amy rolled her head towards Ewan. Her eyes were glassy and weak. She tried to smile. "I love you always, Ewan."

Amy's eyes fluttered and then closed and she let out a last gasp of air.

"Amy?" Ewan said, shaking her shoulders. "Amy, wake up!"

Ewan felt his throat tighten and tears roll down his hot cheeks.

Ewan lowered his face to Amy and kissed her on the lips, but the kiss tasted metallic. Not like Amy at all.

Why? Ewan wondered. *I've even been robbed of a last kiss. Why?*

A Friend in Need . . .

Stu Baillie moved through the long, dark corridors of the school quickly and efficiently. His feet squeaked softly along the grey linoleum floors.

The school was empty and even the vending machine had been stripped of everything. He couldn't even find a single pen or a pencil in this place, let alone any medication. That pathetic man had been lying to him after all. But he didn't have anything better to do other than search for the medication and so he hoped against all odds.

The stucco walls, layered in thick dust, were a yellowish-white colour and hung on them were rows of graduation photos stretching as far back as the thirties. Stu wondered how many of the people in the pictures were still alive and how many had been wiped out by the epidemic. Was it possible every single person in the photographs was dead? Of course it was possible, even likely. Not many had survived the Outbreak and those who had survived didn't know why.

Why had Stu Baillie been spared? Stu couldn't find an answer. Why had that lying bastard been spared? What made them similar? Did they have similar genetic makeup that predisposed them to live? Stu doubted he would ever know the answer and he doubted even less that he cared.

Stu was dressed in the purple kimono he had taken from a fat old woman back just after the outbreak had begun. She definitely wouldn't need it anymore. His Samurai sword was by his side.

Stu wasn't scared of anything. He had conditioned his mind not to feel afraid. He had mastered the art of empting his brain of everything and being at peace with nothingness.

He knew there were Creatures sleeping somewhere in the school but still he made no effort to stay quiet.

He opened the Principal's office, which was where he had found the doctor. But had he really been a doctor? *Still, what else should I call him?* Stu wondered.

There was a large oak desk in the middle, a smashed lamp sat on it. The doctor's mattress was in the corner and pitiful supplies were piled next to it. Stu kicked an empty tuna container, a bunch of useless wires and a couple of logs probably used to make a fire. No medicine.

Stu tore out the desk drawers but still couldn't find anything. What a pitiful existence the doctor had. It was probably a blessing Stu had left him for the Creatures.

Stu picked up a picture that had fallen onto the floor. The cheap golden frame had smashed but the picture was still in place. It was of a plump, bald man about fifty years old wearing a brown suit and red tie. Not the doctor. Perhaps he was the principal whose office it had once been.

Stu placed the picture back on the desk when he heard the distinct sound of a Creature roaring.

Good, Stu thought. *Let them come.*

Stu took out his Samurai sword from its sheath, smiling at the scraping sound the blade made. He listened and waited. He relaxed his shoulders and closed his eyes, pushing all thoughts from his head. He could hear the quick light steps of the Creatures as they came close.

When he opened his eyes, there was a Creature coming straight for him. Stu bowed towards the Creature and took up his fighting stance. The Creature, seemingly unaware of how lethal its opponent was, clamoured over the desk, knocking over the picture Stu had just put in place.

Stu shuffled forward and with a small slash ripped open the Creature's belly. Thick purplish blood oozed from the Creature's stomach. The Creature roared in pain and lunged at Stu. But the Creature had overshot and Stu sidestepped and cut off the Creature's arm at the elbow. The Creature crashed onto the floor and Stu shuffled forward and cut off the Creature's head.

Stu turned to see several more Creatures had filled into the room. Stu smiled and if the Creatures were human they might have been scared of the smile. But the Creatures had no feelings and they advanced.

"Welcome, Teki," Stu exclaimed, taking up his fighting stance again. His blade rose to the ceiling.

The Creatures were ill coordinated in their attacks. Stu took a step forward between two Creatures, slicing the one to his right and then pivoting and cutting the head off the second Creature. The Creatures seemed undaunted and gradually Stu began to tire. With his lean diet, his stamina wasn't what it used to be and he had to retreat slowly, swinging his sword in defensive swipes. The Creatures seemed to hesitate and this allowed Stu to catch his breath and he attacked again. Soon the Creatures were all piles of meat underneath Stu's feet. He was sweating heavily and mopped his forehead with the back of his sleeve. He listened for any more sounds from the darkness but didn't hear anything and so wiped his blade the best he could on the carpet.

The fight had taken a lot out of Stu and he decided to abandon his search for the medicine and go out into the sun where he was safe. He might come back tomorrow if he had nothing better to do and search some more.

Before the Outbreak, Stu had been stronger and had endurance but with the little food he had to eat, he had lost a lot of his energy and muscle. In the later stages of the Outbreak, he had heard some desperate people had taken to eating the Creatures, causing them to mutate.

Stu eyed the fresh flesh but stopped himself. He couldn't chance it.

Instead he wished he could find something nutritious to eat, something with lots of protein and fibre. Then he could take on a whole army of Creatures.

Stu had no further encounters as he made his way out of the school. Perhaps he had killed all the Creatures in the building. Perhaps they had gotten smart and were hiding from him.

Stu pushed the doors open. The light from the sun hurt his eyes and he squinted to adjust to the brightness. He cupped one bloody hand over his eyes and looked up at the sky, which was teal-blue, cloudless and empty.

He walked slowly down the street, taking his time. He had nowhere to be after all. He sat down on the curb and closed his eyes. In his mind he played out Beethoven on the piano. He often tried to remember the chords. He wished he could find a working piano somewhere in the carnage of the city but the only ones he had come across had been smashed to pieces during the chaos.

Stu sighed and opened his eyes. He sat there for a long time, not moving. It was strange to realize nothing ever moved. There wasn't even a breeze.

So when Stu saw flicker of movement down one of the side streets he first thought it was only his imagination. He sat there not moving staring towards the direction where he thought he saw the movement.

Stu would have remained there if his instinct hadn't told him to move. He stood up and slowly shifted towards a shadow of a building where he wouldn't be noticed. He straightened his spine, put his hand on his sword and waited.

He didn't have to wait before a tall lanky man stepped around the corner. He was wearing a Yankees cap and a long black trench coat. Slung over his shoulder was a rifle.

Stu watched him for awhile. He was walking down the middle of the road, seemingly unaware he was being watched.

Stu wondered what he was doing. Stu guessed he was probably looking for something to eat but then again, perhaps he was just bored and exploring new territory.

It was too bad, Stu thought. *Carelessness always got people in trouble.*

Stu stepped out of the shadows and yelled at the man. "Hey!"

The man whirled around and pointed his gun at Stu. Stu raised his hands to show the man he meant no harm. "Welcome to the desert," he told the man.

The man didn't lower the gun but Stu was undaunted and walked towards the man.

"Stop right there," the man said.

Stu did as he was told and stopped. "My name is Stu Baillie. What's yours?"

The man seemed to consider the question, eying Stu carefully. Probably noting the black bile on his kimono. The man had sharp features, a thin nose and clear blue eyes. He was older than most people Stu came across, perhaps mid-sixties but he looked healthy — or at least as healthy as anybody else in this new world.

"Graham Mayer," he said.

"Well Graham, you want to put the gun down?" Stu said. "Talk like civilized people."

"I see you have a sword."

"Of course I do, it would be foolish not to have some sort of protection. But it's not for people killing. I save it for the Teki."

"Teki?" Graham scrunched his forehead.

"Yes, the Teki who come at you in the night, trying to devour you."

"No Creatures around here," Graham said, tightening his grip on the rifle.

Stu held up his hands. "This blood is from the Teki. We all need to protect ourselves."

Stu took a step forward but Graham stiffened and Stu stopped. "Where did you get the rifle?" he asked.

"It was my father's. He's dead now."

"The Teki got him?"

"No. Looters."

Stu nodded in sympathy. "Do you mind if I put my arms down. They're getting tired."

"No, keep them up."

"What can I do to convince you I'm friendly?"

"Give me your sword."

Stu smiled. "I'm sorry Graham. I can't do that."

"Why not?"

"Because it's not just any sword. This here is a genuine Katana from Japan. It was given to me as a present while I was stationed there."

Graham's eyes became wide. "You were in the army?"

"Actually the air force. It was an exchange program. Those were the days, huh Graham? What did you do before the Outbreak?"

"Why does it matter what I did?" Graham snapped.

"You know what, Graham? I'm going to put my arms down. I don't think you're going to shoot me."

Stu slowly lowered his arms. Graham didn't move. He just stood there with the rifle pointed at Stu.

"You know, I suppose you're right," Stu said. "It doesn't much matter what job you did before the Outbreak. I'm sorry if said anything I shouldn't have. I was only trying to make small talk."

Graham's mouth stretched across his face. "It's time to walk in the opposite direction, Stu."

"Oh come on. Don't be like that. I said I was sorry, didn't I?"

"I'm not going to ask again, Stu. Start walking."

"Okay, okay but let me ask you a question first. Don't you think it's better to stick together? I mean the Teki will be out soon enough. With your gun and my sword we could do some real damage. Don't you think?"

"Get away from me Stu, I'm warning you."

Stu studied the gun. It was an old, worn hunting rifle. Its barrel had specks of rust.

"Okay, I'll leave, but I have to ask you one question before I go."

"What's that?" Graham asked.

"Is that gun even loaded?"

"Of course it's loaded. I don't go carrying around an empty gun for nothing."

Stu took a step towards Graham. "I was only asking because it's very hard to find ammunition these days. In fact, I think soon all the ammunition will be used up and we won't be able to manufacture anymore and that will be a real shame because what would we do without guns?"

"I'm warning you Stu, don't come any closer," Graham yelled, but his voice was full of fear and uncertainty.

Stu slowly took the sword from his belt and held it in front of his body. Graham stood still. But Graham's hands were beginning to waver and this made Stu smile. He was going to have fun watching Graham die.

Stu took another step towards Graham, pressing the point of the sword against his neck. Graham dropped the gun and raised his hands.

"My, how the tables have turned," Stu said, the grin still on his face.

"What are you going to do now?" Graham asked, seemingly regaining his nerves.

"I'm not going to do anything," Stu said, although he had a perfectly good image of watching the Creatures tear at his face.

The Twin Terrors

Ewan dreamed he was being chased through the museum by a samurai. He couldn't see the samurai's face but he was behind him. His footsteps followed Ewan closely. Somehow he knew the samurai was dressed in the armour from the museum's collection. The hallway was dark and cast oblong shadows across the floor. The thick blackness seemed impossibly overwhelming, stretching down endlessly. Gasping for breath and his heart pounding, Ewan had to feel his way through the hallways with his hands.

Suddenly the hallways didn't seem like that of the museum. He was in some sort of tunnel only a few feet bigger than his head. Everything was black around him.

Ewan tripped and fell on his wrist, digging into dirt. He turned to see the samurai standing over him, his sword raised. The Japanese warrior was large and bulky, but his face was cast in shadow. Ewan closed his eyes and raised his hands just as the blade came down on him.

Ewan woke with a raspy gasp of a dying man's last breath. He heard the sound of glass smashing and the sound of feet scampering quickly over the linoleum floor. He looked around and found the illuminated room empty. He had gotten used to sleeping with the harsh lights on a long time ago.

"Timmy?" His voice was weak and dry. Ewan tried to call out again, propping himself up on one elbow and rubbing his eyes. His head was still spinning and his body felt numb. He tried to swing his legs around and at first he couldn't move them but with the aid of his hands he managed to place them on the floor. He examined his bandaged ankle, which was beginning to puss. Was that a good or a bad sign? He wasn't sure.

Ewan grabbed the railing and with a grunt of effort got to his feet. He stood motionless for what seemed a long time, letting his body adjust.

He heard Ashley's voice, loud and shrill. "Justin, Anthony get back here!"

Using the railing, Ewan walked down the hallway, following Ashley's voice until he found her in a room. In front of her was a broken display ad; it looked like several of the exhibits were missing.

Ashley glanced up at Ewan and looked embarrassed. "I'm sorry . . . I think the boys took something."

Ashley had changed out of her dirty clothes and had somehow managed to find an ill-fitting dress. Ewan could see several safety pins strategically placed to crop the waist and bust. Ewan wondered where she had found it but was too embarrassed to ask.

"It's okay. It's not like anybody is going to miss it," Ewan admitted, looking around the room as if noticing the different displays for the first time. They were in the Greece section and he was surrounded by Greek pots, Greek jewellery and Greek weapons. The last thought gave Ewan pause.

"What display is that?" Ewan asked.

Ashley read the caption for the display. "Says here . . . Spartan Warrior." Ashley's eye widened, worriedly. "I'm going to kill those two," she muttered.

Ashley ran towards the hallway and Ewan limped after her. They found Justin and Anthony in the dinosaur section sword fighting with the two Spartan swords they had taken from the display case. One of them was wearing a rusted Greek helmet. They were laughing and giggling.

"Boys! Stop that right this moment," Ashley said. "You're going to hurt each other."

As if on cue, the boy with the helmet broke through his brother's defences and hit him on the shoulder.

"No fair. I had stopped," the injured brother said, rubbing his shoulder. Luckily the blade was dull and brittle and probably couldn't do much damage.

"Life's not fair," the other brother retorted.

They both lunged at each other, steel clanging.

"Now both of you stop this moment," Ashley said. "Give me those swords and Justin apologize to your brother."

Justin gave Anthony a pitiful apology as Ashley collected the swords and the helmet from the boys.

"We are guests here of Mr. Walder," Ashley lectured. "You shouldn't go breaking things."

The boys frowned at Ewan who forced a smile on his face. He hadn't been called Mr. Walder since his teaching days and it brought back memories of bratty kids spitting bits of chewed up paper at each other and petting each other under the desks.

"He doesn't own the museum," Justin pouted, crossing his small arms over his chest.

The twins had identical shaggy blonde hair and small dirty faces. They were a little taller than Tim and perhaps a little older but not by much. Their eyes were wide and innocent.

"That's a very rude thing to say, Justin," Ashley pointed out. "He may not own it, but he's taking care of it."

"What for?" Anthony demanded.

Ashley let out an exasperated sigh and told the kids to go out in the garden and find something to eat.

Ewan doubted there would be anything worth picking but he kept quiet as Justin and Anthony scampered off.

"They are quite the handful aren't they?" Ewan said, as soon as they were alone. He was glad Tim enjoyed reading so much and could entertain himself for hours.

Ashley nodded. "They took their parents' deaths really hard." She paused to consider this. "I guess we all did."

Ewan was about to ask how they died but then thought it was better not to know.

"You want to go find Timmy with me?" Ewan asked.

"I think that's so cute."

"What?"

"You calling him Timmy."

Ewan smiled embarrassed. "I think he's grown out of it but, I don't know, I can't stop. Perhaps it would be easier if Amy was alive."

Ashley walked slowly, allowing Ewan to hobble at his own pace. Ewan walked to ask Ashley about herself but he didn't know what to ask. Everything he could think of – the past – was too painful. He was afraid talking about it would be too painful so he just didn't.

Ewan found going down the stairs a painful chore with his injured ankle but he eventually just decided to hop down them while leaning on the railing. About halfway down he paused to catch his breath.

I'm just in bad shape, Ewan thought as he coughed twice.

"Are you going to be okay?" Ashley asked.

Ewan nodded. "Yeah, fine."

Ashley put her arm around Ewan's waist and supported him from the other side until they reached the bottom.

They found Tim sitting in the lobby of the museum reading a book he had picked from the gift shop about dinosaurs.

He looked up when he saw Ewan and Ashley walking toward him. He flashed a small, boyish smile towards Ashley, ignoring his father.

"Ley-ley, did you know birds are descended from a type of dinosaur called theropods?"

Ashley smiled back and to Ewan it seemed as if together they had some secret they were keeping from him. Inside his chest he felt a tweak of jealousy.

"Tim, you're the smartest person I know."

This made Tim smile even more.

"Timmy," Ewan said. "Why don't you go play with Anthony and Justin?"

"My name is Tim."

"I'm sorry. I keep forgetting."

"I'm okay with my book," Tim declined, returning to reading.

"Yeah, but don't you want to socialize a bit? How long has it been since you've played with somebody your own age?"

"I said I want to read my book, okay?"

Ashley touched Ewan lightly on the arm. "The twins can play a little rough. Perhaps it's best to just let him read."

Ewan pursed his lips. He wanted to ask her what she knew about being a parent. How did she know what was best for Tim? But he didn't want to argue in front of Tim so he just nodded.

"Okay, Timmy. Let me know if you get hungry."

"I know where the food is."

"Okay, get it yourself then," Ewan said.

Ewan gave Tim one last look but he didn't pay any attention and so Ewan turned and limped out the front entrance and into the street.

Coldness sunk in from the blue sky and it made Ewan shiver. Soon it would be winter and the snow would come. It was always the worst time of the year. The days were short and the Creatures seemed more emboldened and they didn't seem to feel the cold. Would the generator hold until then? Would they be able to find more coils to power the museum? And now they had three more mouths to feed — two growing boys. Their little garden wouldn't sustain them.

What was he going to do? Could he ask Ashley and the twins to move on? Where would they go? Ashley had saved his life, after all. Kicking them out did seem a little cold-hearted and besides Tim would never forgive him. He had fallen in love with Ashley already.

And what if Ashley and the kids refused to move on? What if they took over the museum? Could he really trust Ashley? Maybe he should just kill them now. Their flesh would probably give them enough to get through winter.

As much as the thought revolted Ewan, he knew he had to consider it because Ashley was probably considering the same thing. He was weak after all and practically useless.

Although Ashley would be useful against the Creatures, starvation was just as big a problem. He would have to weigh his options carefully but not take too much time deciding.

Ewan took in a deep breath. The coldness filled his lungs and made him cough. He turned to see Ashley had come up beside him.

"Oh land of France, oh blissful pleasant land, today laid desolate by cruel waste!"

"What is that?" Ewan asked. "A poem?"

"Song of Roland. It's an old medieval poem."

"Never heard it before,"

"I learned in grade twelve English class," Ashley said, shaking her head. "It's strange what you remember, isn't it? It seems so long ago."

"To me it seems like yesterday," Ewan said, looking at Ashley.

"I had four sisters, all dead now."

As much as Ewan needed the past, he hated talking about it. He saw no use in it. It didn't make him feel any better, but he managed to mumble the expected sorrow.

"My mother was a heroin addict, my father . . . my father was stupid. He got arrested for passing a note to a bank teller."

"Why are you telling me this?"

"I'm not sure," Ashley said. "Perhaps I want you to know about me. Just in case. . ."

"Just in case what?" Ewan asked.

"You decide to kill us."

Ewan tried to act surprised, but he knew he pulled it off badly. "Ashley, I'm not going to kill anybody. You saved our lives. I won't forget that."

"But winter is coming. There isn't going to be any food," Ashley said. "Ewan, we've put my life – the life of the kids – in your hands. It's hard to trust anybody."

Ewan felt ashamed for his earlier thoughts about kicking Ashley and the two boys out. He said, "And I have to trust you too. You could just as easily kill Timmy and I."

Ashley frowned and put her hands on her hips. "I suppose you're right. What do we do?"

"Maybe we go our separate ways."

Ashley seemed to think about this for awhile. "I'm not sure if I can. The kids are great, I love them but . . . I've been alone for a long time. I would rather take my chances with you."

"Me too," Ewan said.

Neither said anything for a long time.

"Do you think the Creatures starve?"

"You mean if they don't have anything to eat?" Ewan asked. He hadn't considered the possibility that the Creatures were running out of a food source as well. What were they eating anyways?

He knew the raccoons and other small rodents were probably mostly gone which didn't leave much. Perhaps the Creatures were cannibals and feasted on their own.

Ewan knew that most extremely deadly diseases were almost too effective and killed their host too quickly, preventing the disease from spreading. Ewan knew the bubonic plague, perhaps the most feared disease, would spout up quickly but would teeter out just as fast.

Ashley nodded. "Maybe one day they will all starve and die off and we'll be able to reclaim the city."

"Maybe. I don't know. Although, I think we are more likely to starve first."

"Don't talk like that. Think of the children."

Ewan eyed Ashley wearily. "You're right."

"What do you think if we caught one and were able to study it?" Ashley asked.

"Catch a Creature? How?"

"I don't know. There's two of us now. I've been thinking about this for a bit but haven't had anybody to help me. Don't you think it would be useful to study it? We don't know anything about them. Perhaps if we learned something about them we could find a weakness and exploit it."

Ewan was doubtful.

"You want to keep the Creature in a cage or something?"

"Why not? We set up a trap, capture it and study it. Try different substances on it. See if any work. You're a biologist, right?"

Ewan frowned. "Who told you that?"

"Tim of course. He was bragging about you."

Ewan sighed. He couldn't imagine Tim bragging about him. "I'm a high school science teacher. That's all. I don't have the expertise or the equipment to study these Creatures."

"Do you have a better idea?"

"Yes, hide out in here where it's safe. Live for another day."

"I'm so sick of hiding," Ashley said softly, her voice swelling up with emotion. "Let's take the fight to them for a change."

"There is no cure, Ashley," Ewan said. He remembered before the television stations shut down for good the reporters were obsessed with finding a cure. That was all they were talking about and here he was talking about it again.

"How do you know that?" Ashley asked. "Have you done any research?"

"No . . . of course not."

Ashley crossed her arms across her chest. "That's right. Nobody has; at least any meaningful research. Perhaps you can."

65

"I told you, Ashley. I'm just a high school teacher. I'm not that smart."

"What choice do we have?" Ashley said, biting her lower lip. "I saved your life. This is what I'm asking for in return.

Ewan let out a long sigh. He didn't say anything for a while. He looked out into the empty city. Just behind Queen's Park the University of Toronto stood, once full of students. Ewan was suddenly struck by an idea.

"Saint George's Campus is where the biology department is. It's not far from here." Ewan said, smiling. "More specifically the department of Ecology and Evolutionary biology. If things aren't totally trashed we might be able to find something there to study the Creatures with."

Ewan went to grab his backpack and was surprised to find Tim was sitting on the old mattress staring blankly at the wall.

"What's wrong Timmy? You finished your book?" Ewan said, putting a flashlight into his backpack. He expected Tim to reprimand him for calling him Timmy again but didn't even seem to notice.

"Justin and Anthony are orphans."

"They're not orphans. They have Ashley."

"But Ashley's not their real mother."

"That's right," Ewan said.

"If you die will I be an orphan?" Tim asked, looking over at Ewan.

"That's not going to happen."

"Where are you going?"

"We're going to look for some supplies. We'll be back in a bit."

To Ewan's surprise, Tim didn't ask to go with him. Instead he just nodded, still seemingly lost in thought.

"You sure you're alright, Timmy?" Ewan asked again.

"I think Justin and Anthony are only acting out because their parents died," Tim said, seriously.

This made Ewan laugh. It was a much-needed release.

Tim stared at him angrily. "What's so funny?"

Ewan went to rustle Tim's hair but Tim managed to dodge Ewan's grasp. "You're just wise beyond your years, Timmy."

Tim nodded, as if he was accepting this. They didn't say anything for a while. "Why can't the Creatures come out in the daytime?"

"Tim, I told you already. It's because of their eyes."

"Yeah, but how can a disease do that to a person?"

Ewan put a hand around Tim's small shoulder. This time Tim didn't resist. "If I knew we might have been able to stop it."

"But not anymore?"

Ewan sighed. Tim was spending too much time around Ashley. It had been a long time since Ewan had any kind of hope and he wasn't about to start up again now. "I'm not sure. Maybe."

Tim nodded as if he was thinking deeply. "Dad, can you tell me about sharks?"

"Why do you want to hear about the sharks?"

"Please, Dad."

Ewan sighed and sat down beside Tim. His thick hair was matted with mud and dirt. His clothes were ripped and worn. Ewan made a mental note to find Tim some new clothes when he had time.

"Don't you think it's interesting?" Tim asked.

"Of course, Timm—Tim. I'm the biologist, remember," Ewan reminded him. "There have been five extinctions since the beginning of the Earth. Sharks have survived three of them. They are over three hundred million years old."

"Do you think they are still around?" Tim asked.

Ewan nodded. "At this rate they'll outlive humans."

"Ewan, don't say that!" Tim scolded.

"Sorry," Ewan said. "Perhaps you would like to be my father instead. The job is still vacant, no matter how many applicants I have interviewed."

Ewan thought Tim was going to scold him again for being too morbid but instead he laughed which made Ewan smile. He never got tired of hearing Tim laugh. It happened so infrequently.

"I also read up on Dragonfly's eyes," he said.

"Yeah?"

"Apparently they have 360 degree vision and can see UV light and a special set of eyes for polarized light that helps them navigate the sun's glare."

Ewan nodded. "Yes, that's true."

"So why is a small insect more advanced than humans?"

"I don't know, Timmy," Ewan said, wondering if there were any more Dragonflies left in the world or if they had gone extinct. "It's a funny world."

"I'll say," Tim agreed, which made Ewan hold him tighter.

Ewan loved it when Tim wanted to talk about sharks and dragonflies. He was glad he was able to pass along some of the wonderment of the world, even if it was slowly disintegrating in front of them.

Ashley Vulfriezer walked several paces in front of Ewan. His ankle still hurt when he put pressure on it and so he travelled slowly. Ashley's pistol was stuffed into her waist and Ewan was spinning Ol' Bessy around in his palm distractedly.

They were walking on Bloor Street where some of the best shopping had been in Toronto. Ewan remembered when the streets were packed with cars and people clustered the sidewalks with their shopping bags, talking on their cellphones.

The street had been nicknamed the Mink Mile for its pricy clothes, but now any fur coats that had once been on sale had long disappeared and most of the glass panes that had displayed decadent merchandise had been smashed and the stores looted.

They turned left onto Devonshire. Ashley was wearing brown work boots and tight blue jeans. Ewan couldn't help but stare at her butt as she took long strides. How long had it been since he had seen a female in person?

"Oh Amy, forgive me."

Ashley stopped and turned. "What was that?"

"Nothing," Ewan said quickly. "I'm just used to talking to myself."

"You were talking to your wife, weren't you?"

Ewan stumbled. "Just forget it."

Ashley smiled. "What was she like?"

"Why are you so curious?"

"I just want to know my competition."

Ewan frowned. He was sure he hadn't heard her right. "Excuse me?"

"Well, we'll need to breed to preserve humankind so technically she's my competition."

Ewan stopped walking. He suddenly felt woozy. "I'm not sure . . . what I mean is—"

Ashley laughed. "Relax. I'm just joking."

Ewan forced a smile even though as he felt the blood rush to his cheeks. "That was just mean."

Ashley laughed again. It was a high, fluttery sound and Ewan couldn't help but enjoy it.

"I've only been talking to the twins for the past year. It's good to have an adult conversation."

"I wouldn't actually call this an adult conversation."

Ashley smiled. "Yeah, but that look on your face was priceless."

There was a sudden gust of wind that picked up and Ewan shivered. Ashley rubbed his arms.

"You're cold. You have goose bumps," she observed.

Ewan smiled. "I'll be okay. Let's keep moving."

Ashley nodded and they continued their trek.

The truth was Ewan felt the coldness in his bones and his joints felt stiff and with each step a pain shot up through his ankle.

"You know," Ewan said, just to have something to say. "Goosebumps are leftover from an evolutionary process when humans had fur. Little tiny muscles would raise the fur and help insulate us."

"Really?" Ashley said. "I wish I could grow some fur now."

Ewan laughed. "You would look awfully funny with fur."

"Tim was right."

"About what?" Ewan asked.

"You're just full of useless facts."

"At least I don't have medieval poems memorized."

Ashley kicked at a rock and watched as it skipped over a crack in the sidewalk. "It's one of the oldest pieces of French literature. That's got to count for something."

They walked in silence for awhile, sticking to the middle of the road, walking between the burnt cars to avoid any of the darker shadows. Ewan had seen some of the Creatures navigating the dark alleyways in the daytime and so it was safer to stick to the main routes. As long as there was sun.

"You think we'll ever find some more ammo?" Ewan asked.

Ashley shrugged. "Not sure. I think most of it has been used up."

"Maybe we should try and make some bow and arrows," Ewan said, jokingly.

But Ashley turned towards Ewan. "That's actually not a bad idea."

"You're serious?" Ewan said.

"Crossbows would be better. We can be like Buffy the Vampire slayer."

"I don't even know where to begin."

Ashley smiled. "We learn like our ancestors did."

They got to King's College Circle where Saint George's Campus was and there they stopped. The campus looked like a building from Oxford or Cambridge. It was made of stone and had a churchy look with moss growing on the side and steeple stretching skywards. Leafless trees stood in front of the building, their branches like thick knarred fingers.

"What do you think?" Ashley asked. "Will there be Creatures in there?"

"I would think so," Ewan replied. "But hopefully they'll be asleep and we can get in and out of there no problem, without waking them."

Ashley stared at Ewan. "You don't really believe that, do you?" she asked.

Ewan shrugged. "Not really but it's easier than the alternative."

"Do you even know what we need?"

Ewan shook his head. "Not a clue. Anything that will help us study the Creatures would be a start."

Ewan glanced at Amy and then back at the ominous building. Neither wanted to move forward yet they knew they couldn't go back either. They still had plenty of sunlight but they knew it wouldn't last forever.

"Looks like something Count Dracula would live in, doesn't it?" Ashley said.

"Just remember you're Buffy." Ewan tried to laugh but the nervousness swelled around in his stomach, making any normal noise all but impossible.

"Ewan?"

"What?" Ewan demanded, sounding a little harsher than he meant to.

Luckily Ashley didn't seem to notice. "Do Hydra's really live forever?"

Ewan looked at Ashley confused, not knowing what she was talking about.

"Tim said there was this animal that lived forever — this Hydra."

"Tim told you that? I didn't think he had been listening."

Ashley nodded.

Ewan studied her closely. Her hard brown eyes seemed strange somehow. Her toughness seemed to have dissipated somewhat and replaced with . . . what? Maybe it was motherliness, a need to protect and nurture.

"It's still not conclusive. Nobody really knows," Ewan replied.

"How can you measure immortality? I mean how do you know if an animal lives for five hundred, six hundred years? Or if it lives forever?"

Ewan shrugged, wondering what Ashley was getting at. Why was she bringing it up now?

"I don't know Ashley."

"Sorry."

"Sorry for what?" Ewan asked.

"Sorry for saying you're full of useless facts."

Ewan laughed. He was happy to have someone to talk to that wasn't Tim.

They walked up the large front steps to the wooden double door. Their footsteps echoed dully on the hard surface. Ewan put his ear to the door but couldn't hear any movement.

"No talking from now on," he whispered to Ashley who nodded.

"Okay Xander."

"Xander?"

"Yeah, he was Buffy's sidekick."

Ewan took a deep breath and reached for the handle but instead he came in contact with Ashley's small hand. She had reached out and grabbed his and gave it a quick squeeze. Ewan raised his eyebrows as if questioning her. She gave a small smile and nodded.

Ewan put his hand on the handle and turned. The door creaked when he pulled it open. A powerful damp musty smell filled Ewan's nostrils and he had to stifle a cough.

Neither Ewan nor Ashley moved. The darkness that lay before them was thick and daunting. They listened again but didn't hear anything.

Ewan felt his heartbeat quicken and his breathing become shallower. He could still feel the clammy warmth of Ashley's skin against his. It lingered in his senses, tingling his skin.

Ashley slowly took out the flashlight from her pocket and shone it into the hallway. The bright incandescent light flooded the room. The grey room was large and cavernous with large stone pillars holding up the ceiling. The room appeared to be empty.

Ewan turned on his flashlight and his light joined Ashley's. Ashley stepped in first and Ewan followed. She held her gun out in front of her as she slowly stepped into the hallway.

There was an overturned desk in the right hand corner. A sign above lead them to the elevator. Ewan knew enough about universities to know there wouldn't be any congruent layout or any systematic way of quickly sweeping the building.

Ewan tapped Ashley on the shoulder and pointed to a corridor to the left. That was where the steps were that would lead them to the classrooms and labs.

Escape

Stu took Graham through the front entrance of the zoo, across the empty parking lot. Somehow Stu expected to hear the roar of lions or the distant gawking of a crane. How was it he hadn't become accustomed to the silence yet? Maybe it was just humans weren't conditioned for the silence.

Stu had come to the zoo long after all the animals were gone. He wondered what happened to them. Had some poor zookeeper released them after the city fell apart? And if so, were they out in the city somewhere? Had the Creatures gotten to them? Or were some of the predatory animals still out there?

Stu had used some rope to bind Graham's hands and was walking several paces in front.

"This is where you live?" Graham stopped and looked up at the sign that was now weathered and dilapidated.

"This is where I've made my home. It makes a good fortress against the Teki."

"You mean the Creatures?" Graham asked. "Why do you call them that?"

Stu pushed Graham forward, and he stumbled and fell on the pavement. His Yankees cap fell from his head. Stu waited for Graham to move but he didn't.

Stu sighed and prodded Graham with his foot. "Come on, get up."

Graham tucked a knee under his body and managed to rise to his feet. He had gravel in his hair but otherwise didn't appear hurt. He stared at Stu while casually dusting himself off. He then bent down and grabbed his hat and put it back on his head.

Stu stared thoughtfully back. He didn't see anger or hatred in Graham's eyes, the usual reaction from captives. No, there was a look of cool calculating.

"You know my father," Graham said, turning and walking across the bridge that passed over a small pool of water. "He used to come home drunk from the bar, and for fun he used to come beat on my sister and me. Sometimes he just used his fist and sometimes, if he had a particular bad day, he would use his belt."

Stu smiled behind Graham's back. "So what are you saying? You're used of being pushed around, pussy?"

"Trust me, you couldn't lay a beating down like my old man."

"Is that an invitation to try?"

Graham shrugged. "Isn't that the reason you tied me up?"

Stu laughed. "You don't know the half of it."

They walked towards the Siberian Tiger exhibit. A swarm of large flies hung around the cage in a black cloud. Stu swatted them away, wondering if they were infected with the same disease the Creatures had.

Stu was strong, he was a survivor. He would do what it took while others simply gave up and died. Everybody else, including Graham, was weak.

The Outbreak had provided Stu a chance to become great. One day he would be charged with rebuilding civilization and he would be the leader. He just knew it deep down in his gut.

"You're going to feed me to the Creatures aren't you?" Graham asked.

Stu looked at Graham surprised. Nobody else had guessed their fate until it was too late. Nobody else realized how deprived Stu really was. He would have to be careful with this one. He was smarter than the rest. Perhaps it came from having an abusive childhood.

"Why do you say that?" Stu asked.

"Because that's what I would do if I were you."

"Have you fed anybody to the Creatures?"

"No, of course not. You're the first person I've come across in two years. But I've always wondered what it would be like."

"It's like being God," Stu said. "Having life and death over another human being is the ultimate power."

Graham nodded. "I guess that's how my father felt. He had power over our lives. He could cause us pain or not. It was his choice."

"Was he really killed by looters?"

Graham didn't answer for a while but eventually he shrugged. "I killed him with a steak knife. He was drunk and I told

74

my mother that looters had broken in. People were dying all around us. It really wasn't that hard."

"And what did you feel?"

Graham shrugged. "Nothing. Not a thing. I wasn't happy, I wasn't sad. I might as well have been, I dunno . . . playing a video game."

Stu never remembered his parents. His father had killed himself and his mother had died of AIDS shortly thereafter so he'd been raised by his aunt who lived in Etobicoke. Stu lived as an unwanted second-class citizen and had been constantly bullied by his aunt's two older boys. His aunt never knew her two sons bullied him. Stu stayed silent, fearful of the repercussions. His aunt spent her entire day at her job and came home too exhausted to care for the kids. Stu knew she wouldn't be able to offer much protection anyways

Sometime just after Stu turned thirteen, he discovered martial arts. Having no money to actually join classes, he learned on his own by befriending some of the kids in the class and begging them to teach him. In return he would run errands for them or cover for them when they were out late or with their girlfriends.

Stu shoved Graham into the tiger cage and locked the doors. Stu looked up at the sky, which was a deep blue and cloudless. It wouldn't be long before the sun would begin to set. Stu looked back at Graham who was staring intently at him. Neither of them said anything. Stu realized Graham was looking for a way out, an angle he could use.

Stu realized Graham wasn't the type to beg for his life. He would remain calm and try to look for a way out.

What a disappointment, Stu thought.

It would take a lot of the fun out the whole thing. Stu loved watching people squirm. But he also respected Graham for remaining brave.

Stu spent the rest of the afternoon scrounging for food but there wasn't much around. He wondered if he should just kill Graham himself and eat him but the thought was still repulsive no matter how much he tried to justify it. He had seen people do it but he wouldn't sully his body with human meat.

When Stu returned to the tiger cage Graham was sitting on a rock, his feet curled up, and his hands still tied behind his back. He was shivering from the cold and looked small and sickly.

Stu hadn't noticed how quickly the temperature had dropped, but it was getting colder, especially during the nights.

When Stu opened the cage, Graham didn't look up. He just sat there shivering. Stu stood there vexed. Maybe he should leave Graham there for another day or so. Maybe then he would start begging for his life.

But no, Stu thought. *Might as well get it over and done with.*

Stu walked over to Graham. "Time to get up," he said. "Time to meet the Teki."

Finally Graham looked up at Stu. There was something in his eyes that gave Stu pause. Usually people felt defeated and scared, but there was something else there. Stu thought it looked like resolve.

All of a sudden Graham jumped up from the rock with a speed that only moments ago seemed impossible. His hands became free and in them was a large rock.

What happened to the rope? Stu wondered how he had freed himself.

Stu began to draw his sword but before he could do so, Graham hurled the rock at him. Stu had no time to duck and it hit him hard in the forehead and a wave of pain swept over him. His vision became blurry. He tried to recover but the pain and dizziness overtook him and he collapsed to the ground.

Stu could hear Graham's heavy footsteps as he ran past Stu and out of the cage.

Stu clutched his head and tried to get to his feet. It took him several tries before he could orientate himself. Just in time to see Graham run down the pathway towards the exit.

Stu cursed himself for not being more alert and ran after him. How had he become so sloppy? He was used to stupid, feeble people. Graham was different. Stu had known that. But that was okay. Graham had nowhere to run to. He was dead either way.

Stu drew his sword and charged after Graham. He lost sight of Graham as he turned the corner around the old butterfly exhibit. He kept running only stopping when he got to the gift shop. There he stopped and looked around. There was still no sign of Graham. Stu looked beyond to the parking lot but there was nothing moving. He listened but only heard his heavy breathing.

What if Graham had double backed? That's what Stu would have done. He turned around and headed back down the path towards the tiger cage, his sword held ready.

He looked up at the sky, which was turning purple as the sun slowly disappeared behind the horizon. It wouldn't be long before the Creatures came out.

Still Stu did not rush. He walked slowly, quietly, listening at every step for any sound of movement. He heard nothing.

There were many places Graham could be hiding and there was no way he could get to them before the Creatures started to appear. Stu tried to remember if there was anything that Graham might be able to use as a weapon. Stu had kept an M-16 at the guest services but it had run out of bullets long ago.

Stu debated whether he should just go into one of the cages and wait until the morning. Would Graham be able to survive the night? Stu gave him about a fifty-fifty chance. Anybody who had survived this long could probably find some place to hide. It would be a waste if Graham was killed by the Creatures and he wasn't there to watch.

Stu checked the Indo-Malaya pavilion. Inside it was dark and stank of decay. The building had turned into a large morgue of foreign plants and animals. Once they had no human protector there was no way they could have survived.

Stu made his way through the building sweeping each nook and hallway. He wasn't afraid of being ambushed by any Creature. He made sure the zoo was clear every morning. He hadn't found a sleeping Creature in at least a year. They seemed to realize the zoo was a dangerous place to be and only came for feeding time during the night.

Stu stepped out of the pavilion, surprised to see the sky had turned dark. He felt a presence above him and turned around just in time to see a Creature jump from the rooftop. Stu crouched for balance and thrust his sword upwards. The Creature came down, impaling itself on the sharp blade.

Stu pulled the sword free and quickly crouched back into an attacking position but he was alone. He lowered his sword slightly and continued deeper into the zoo.

Again he considered whether he should lock himself up and get some rest but he wasn't comfortable with Graham on the loose. He knew he could defend himself against the Creatures, just so long as too many didn't attack him at once.

He knew out in the open he was vulnerable because the Creatures could easily surround him. He had always fought the Creatures in rooms and hallways where he could easily defend against their vast numbers by keeping his back against a wall but here he would have no such advantage. Still he was up for the challenge.

Stu made his way along the path, past the rainforest until he came to the rhino overlook without any incident. In the paddocks below there was a carcass of a rhino that had been picked clean by the Creatures.

Stu heard a noise from behind and saw about a dozen or so Creatures charging for him. Stu did something he'd never done before when facing the Creatures: he turned and ran back the way he'd come.

There was a building in front of him and he knew if he could defend the entrance he would be fine. He looked behind him and saw the Creatures gaining on him quickly. He picked up speed, his legs pounding on the pathway, his lungs hurt from inhaling the cold air.

Stu was almost at the building when he stumbled, losing his balance slightly. It was just enough to slow his momentum down and he knew he wasn't going to be able to make it to the building. He turned and slashed the first Creature, cutting its body open. He tried to back away, all the while defending himself from the Creatures.

The Creatures were flanking him and soon he would be surrounded. The battle seemed to be going in slow motion. Attacking and defending. The Creatures' snarls cut short as he slashed them. He was determined not to show fear and to take as many of the Creatures as he could. He sidestepped and attacked. He spotted to his left, out of the corner of his eye a Creature hurling its body at him. He knew he was too late to bring his sword around.

This is it, he told himself. *This is how I die.*

But it wasn't to be. A pitchfork seemed to come out of nowhere and pierced the Creature's neck. The Creature seemed to hover in midair and then fall to the ground. Stu looked and saw

Graham standing there, no more than five paces away from him, defending against the Creatures, which were going berserk with fury.

Stu circled so his back was against Graham's. Together a Creature wouldn't be able to sneak up on them.

"We need to make our way to the building," Stu said, breathless. He was getting tired, his limbs burned from exhaustion.

They fought their way until they were at the entrance of the door. Stu admired Graham's use of the pitchfork, spearing and parrying with it with skill.

Stu kicked the door open and together they stepped in.

"What now?" Graham asked.

Together they could easily defend the door – at least for awhile but the Creatures kept coming and there was no way they could do it the entire night.

"We need fire," Stu said.

"Okay, I'm going to look around. You think you can defend the doorway?" Graham asked.

Stu laughed confidently, although he wasn't so sure his strength would hold up.

Graham nodded and disappeared running down the hallway and Stu concentrated on conserving his energy.

The Creatures seemed hesitant on attacking him now as if they just realized the futility of the effort. He could hear their heavy footsteps on the roof, no doubt looking for ways to get in. He wondered if they would find tiles missing or a broken window. In all likelihood they would find some way into the building, but there was no use thinking about it so instead he decided to concentrate on his breathing and relaxing his aching body.

The adrenaline was still coursing through his body. He loved wielding the blade: the poetry, the agility. It gave him such a rush.

Stu smiled. "Come on Teki, you too scared of the Samurai?" he whispered.

Suddenly Stu heard Graham call him. "Stu, come quickly!"

Stu glanced back to the darkness. He wondered if it was some sort of trap. What was Graham up to?

Stu glanced back again and saw a small speck of light glowing down the hallway. What was happening? The speck of light was getting bigger. Stu lowered his sword and bolted towards the light. It took a moment for the Creatures to realize he was gone but once they did, they swarmed into the building.

Stu ran down the hallway. As he got closer he realized the whole wall was on fire. How had Graham accomplished that? The fire quickly spread across the support beams overhead and thick, dark smoke filled the room.

The Creatures hung back, afraid of the fire. Stu watched as the fire spread to engulf the entire hallway. Graham stood next to the wall. In his hand he had a torch and a cloth covering his mouth. Although they were safe from the Creatures they were at risk of dying from carbon monoxide.

The University

Ewan and Ashley walked through the university, going from room to room, hallway to hallway, floor to floor. The classrooms were conventional with long desks and stools pushed up against them. To Ewan the place felt eerie. Everything was silent and unmoving with the faint smell of undefined chemicals. There were layers of dust everywhere and cobwebs strung from the neon lamps but a part from that, everything was neatly in place as if the students had just gone away for summer vacation and would be back any moment.

Ewan wasn't even sure what he was looking for. It seemed a fruitless exercise but perhaps it would appease Ashley. Besides, it was better than doing nothing, he reasoned.

In one of the classrooms there was a diagram of an atom with half of its parts labeled as if the professor had been interrupted mid-lesson.

Ewan thought of his own students and how obnoxious they had seemed at the time; not caring about the workings of the body or the living, breathing Earth around them. They had seemed so entitled, so wilfully ignorant but now he missed them and would give anything to have them back.

Ewan checked underneath the desks and all the drawers and cupboards. He found a broken microscope and a couple scalpels but nothing of use. He took the microscope and stuck the sheathed scalpels in his pocket.

Ewan was walking out of the classroom when he spotted a familiar name on one of the doors: Doctor Winkler. Ewan knew Doctor Albert Winkler from the days before the Outbreak but Ewan didn't know he worked for the university. Amy had worked for him as a researcher in his own private company before Amy and Albert had a falling out.

Ewan stepped up to the door and placed his hand on the handle. It was cool to the touch.

Do I want to go in? Ewan wondered. *What will I find?*

But curiosity got the better of him and he lightly turned the handle and swung the door open.

The office smelled musty, stale and rotten, not unlike the rest of the campus but the fumes seemed even more intense as they gushed out into the hallway.

Ewan took a step inside the small, windowless office and instinctively he reached for the light switch but of course it wasn't working.

In the corner of the room was a desk with an IBM computer sitting on it, miraculously and seemingly intact. To the left of the computer was a picture of Doctor Albert Winkler and his family, with the frame broken. Next to that were stacks of paper covered in layers of dust.

Ewan brushed them off and started to read them. They all had to do with experiments relating to Genetically Modified Organisms. It was Doctor Winkler's speciality and Amy had done her Masters' thesis on the subject but Ewan had little understanding of the subject. He put the papers back and went through the drawers. He found pens, pencils, paperclips and assorted other stationary. He opened several more drawers, finding old scientific magazines, graphs and more research papers.

At the very bottom drawer he found another picture frame of Albert standing with his arm around Amy. They were in some sort of lab; both were smiling for the cameraman. This discovery hit Ewan like somebody had suddenly pumped his stomach.

Ewan had never seen the photograph before and he wondered when and who had taken it. He ran his fingers across the surface of the photograph.

"Amy, I miss you more than anything," Ewan proclaimed.

Ewan took the picture out of the frame, folded it and put it his pocket. He then left the office, shutting the door behind him, shutting out those painful memories.

It took them a couple of hours to search the entire building. Remarkably there were no sign of Creatures anywhere.

"What caused the Outbreak?" Ashley asked, after they had cleared the building. They had found one working microscope with the entire lens intact but that was the only working piece of equipment they found. Ewan already knew it wouldn't be powerful enough to see any sort of cell tissue or virus but he took it so Ashley wouldn't feel their trip was in vain.

"Your guess is as good as mine," Ewan said, feeling slightly rejected. Despite everything he had told himself, he had really hoped to find something that would be helpful but like everywhere else the lab had been raided and gutted.

"You're the biologist."

"I told you I was a high school teacher," Ewan pointed out, "Not some university genius, and even they weren't able to figure out much."

Ashley put a hand on Ewan's shoulder and Ewan turned to look at her. Her brown eyes were large and silently pleading with him to come up with some answers, to make sense of the world but seeing the labs had done something to him.

At one time he had wanted to become a doctor, to do meaningful research, not just preach to the heathen students but he had run out of money and with a young family he had made the logical choice to get a job and not sink deeper into debt.

Ewan took a deep breath. "It probably came from a mutation of some other virus — most likely the H5N1 or SARS virus but how it mutated so quickly to resist any drugs or treatment is really a mystery. I heard that a Dutch team had experimented with a new strain of H5N1 that was extremely deadly to humans."

They walked back to the ROM in silence, each deep in their own thoughts. Ewan had gone over in his mind all the different types of diseases he knew of and none of it had made any sense. He had given up hope long ago so why was he thinking about them now? He didn't want to think Ashley had anything to do with it.

The afternoon light was fading and soon the Creatures would be waking and prowling the city looking for food.

When they got back to the museum Justin and Anthony came running out to meet them, their faces all red.

"Tim went to the woods," they said in unison. "We tried to stop him but he was determined. Said something about a guardian angel."

"Guardian angel?" Ashley asked, knitting her brow.

Ewan let out a low, painful growl and looked up to the sky. "This is your fault," he accused.

"My fault?" Ashley said.

Ewan glanced over at her with an embarrassed look. "Uh . . . Sorry, no. I was just talking to myself again."

"What was this guardian angel thing?"

Ewan sighed deeply and told Ashley the story of how something saved them from being eaten by the Creatures before they had made it back to the museum.

"What do you think it was?" Ashley asked, after Ewan had finished.

"I'm sure it was some kind of animal. I don't know — a lion maybe."

"I don't think even a lion could fend off a horde of Creatures?" Ashley speculated, dubiously. "Besides where would a lion come from?"

Ewan shrugged. "Whatever it was, Timmy is probably trying to find it again."

"Why didn't you tell me about his earlier?"

"Why would I?"

"Because this thing, whatever it is, is obviously on our side. Maybe it could protect us."

"I don't think so," Ewan argued. "I don't think it saved us out of some Christian charity."

"Then why would it just spring in front of the Creatures like that? Putting itself in harm's way?"

Ewan was beginning to get irritated. "Ashley, I don't know, okay? But what I do know is it wasn't Jesus reincarnated."

Ashley frowned, biting her bottom lip. "Come on, we better stop arguing and go find Tim before it gets too dark."

Ewan looked up at the deep metallic blue sky. "Too late," he said. "You have to stay here. I'm going after Timmy."

"No," Ashley said. "I'm going with you."

"Stay. Protect Justin and Anthony they need you."

"But what about you?"

"You can come look for me in the morning when it's safe."

Ashley gave Ewan the flashlight and her gun. He stuffed both guns in his belt and ran as fast as he could back the way he had come. His lungs soon were choked with air and he started coughing but he kept running. Tim couldn't be that far ahead but he saw nothing. He stopped at the edge of the forest. The trees and the darkness loomed in front of him. He could hear the distant movement of the Creatures now stirring to life but could not hear any scuffle or movement that could be attributed to Tim. Was it possible Tim had gone someplace else? No, Tim would want to find the thing that had saved their lives and Tim would think the answer was in the woods.

Should he call out? Did it matter anymore? Was Tim even still alive?

Ewan's ankle burned and ached from the strain he had put on it but he did the best to ignore it. He took a deep breath and ran into the forest. Soon shapes started moving and Ewan could feel himself being surrounded but he kept running. He had no choice. He felt footsteps behind him and when he looked back he could see about a dozen or so shadows chasing him.

"Timmy?" Ewan yelled. "Where are you Timmy?"

Ewan tripped on a stump and fell onto the mossy snow-flecked floor. He rolled onto his back just in time to see something jump on him. He raised his gun and blindly fired. The loud crack echoed through the trees and the Creature's face exploded, its body falling limp on top of Ewan. A thick dark substance – not blood exactly – spilled onto Ewan.

Ewan managed to scramble to his feet, desperately trying to scrub the Creature's guts away from his face and neck. He turned on his flashlight and shone it at the Creatures. The light blinded the Creatures momentarily but they kept coming. Ewan could hear them all around. They were surrounding him and soon there would be no way to go.

Ewan stopped, panting heavily, cold droplets of sweat poured down his forehead and neck.

"Timmy?" Ewan yelled. "I'm here, Timmy."

Finally after what seemed like an eternity he heard Tim's high-pitched voice full of fear, float through the trees. "Dad! Help!"

When Ewan heard those words something happened in his inner core, something he failed to be able to explain. He no longer felt any pain. In fact, he didn't feel anything at all. Ewan screamed and started running towards the direction of Tim's voice.

Ewan fired ol' Bessy blindly into the swampy darkness. He couldn't hear anything above the shattering cracks of the gun. He fired until he was out of bullets. He then shoved the gun back into his waistband and took out Ashley's gun and kept moving.

Ewan didn't know where he was going or where the Creatures were. He just tried to run towards Tim's voice, which now seemed like a dream.

Eventually he came to a clearing in the woods. He didn't know where he was. He felt like he was deep within the forest but he didn't have any bearings. There was a small single-story brick house in the middle of a clearing. Had it always been there? It looked like it was some sort of grounds keepers' house.

Ewan was staring at the building when he saw Tim come around the corner. His tiny shadow was against the dim moonlight but Ewan knew it was him.

Tim moved slowly, almost as if he was in some sort of trance.

"Timmy?"

But Tim didn't turn around. Ewan saw Tim try the handle of the front door but it appeared locked so Tim knocked.

What was he doing? Ewan wondered.

The door to the building slowly swung open and a large figure appeared but it was too dark for Ewan to see anything other than a vague ghostly shape.

There's no such thing as ghosts, Ewan thought.

Tim looked up at the looming figure. The figure stepped back as if inviting Tim in. Tim took a step in and the door was closed behind him.

"No," Ewan said, but his voice seemed distant and hollow. His lungs still burned but he managed to run towards the building. He heard the Creatures behind him, crashing through the woods.

Ewan tried the handle but the door was locked. He pulled on it and banged on it but nobody answered.

"Timmy," Ewan screamed. He was heaving and he started to cough. He dropped to the ground.

"Amy . . . I'm sorry," Ewan whispered.

"You've got to protect the children," Amy told him.

"It's going to be okay," Ewan said to her. Inexplicitly he could smell her strong scent wafting up his nose.

She smiled at him. "Ewan, listen closely because you're going to wake up soon. Protect them."

"I can't. He's gone. He's dead."

"No, Ewan, he's growing. He needs you."

Amy began to fade in front of him.

"No, Amy, don't go. Stay with me a little longer. I need your courage."

But she faded away and Ewan was left in the darkness. Somehow Ewan struggled to his feet. Every joint in his body hurts every muscle, every fibre.

Ewan turned to face the Creatures who were slowly approaching him. They seemed hesitant, cautious perhaps of the house. He fired, hitting the Creatures until Ashley's gun was out of bullets as well.

This was it. Ewan looked around him, taking in a deep breath. He had no energy to try to make a run for it. He could only think about the hideous fate that awaited him. In the beginning he had seen people torn to shreds by the Creatures, limbs ripped off, blood soaking the floor. The pain would be excruciating but luckily short.

Suddenly there was a bright hot light that first hit Ewan's back and then spread across the woods. For a brief moment Ewan wondered if he was in heaven. Had he died? But then Ewan felt himself propelled across the clearing and landed just under a tree. His face hit the dirt and he felt something crack in his shoulder.

When he lifted his head he saw the ground keepers' house was on fire and a few of the Creatures were running around burning, screaming hideously.

Ewan forced himself to one knee, holding his left shoulder with his right hand, and somehow managed to climb to his feet. Was it the guardian angel again? Had it rescued him again?

Ewan snapped off a piece of the tree and he brought it close to the burning pile that had used to be a building. With one end he touched the branch with the burning fire until the branch was lit up. It burned hesitantly but then gained life and Ewan held it upright to prevent the flames from descending to his arm.

Somehow Ewan made it to the edge of the forest with the burning branch. He turned but could not see the smoke in the night sky. He touched the flame with the base of the tree until the flame caught and engulfed the tree. Ewan watched as the fire jumped from tree to tree, spreading quickly. He had lost both the guns when he had been thrown. They had probably been lost in the fire somewhere.

"Let everything burn," Ewan muttered to himself. Hopefully the fire would take some of the Creatures with it.
Ewan turned and walked slowly towards the museum.

The Pact

Graham and Stu took turns watching and stocking the flames while the other slept. The flames and the light kept the Creatures away. They managed to keep the flames going until the morning light appeared.

The Creatures, frustrated, melted back into the shadows.

Stu woke up to find Graham pointing his own Samurai Sword at his chin.

"What are you doing, Graham?"

"You were going to kill me," Graham said. "Feed me to the Creatures."

"No, I wouldn't have done that to you."

"That was your plan. You told me."

Stu propped himself up on his elbows. Graham held Stu's gaze.

"Graham, if you were going to kill me you would have done it in my sleep."

Graham didn't move for a moment and then suddenly he lowered the sword. "I don't want to kill you if I don't have to, but I need to be able to trust you."

"You can trust me," Stu said.

Graham raised his eyebrows. "How?"

"Because you're still alive." Stu produced from his kimono a pair of throwing stars and showed them to Graham. "These would have been embedded in your throat."

"I want to call a truce."

"What sort of truce?"

"Let's work together. Why kill each other when the Teki are out there?"

Stu smiled at Graham's words. "To tell you the truth Graham, you're the only person I've come across that deserves to live."

Stu stood up and dusted off his kimono. "You think you could give my sword back?"

Graham hesitated but then handed the sword over. Stu put the sword back into his belt and then placing his hands stiffly by his side he bowed to Graham. "The samurai have something called Bushido, loosely translated as way of the warrior. Honor, trust and loyalty are very important."

"How did you become so knowledgeable about samurai?" Graham asked.

Stu shrugged. "I don't know. I started off learning martial arts as a teenager and it just grew from there.

"I'm exhausted," Graham said suddenly, and he collapsed to the floor. It wasn't long before he fell asleep.

Graham and Stu walked slowly through the forest. Stu hummed Beethoven as they walked. Stu had no greater pleasure than humming Beethoven, not even watching people die could compare to the beauty of Beethoven.

"That's Beethoven?" Graham asked.

Stu frowned. It had been years since anybody had interrupted him while humming and he didn't appreciate the interruption anymore than when he had been riding along in the ambulance.

"Yes, it's his Fifth Symphony," Stu said. "You like classical music?"

"Oh yeah, sure. I used to be on the symphony board."

Stu found this talk of the past dizzying, almost fantastical as if it had all been part of some dream state that hadn't actually happened.

"I think you and I are going to get along just fine," Stu said.

They were surrounded by scarred trees and frozen mud and beyond empty skyscrapers. Large snowflakes started to fall and stick to the cracked road and mix with the black ash. It was the first snowfall of the year and it was early.

To Stu, the surrounding area looked like what he imagined the trenches of France to look like in the First World War, which he had studied in school. It had been one of the few topics that interested him.

"Do you usually find anything to eat?" Graham asked.

"Maybe a mouse if I'm lucky," Stu said. He stared across the horizon, looking for movement. But there was nothing, just barren land. He was hungry and cold but he did not want to show weakness in front of Graham. To compound the problem Graham didn't seem to show any aptitude for hunting which meant Stu would probably have to hunt for the both of them.

Perhaps this alliance won't prove beneficial, Stu thought.

Stu had picked the surrounding wooded area pretty much clean of all wildlife and Stu found he had to go further and further for food.

They came out of the woods and onto a street with rows and rows of small family houses that had once been filled with life and warmth but now stood empty and ominous.

There was a bent sign post that read McLevin Avenue. They walked further and passed a track-and-field and then a baseball field that had grown over. The stands had mostly collapsed and the large spotlights had been tipped over. Stu had always despised baseball and most sports and so he looked at his dilapidated surroundings with grim satisfaction.

There they picked up speed for several hours, only stopping briefly once to take a few sips of water at midday. Eventually they came to a rail yard. There were dozens of parked train cars, rusted and blackened by the weather and the years.

"Shall we take a look?" Graham asked. "Maybe there is something we can eat inside one of them?"

Stu nodded. "Okay, just be weary of the Teki."

They decided to walk part way around, observing for any movement, perhaps a rat or a small animal but they saw nothing.

After watching for several moments they moved towards the tracks. The engines on most of the trains had been destroyed but there were a few locomotives still standing, red with rust and blacked with ash.

Stu and Graham didn't say a word as they walked around the yard. There was nothing there so Stu climbed up on one of the cars and opened the hatch and immediately he heard a piteous screech he knew were the Creatures. Stu climbed down and tried the next car down and was met with the same death-throw.

Stu glanced at Graham. "All these trains are filled with Teki."

They spent the next thirty minutes opening up all the hatches and exposing the Creatures to sunlight.

They reached the train at the very center of the yard. It had long round cars and on the side of them it read: PERPETUUM INDUSTRIES: The Future is Now.

When Stu opened the hatch of the first car he found it empty. He peered in but there was nothing. There was nothing for several more cars and then on the seventh car Stu found the car was still filled with a thick black substance.

"Hey, this one still has oil in it," Stu said.

Graham's eyes went wide. "Jesus . . . how much do you figure is in there?"

"Well it's filled all the way to the top so I would say quite a lot," Stu said, climbing down to the ground.

"We need to find something to transport it in. We need to find some containers. We can get some heat"

"I don't think it's refined. Will it work in a generator or a car?"

Graham shook his head. "There isn't much we can do without it being refined."

"So it's useless, is what you're saying?"

"No, we just need to refine it first."

"How the fuck do we do that?" Stu asked.

"Refining oil is basically just heating it up to extreme temperatures. If we can do that then we should have enough gas to last us for a couple of years, depending on how we conserve it."

"How do you know this?" Stu asked.

"I have a degree in engineering. . . I used to work for Perpetuum."

"You worked for Perpetuum Industries?" Stu asked. "Why didn't you say so?"

Graham shrugged. "Why does it matter now?"

Stu paused to consider this question. He supposed it didn't but why had he gone on talking about his father and failed to mention he was an engineer? Stu saw some use in their alliance after all.

"Do you think you could refine this oil?" Stu asked.

Graham shrugged. "I don't make any promises but if we can find something to heat the oil then yes. What we need now is something to transport the oil in."

They walked across the train tracks, following their own prints in the dirty snow that was only beginning to stick on the ground until they hit a residential area of town. The snow had stopped falling but it was now several degrees below zero and the cold cut to the bone even with the sun, which was beginning to set. They didn't have much time to collect the oil and get back to the zoo.

They entered a wooden white house with flecked paint and rotting baseboards. Stu drew his sword and proceeded to move through the building. Graham, who had a large butcher's knife, was careful to stay a few steps behind Stu. The house smelled like a mixture of rotten meat and wet wood.

Stu slowly crept though the living room first. There was an old sofa on an old carpet that had been stained with blood but had long ago since dried. Stu wondered what sort of catastrophe had occurred. Had a Teki found something to devour or had it happened before? There had been plenty of looting and plundering beforehand.

They crossed the room and entered into the back of the house where the kitchen was. There was broken white tile on the floor and mold in the sink. Layers upon layers of ash and dirt covered the floor and walls. Next to the sink was an intact glass vase that had probably once held flowers. Graham walked over to it.

"Perfect," Graham said, picking up the vase and examining it. It was covered with dust and Graham used his shirt sleeve to try and clean it off. He tried the tap but of course there was no water.

"Alright, let's get out of here," Graham said, turning back to the living room but Stu raised his hand.

"Wait one moment."

"What is it?"

"I hear the Teki," Stu said. "They are upstairs."

"Okay, let's get out of here then before they realize we're inside."

"A samurai doesn't run from a fight."

Stu shuffled to his left and looked up at the ceiling as if he could almost see right through it.

"Stuart, we don't have time to hunt Teki."

Stu's eyes narrowed and his mouth stretched across his face. "It's Stu. Only my father called me Stuart."

Graham held up his hands. "Of course."

93

Stu exited the kitchen and found the stairwell in the next room. He slowly ascended. Graham sighed heavily and decided to follow him.

The second floor was rotted and creaked and groaned under their weight but that didn't stop Stu from agilely moving across the main support beam, avoiding the weak areas.

They entered the master bedroom first. It was filled with dust and ash. The curtains were drawn shrouding the room in pitch darkness. A sure sign the Teki were about.

Stu crouched and sniffed the air, smelling firewood and metal. He slowly entered the room, his sword raised to strike. He crept towards the window and opened the curtains letting a ray of light into the room. That was when he saw the Teki lying on the floor, its body slashed open by some sharp instrument.

Stu motioned Graham to approach. He then bent down and examined the body. Thick black liquid still oozed out of the Teki indicating the kill had been recent.

"Interesting," Stu said. Perhaps there was something other than the Teki in the house.

Stu stood up and raised his sword again. He stood perfectly still, his eyes half closed for what seemed like an eternity. Eventually he moved towards the sliding closet. Stu grabbed the handle and slid the door open, stepping backwards.

Something leapt out at Stu with a piercing cry but Stu managed to sidestep the creature which then slipped on the carpet, almost losing its balance.

Graham raised his knife and was about to slice the attacking Creature when he realized it wasn't a Teki but a human. A female at that. In her right hand she held a knife almost identical to the one Graham had.

Stu pointed his sword at her neck. "Don't move," he ordered.

The woman stood motionless, her thin hands raised in the air. She had dark skin and looked like she was in her mid-forties. Her cheekbones were high and her chin was small and angular. She stared at Graham and Stu with sunken brown eyes.

"Who are you?" Stu asked.

"My name is Krista," she said in a thick accent.

"Did you kill the Teki?"

Krista's eyes darted between Stu and Graham, wide with fear. "The what?"

"He means the Creatures," Graham interjected.

"Yes, sure, killed it."

Stu had never encountered a woman before, not since the Outbreak. He had thought they had all been eaten or killed.

"Give me your weapon," Stu said.

"No," Krista snarled.

Stu pushed the edge of his samurai sword against Krista's neck until she started bleeding. She dropped the knife.

Stu examined Krista closely before turning to Graham. "What do we do with her?"

"Why do we have to do anything with her?" Graham asked, not looking at Krista. "We need to get back before it's dark," he reminded Stu.

Stu nodded, smiling at Krista. It was a terrible smile, a sinister smile that seemed mechanical and false, as if Stu had learned how to do it from a robot. "He's right," Stu said. "We shouldn't be debating this."

"Please, let me go," she pleaded. "I didn't mean to attack you. I was just scared."

Stu didn't move for a long time. Graham just stood there watching Krista who stood shaking slightly.

"Graham, what were you saying earlier about rebuilding civilization?"

Graham frowned, looking confused. "What about it?"

"Graham, I want you to make sure she doesn't try anything stupid, got it?"

Graham took a step towards Krista. "Sure thing, Stu."

Stu sheltered his sword and opened his kimono part way. Underneath he was naked. His body was shrunken and shrivelled from malnutrition. He moved close to Krista who started screaming. Graham didn't move. He just stood there mesmerized as Stu started to tear at Krista's ragged clothes until she stood there naked. She was all dangling flesh and bones. Her breasts were almost non-existent and her hips jutted out unnaturally.

After awhile Krista's screams became whimpers. When Stu pushed her back onto the bed, she didn't resist. She even spread her legs almost willingly, as if she was determined to get it over with

95

and Stu inserted himself into her. Stu stared down at Krista who had closed her eyes tight.

She wasn't pretty. Stu could smell her stale breath and it almost made him sick. Stu took no joy in the act and finished quickly as possible. He wiped himself off on the bed sheets and closed his kimono.

"Get dressed," he told Krista, who laid still, unmoving.

Graham looked questionably at Stu but didn't say anything.

"We're taking her with us," he announced.

They walked back to the train station. It was slow going. Krista, stumbled along and Graham had to hold her from falling. The dead city was quiet except for a small wind that blew through the trees.

"Let me go," Krista requested.

"Why don't we just release her?" Graham asked Stu.

"Safety in numbers," Stu said, without looking back.

The sky was a dark blue. They only had a couple hours at best before the sun went down.

"Maybe we should give her a weapon," Graham said. "The Creatures will be out soon."

"That's not what I meant by safety in numbers," Stu said. "The Teki come, we offer her as a sacrifice."

They found the train car and Graham climbed the ladder to the top where he opened the hatch and dipped the vase into the crude oil. With the vase filled, he climbed back down to the ground.

"Okay, let's go," Graham said.

They walked quickly back to the zoo. Krista seemed to accept her fate and walked quietly along with them, her head bowed. They didn't say anything for a long while but continued along their trek.

After about forty minutes they stopped to drink from their water supply. The sun was into its death throes, casting streaks of pink and purple through the air.

"We better continue," Graham said, staring up at the sky.

"So what did you do at Perpetuum Industries?" Stu asked.

"Why does it matter?" Graham asked, starting to walk again. Stu and Krista followed him.

"I guess it doesn't matter, really."

"I was chief technology officer."

"Sounds like an impressive title."

Graham shrugged. "I suppose."

"You're Graham Mayer," Krista said, speaking for the first time.

Graham turned and stared at Krista, who looked back at the ground.

"Do you two know each other?" Stu asked.

"I don't think so," Graham said. "Do we?"

"No, I just remember you from the news."

Stu turned to Graham. "You were on the news?"

"Yeah, a couple of times."

"What for?" Stu asked.

Graham shrugged but Krista spoke up, "He was on CNN talking about the Perpetuum car."

"There was a Perpetuum car?" Stu asked.

"In its prototype stages yes."

"And what happened to the prototype?"

"There were six actually. The army seized them when martial law was declared. I don't know what happened to them."

"You think they are still in the city somewhere?"

Graham shrugged again. "I doubt it. I'm sure they were destroyed with everything else."

"But what if they were still around? Maybe just lying in somebody's garage unnoticed?" Stu asked.

"And what if they were? We have no way to find them," Graham said. "And trust me, I've looked for them."

"What else did Perpetuum have?" Stu asked.

"Nothing much else."

"We need to go to the Perpetuum building."

"There's nothing much there," Graham said. "Trust me, I've looked. I think first we need to concentrate on refining this oil. Get a gas car to work first and then plan our next move.

Suddenly there was a sound from the distance. It sounded like a dozen bears awaking from hibernation but they knew it was the Creatures. Stu dug into his bag and produced a flashlight which he gave to Krista. She took it tentatively. Graham took out his own flashlight from his bag.

Stu turned to Krista. "You think you could run for it?" Krista nodded.

Stu scanned the row of houses, imagining the Creatures pouring from them at any moment. "Okay. Graham, you take the lead," Stu said. "I'll bring up the rear."

They made their way slowly at first but when the first Creatures appeared from underneath porches and from the houses Graham started to run, balancing the vase of oil, his knife and the flashlight and the other two followed.

They made it to the woods but they were quickly surrounded by Creatures who leapt at them in the darkness. Graham slashed at the Creatures and Stu dispatched them with the sword.

They made slow progress, careful to cover each other's backs but eventually made it to the outskirts of the zoo.

"Where to?" Graham asked.

"Follow me," Stu said, taking the lead. They were all covered in guts and the Creatures' black blood.

Stu ran towards the tiger cage and the other two followed. They were almost there when Stu heard Krista scream. He turned and saw a Creature had toppled Krista and would soon be on her. Stu threw Graham his bag.

"Keys are in there," he said, turning and charging the Creatures. With one smooth stroke Stu cut off the head of the nearest Creature and then with a smooth movement he thrust the sword into the stomach of another.

Stu took Krista's hand and pulled her up. "Come on," he said. Krista got up and together they started to run. Stu sliced at any Creature that got close to them.

Through the darkness, Stu saw Graham about twenty yards in front of them. A Creature jumped from one of the fences but Graham managed to dodge and stab the Creature twice. The Creature stumbled but didn't fall. Graham kicked it and finally the Creature collapsed.

Graham reached the cage first. He put down his flashlight, the vase of oil, and stuck his butcher's knife in his armpit. He then dug into Stu's bag and found the keys. A Creature jumped on Graham's back and sunk its teeth into his shoulder. Graham yelled and dropped the knife. He grabbed the Creature flipped it over his shoulder and rammed it up against the fence.

"Graham, look out," Stu yelled, breathlessly.

Graham turned just in time to avoid another Creature. He used Stu's backpack to hit the Creature. The contents of the backpack went flying but it managed to momentarily stun the Creature enabling Graham to pick up his fallen knife and with a great burst of adrenaline he attacked the Creatures.

Stu and Krista reached Graham and together they were able to unlock the cage, collect most of their things and enter. A few Creatures managed to follow them but Graham was able to close and lock the cage while Stu quickly decapitated the Creatures.

After they were safe they collapsed onto the ground, breathing heavily.

Without Tim

Ewan opened his eyes and at first he didn't comprehend where he was. His head hurt like it had been put in a clam and his stomach was turning with nausea. He could taste copper in his throat and he knew it was from blood. He tried to move and at first he couldn't. He couldn't even feel his limbs and at first he thought he was frozen with frostbite. But gradually the feeling in his hands and feet returned. He tried moving his shoulder and found that it was stiff and painful but not excruciatingly so.

Thank God for small mercies, Ewan thought.

Why hadn't the Creatures torn him to shreds? Why was he still alive?

Ewan blinked rapidly and looked up at the sky. The yellow sun was peaking up above the burnt trees and the blackened skyscrapers.

The sun, Ewan thought. *The sun saved me.*

Ewan tried to get up; on the first few attempts he collapsed back to the Earth, a dizzy blackness kept overcoming his vision, but on the third try he managed to climb to his feet. He looked over at the park. Most of the trees had crumbled into ash or blackened from the intense heat. Miraculously the fire seemed to have run its course and had not spread.

Ewan spent the next hour combing through the forest. He found many bodies of the Creatures but he couldn't find the remains of Tim.

Was it possible he had survived?

No, he remembered the explosion. But what had caused it? Maybe something had spontaneously combusted. Ewan had heard about such things but he had never believed in it. No, something had been in the ground keeper's. Ewan had seen a figure open the door. The memory was coming back to him. Some sort of suicide bomber? Ewan touched his temple with his thumb and forefinger. Something just didn't make sense.

Ewan heard somebody call his name. He turned towards the sound and found Ashley running towards him. She gave Ewan a hug which crushed Ewan's shoulder. He gave out a loud yelp and Ashley jumped back.

"I think I've dislocated my shoulder," Ewan said.

"I'm sorry," Ashley sympathized. "Can you move it?"

Ewan tried to raise his arm but the pain was unbearable.

Ashley prodded her fingers along Ewan's chest and up towards his shoulder. Even though it hurt, he loved her strong, warm touch almost pulsate through his body. Ashley shifted her hand up to the cavity between Ewan's chest and shoulder. Ewan sucked in his breath.

"We need to put this back in place."

Ewan looked at Ashley but her eyes seemed larger than normal and Ewan was scared of what he would find in them.

"Okay."

"If you want maybe we can find some Advil."

Ewan shook his head. "No, I don't think there's any left. I need you to do this. Quickly."

"I thought when you didn't come back. . ." she let her voice trail off.

"Timmy," Ewan whimpered.

"What happened?" Ashley asked.

Ewan told her everything starting from when he saw him knocking on the ground keeper's house to the explosion.

"Is Tim still alive?" Ashley asked.

Ewan opened his mouth to answer but he couldn't answer. No, he couldn't entertain the idea that Tim was dead. He must be alive, somewhere.

Ashley stared at him for a long time, not saying anything. "Do you believe in God, Ewan?"

Ewan, still not able to speak, shook his head. Tears rolled down his muddy cheeks. He was crying. Ewan couldn't remember the last time he had cried. He had never shown his emotions, not even as a kid. His parents had told him even as a baby he hadn't cried much. And when the world went insane like a rabid dog, Ewan didn't cry for humanity. Was it Amy and Sophie? Yes, that was the last time and the only time in his memory he had shed tears.

Ashley stepped closer to Ewan. He could smell her strongly, a mixture of sweat and dirt but strangely he didn't mind the smell. It was good to have somebody just near. She raised her thumb and wiped away his tears. Suddenly she leaned in and kissed Ewan. Her lips were parsed, salty, and crusty but it felt good.

When Ashley leaned back Ewan stared at her, wondering what she was thinking. What was the kiss for?

"Don't lose hope," Ashley said.

Ewan couldn't think of anything else to say so he just nodded.

"Now, lie down on your back," Ashley said.

Ewan did as he was told. He stared up at the cloudy, white-blue sky.

"What's your favourite memory?" Ashley asked. Her voice seemed far away, carried by the light breeze.

"Of my wife. There were so many good memories. "

Ashley dug her heel into her Ewan's armpit and took hold of his wrist. "Tell me about it."

"Why?"

"So you'll relax. How did you two meet?"

"We met in school. She was in Ecology 2130 class. When I first laid eyes on her I thought she was the most beautiful-" Ewan's words were cut off by a loud snap and a sharp pain that spread over his upper body. He let out a loud yelp. His eyesight dotted with black dots before he was able to regain focus.

"I think I got it," Ashley said, standing up and feeling Ewan's shoulder. "How do you feel?"

"Better," Ewan admitted.

Ashley helped Ewan up. "Come on, let's get back to the museum. You must feel exhausted."

Ewan did feel tired but his mind was still filled with thoughts of Tim to worry about himself.

They didn't say anything on the way back. Ashley, who was usually alert, stared down at the ground. Ewan forced himself to take each step, each muffled effort echoed through the empty city.

Back at the museum, Ewan went to the washroom and looked at himself in the mirror. He looked more like one of those Creatures than a human. His shirt was soaked with blood and mud. His skin was translucent from lack of nutrition and his eyes blood shot. His hair was matted back against his skull.

Ewan stripped off his clothes and filled the bathtub with rainwater he had stored up. He forced his aching body into the icy cold water. Long ago the pipes had burst from the cold and had stopped working. Tim always used to complain but Ewan never minded cold baths. But now, for the first time since the Outbreak, Ewan wished he could heat the water, but he knew they had to conserve energy for the lights.

Ewan pulled the plug and watched as the water swirled and disappeared down the drain. He wondered where it went. It probably leaked out some crack somewhere down the line.

He climbed out and towelled himself down. He looked better without all that blood and dirt splatter. He parted his hair with his fingers.

Seeing a normalized version of himself made him break down again. He felt his body slide away from his soul and all of a sudden he felt as if he was in two places at once.

I'm losing my mind, Ewan thought.

"Timmy," he whispered. "Timmy."

He smashed his fist against the mirror. A sharp pain ran up his fingers and wrist but he ignored it. He smashed the mirror again and again until the mirror broke and shards of glass pierced his hand. Then his body seemed to snap back within itself and he felt alright, a bit sick but alright. He took a deep breath and leaned against the sink and sobbed until what little energy he still had drained from his body.

After he picked out the slivers of glass from his hand and examined his various bite marks. He looked at his ankle. The wound had already started to scab over and looked on the way to healing. The second bite marks were fresh puncture wounds on his shoulder and they were swollen and red but strangely they didn't hurt that much. Maybe he was becoming immune to their teeth. Lastly he looked at his dislocated shoulder. He rotated his arm in his socket and concluded that there would be no lasting effect.

Ewan dressed and walked slowly up the two flights of stairs to the room he and Tim used as a bedroom. He looked down at the two empty mattresses and thought of Tim. He couldn't believe he had lost him too. Why had he survived when his entire family had died? Why did he have to be the one? Was it some sort of fate or just dumb luck that tortured him? He would trade his life for any one of theirs. Why couldn't he?

Ewan found some gauze, tape and bandages in a bag by the foot of the mattress. He cleaned the teeth marks with the gauze and then wrapped them with bandages. They were sloppy jobs and he could have gotten Ashley to do it but after the kiss he didn't want to see her.

He rested his head on the mattress and pulled up the blanket to his chin. He shivered for awhile but eventually exhaustion overtook him and he fell asleep.

It didn't take much for Ewan to dream of his family. They were in a park together, playing on the swings, laughing. Ewan could smell the freshly cut grass. The sun was giving off a pulsing warm glow, hitting the cedar trees and the swing set. A light breeze picked up and flowed through Ewan's hair.

"Higher, Daddy, higher!" Sophie squealed as Ewan pushed her. Sophie kicked out her legs, pointed her small toes into the sky. Tim was swinging next to her.

"It's my turn," Tim said, frowning at her sister.

"In a minute," Ewan told Tim.

Amy walked over and leaned on Ewan's shoulder. She was wearing a tank top and cut-off jean shorts that showed off her glistening brown legs.

"You can't stay here forever," Amy said.

Ewan turned to look at her. In the distance he could hear the distant sound of traffic.

"I know," he said.

Sophie was laughing but her voice suddenly sounded muffled as if he was listening to her from under water.

"You need to find them," Amy said.

Ewan looked around. Sophie and Tim were both gone. The park was empty. His family was gone. Ewan yelled but nobody answered. The sound of traffic suddenly stopped and there was nothing to listen to.

Ewan wandered around the park in search for his family but the park was empty. He returned to the swing set. The swings were still swaying back and forth as if Sophie and Tim had just stepped off.

Ewan heard a loud yell from behind him and turned to see a Samurai warrior in full battle armor running towards him, his sword raised over his head.

Ewan turned to run. He sprinted across the park, past the sandbox and playground. He reached the chain link fence and breathlessly he climbed over it. On the other side he glanced backwards at the Samurai and Ewan realized he was gaining on him.

Ewan ran across the street, cutting across the front yards of some houses. He ran a few blocks but realized he couldn't keep up the pace. His heart was pounding in his chest and he was increasingly getting shorter of breath.

He decided to duck between two houses and went down the side path towards a laneway. He looked over his shoulder. The Samurai hadn't followed him. Ewan looked around, slowly catching his breath. The backyard was small with a row of daffodils in front of a neatly trimmed hedge. To his left there was an old garage with a roof that badly needed fixing up. Ewan turned the handle to the garage and opened the door. It creaked open on its rusty hinges. Inside it was dark and damp. He could smell the mold.

Ewan stepped inside and flicked on the lights, illuminating the garage. He walked further inside and found himself surrounded by darkness. He put his hand out in front of him, grasping at nothing. He reached to the side and found his fingertips reach a cold smooth surface. He stumbled along for what seemed like a long time with nothing but darkness to guide him, all the while feeling the walls of the corridor.

Finally, he saw a light up ahead. It was a yellowish glow, as if coming from a street lamp. Ewan stepped closer and saw something shift in the dim light.

The Samurai was standing in front of him. He had glowing red eyes staring out at him behind a silver mask. The Samurai raised his sword and Ewan closed his eyes and raised his hands as if they would protect him.

Ewan woke with a gasp. Ashley was sitting cross-legged bedside him. She leaned in and took his hand.

"Everything alright?" she asked.

"Yeah, just strange dreams."

"You were muttering in your sleep."

"It's just this Samurai keeps chasing me. It's all very weird."

Ashley smiled. "Maybe you've been hanging around the Asia exhibition too much."

Ewan laughed. It hurt but he didn't mind. He preferred not to think about his dream turned nightmare. "How long was I out?" Ewan asked.

"A long time."

Ewan propped himself up on his elbow. "And how long have you been sitting here?"

Ashley shrugged. "I don't know. A couple of hours at least."

Ewan rubbed his forehead. "Do we have enough food?"

Ashley stroked Ewan's head. "Don't worry about that right now. We'll be fine for awhile."

Ewan wondered if that was true or not.

Oil

Stu slept better than in recent memory, but still he wished they had something to make a fire with. The ground was cold and it got colder during the night. As usual he had a dreamless night. He had once been told everybody dreamed, you just sometimes didn't remember them. Stu didn't think that was true. Other people dreamed, perhaps, but not him. He didn't know why he had been chosen – only that he had. Like he had been chosen to rebuild humanity. Graham had been right about that. It was his burden to rebuild everything, only he would build things his way. People wouldn't be so wasteful, so destructive. They would be obedient and loyal.

Stu woke to find Graham and Krista already up. They were sitting across from each other, their legs tucked up under their chins, silently staring at each other.

Stu got up, stretched and looked at his companions. He felt refreshed and in a good mood, despite the cold. "You guys don't want to get acquainted? We're going to spend a lot of time together. We might as well know something about each other."

Stu nodded towards Krista. "We learned a lot about Graham yesterday. Why don't you tell us a little about yourself?"

Krista didn't move but instead just sat staring at Graham.

Stu smiled. "Come on, Krista. Where are you from?"

"I'm from South Africa, from Johannesburg."

"Johannesburg? How long have you lived in Toronto?"

"About ten years. Moved here when my boy was born."

"Stu clucked his tongue with the roof of his mouth. "The problem with this fucking city is everybody is a fucking foreigner. Nobody was actually born here."

Krista's eyes moved to Stu and he felt a keen sense of hatred in them.

"Why don't you just kill me?" she said. "Just get it over with."

Stu stepped towards her. "You can thank Graham over there for convincing me to spare your miserable life."

Krista cringed as if she'd been struck which made Stu laugh.

"Now, I want you to take off all your clothes."

"No, I won't do this again. I would rather die."

"You know I feed people to the Teki? You can ask Graham," Stu said. "Would you like to be one of them?"

Krista looked from Graham back to Stu as if she didn't quite believe them. After several moments she took off her ragged clothes until she stood there naked. She clasped her arms around her small breasts, shivering.

Stu watched her. Nobody moved. Nobody said anything.

Graham was the one who broke the silence. "Just get it over with Stuart."

Stu stared at Graham. "I told you, nobody calls me that."

He approached Krista who had gone from shivering to shaking, although whether it was from fear or the cold, Stu didn't know. He turned Krista around and bent her over. Like before, she didn't resist.

It was over in about a minute and Stu pulled his pants back up. Krista quickly got dressed. She sat in the corner of the cage, staring down at the ground.

Nobody said anything for a long time. Dust flew into the cage and scattered around the rocks.

Eventually Stu looked at Graham. "You said you could refine the oil."

"Maybe. But like I said, I make no promises."

"How about gas?"

Graham nodded. "If I can refine the oil I can make some sort of gas too."

"What's your plan?"

"It will be dangerous."

"But if we get oil and gas then we can start the cars again and we can travel further without worrying about the Teki."

Graham nodded again.

Stu unlocked the cage. Graham stepped out but Krista didn't move from the ground.

"Come on Krista," Stu said.

But Krista refused to move. Her shoulders hunched over and her eyes downcast.

Stu sighed heavily and marched over to Krista, grabbing her by her boney elbow and pulled her to her feet. Krista screamed and bit down on Stu's hand. Stu took a step back, shocked. His hand started to bleed. Krista yelled as if suddenly possessed and jumped on Stu who tumbled to the ground. Krista started to hit him with her open palms.

Stu took the blows calmly and after recovering from Krista's outburst, managed to roll over and onto of Krista.

"You crazy bitch," he said, fiercely. He grabbed his Samurai sword and pulled it from its sheath. "For that I'm going to cut off your ears."

"Stop," Graham yelled.

Both Stu and Krista looked up at Graham.

"Let's stop this right now. We need to work together. Why are we fighting each other when the real enemy is out there?" Graham pointed towards the forest, past the parking lot.

Nobody said anything for awhile and then finally Stu stood up, wiping the blood from his hand on Krista's shirt.

"Fucking rapist," Krista muttered.

"You can thank him for saving your ears," Stu replied. "And your life."

"Let's go find something to eat," Graham said, turning away from his two companions. "I'm starving."

The thought of food managed to quiet everybody and they followed Graham as they walked out past the gates of the zoo, past the parking lot and towards the forest.

The sun cast long, skinny shadows against the undergrowth but did not warm the Earth. A cold breeze picked up and flapped against the travellers.

"Be careful," Stu said, drawing his sword. "There could be Teki in these woods."

They entered the forest. Their feet crunched branches and twigs. They looked around for threats and when they didn't find any they moved deeper.

They searched for hours but in the end, they didn't find much except a few mushrooms which they shared amongst themselves.

"If we go further out we might be able to find something else," Stu said. "I think I killed pretty much every rodent in these woods."

"I think we need to start refining if we're going to finish by sundown," Graham said, looking up at the clear sky between the trees.

"Alright, what do we need to do?"

"Do you have any shovels back at the zoo?"

Stu nodded. "Yeah, I'm pretty sure there are some still left."

"We will also need to find a hose or a tube and some kind of pocket."

They walked back to the zoo in silence. They found a couple of shovels, a large bucket and a hose in the Australian Pavilion. But when Graham examined the hose he shook his head. "We need a hose that will stand up to intense heat." Graham looked around the zoo until they came to one of the bathrooms next to the Giant Panda Shop.

Graham smiled and said, "I think I have an idea."

They entered one of the bathrooms. It smelled of copper, rotten wood, sewage and mold. Krista shook her head and tried to duck out but Stu pulled her back in. "I don't want you going anywhere."

There was a stall on the left and two cracked urinals in front of them. Graham walked over to the stall and examined a piece of pipe that led from the toilet into the wall. It had been rusted with years of disrepair. Graham bent down and tried to unscrew it but the bolts were rusted together. They tried another washroom across the zoo at the Indo-Malaya Pavilion but those pipes were rusted as well.

"I can probably find a wrench around here," Stu said.

"We should split up," Graham said. "It will be faster."

But Stu shook his head. "No, I don't want to let Krista out of my sight."

"You're never going to let her out of your sight? Won't that be impractical? To watch her all the time?" Graham said.

"We can't trust her not to run away."

"Why not let her go?" Graham asked. "What good is she if she wants to go?"

Stu looked at Graham evenly. "Because I want her to have my baby," she said.

Graham stared at Stu for a moment, his mouth half open, as if he didn't understand. There was a long silence and then Krista started to cry.

Stu smiled at their reaction. "You said we should rebuild civilization. We will need children to do that."

Nobody said anything for awhile until Stu turned to Krista. "You should cheer up. It means you get to live for at least another year. After that we'll see."

"You're a monster," Krista screamed. "A complete monster."

She lunged at Stu but this time Graham was able to catch her before she got to Stu.

"Krista, don't be stupid," Graham said.

Stu took a step toward Krista who turned her head away. "That's right, Krista, don't be stupid."

"Stuart, don't taunt her."

Stu glared at Graham.

He's getting too mouthy, Stu thought. *I'm going to have to deal with that sooner or later.*

But he knew he should only fight one battle at a time so Stu forced himself to relax. "Okay, let's stop wasting time and go find that wrench then."

Graham took Krista and Stu went searching for a wrench by himself. Thirty minutes later Stu found a toolbox stored underneath the first aid center, next to the African Rainforest Pavilion.

He went to Graham and Krista who were wandering around the Gift shop. All the shelves had been broken but there was still some merchandise sprawled across the ground. Stuffed lions and giraffes and plastic sharks and picture books were piled up. The cash register had been upturned and tossed to the floor as well. Its contents plundered a long time ago.

"Let's go," Stu said.

Together they went back to the bathroom in the Indo-Malaya Pavilion. Graham tried first but it was Stu who eventually managed to twist the bolts off the pipe and pry it loose.

"Now we just need something to make a fire with," Graham said.

Stu smiled. "I know just the thing."

They went back to the tiger cage and Stu pulled out some steel wool and a battery.

"You can start a fire with that?" Graham asked.

"Yeah, I learned this trick back in Boy Scouts."

They went back into the forest and together they searched for the perfect spot, eventually finding a small clearing that would work. They all started to dig, even Krista helped. There were patches of snow and the ground was frozen solid. It was tough going at first but gradually they made a hole about six feet deep and a circumference of five feet.

"I think that should be deep enough," Graham said, surveying their work. "Now comes the tricky part. We need to find lots of dry wood."

For the next hour they searched to find branches and twigs that were dry enough to be used as timber. It was painfully slow work but eventually they had enough and they threw it into the pit.

"Let's hope it doesn't start snowing," Graham said, looking up at the clear, cloudless sky which was white as the colour of whipped cream.

"I think it's going to hold off for now," Stu said.

Graham doused some of the oil onto the wood in the pit.

"What are you doing?" Stu asked. "You're wasting precious oil."

"It's useless if we don't get a strong fire going."

Graham then fed the pipe from the bucket to the vase. "Okay, light the fire," he told Stu. He then turned to Krista. "You might want to stand back a bit for this. It could be dangerous."

Krista nodded and climbed out of the little pit they had dug. She stood there staring down at them. Graham nodded towards Stu who bent down towards the stack of wood and started rubbing the battery against the steel wool. It didn't take long for the steel wool to start burning. Stu dropped the wool into the pile of wood and immediately the wood, aided by the oil caught flame and started to burn. It gave off a strong tar smell yet it was warm and inviting against the bitter cold that surrounded them.

Graham tilted the vase so it was on its side and adjusted the pipe so it was on the very top. The oil came close to spilling but Graham managed to balance the vase so nothing was spilled.

Graham then calmly walked up to the open flame and with a gentle toss threw the vase onto the fire. The fire roared. Graham jumped backwards, feeling the heat.

The vase had landed perfectly perpendicular; it's landing softened by the twigs. The pipe was still inserted inside the vase.

"Okay, we need to keep this fire hot," Graham said. "You two go get some more wood."

Stu and Krista went back into the woods and gathered any dry wood they could find. When they returned they saw Graham smiling and hopping around the fire. He showed them the bucket. There were only a few droplets of a clear yellowish substance draining from the pipe and into the bucket.

"It's gas," Graham said. "I don't know if it'll work in an engine yet but it's gas!"

Stu stared down at the bucket. His stomach was suddenly twisted in knots. Possibly it was from hunger but there was another possibility as well. The possibility he was awed by something that seemed so trivial. It almost seemed impossible that this . . . this thin yellowish substance was one of the most fought over liquids in human history. How many wars had been started because of gas and oil? How many lives lost? And here he was standing, watching as it dribbled into a bucket that had probably once been used to bring dead fish to feed the dolphins. It was a humbling experience, yet also an exhilarating one because he had what nobody else had. The power of mechanism. The power to start machines and in turn that meant the power to rule.

Part Two: The Creatures

Lost Hope

For the next couple of weeks Ewan ate very little and only drank water when Ashley insisted. As a result, Ewan grew even thinner and even frailer. If he ran his hands down the front of his body he could feel each protruding rib and pelvis. His hacking cough became more pronounced.

Time seemed to taunt him. He had no way of measuring it, no way of grasping it, but it seemed to move slower than ever before, inching its ugly, little body along bit by bit forward.

Why can't I just die? Ewan asked himself. *If only I had something to kill myself with. If only I wasn't such a coward.*

He focused on Amy. He wanted to join her so badly, leave all the pain and suffering behind. He missed her so much. He wanted to run his fingers through her dark hair, feel her soft cheeks, her mouth, her smooth forehead.

Ewan looked around to see if he could use something as a weapon, perhaps make a noose but there was nothing. He was too weak to be able to kill himself.

Ashley would come in and change the bandages on his ankle and shoulder, checking out how he was healing. Despite Ewan's lack of nutrition his various wounds were getting better, then one day he got a high fever.

Ashley found him in his sleeping bag, his hands tucked underneath his armpits and his teeth chattering. She bent over and felt his forehead.

"Jesus, Ewan. How long have you been like this?"

"I don't know."

"Alright. I'll be right back."

Ashley disappeared and came back with some soup and a glass of water.

"You have to eat this."

"Save it for the boys."

"I'm not just going to let you die," Ashley said.

"It's . . . what I want."

Ashley fed Ewan the soup and he reluctantly ate it. She then gave Ewan the water. It looked silted and discoloured but Ewan didn't care. He drank it but it tasted strange.

"Did you put something in this?' Ewan croaked. Coughing again.

"I crushed up our last Advil."

Ewan closed his eyes. "Ashley, why?"

"Don't argue just drink."

Ewan sighed and took several more sips of the water before he handed it back to Ashley. "I can't drink anymore," he said.

The next day the fever broke and he felt better, although he still didn't eat much.

He spent his time staring up at the ceiling panels thinking more and more about Amy, Sophie and Tim. More often than not they appeared in his dreams. Sometimes the strange Samurai warrior appeared also, chasing them on and on, through their house or through the park.

"You need to eat," Ashley insisted again, one evening. She was dressed in a loose pink blouse and dirty jeans. Her small breasts were pressed up against the cotton, outlining large nipples. Her long brown hair was tangled and fell across her face.

She had been such a fixture that Ewan sometimes forgot she was a woman. The kiss they had shared seemed like a distant memory.

"Save the food for the boys," Ewan said. He was lying on the mattress. All of his strength had left him and he doubted he would be able to get up even if he wanted to. "They need it more than I do."

"Don't talk like that Ewan," Ashley said, kneeling beside him. "I need you."

"For what? I'm no use to anybody."

Ashley didn't say anything for a moment, her intense eyes searching Ewan's while he ran her fingers through his grubby hair.

"What are you doing?" Ewan asked.

But Ashley didn't say anything; instead she leaned down and kissed Ewan. It was a soft tender kiss. Ewan closed his eyes, feeling her lips against his. But in the darkness he saw Amy looking at him. She wasn't looking at him in a disapproving way. It was more of a desperate look, like the last moment before she sighed her last breath away. But what she was pleading for, Ewan didn't know. Did she want him to stop? To continue? He didn't know.

He opened his eyes again and put both hands on Ashley's shoulders and tried to push her back but he was so weak he didn't have the strength.

"Ashley, stop."

"What?" Ashley asked. "The kids are downstairs."

"I can't do this."

Ashley sat back on her heels. "Trust me, it'll do you some good."

Ewan shook his head. "No, I don't think it will."

Ashley looked at Ewan incredulously. "Is it because of Amy? Is that why?"

Ewan turned to look away. "Don't say her name like that."

"I had a boyfriend too, you know, except you never ask about him. His name was Lucas"

Ewan felt very exhausted and he really wanted to be left alone. "Ashley, forgive my language, but I never asked because I don't give a shit."

Ashley stood up with her eyes blazing. "Amy's dead and I'm right here. You think you can't go on living like this? I can't either."

She turned and walked out the door. Ewan felt bad for what he said but it was the truth. He had enjoyed their kiss but he didn't want to get to know Ashley. None of them were going to see old age. The Creatures were going to get them sooner or later and there was nothing they could do about it. He had fought it for Tim's sake but now that Tim was gone he had no reason to live.

Ewan fell asleep and he dreamed of Amy. They were in the grocery store. She had the shopping list in her hand and was pushing a cart full of groceries.

Ewan tried to sneak a bucket of ice cream into the cart but Amy caught him.

"It has Titanium dioxide in it which can cause respiratory cancer."

Ewan eyed the ice cream sadly as Amy put it back on the shelf.

"How can something I never even heard of be so deadly?" he asked.

"Trust me," Amy said. "The world is full of deadly things you've never heard of." Amy turns around and grabs a book out of a section devoted to vegan life style. "Here, in this book by Monika Baechler, Three Lions and a Gazelle, the author explains her battle with her family accepting that all manufactured food, meats and genetically modified foods are the future cause of many diseases." Amy handed the book to Ewan who looked at it for a few moments and frowned. "Soon, we can't eat anything anymore…" He reluctantly put the book into the shopping cart and looked around the isle but couldn't see the children. In fact, they seemed to be the only ones in the grocery store. "Where are Tim and Sophie?"

"Don't worry, they're still alive."

"How can you be so sure?" Ewan asked.

"Because a mother knows," Amy said, turning, wrapping her arms around Ewan and leaning in to kiss him. It wasn't like Ashley's kiss. It was softer, sweeter, her lips tasting like blossoms.

Ewan woke up with a start. The lights had gone out and he felt a presence in the room and immediately went for his revolver.

"Relax, it's just me," he heard Ashley say, holding up her hands.

Ewan relaxed, letting out a gush of air from his lungs.

"Sorry," Ashley said. "I didn't mean to startle you but I don't know how to fix the generator."

"It's easy. You just need to replace the coils."

"Do you think you could show me?"

"You'll find the coils in the basement-"

"Why don't you just show me?" Ashley insisted.

"Because it'll be faster if I just tell you."

"Ewan, the boys are scared. I don't think we have a lot of time. Could you please just show me?" There was an urgency in her voice that Ewan had never heard from her before.

Still Ewan didn't move. He could only see a bare outline of her in the darkness but he could hear her quick, heavy breathing. He didn't care if he died or not, but he didn't want to be responsible for Ashley's and the boys' deaths as well.

"Alright. Help me get up."

Ashley took Ewan by the hand and with the other hand braced against the wall he managed to get to his feet. He felt extremely weak and dizzy. He took a few hesitant steps towards the door but stopped halfway.

"You sure you don't want me just to tell you?" Ewan asked.

"Come on, you can do it," Ashley said.

Ewan made it to the hallway. Stepping out of the room, he felt a little more stable on his feet.

"I'm sorry," Ewan apologized, as they reached the stairs.

"For what?"

"For what I said earlier, about your boyfriend. You're right . . . I guess I was just so absorbed in my own misery."

Ewan gripped the railing with one hand and Ashley's arm with the other and slowly they made it down the stairs, one step at a time."

"Nick Carraway said you can't create the past. Maybe we should just forget it as well."

"Who's Nick Carraway?" Ewan asked.

"The Great Gatsby? Surely you've read it."

Ewan shook his head confused. "Wasn't it a movie?"

"It's a classic. Written by F. Scott Fitzgerald."

"Sorry, I was the kid who took apart the television and assembled it again, not one to read classical novels."

They made it down the stairs but they still had two flights to go and Ewan was breathing heavily. "I . . . don't . . . think . . . I can . . . make . . . it," he panted.

"It's okay, why don't we rest for awhile?"

"But what about the Creatures? Where are the boys?"

"I gave them lots of candles to burn. They should be okay for awhile," Ashley said. "Besides I don't hear any Creatures yet. I don't think they've figured out we've gone dark yet."

In the darkness, they found a metal bench close to a ten-foot totem pole and just beyond that Ewan could see the silhouette of the stuffed five-thousand-pound white rhino that had lived in the Toronto Zoo. Ewan knew around the corner was a meteorite on display that had fallen in Tagish Lake.

"What was his name?" Ewan asked, still out of breath.

"Whose?"

"Your boyfriend?"

Ashley looked away from Ewan. "Lucas . . . Lucas Goldsmith. He was actually the one who introduced me to many classical novels, including the Great Gatsby."

"You want to forget him too?"

Ashley seemed to consider this in the darkness. "I don't want to . . . but what's the use remembering him or anybody?"

"Maybe I'll read that book one day," Ewan said.

Ashley nodded but didn't say anything.

For the first time in what seemed like forever Ewan felt comfortable in the dark. Maybe because he had come to terms with death and if Creatures were out there somewhere just lingering in the shadows there was truly nothing he could do about it. He didn't have enough energy to run or enough strength to fight.

Through the glass panels Ewan could see the night was cloudy. There was no moonlight and Ewan couldn't see further than maybe twenty meters but he felt at peace. It was beautiful. Even serene. The floor was cloaked completely in darkness. Nothing made a sound. Not even a groan from the glass or a whisper from the metal beams.

"I suppose we should get going," Ewan said.

Ashley mumbled in agreement and took Ewan's hands to help him up.

They made it to the basement. Ewan was coughing and hacking from the exertion but he was surprised to find he was glad to be out of his room. And even more surprised to find he was happy Ashley was standing next to him, supporting him.

Ewan took a spare coil from the box on the workbench and pressed the button to open the generator's tray. The right coil had completely burnt out. Ewan took it out and replaced it with the fresh one. He closed the tray and in a few moments the generator started to hum softly and the lights flickered once and then came back on.

Ashley smiled and patted Ewan on the shoulder. "Good job, Ewan."

Ewan smiled back at her and for the first time Tim had disappeared into the woods he felt almost happy.

Ashley helped Ewan back up to the main floor.

"Help me to the lobby," Ewan requested.

They passed through Samuel's Hall to the main entrance where Ewan sat looking out the glass door. The snow was falling in large fluffy white snowflakes. It looked beautiful on the dead, dark city.

"I just want to look outside for a while," she told Ewan.

"Do you mind if I join you?"

"No, be my guest."

They sat behind the big desk in the lobby that employees of the museum had once used to sell tickets to patrons.

"Before you asked me if I believed in God," Ewan said, after a long silence.

Ashley nodded. "I know you're a scientist but even scientists believe in heaven."

"Are you a believer?"

"I first went to church when the Outbreak got really bad. When the Creatures started appearing. I remember the churches were pretty full. I think a lot of people turned to God then."

"Why?"

"Why did I turn to God?"

Ewan nodded.

"Because if I don't have faith then what do I have?" Ashley asked.

Ewan didn't know the answer and so they sat silently for a while. Ewan thought of Tim out there. It was probably several degrees below zero and Tim hadn't taken any warm clothes with him. Could he survive out there? Maybe he had started a fire that had kept the Creatures away. In his dream, Amy said he was still alive, but how was that possible?

"Do you believe in premonitions?"

Ashley shrugged. "I don't know . . . I wouldn't call them premonitions."

"Signs from God?"

"Maybe."

Ewan told Ashley about the dreams he had about Amy, Tim and Sophie.

"If you're asking what it means I don't know," Ashley said.

"I don't believe dreams mean anything," Ewan said. "They are just active neurons firing randomly . . . but I just can't shake this dream. I've never been one to remember dreams but this one is . . . so vivid."

"I'm hungry," Amy said, abruptly. "You want anything to eat?"

Ewan nodded; for the first time in a long while he felt the pang of hunger in his stomach. "Sure."

Amy smiled, got up and disappeared through the hallway. She returned with some roots and passed them to Ewan.

"Here," she said. "I've been saving these for you."

Ewan took the roots and bit down on them. They were hard and tasteless but they satisfied his stomach. Amy also got Ewan some fresh water which he drank quickly.

"Not so fast. You'll get sick."

Ewan shrugged. "You mean more sick than I already am?"

Amy didn't respond, instead she sat down beside Ewan. "You can find a cure or maybe a disease that will kill those . . . animals."

"For the last time, Ashley if there ever was such a thing then there is no way I could find it without some kind of super lab."

"Then let's find you one," Ashley suggested. "There must be some sort of lab down in Nevada or someplace?"

"Even if there was one, we would never get past the Creatures. We would never make it. Not in our condition."

"Maybe we should go south to a warmer climate," Ashley said.

"Ashley, you're not listening to me. There's no way we could survive the nights without the genie."

"What would you rather us just starve to death here?"

Ewan turned away. He had no answer. They either were going to die a slow and painful death from malnutrition or they were going to be ripped apart by the Creatures. Neither seemed very preferable but Ewan saw no other alternative.

Building an Empire

Outside the snow was coming down on the 401, covering the ash and the grind, obscuring the view of the road. But that didn't stop Graham from pressing the gas pedal to the floor. The Alfa Romeo Stelvio's powerful turbo charged Ferrari engine kicked into high gear, letting out a roaring hum from this sport utility vehicle. It was beautiful, almost song-like – not Beethoven of course – but it had its own simple purity to it. It was the sound of hundreds of small working parts, working harmoniously together. It was the sound of a revived generation, rising once again from the burnt ashes of civilization.

The wipes scraped furiously across the front windowpane as thick crystallites of snow fell and then quickly melted to liquid.

Stu, who was sitting in the passenger's seat, felt the small of his back press against the leather seat. He smiled at Graham who was hollering like a little kid.

He probably hasn't had this much fun in years, Stu thought to himself.

Over the past few weeks they had diligently shuffled the oil from the train back to the zoo where they refined it as best as they could and now they had several barrels of gasoline stored up. Stu estimated it was enough to last them seven or eight months depending on how they used it.

Graham had said their imprecise homemade gas would eventually wreck the engine but it didn't matter. They had hundreds of vehicles to choose from. Each only needed some fuel to get it up and running again.

Stu watched as the speedometer reached a hundred miles per hour. Krista was in the back and, when Stu glanced at her in the mirror, she looked a little pale.

Well, can't please everybody all the time, Stu thought.

Graham got off the highway and turned north onto McCowan Road. They passed a small park with clusters of Spruce trees and past an old Television station.

Graham had wanted to find a more practical car that was more fuel-efficient but Stu had always wanted to drive an Alfa Romeo Stelvio and so had convinced Graham to at least test it out. It seemed once Graham had started to drive it he was sold.

They continued along McCowan Road for several minutes, traveling along rows of houses, past Finch Avenue.

When a park came into view, Graham hit something in the road and the car suddenly spun and fell into a ditch. The airbags deployed and Stu felt himself thrust forward only to be yanked back by his seatbelt.

Dazed, he looked around him. Everything was spinning; Graham was unconscious next to him. His head was bleeding. Stu couldn't see Krista.

Stu felt Graham's pulse and found it was normal. He would survive.

Stu opened the door and stumbled out. The cold wind hit him like a wet towel and immediately he started to shiver. There were large stakes fashioned out of wood stuck into the ground and below him large pools of thick black bile stained the snow. What was it? It was dark and glossy like oil but it smelled like feces.

Stu turned and looked at the car which had fallen about seven feet into a large ditch. The car's front had been totalled. Graham must have not been able to see it with the snow cover.

He opened the driver's door and pulled Graham from the car. Next, he looked around for Krista but he couldn't see her anywhere.

She probably thought she could escape but then he heard her scream and saw her come sliding back down the ditch towards Stu.

Stu, puzzled, laid Graham down on the snow and calmly walked towards Krista who stopped just in front of him.

"There are men with bows and arrows," she panted, out of breath. "They were shooting at me."

Stu climbed back into the ditch, realizing as he did so that the ditch was too smooth to be put there by any act of nature. He now realized what the spikes were for. Somebody had purposely dug the ditch here to trap the Creatures. And by the looks of the black bile that oozed from the Creatures the trap had been successful.

Stu peeked his head out from the ditch and surveyed the surrounding territory. The sky was the colour of milky coffee. There was no sunlight but the blankets of snow illuminated the surrounding world. The park was populated sparsely by spruce trees, frosted in white.

Stu stared out but he could see nothing. No danger. What had Krista seen? Was she just trying to scare him?

A small wind picked up the ice and snow and ash and flung it across the clearing. There was a dilapidated structure behind the trees and to the right was a parking lot still with a couple of cars parked in it.

Stu continued his sentry but still he could see nothing. But then he stared at a large clump of snow that seemed to move. Stu stared at it again and some sort of figure appeared from the snow and an arrow grazed his ear. Stu ducked down, swearing.

He climbed back down towards the car. He reached in and took his sword from the floor where it had fallen before turning towards Krista and Graham, who had fortunately woken up and was brushing the snow off of his clothes.

"What's going on?" he asked.

"There are some fucking idiots out there shooting arrows at us," Stu said, angrily.

"What do we do?"

"Good question," Stu answered, surveying the useless car.

If they could somehow siphon the gasoline from the car they could perhaps take one of the cars in the parking lot and escape. But the trick would be to get across the open field without being shot.

"Graham, do we still have that hose in the trunk?"

Graham understood exactly what Stu wanted to do but he shook his head. "It won't work."

"Why not?"

"The SUV has an anti-siphoning mechanism."

"There's no way it can be disabled?"

Graham shrugged. "Perhaps."

"Try it. I'm going to keep these savages at bay." Stu promised, smiling. He liked the word savages. It described their attackers perfectly. They were just a bunch of uncivilized savages and he would kill them all, very slowly, very painfully.

He peeked his head back up over the edge of the ditch and saw three men dressed in large, dirty fur coats slowly approach them. Each man had a cross bow at the ready. The one closest to Stu fired his weapon but Stu was ready and ducked before the arrow came into range.

Stu took out two throwing stars from his sleeves and raised his head again. He saw the first savage reload his weapon. This time several arrows came at Stu who ducked again. He quickly popped back up again and threw the throwing stars at his assailants. The throwing stars hit their marks and two savages clutched their throats as globs of blood splashed out onto the white snow.

The third savage just stood there, as if bewildered at what just happened. Stu ducked back into the ditch but as he did so he pulled a third throwing star from his kimono and held it at the ready.

When he glanced over the edge of the ditch he saw the third savage had retreated to the safety of a nearby tree.

"Why don't you come and get us?" Stu taunted the man but he got no answer.

Stu waited but the savage didn't appear. He turned to see how the siphoning was going.

Graham had a crowbar in hand and was jamming it down the fuel line. He then dropped the crowbar and picked up a rag and the hose and stuffed them into the gas nozzle and began to suck the gas out. Krista, her body tense, was holding the gas can at the ready.

Stu nodded his approval and turned back his attention to the savages. He was confident he could hold them off but making a dash for the parking lot was another matter.

Should they wait until the cover of darkness? Perhaps it was safer to deal with the Creatures than the humans. But he didn't want to wait for hours in the freezing cold for the sun to go down.

Besides he wanted to teach the savages a lesson. He didn't want to escape. He wanted to annihilate them.

Stu watched as six more savages came out from the dilapidated building just beyond the spruce trees. He watched as they split up into two groups and started to circle around the ditch. They would flank them and create two new attacking angles.

Not a bad move, Stu thought.

He had to formulate a plan and quickly. Perhaps he could draw the savages away from the ditch, allowing Krista and Graham to get the gas to their new vehicle. Perhaps not the best plan but it would have to do.

He turned and quickly told Graham and Krista his plan.

"But what about us," Krista said.

"I have no time to argue," Stu said, turning and focusing on the terrain ahead. He put his sword away and quickly climbed over the ditch. He sprinted towards the dilapidated building, hoping his brazen full frontal assault would confuse the savages. It seemed to do just that as no arrows came in his direction until he was almost at the first tree.

One arrow flew past him, another hit the tree Stu was running for, but the third arrow struck Stu in the shoulder. He felt the pain almost immediately spread across his upper body but he didn't slow down. He knew if he did, it would mean certain death.

He dove and crawled behind the tree just as a few more arrows flew past him. Stu pulled the arrow from his shoulder, feeling the blood trickle down his back. He prodded the wound with his fingers. Luckily it didn't seem too deep but it hurt like a son-of-a-bitch.

He had seen plenty types of wounds as an ambulance driver. When somebody was shot or stabbed they generally went into shock. Once Stu saw a gangster who had been stabbed through the eye. He had stared up at Stu as if nothing had happened.

Stu took a moment to mentally check himself over. He seemed okay but adrenaline was coursing through his body and he knew that was a bad indicator of his true state. Still . . . there was nothing he could do about it now.

He concentrated on his surroundings. He suspected more savages to shoot from the building but he couldn't see any movement. Peeking from behind the trees, he saw the two groups of savages had stopped and seemed more concentrated on Stu than Krista and Graham in the ditch.

Good, Stu thought. *Come get me.*

He had nine throwing stars left. It would be more than enough for the seven savages. Stu ran to the building, careful the savages weren't able to get a clear shot.

Without slowing down he shouldered the doorway which broke easily under his force. Stu crashed to the ground but quickly oriented himself and got behind the brick wall. The building smelled like urine and decaying matter. Weeds and moss had sprouted through the floorboards. In the corner there was the remains of a fire and several backpacks that were no doubt full of supplies. Stu wanted to go through them but he knew that he had to concentrate on the immediate threat of the savages.

"Victory goes to the one with no thought of himself," Stu said to himself. It was from Sun Tzu, the Art of War, a book he had read many times. He had to focus and not let distractions seep into his mind. He had to kill the savages.

He heard the sound of footsteps and looked through a broken window. Four savages were running towards him. They stopped and raised their crossbows but Stu was quicker, hurling two throwing stars at them. One caught one savage in the throat but the other dropped to one knee and the star passed over his head.

Stu drew his sword and waited behind the wall of the building. One savage climbed through the window while the other came through the doorway. Stu grabbed the savage from the window and sliced open his throat. He then rotated the corpse to shield himself from the arrow shot from the doorway.

Stu threw down the corpse and ran towards the savage in the doorway. Stu's attacker drew a short knife but it was no match for Stu's samurai sword. Stu bent low and with one fluid movement cut the savage's head off. Blood poured down the body and onto the rotten floor.

Stu ducked his head out the doorway. The remaining savage shot his arrow but it hit the building wall harmlessly.

Before the savage could reload, Stu charged him. The savage fumbled with his arrows as Stu gave a loud, blood curling battle cry. The savage managed to wind back his bow and was just about to bring it up before Stu threw another throwing star, this one hitting the man in the throat.

Stu didn't slow down as another savage appeared from behind a tree and fired. The arrow went just past his arm. Stu pivoted and threw a throwing star. The star missed and dug itself into a tree.

Stu picked up the dead man's crossbow and fired it but he was untrained and the arrow shot wide.

Stu dropped the cross bow and reached for another throwing star. But before he could throw it heard the unmistakable sound of a car engine.

Graham and Krista had gotten a car started. This strange and foreign noise seemed to unsettle the savage and he turned and ran back into the woods.

Stu ran towards the parking lot. A sleek, black Audi A9 pulled up beside Stu and he got into the back.

"Let's get out of here," Stu said.

In the driver's seat Graham nodded and stepped on the gas. The car lurched forward over the snowy park and back onto the road.

"Maybe go a little slower this time," Krista suggested.

Graham looked over at her and laughed. "Yeah, probably a good idea."

Stu stared out the window but he wasn't paying attention to the winter or that the daylight was slowly seeping into darkness.

No . . . all he thought about was revenge.

The Good Professor

It snowed heavily all day and in the night the snow was so fierce only a few of the Creatures ventured out. Ewan could hear them as he lay awake. The screams and moans pierced through the wind that shook the museum walls.

Ewan imagined Tim out there, somewhere while he was stuck in a tiny room, staring up at the ceiling, trying to fall asleep. But the more he tried, the more sleep alluded him.

Eventually Ewan did fall into a deep slumber. Again he dreamed of the samurai chasing him through the museum. Ewan ran but there was nowhere to go, nowhere to hide.

The next morning Ewan woke up but he didn't get out of bed. He was beginning to hate the bright neon lighting that kept the Creatures away. It no longer gave him any comfort and seemed to pulse inside his head and drive him crazy.

He remembered the samurai but he had also dreamed about Amy who had told him again that Tim and Sophie were out there still. But that was impossible. He knew they were dead. Weren't they?

Amy opened the door and smiled down at him. She was wearing pajamas that bunched together at the wrists and ankles. Her dark hair was tangled and fell across her forehead and shoulders.

But then the image of Amy faded and was replaced by Ashley. Ewan closed his eyes and then opened them. Was he going crazy? He had heard of people going mad with sorrow but he thought it only happened in really old movies.

"How you feeling?" Ashley asked.

"Terrible."

"Did you have that dream again?"

Ewan didn't have to answer which dream. He nodded.

"Ashley?"

"Yes?"

"Can you do me a favour?"

"Of course," Ashley said, seemingly pleased by this prospect.

"What was that novel you mentioned?"

"Novel? Are you talking about the Great Gatsby?" Ashley asked, sitting down beside Ewan.

"Yeah, I think so," Ewan said. "Do you think you could read it to me?"

"I would . . . but I don't have a copy but I could probably find one somewhere."

"I think that would be nice."

"And we also need to find some food. We're out."

Ewan tried to laugh but it got stuck in his dry throat. "What do you think you'll find?"

"I don't know, but what I do know is there's nothing to eat here and the kids are driving me crazy."

"You should let them die. It will be kinder than letting them live in this world."

Ashley backhanded Ewan across the cheek with a loud thwack. "Don't say that. Don't ever say that!"

It took a moment for Ewan to recover. "Am I wrong?" he asked.

"Isn't some life better than no life?"

"Is it?"

"I lost my family too, Ewan. I lost everybody just as you did. I've let you mope around here too long."

"What else is there to do? We can't go out there."

"What choice do we have?"

The wind had picked up some and blew snow against Ewan's body. Even with the insulated Gortex shoes and Mammoth jacket and the balaclava pulled over his face, he was freezing to the bone. He didn't have much flesh on him to begin with which didn't make dealing with the cold any easier.

Ashley was walking silently beside him and she didn't look like she wasn't doing any better. She was shivering and moving slowly in the snow as it piled up on the street.

They each carried a small bag that contained water, some matches and spare batteries for their flashlights. Ewan had a large knife and Ashley clutched a machete tightly in her hand.

They were making their way down Bloor Street and Ewan remembered a time when four snow ploughs would drive down the street and clear the snow. Now the only sound was the wind blowing the snow through the buildings.

Why did I agree to this? Ewan wondered. *What are we going to find?*

Ewan and Ashley walked on, past some tall buildings, past a broken and disintegrating United Church, past a coffee shop, and past a cinema and into Koreatown. In Koreatown, the buildings were all two-stories made of stained-brick. Colourful Korean shop signs hung above entrances. Most of the windows had been smashed.

Ewan and Ashley decided to split up. Ewan took the north side and Ashley the south. Ewan entered a restaurant through the smashed window. He wasn't hopeful he would find anything but still, what better place to start than a restaurant?

Inside he hoped not to be subjected to seeing the old pictures of different Korean dishes that still hung on the wall. All the writing was in Korean. Ewan went to the back of the restaurant. The strong urge of food overpowered any caution he had. He opened the large walk-in fridge and shone his light in. A Creature was curled up in the corner. It let out a low groan when the light hit it. Ewan quickly closed the fridge and looked around for something to brace against the door. Before he could find something he saw a Creature crawl out from under the counter.

Ewan flung himself on top of the Creature and stabbed it repeatedly with the knife. Reddish-black goo sprayed from the Creature as it screamed hideously. It swiped an arm at Ewan's face but Ewan leaned backwards so its claw missed. Ewan raised his knife again and brought it down. As the knife sunk into the Creature's flesh, Ewan thought of Tim and that gave Ewan, who was breathing heavily, extra strength to drive the knife deeper. Eventually the Creature lay still.

Ewan jumped up and ran out towards the street where he knew he was safe. As he got into the light, he saw Ashley appearing from one building. She was covered in the Creature's black bile.

"I think maybe we should stick together from now on," Ewan said, and Ashley nodded.

They randomly selected buildings to go into but nowhere did they find anything to eat.

"Ewan?" Ashley said, once they were out in the street again.
"Yes?"

"Have you ever eaten a Creature before?"

Ewan shook his head. "No but I know people who have."

"And?"

"They turned into them."

"You think there is a correlation?"

"Yes I do."

Ashley paused. Ewan stopped as well. The cold was worse when they weren't moving.

"We are desperate," Ashley said.

"We should keep moving."

They continued through Koreatown. On one the street lamps there still was a tattered Korean flag flapping in the wind, half covered with snow.

"Maybe we should try it."

Ewan shook his head. "I wouldn't chance it. It's a fate worse than death."

"But we've made it this long. We must be immune."

"We may be immune through the air but if we digest the virus, that's a whole different matter."

They got to the Bloor/Gladstone Library. It was made of rust-coloured bricks with intricate patterns across the top. As with the ROM – and much of Toronto – the older building had been connected with a newer glass rectangle structure. It was a city that sometimes tried to be too many things – old as well as new, modern yet historic.

"You sure what did this?" Ewan asked.

Ashley nodded. "It's been a long time since I read Fitzgerald."

"Who?"

"He's the author."

"Right." Ewan was glad his face was covered behind a balaclava because he was sure he was blushing. "I was just testing you," Ewan said.

Ashley laughed and gave Ewan a playful shove. "Come on. Let's get this over with."

They entered the building. The inside was painted a bright white with large chandeliers hanging overhead. Luckily the large U-shaped windows let in plenty of light so there weren't many places the Creatures could hide.

As they walked into the building they saw many of the books had been tossed onto the ground and left in large heaps.

"How are we ever going to find anything?"

"Have a little faith," Ashley said.

"That's something I don't have."

They walked across to the modern part of the library where they found the fiction section.

Ewan started looking through the rows while Ashley started sorting the piles.

"So what makes this book a classic?" Ewan asked.

"It's all about the American dream."

"The American dream?"

"You know — of owning a big house, marrying the right girl or guy, those sort of things."

Ewan thought about it for a while. He wondered what Fitzgerald would write about now. What would the American dream be now?

Ewan eventually found the book, which was still on the shelf where it was supposed to be. It had a dark-blue hardcover with a golden trim. Two weird-looking eyes were on the cover. Ashley took the book and put it in her bag.

"Alright, let's go," Ashley said.

"Do you want to look around for food here? I'm sure the libraries had a fridge or something."

Ashley nodded. "Okay."

They found the staff room back in the older part of the library. It had a kitchen table with a couple of chairs. In the corner there was a small fridge; it looked as if it had been picked through a long time ago. They searched the cupboards but they were all empty.

They continued their journey for several more hours. Sometimes they walked long distances and sometimes they would spend long periods of time in just a few buildings. Eventually Ashley managed to catch a couple of rats in the cellar of one building.

Ewan took out a water bottle and took a sip of water. Feeling a little weak and dizzy, he put an arm out against the wall.

Ashley turned to look at him. "Maybe you should eat one of the rats now."

But Ewan shook his head. "No, save it for Justin and Anthony."

They decided to return to the museum. They still had several hours before it got dark but they had taxed a lot of their precious energy and they didn't want to push it.

They walked slower now than before. The snow was almost up to their knees now and it was very exhausting work. The snow was falling at an even faster pace now, making visibility poorer.

They walked for an hour before Ewan begged for a rest.

"Okay," Ashley said, uncertain, looking up at the sky.

They found shelter under an awning. They decided not to go into any of the buildings even though it would be warmer just in case Creatures were lurking in the dark. But even out of the snowfall the cold seeped in through Ewan's thick jacket and he rubbed his hands together, trying to keep warm.

"Maybe we should build a fire," Ashley said. "I'm sure I can find some wood in one of these buildings."

"No, it's okay," Ewan said. "We have to keep moving."

They picked up their bags and continued their walk. A couple of moments later, Ashley put a hand on Ewan's shoulder and they both stopped.

"Did you see that?"

"See what?"

Ashley pointed down one of the side streets. "I thought I saw a Creature."

"A Creature? That's impossible. It's too light."

"Maybe it was a human," Ashley said. "Should we go and investigate?"

Ewan shook his head. "I can't."

"You sure you don't want the rat?"

Ewan hesitated this time. His whole body ached with hunger and he thought he could devour the entire rat whole if Ashley gave it to him. "Maybe just give me a piece."

Ashley took the rat out of her bag and with her knife she sawed off a fleshy part of the rat and handed it to Ewan who put it in his mouth.

Ewan remembered when he had argued with Tim about whether they had seen a rat or a mouse. It seemed everything reminded Ewan of Tim.

The raw meat was tough and tasted disgusting but he was too hungry to care. He swallowed it after a couple of bites and immediately he felt sick.

"I'm glad your appetite has returned," Ashley said.

Ewan didn't answer. He saw something move in the shadows to their right.

"They're out," Ewan said, pointing to where he had seen the movement.

"You want to go kill it?"

Ewan shook his head. It was best if they conserved their energy. "No, let's just keep going."

He felt a little better now his stomach had seemed to find some way to digest the raw rat meat and they continued towards the ROM.

They walked as quickly as they could but they were slowed down by the snow. They got to Manning Avenue before Ewan turned and saw a large figure coming quickly towards them. Ewan couldn't see it well through the snow but it was brownish in colour, it's face hidden by shadow, and somehow it seemed to glide towards them.

"Run," Ewan told Ashley, taking her by the hand.

They ran as hard as they could for several minutes but they didn't get very far before Ewan had to stop. He was breathing heavily and his heart felt like he was going to explode. Ashley turned, levelled her pistol at it and fired.

The loud gun cracked in Ewan's ear and he felt a sudden rush of blood swirl towards his head. He tried to grab hold of Ashley but he missed and tumbled to the snowy floor and lost consciousness.

Ewan was in bed next to Amy. The bedside lamp let off a warm glow that allowed Ewan to work on his student's papers. Amy was wearing her white dressing gown, her Earthy brown hair spilled onto the pillow. Ewan knew she was reading a scientific journal on her e-reader.

Amy turned towards Ewan. "Did you know humans are the only animals that sleep on their backs?"

"My wife is full of wonders," Ewan said, smiling. "You know most wives read harlequin romances before bed. Nope, not my wife."

Amy smiled, showing a small row of white teeth. "Why would I want to read about a silly cowboy when I've got you right here?"

Ewan laughed and leaned over to kiss Amy. She tasted of mint toothpaste. "Maybe, but I forgot my cowboy hat and let my abs of steel go a little. I hope you don't mind."

Amy patted Ewan's belly and it let off a low thwacking sound. "Only fools need abs of steel," she said.

"I love you so much, Amy. I don't know what I would do without you."

"Probably marry one of your hot little high school students. Bet one of those teenagers has a crush on handsome Mr. Walder."

Ewan laughed again but felt uneasy. "Don't be crazy, Amy. You know I love our family too much."

Amy smiled and turned back to her e-reader. "I know dear, I was only teasing."

Ewan couldn't have been out very long before he opened his eyes and came back to reality. He looked up at the greying sky and wished he could go back to Amy in his dream. Where he could be a cowboy and have abs of steel.

Ewan glanced around and saw Ashley kneeling over him and next to him was a man wearing a wool hat and synthetic fur surrounding his hood. The man was perhaps sixty or seventy years old. He had a bulbous nose, large intelligent blue eyes and a white beard with small ice crystals lodged in it. In his hands he held a pair of red skis and poles.

"I . . . know. . . you," Ewan said.

The old man suddenly look frightened, almost dumbfounded. "I know myself too," he said.

Ashley looked at the old man then back at Ewan. "He seems harmless enough, whoever he is."

Ashley helped Ewan up who still felt unsteady on his feet.

Ewan concentrated on the old man. He did seem harmless enough but years of not trusting anything made him suspicious. How had he known this man?

"Why were you following us?"

The man wrinkled his forehead as if concentrating hard. "Names are so constricting. Without an identity you can choose to be whoever you want to be. Tomorrow I can be a Ned or and Ali or even a Michelle."

Ewan took an unsteady step towards the man who jumped back as if slapped. He didn't run however. "Speak sense, old man."

Ashley turned to Ewan. "Be gentle on him. He's obviously . . . not. . ." Ashley didn't finish the sentence.

The old man frowned, almost comically. "No, that doesn't sound right. I don't think my name is 'old man'."

Something finally clicked in Ewan's brain. "You're Doctor Albert Winkler," he said.

The old man's face lit up. "Yes, by Jove, I think that is it. Albert . . . Winkler. I remember my birth name."

Ewan turned to Ashley. "I don't believe it. This man was my wife's boss."

"I was somebody's boss?" Albert asked. "No, I don't think that was likely." Albert paused. "I bet you can't remember your name?"

"It's Ewan and this is Ashley."

"Ewan and Ashley!" Albert said, seemingly taken aback. "Well then for extra points I bet you can't remember your family member's names . . . Of course family names are for further identification of populous of at least five or six thousand. We're just three, now aren't we?"

"We also have kids, Justin and Anthony and my son Tim is out there somewhere."

"Excellent," Albert said. "We have enough then to start to rebuild civilization. Come with me."

Albert put the skis on the ground and attached his boots to them. He pushed himself off.

"Wait," Ashley said. "What about the Creatures?"

The sky was getting dark and soon the Creatures would be out.

"Don't worry about the mutants. We will be fine."

138

Ashley looked at Ewan. "What do you think?"

"I think we should leave him and go back to the ROM."

"I want to know where he's going."

"The kids will worry if we don't get back."

Ashley nodded. "You're right. Why don't you go with him and I'll go tend to the kids."

"Me?"

"You don't trust him?"

Ewan shook his head. "He could be leading us into a trap."

"He's out of his mind crazy. I think you can handle yourself," Ashley whispered, although Albert was about twenty meters in front of them and in no danger of hearing them over the noisy wind.

"But that's the point. It could be just an act."

"You knew him from before. What do you think he was capable of?"

"I know he got funding from Albros."

"From the Albros Corporation?" Ashley frowned, now seeming unsure. "Then maybe he knows how to get a cure."

Ewan wanted to remind Ashley they had been over the subject before but he held his tongue. Instead he looked at Albert Winkler now just a snowy figure in the distance. He was motioning for them to follow him.

Maybe he is Tim's only chance, Ewan thought.

As if Ashley knew what he was thinking, she touched him lightly by the elbow. "We need to take some risks if we want something more."

Ewan nodded. He was curious to see how this man had survived. It didn't seem he was starving or had suffered any other effects – at least physically – from the Outbreak.

"Alright. You go to the kids. I will go with Winkler."

They didn't have much time. The cloudy sky was a bluish-grey and visibility was becoming even more difficult.

"Here, take the gun," Ashley said, holding out the pistol but Ewan shook his head.

"Be safe," Ewan told Ashley.

"You as well," Ashley said, sticking the gun in his waistband and turning and walking a little more quickly towards the ROM.

Ewan called out to Albert but he wasn't sure if he heard him. He started to jog towards the small figure of Albert.

Ewan had only gone a couple blocks when he heard the indistinguishable cry of a Creature.

Ewan tried to quicken into a run but his heart was beating too quickly in his chest. There was no way he could sustain his pace. He paused, bending down to put his hands on his knees.

He looked up just in time to see a Creature jump from a second floor window and onto the street, just about twenty meters in front of Ewan, cutting him off from Albert.

"Albert," Ewan yelled, although he knew it was futile.

He briefly thought about turning and running after Ashley. At least he had a chance to catch her and she had the gun.

But then Ewan thought about his son and what Ashley had said.

We need to take some risk if we want something more.

Ewan looked around for something he could use as a weapon. Next to him was a smashed up car and inside in the back seat, remarkably, was a set of undisturbed golf clubs. Ewan reached in and grabbed the largest one.

He supposed after the Outbreak nobody had a chance to go golfing.

Ewan charged the Creature, swinging the club with all his strength. Ewan connected with the side of the Creature's face, but despite the fierceness of the blow, the Creature was only momentarily stunned. Ewan swung the club again. This time he heard a crunch as bone cracked inside the Creature's skull. Ewan swung a third time and this time the side of the Creature's face caved in, but this didn't stop him.

The Creature lunged at Ewan who blocked it with the club's shaft. He pushed the Creature off and hit it again. This time the Creature fell backwards and Ewan was able to sidestep the Creature and run.

Other Creatures were coming out of doorways and soon Ewan would be overrun. He ran the way he had seen Albert go.

He got to the end of the block; he couldn't see Albert but his footprints were fresh in the snow and easy to follow. Ewan ran west two blocks before he had to turn right. Eventually he turned down an alleyway and saw Albert.

Ewan continued to chase after him. Albert wasn't fast and Ewan was able to get in with about twenty meters of the doctor and again Ewan wondered how he had survived for so long.

A Creature appeared in front of Albert and Albert turned and ran down another street.

Ewan cursed and increased his speed. The Creature had now obviously spotted Ewan and was running straight towards him.

Ewan didn't slack his pace and met the Creature straight on, just as he had done before. This time he swung for the Creature's knee. The club connected and the Creature buckled and with a second blow it fell.

Ewan had lost his bearings and was now completely disoriented. His only option was to continue to follow Albert so he turned right, down the same street Albert had disappeared down. Again in a couple of minutes Ewan could see Albert again, scampering along with quick short steps.

Albert came to a small parking lot which he cut across and ran into a small building on the corner. Where was he going? He would surely meet some Creatures inside and that would be the end of him. But again Ewan had no choice but to trust Albert and so he followed.

Creatures appeared from behind cars, a couple jumped up onto the hoods and over towards Ewan. Ewan managed to weave himself around the parked cars, avoiding the Creatures until he reached the building.

Ewan entered and found himself in a small corridor lined from floor to ceiling with mirrors. He hesitated, a little startled at his own image. His clothes were covered in dirt, snow and black bile.

Ewan was jarred from his own reflection by a noise behind him. He turned and saw that a Creature had managed to get in after him but the Creature seemed more dazed by the mirrors than Ewan had been. The Creature covered its eyes just as an overhead light came on. The Creature gave a hideous scream, clawing at its face and tried to back away from the light but it kept smashing into different mirrors.

The Creature kept up its high-pitched screams, finally dropping to its knees and withering on the floor. Ewan almost felt sorry for it as he stepped up and with several downward swings of the golf club smashed the Creature's skull into bits. Black bile slowly seeped out onto the ground.

Ewan turned and continued forward through this funhouse – or whatever it was.

Only Albert would be able to create something so brilliant, Ewan thought.

Ewan turned the corner and stepped right into a mirror.

Damn, Ewan thought, rubbing his forehead. *I'm going to have to be more careful.*

Ewan found the correct path and walked forward. In about twenty paces he found a door which he opened and found he was in a room which was covered with a bouncy, pillow surface. He felt like he was in one of those insane asylums he had seen on television before the Outbreak.

Ewan bent down and touched the soft, rubber material. It was almost jelly-like in how it sprung up after Ewan released his finger.

Ewan stood up and turned his attention to a five-foot wide model of the RLV Silverback Mark III Spaceship. Ewan walked up to the model and ran his fingers along the top. It looked much like the NASA space shuttle except its wing span was larger and on its side was the familiar emblem of Perpetuum Industries and the tagline: The Future is Now!

Ewan remembered about five years ago Perpetuum had launched its first successful space tourism program, shuttling some of the world's billionaires into space at over a million dollars a ticket. It was the first time a private company and private citizens had been into space and there had been a lot of media coverage at the time.

Ewan wondered what the spaceship model was doing in this strange room.

What is this place? Ewan wondered, not for the first time.

Ewan made his way across the padded floor to the doorway. He opened it and found it lead into a spinning tunnel. The room was dark except for a few spinning red lights. Ewan took an unsteady step forward before he realized the second half of the tunnel was spinning in the opposite direction.

Ewan glanced back through the doorway he had left open and wondered if he should go back to the room covered with the soft-pillow material. But he decided he had to find Albert. Perhaps Albert could help him find Tim. Despite the man being half crazy, he was probably the only one who might know what had happened to him.

Ewan took another small step but this time he lost his balance and fell to his knees. His body rotated with the tunnel before falling back to the middle. Ewan put both hands down and lifted his body to a standing position. He tried to take another step but he lost his balance again and fell hard to the floor.

Ewan retreated to the room he now thought of as the pillow room. He checked himself but he seemed relatively uninjured by the experience. Ewan took a deep breath. He was frustrated by the whole building; none of it made sense.

He looked back towards the tunnel and decided he would run across it. He took several steps back and took a running start. He managed to get halfway through the tunnel before he twisted his bad ankle and fell forward, bracing his fall with his hands. He lifted his head and managed to crawl to the end.

With some difficulty, Ewan got up and managed to turn the doorknob to open the door and tumble into the next room.

Ewan stood up and saw Albert standing in the middle of the room. He was leaning over a set of test tubes and glass beakers. Dark liquid churned in one beaker lit with a Bunsen burner.

The room was large and sparse with only one dim overhead lamp. Behind Albert was a huge computer that seemed to be made up of spare parts taken from different machines. Above the machine were three large computer monitors that showed different angles of the streets outside of the funhouse.

Ewan couldn't believe it: Albert had a security network.

Ewan turned to Albert who glanced up from his test tubes and gave a small surprised shout. "Good lord! Who are you? . . . Oh you're that Ewan guy."

"Yes, Ewan Walder."

"Yes, him too."

Ewan dusted the dirt off his grubby jeans and stared at Albert's experiment. The liquid began to bubble in the beaker and started to rise.

"You like it?" Albert asked, a small smile on his lips.

"Is this the cure you're making?"

Albert shook his head and laughed. It was a loud, boisterous laugh. "Not quite."

"Do you remember my wife? Amy Walder?"

Albert turned down the flame on one of the Bunsen burners before looking curiously at Ewan. "The name . . . it sounds familiar. . . but the past . . . I don't remember much."

"Do you remember inventing the Perpetuum generator?"

Albert creased his deeply wrinkled forehead and shook his head. "I heard there was this company . . . once. Perpetuum Industries."

"Amy said it was you who invented the generator and Graham Meyer turned it into a business."

Albert stood up completely and turned his whole body to face Ewan. He frowned deeply and said sadly, "I don't remember any Meyer."

Ewan remembered reading an article about it many years ago. Albert Winkler had invented the generator and was about to install it at the University of Toronto for a fraction of the cost when he met Graham Meyer who patented it and started to sell it to companies. Turned it into a business. The company quickly grew to be worth a trillion dollars and then, in a stunning Brutus-like maneuver, Graham Meyer persuaded the board of directors to kick Albert Winkler out of the company.

Albert shook his head again and returned to his tubes. He poured the liquids from the tubes into a beaker, stirred and then held up to Ewan.

"Drink it," he said.

"What's this? The cure?"

"Just drink it."

Ewan took the beaker and reluctantly took a sip. The hot liquid hit Ewan's tongue, tasting sour and filthy. He spit it out onto the ground, but immediately regretting doing so. He wiped his mouth with the back of his hand. "Christ, that tasted awful. What did you put in there?"

"It's supposed to be soda pop."

"You're trying to make soda pop?" Ewan asked feeling his anger rise. "The world is full of shit, Creatures trying to kill all of us and you're making what? . . . soda pop?"

Albert took the beaker back and took a sip. He frowned and spit out the liquid just as Ewan had done. "Hmm . . . I think I took a step back there."

Albert put the beaker back on the lab table. Ewan took Albert by his shirt and shoved him up against the wall and cocked back his fist. "Tell me one good reason I shouldn't beat you to death?"

Albert laughed, crazily and this made Ewan lose his senses. He brought his fist forward as hard as he could and smashed his fist against Albert's chin. A bolt of pain ran through Ewan's fist and up his wrist. He stepped back clutching his knuckles. Ewan hadn't hit anybody since grade school and now he remembered why.

Albert let out a tiny yelp and threw up his hands. His body reeled backwards and he probably would have fallen if he hadn't been already leaning up against the wall.

"Why did you do that?" Albert asked, feeling his jaw.

Ewan, who hadn't hit anybody since grade school, stared at his knuckles which were already beginning to swell. "I'm sorry. I just couldn't believe it."

A sound like an egg timer dinged from somewhere on the table. Ewan turned to locate the source of the sound.

Albert took his hands away from his face. "Dinner time," he said. "Why don't you stay? Especially since you can't go out now."

Ewan was hungry and, apart from the piece of rat, he couldn't remember the last time he had eaten a real meal. Perhaps Albert had some real food.

Ewan followed Albert through a doorway into another smaller room. In the middle was a set of chairs and a square table.

"On the menu tonight, spaghetti in tomato sauce and mashed potatoes with gravy."

"Sounds good," Ewan said, his mouth already beginning to water. "Really good."

Albert opened a cupboard in the corner and took out two cans and gave one to Ewan. Ewan read the label.

"Baby food? This is what you call spaghetti?"

Albert produced a can opener from the cupboard and began to open his can with it. "It's the most natural food on the shelf nowadays. Riddle me this, Walder: what food would you say is most scrutinized in our society?"

Ewan shrugged. Amy had probably told him at some point but he had filed that in some department of his memory long forgotten.

"Baby food," Albert said, in a tone he had probably once used on his students. "Less toxins and you don't need to refrigerate it."

Ewan wanted to tell Albert that society was gone but his words would probably only be lost on the doctor. Albert passed the can opener to Ewan who began to eagerly open his can. Baby food or not, he would eat it.

"You know it's funny," Ewan said, tipping the can and empting the contents down his throat.

"Careful now," Albert said. "You're malnourished. You want to eat slowly."

"Do you remember when we used to have a choice of what to eat? My whole family used to be first vegetarians and then we went vegan. We could actually choose not to eat meat or drink milk. Now . . ."

Albert nodded enthusiastically and it reminded Ewan of a small child who knew the answer to some math problem. "Yes, yes, I've been a vegan since I was seven."

"Seven?"

"Yes, my parents were scientists. Both worked for U of T. They understood the benefits before the whole hippy thing."

Ewan put the tin can on the table. "You have any more?"

Albert nodded and got up from the table. "My father always used to say flesh eating turns into flesh eaters."

Ewan frowned. "Your father used to say that?"

"You want spaghetti or something different this time?"

"How about fish and chips?"

"Yeah, I've got that." Albert ran his fingers along the row of cans and finally picked one up from the end and handed it to Ewan who took the can opener and dug the teeth into the lid.

"You know, Amy never said you were this . . ."

"What? Crazy? Is that what you mean, chap?"

Ewan smiled. "Eccentric."

Albert laughed and sat down opposite Ewan. Ewan finished the baby food. It didn't taste anything like fish and chips but it hardly mattered anymore. His stomach started to ache but the sudden injection of nutrients felt like a shot of heroin was coursing through his body.

"Amy . . . Amy Walder," Albert said, his face deep in concentration.

"You don't remember her, do you?" Ewan looked down at his lap. He couldn't look Albert Winkler in the eyes. He didn't want him to know how much it hurt him that her memory had faded from consciousness.

"Yeah . . . sure. You said I was her boss."

Ewan nodded. He dug into his pocket and produced a small wallet-sized photograph of her in the park and handed it to Albert. He wished he had the photograph he had found in Albert's office. Albert took the photograph with both hands and held it close to his face, studying it closely. "She was your research assistant at the university after you left Perpetuum Industries."

"Yeah, sure," Albert said, nodding twice. "Great looking gal."

"Can I ask you a question?"

"Of course, chap."

"Amy quit because she found out you were taking Albros funding. She said it was the equivalent of taking money from the devil to study hell."

Albert laughed. "She must have been a special gal."

Ewan nodded emphatically. "That she was."

"Tell me Walder guy, do you know how to start a fire?"

Ewan frowned, thrown by the question. "What do you mean?"

"Can you take two twigs and rub them together to make a fire?"

"Uh, no . . . Do you?"

Albert shook his head and laughed. "Not a clue, chap. Not a clue. Isn't that wonderful?"

Ewan rubbed his cheeks, suddenly tired of the old man. "Tell me, why is that wonderful?"

"Our ancestors were smarter than we are, right now in this time. We have cars and planes and weapons and computers all sitting around this great city of ours, yet we can't use them. Our ancestors in the Stone Age were better off than we are right at this moment in time. They could hunt, make fires, and make tools. If only they could

147

see us now they would probably laugh at how helpless we've become."

Ewan nodded, thinking, *Yeah they didn't have to contend with millions of flesh-eating Creatures.*

But he didn't say that. Instead he said, "I can't disagree with you there old man . . . But why is it wonderful?"

"Chap, didn't you ever want a second chance at something?"

Ewan shrugged. "Not badly enough to wipe out the entire population of Earth."

"Now we can rebuild and make it right this time. No wars, no pollution, no geo-political nonsense!"

Suddenly the lights went off and the low hum of the lights ceased. In the darkness Ewan got to his feet. "What the hell! Your genny coil has blown!"

Sneak Attack

Stu decided blitzkrieg would be the best option and so they laid low in the car and Graham pressed the gas petal. The car propelled them forward through the parking lot, over the speed bumps, over the curb and onto the snow-covered grass towards the park's single dilapidated building.

Krista was in the seat, covering her head with her hands. Her mouth was open as if she wanted to scream but no words came out.

Stu had placed his sword between the seats and had two Molotov cocktails ready to be lit. Surely they had heard them coming from a long way off, which was why they now had to move quickly.

Graham suddenly hit the brakes. The Audi fishtailed and then skidded across an icy patch and Graham struggled to control the wheel. The car slowed and then smashed into a tree. The crash jarred Stu, making him lose his concentration and orientation, but only for a moment as he struck a match and lit the first Molotov cocktails. He threw it through the window at the building about ten meters in front of them.

The bomb hit the brick wall just above the window and erupted into a fireball of gas and flames but the fire quickly fizzled out. Stu didn't wait. He lit the second cocktail and threw it. This time he hit the roof, a more flammable substance and it burned quickly.

Stu drew his sword and readied his throwing stars. The savages would be forced out of the building. Stu waited, watching until the roof collapsed inwards.

Nobody came out.

"Guess they moved on," Graham said, getting out of the car.

"Get down," Stu said. His eyes were alert, scanning between the trees for any movement. But he couldn't see any threats.

Graham took his knife out and walked slowly towards the burning building. The interior had now caught fire and thick columns of black smoke rose into the light blue sky. If there was anybody nearby they certainly could see the smoke. Would the savages ambush them from behind?

Stu got out of the car as well and took out his sword. He again scanned the distance all around him but still couldn't see anything.

Graham circled the house and Stu searched the surrounding area for any sign of the savages but there were no fresh tracks. Stu sighed and put his sword back in his belt. Together Graham and Stu walked back to the car.

"You were right," Stu said, begrudgingly.

Graham glanced furtively at Stu. "It was worth a shot."

Graham had told Stu that the savages had almost definitely moved on to some place safer. Stu had hoped he could catch them and slaughter them all. But now they had escaped punishment.

"We should go find some food before it starts to snow again," Graham said.

The temperature had dipped significantly over the last couple of hours and icicles hung on the trees like crystals, refracting the light, creating colourful patterns on the snow.

When they got back to the car, Stu looked around for Krista but she was nowhere to be found.

"Damn it, we've lost Krista," Stu said.

"She couldn't have gone far." But as soon as Graham spoke, Stu saw Krista walking towards them from the direction of the road. She seemed like a pathetic figure, her head bowed and her hands stuffed in her pocket.

"Where did you go?" Stu asked.

Krista shrugged. "Just checking out which direction they went."

Graham frowned. "How do you know they went that way?"

"Easy, their foot prints. Course you guys made it a little more challenging with the car and your own prints but there's four sets of prints clearly heading south west."

"How do you know they're not footprints from the Creatures?" Graham asked.

"The Creatures have a very distinctive footprint and their stride is much different. These tracks are clearly human."

"How do you know about tracking?" Stu asked

150

"My uncle used to love to hunt. He would always show me some things to watch out for. I don't know, just in case, I suppose."

Stu stepped up to Krista who backed up against the car, her eyes wide now with fear. "What?" she asked.

"Do you think you could track them?"

"Stu, forget it. They're gone."

But Krista nodded. "Yeah, I could figure it out. It's not so hard in the snow."

"Then let's go," Stu said, walking around to the passenger's side.

"Stu, we have nothing to eat."

"We can feast on their dead bodies. I said let's go."

Graham glanced at Krista but her face remained impassive. Eventually Graham sighed and everybody got into the car.

"How are we going to track them using a car? Wouldn't it easier on foot?"

"I think the tracks will be easy enough to follow."

Graham turned on the engine. It sputtered and came to life. The gas they used clearly wasn't very good for the engine but it didn't matter. They had hundreds of cars to choose from, cars littered on the side of the road, abandoned when gas ran dry from the pumps and nobody came to refill them.

Graham slowly followed the path with Krista guiding him. Occasionally they had to veer around a cluster of trees or some rocks and they had to stop the car and Krista had to get out to search for the footprints but she always found them again. The footprints cut across large neighbourhoods, all the time heading towards southwest. Luckily the savages seemed to keep to the main roads so it wasn't too hard to follow them and even Stu thought he could distinguish their footprints from the many prints from the Creatures.

"Where do you think they're heading?" Graham asked Krista after awhile.

"Some place safe from the Creatures, no doubt."

They hit the 401 Highway and the savages seemed to have walked along the road before they got off near Morningside Avenue but there Krista couldn't pick up the trail again. Their footsteps seemed to have almost disappeared in the snow.

"Perhaps they stopped here for the night?" Graham suggested.

Graham looked around. "I believe there is a U of T campus here. Perhaps they stopped there."

They drove a little further south and they came upon a greyish-brown building with the familiar University of Toronto Coat of Arms over top of a big doorway.

"Why would they go in there?" Krista asked. "It seems like they would have stayed outside and built a fire for the night."

Stu shook his head. "I don't know. That would have attracted Teki from within a hundred miles."

"But the fire would have kept them safe," Krista said.

"If I was them," Stu said. "I would have found a safe hiding spot, some place the Teki wouldn't be able to find them, just like the Teki do to us in the daytime."

"And you think they probably hid out in a university? That place would be full of Creatures."

"Let's just see if we can find their tracks again," Graham said.

"We should leave the car and split up," Krista said.

"Why? So you can run away?" Stu said.

"I could have run away back at your stupid ambush."

Stu slapped her across the face. Krista lunged at him but Graham caught her and wrapped her around with his large, lanky arms. Stu drew his sword and held it in front of him, ready to strike.

"Why do you always try to stop me?" Krista screamed.

"He'll kill you," Graham said into Krista's ear.

"What do I care?" Krista said, half crying, half shouting. "This isn't life. This is fucking purgatory."

Stu smiled. "Go ahead commit Seppuka."

"What the fuck does that even mean? Why don't you speak English?"

Graham was the one who answered. "It's a ritual suicide for samurais."

"Go ahead Graham. Give her your knife so she can disembowel herself."

But nobody moved for a long time, each eying the other until Stu finally sheathed his sword. "That's what I thought," he said. "Now let's find those tracks."

They searched for over an hour before Krista found the tracks. She called Stu and Graham over and pointed out the set of footprints that was trampled under tracks from the Creatures.

"You sure?" Graham asked.

They followed the tracks on foot as they went through the campus, heading directly westwards.

"I would bet my life on it," Krista said, stopping at the edge of the campus, looking at the rows of ash-red houses that went on into the horizon.

Graham turned to Stu. "You're bleeding," he said.

Stu gently touched his shoulder and realized the bandage he had put on earlier had soaked through with his blood. He would need to find a replacement.

"Shall I get the car?" Graham asked.

But Stu shook his head. "No, let's follow these for awhile and see where they lead us."

"At least make sure it's not infected," Graham said.

"I'm fine. Let's keep walking."

They walked on for about twenty minutes. Their shoes squeaked on the snow as they trudged through alleys, streets, lawns and backyards. The snow had buried much of the debris and ash and glass that coated the sidewalk and formed a beautiful, undisturbed surreal white coat across the city.

"Graham, go back and get the car. We're going to continue on and meet you at the main road. I think it's called Ellesmere or something like that." Stu pointed to his right and in the distance they could see what had once been a main artery through the neighbourhood but now stood silent and vacant. "If we get split up meet back at the university campus."

Graham looked up at the sky and found it clouding over. "It's going to get dark soon. Maybe we should find a safe place to stay for the night and continue our search tomorrow."

"No," Stu said. "We push on. I'm not afraid of the Teki."

"Let me go with Graham," Krista said.

"You have to stay here and help me with the tracks."

Stu noticed Krista give Graham a pleading look and Stu thought Graham would try and persuade him but instead he just said, "Alright I should be there in about thirty minutes."

Stu watched Graham trek slowly back the way they had come through the snow before turning to Krista. "It's just you and me now."

Krista stood silent, her body straight as if at attention.

"Don't worry, I'm not going to hurt you."

They continued to track the savages as they continued westward.

"Where do you think they're heading?" Stu asked.

Krista shrugged. "Who knows?"

"If you were to stake your life on it?"

"My life?" Krista stopped walking and looked at Stu. "The people we are tracking are a hunting party and they're going back to their base camp. And before you ask me now, I don't know where that would be."

Stu nodded thoughtfully. "We should probably head towards the road so we don't miss Graham."

They turned north and walked up the street until they hit Ellesmere Road. They walked on in silence for a few minutes before they heard the distant, unmistakable sound of a car engine in the distance. It was the only sound above the wind and seemed to echo from the brick houses, amplifying the sound.

"We certainly can't sneak up on anybody," Krista commented.

Stu nodded as they waited. When they weren't walking the cold seeped in through their clothes and Stu began to shiver.

I wonder what the temperature is, Stu thought just as he spotted a black dot in the distance, racing towards them on the road, kicking up shards of ice and snow.

Graham braked and stopped next to them. Krista opened the back door but Stu stopped her. "Why don't you sit up front for a change? I will sit in the back."

Krista didn't respond, but just nodded and walked around to the passenger's seat. Stu climbed into the back. He was glad of the warmth and the comfortable seats. It was one of the few luxuries he missed from before the Outbreak.

"Where to?" Graham asked.

"We continue west until we find the home base."

"Home base?"

"The home of the savages," Stu said. "And go slow. You can bet they've booby-trapped around their base."

Graham continued on Ellesmere Road until they reached the McCowan Road. To their right was a small cluster of skyscrapers.

"I think that's Scarborough Town Center," Krista said, pointing to the skyscrapers.

"We're not far from the train tracks," Graham commented.

Graham turned right on McCowan Road and headed towards the city center.

"You think that's where the savages are?" Graham asked.

"Possibly."

They stopped at Progress Avenue. There they decided to get out and proceed on foot once again. The temperature was dropping even more as the sun moved behind the clouds.

"Stu we should come back. If the savages really have a base here then they know we're here and they have the drop on us. It's better to fight on our terms."

"We'll just do a little reconnaissance and if we're out gunned then we'll fall back, but at least we'll know where they are."

A line of ice-covered trees grew down the center of the boulevard. To the right was a line of old brick houses and to their left was a set of modern skyscrapers, rusted and broken. It was almost as if they were on the dividing line between the old and the new.

They walked along Progress Avenue. It was a winding road that made its way on the outskirts of a large shopping mall with empty parking lots. They walked slowly, carefully through the snow. Stu carried his sword in front of him, searching the windows and the snow banks for movement.

They took cover behind a row of trees and walked underneath their shadows for a while until they came to a clearing. A neon sign, long burnt out, hung in the distance advertising a line of clothing.

Stu and Graham stopped and surveyed the area but Krista kept walking out into the open.

Graham glanced at Stu. "You want to follow her?"

"Just wait."

Stu looked around but there was nothing to see but the parking lot and a few cars covered in layers of icy snow.

He nodded and they followed Krista, still looking around for threats.

"There are a lot of human tracks here," Krista said, crouching down and examining the snow. "More than just the four we've been tracking."

"You think they are inside the shopping mall?" Stu asked.

"I think it's time we go," Graham said, glancing nervously around.

Stu walked up to Graham. "Are you a coward?"

"Just practical."

Just then an arrow flew from behind a parked car, passing through the narrow gap between Graham and Stu. They both flung themselves to the ground. Krista took two steps running back the way they came when an arrow hit her in the arm. She let out a low yelp and fell to the ground. Her blood poured onto the snow.

"Son of a bitch," Stu said, pushing himself into a crouching position. He picked up the sword he had dropped and got ready to attack the savages hiding behind the cars.

Just as Stu dug into his pouch and got out his throwing stars a voice spoke from behind the cars. "My worthy opponents, you are surrounded. It is best if you surrender now."

Stu glanced around him and saw a dozen figures stand up from the snow. They were wearing large white parkas that camouflaged them and each of them had a bow and arrow ready to fire.

Stu looked at Graham who was staring ahead impassively. He glanced at Krista who had rolled over and was now just whining softly as her shoulder oozed blood onto the snow.

A man stepped out from behind the car. He had on the same white parka but over his face he wore a large wooden mask in the shape of an eagle's head. It was brightly painted like a First Nation's mask Stu had seen hung up in art galleries. In his right hand he had a sword and in his left a butcher's clever. He was a large, broad-shouldered man with a thick, black neck.

Stu turned to Graham. "What do you want to do?"

Graham surveyed the savages in front of him. "Do we have a choice?" he asked.

Stu nodded and stood up, his sword raised in front of him. He closed his eyes, feeling the beating of his heart and willed it to slow down. He steadied his breathing and tried to relax all his muscles in his body. His old sensei had told him he must not even feel the grip of his sword.

If I am to die today, Stu thought, *let me die with honour.*

He opened his eyes and stared at the large, powerful man standing in front of him.

"Are you the leader of these savages?" Stu called out to him.

"We are no savages and I do not have the pleasure of being our leader," the eagle-headed man said. He spoke in a heavy Caribbean accent, his voice deep and resounding.

"What is the name of your leader then?"

"We call him the White Chief. He is a wise and just ruler."

Stu opened his eyes and studied at the eagle-headed man. Although he was heavily armed and would have superior reach with his long arms, Stu knew he could beat him with his agility and speed. He had done it many times before with stronger men, turning their strengths into weaknesses. His old sensei had taught him how to do that too.

"You say the White Chief is a just ruler. I am a man with honour. I challenge you to one-on-one combat. The winner will walk away unharmed."

The eagle-headed man laughed. "You think I'm stupid? You have entered sacred land. You cannot walk away freely. I urge you to drop your weapons and come with us."

Graham spoke up for the first time. "What do you intend to do?"

"That is for the White Chief to decide."

The Outbreak

Ewan wrapped his arms around Amy's warm body, feeling the slow movement of her chest against his own. He should have been marking papers, seemingly endless papers, but his eyes were droopy and all he wanted to do was fall into slumber next to his wife.

Yet he couldn't fall asleep, something kept him awake.

Then a thud came from the ceiling, waking Amy with a small gasp.

"What was that?" she asked

Ewan closed his eyes and buried his head into the crevasse between her neck and shoulder. She smelled fresh, like a spring garden after watering.

He knew it would soon be over — this dream this nightmare . . .

Whatever it was, he wanted to enjoy every single moment before he was catapulted back into reality.

"Ewan did you hear that?"

Yes, my love. I heard it. But I can't stop it.

Ewan opened his eyes. He was in a dark cavernous room. Amy was gone. Sophie and Tim were gone. Albert was standing over him, smiling wildly.

"You sure it's safe to turn out the lights like that?" Ewan said.

"We're as safe as . . . what's a good analogous situation?"

"I can't remember the last time I slept with the lights off," Ewan said.

Last night Albert had explained how the Creatures' higher functioning brains had somehow been shut down and because of that they couldn't find a way through the funhouse mirrors. Albert shut down his generator at night to preserve it.

"I have to show you something," Albert said.

"What?"

"You just have to see it."

Ewan got up, stretched and walked back through the doorway to the room he thought of as the lab.

Albert got to his table and turned to face Ewan. "I made a mistake . . . We all made a mistake."

"What do you mean?"

"It wasn't a virus. It wasn't a disease. That's why it couldn't be cured. There is no cure."

"If that's all you've got you should have let me sleep," Ewan said, turning to return to his mattress. He didn't realize how much he missed sleeping with the lights off.

"Wait, chap. Wait."

Ewan stopped and turned back to Albert. There was something different about him. His face was in full concentration and his eyes seemed deeply focused.

"Tell me Ewan, have you ever listened to outer space?"

"What do you mean?"

"I mean the High Frequency Active Auroral Research Program. Publically HAARP was designed to analyse the Ionosphere and use it for better communication systems in reality it was used to try and communicate with alien life forms."

"So you're saying the Creatures were created by some alien life form?"

Albert shook his head. "In 2025, the Albros Corporation was founded by retired Naval Officer James Marcus, who was part of the HAARP team. Originally he wanted to improve on non-perishable food sent into space. He created something called the Marcus meal which now almost every astronaut and tourist eat when going into space."

"Amy said he created the most advanced, cheapest seeds in the world," Ewan remembered.

Albert nodded. "Yes after the Marcus meal he turned to GMOS. This is where Retired Naval Officer James Marcus became a billionaire. There was only one problem: they started to change the genetic makeup of every person who consumed them."

Ewan held up his hand. "No wait. I'm no fan of Albros, my wife was even less of one, but I'm sure the WHO wouldn't have allowed Albros to sell anything that was unsafe."

"It passed all the regular tests. Nothing abnormal was detected in the food."

"So Albros created the Outbreak?"

"It would seem so."

"Shame on you," Ewan said. He wanted to throw Albert against the wall, or better yet toss him out and let the Creatures feast on him. "Amy was right. How could you take money from these people?"

Albert looked down at the ground. "I'm sorry, chap. I let the world down. I know."

Ewan started to pace, to get some of the nervous energy that was building up in his muscles. He couldn't believe that just with a few nutrients his whole body felt better.

"But I don't understand it. How did we survive? How did you, Ashley and the boys survive?"

"You said yourself you were a vegan. Did you eat genetically modified organisms?"

Ewan shook his head. "No, Amy would never have allowed it."

Albert nodded thoughtfully. "That probably had something to do with it, but there are probably several components to it."

Ewan thought about how Amy always insisted on spending extra money on organic products. Was that why he was still alive today? Because of the organic vegetables Amy forced him to eat?

Ewan sat down and rested his hands on his head. He had told Ashley there was no cure, that he would need a super lab to find a way to stop the Outbreak. For the first time since Amy had died he had reason to hope. In front of him was the man who created the Perpetuum generator had possibly the most brilliant mind since Stephen Hawking. Was Doctor Albert Winkler too crazy to help him?

After breakfast, Ewan managed to drag Albert Winkler back to the Royal Ontario Museum. Ewan had to practically threaten him with torture to get him to come with him.

"No, no, I must work on my soda pop," Albert wined.

"No, you're going to help me."

"But you need the soda."

"No, soda is on my top ten list of worst inventions of all time," Ewan said, pushing Albert through the door and out into the sun. A sharp yellow light sparkled on the dead city and on the white snow that layered the cement and the brick and concrete.

It would have been beautiful if it weren't so eerie. The smog and pollution had cleared the first year of the Outbreak as Mother Nature repaired herself from the damage from humankind.

Ewan took Albert by the arm gently but firmly, leading him into the large entrance hallway of the ROM.

"Ashley?" Ewan called out but there was no answer.

Ewan and Albert found her staring at the large T-Rex on the second floor.

"Oh, hey, you're back," Ashley said, smiling.

Ewan glanced up at the T-Rex skeleton trying to find out what Ashley had been so mesmerized by. "You alright?"

"Yeah, yeah. Just thinking of the extinction of the dinosaurs . . . and wondering if we're going to be next."

Ewan took off his backpack and gave Ashley a couple of cans of baby food he had taken from Albert's cupboard. "Well not for awhile yet."

Ashley grabbed the cans excitedly. "Food?"

Ewan just smiled and nodded. "The good doctor has enough to last us awhile."

They went and found a can opener in the staff room and Ashley quickly opened up the can while Ewan went and found the boys. "Don't let Doctor Winkler leave," he said.

Ewan found the two boys upstairs drawing on the wall with crayons. He knew he should have scolded them but he just didn't have the energy. The boys dropped the crayons and raced downstairs when they heard Ashley had food.

Ewan smiled and followed them down the stairs.

When was the last time I smiled? Ewan wondered. *When was the last time I was happy?*

After Ashley and the boys had finished eating, Ewan said, "Doctor Winkler might be able to help us with the Creatures."

"But I only make soda pop, chap!"

"Not any more you don't."

Ewan explained to Ashley what Albert had told him about the Outbreak about how Albros food had changed the genetics of people who ate it.

"So these Creatures were caused by mutation in our food supply?" Ashley asked.

Albert looked around the museum. "You know what chemtrails are?"

Ewan and Ashley exchanged glances.

"No what are they?"

"Albros and other large companies used the technology of chemtrailing a.k.a. geo-engineering since the late 70's. They controlled the weather worldwide, created storms, droughts and floods. But Albros went a step further by spraying chemicals at high altitude of over 15,000 meters in our stratosphere containing boran, aluminum, strontium and genetically created substances. The jet streams and the global weather system distributed this toxic mixture worldwide and through rainfall, covered fields, destroying any non-GMO crops so farmers were forced to buy from Albros. Another company came up with toxic aerosols containing viruses and even genetically modified cells to depopulate portions of the poor world. Over 60 companies committed illegal and ungoverned aerosoling worldwide and these toxic mixtures … well … they mixed up."

"How do you know this?" Ashley asked.

"You don't believe me, do you?"

"No, it's not that," Ashley said quickly. "I do remember whistleblowers coming forward about this but governments worldwide explained that it's because of climate change, because we produce too much CO_2 and that these chemtrailing planes are just weather control, cooling the planet."

Albert coughed slightly and drew in a deep breath. "That is correct, the whole CO_2 scare was just another hoax or a way for them to rape humanity of money to further their real evil plan on controlling first the weather and then the food. President Kennedy once said, that the ones who control the weather control the fate of the world. It's just like when they added fluoride to the drinking water. A neurological substance to dumb people down … or artificial sweeteners like Aspartame to make people lose memory. All this was part of Albros's plan and the final step was controlling every single food item we consume."

"Is there any proof of that?"

"Proof is in the pudding as they say. Did you know they had a secret lab in the city?"

"Can you take us there?" Ashley asked.

Albert scratched his dusty beard. "That would be difficult. Very difficult indeed. I don't know where it is."

Ewan stepped up to Albert, shoving him against the wall. "Are you lying to us? You better not be lying doctor!"

"I swear I'm not, old chap," Albert said, cowering. "I don't know where it is!"

"Ewan, stop it," Ashley said, putting a hand on Ewan's shoulder.

"No, I'm not going to let him get off so easily. He's holding something back. I know it," Ewan said. "And if this is the only way I can get Tim back then I'll do what it takes." Ewan turned back to Albert. "How do you know about the lab?"

"I'm not sure, chap. The memory is a little hazy! Surely you can understand that? The neutrons aren't firing as quickly as they used to."

"Well you better get them working," Ewan said, shaking Albert.

"Ewan stop it," Ashley said, behind him, her voice high and panicky.

Ewan released Albert. "I want you to think about it doctor."

Ashley was writing in her journal when Ewan approached her. "What are you writing about?" he asked her.

Ashley closed the book and looked up at Ewan. "Nothing important. It just keeps me sane that's all."

"I'm sorry about before," he said.

Ashley was sitting in the main entrance. The afternoon light poured through the glass doors, spilling onto the floor. Outside it must have been ten or eleven degrees below zero but using the generator's power, inside it was warm and comfortable.

Ewan had left Albert to wander through the museum. He went from exhibition to exhibition like a kid, reading every plaque, every stand, ever caption.

Ewan realized Albert would be able to escape easily enough but short of locking him up there was no way he could prevent that. And if Ewan wanted Albert's help then he realized he would have to give it freely.

Ashley didn't look up at Ewan but continued to write. "You're concerned for Tim. I get it."

Ewan could tell by the tone in her voice that she was still angry. Ewan pulled up a chair next to her and only then did Ashley look at him. Her eyes were red and swollen with tears.

"What's wrong?" Ewan asked.

"You don't think I miss Tim too? You mope around like you're the only one in a bad situation. What about Albert? He's half demented, probably from living alone without anybody to talk to."

"You're right," Ewan conceded, looking away from Ashley. Ewan thought for a moment. "Ley-ley, remember when you told me not to lose hope?"

Ashley smiled widely at Ewan's use of Tim's nickname for her. "Of course," she said.

"Well I did. I'm sorry. If I could have killed myself painlessly then I would have. But now we have Albert and locked inside his mind somewhere is a way we can beat the Creatures. Maybe there is no cure. I don't know . . . but maybe there's a way we can beat them and live a normal live."

Ashley put down her pen, rubbed her eyes and looked at Ewan. "I don't want you to take this the wrong way . . ."

Ewan shook his head. "I will do my best."

"How do you know Tim is still alive?"

"Because I can feel it . . . I know that doesn't make much sense but I know he's still out there."

"You said Creatures took him?"

Ewan shook his head. "They weren't exactly Creatures . . . They might have been human, I don't know. They were tall — maybe eight or nine feet…"

Ashley didn't say anything for a while but then she nodded. "Okay. You really think there is a secret lab somewhere in the city?"

Ewan shrugged. He didn't want to think of Albert as his only hope but even in his demented state he was still a genius. Ashley had to write in her journal and Ewan knew he had to believe Albert Winkler. He remembered Amy in his dream and he knew if Amy was correct and Tim was alive then he would be found through Albert. That was all there was to it.

"I don't know if we can trust anything Albert says, but then again," Ewan said. "Do you have a choice?"

Ewan laid a map of the city down on the counter at the front of the museum. Oddly enough Albert Winkler was still with them.

"Alright," Ewan said. "My hypothesis is that if we track down where the Outbreak first occurred and from that we might be able to pinpoint the origins of the disease and find a perimeter for this secret lab."

"You think perhaps it was tested on Albros employees first?" Ashley asked.

"I think that is the most likely theory."

"Are we going on a vacation?" Albert asked, studying the map closely.

Ewan frowned. "Of sorts."

"Good, I like vacations."

"Albert," Ewan said, slowly and clearly. "Do you remember when the first people started mutating?"

"You want to know the tipping point."

"The tipping point?" Ewan asked. "What are you talking about?"

"The tip on the end of something pointy, chap."

Ewan sighed and rubbed his temples, resisting the urge to look at Ashley. "What are you talking about old man? Please try and make some sense."

"Sense? What is sense? How do we know what sense is? To be in a world full of mutated organisms."

Ashley smiled, taking the tension out of the room. "He has you there, Ewan."

Albert looked at Ashley and smiled back at her. "You know it's not a bacterial or viral infection. It's a mutation. I've explained this a million times already."

Ewan threw up his arms. "We are arguing over syntax. I don't know what else to call it," Ewan said, trying to hide his frustration.

"But he's right," Ashley said. "If the mutation was changed by the shit Albros put in the food maybe it wasn't airborne at all as the scientists suggested."

Ewan shook his head. "Albert said that was part of the equation but that something changed in the genetic makeup and somehow we are all immune. Otherwise we would be all dead by now or mutated."

"I said that?" Albert asked. "I never knew I sounded so smart."

"We track down the source and we'll be bound to find some answers," Ewan said. "Albert do you remember where the first cases were reported?"

Albert frowned and stared at the map. "Sorry old chap. As I said, my memory isn't my best asset these days."

Ewan sighed. "I remember when it hit the news it was in central Toronto but I have a feeling it started on the outskirts."

"The outskirts would be a good place for a secret lab."

Ewan stared at Albert but the doctor didn't say anything.

Would they be able to make it from the middle of the city all the way to the edge without being killed? And what if they were wrong? What if they had the wrong location or worse there was no secret lab?

Ewan started to fold the map. "Maybe it was just a crazy idea," he said.

"Wait," Albert shouted, making Ewan pause and look at the doctor.

"The Outbreak started in York."

"In York?" Ashley said. "You sure?"

Albert shook his head. "I can't be sure of anything these days but I think so. The first case went to Sunnybrook Health Science Center."

Ewan unfolded the map and looked at the Sunnybrook Health Science Center. It was a large complex with a cancer, emergency and heart center, along with other specialties. It would be an ideal place to have a lab, but how secret would it be there?

Ewan turned to Ashley. "What do you think?"

Ashley didn't say anything for a long time. "We could probably make it there in two days, worry about one night out. It wouldn't be that hard to check out."

"There's still some gas left in my car. I've been saving it for a rainy day. I think this is it."

"You sure you want to use the last of your gas? I mean what if we need it?"

"We do need it."

"You know what I mean," Ashley said. "Maybe we should keep it . . . you know, in case we need to escape."

Ewan nodded. "The car might not even work in these conditions. Let me test it out before we make any decisions. In the meantime pack everything you need. We leave tomorrow at first light."

"Don't you think we should wait until the snow clears?"

But Ewan shook his head. "Timmy doesn't have that long."

Ashley nodded, but averted her eyes. Ewan knew what she was thinking: *if he's still alive.*

"What about Doctor Winkler?"

Ewan looked at Albert. "We take him with us."

To Ewan's surprise, Albert let out a high-pitch almost girlish giggle. "Good! I like vacations."

"This isn't going to be a vacation, doctor," Ewan said grimly. "We are going into the heart of enemy territory."

The White Chief

The savages had bound their captives' hands and taken them around the side of the shopping mall. They halted about twenty yards in front of the entrance.

"Why are we stopping?" Stu asked one of the savages, but instead of an answer, the savage just backhanded him. Stu reeled from the force of the blow but quickly recovered and launched himself at the savage. Stu's only weapon was his teeth and so he opened his mouth and bit down, finding a piece of the savage's cheek and Stu clenched and tore with all his might. The savage, not expecting this fierce attack, dropped his bow and fell backwards, blood spewing from his wound.

Stu would have been on top of the savage if the other savages hadn't stepped up to him and started punching him. Stu struggled to stay upright. He didn't want to look weak in front of them but a swing from a stick smacked Stu on the top of the head and he crumpled to the ground. He struggled to remain conscious as his vision blurred.

Stu tried to roll over onto his side but the savages circled him and started kicking him mercilessly. Stu curled up, trying to protect himself, his wrists still bound but he felt a crack as his ribs broke. Still he refused to cry out in pain. One kick caught him in the chin and he felt a tooth in his throat.

"Enough, enough!" came a voice and Stu looked up to see the black man in the eagle's mask standing over him.

Stu struggled to his knees.

"Attack him when he is unprepared, appear when you are unexpected," Stu said, smiling. It was painful to breath and he felt blood running down his chin and dripping into the snow.

"I know Sun Tzu, samurai."

"You impress me, savage."

"I told you, we are not savages, we have retaken this land."

"If you are not a savage then why don't you show me your face? Only cowards hide behind masks."

The man with the eagle mask laughed and turned to his soldiers. "If he tries anything like that again, cut off his right arm."

Stu didn't say anything but just watched as the front door to the mall opened and a thick wooden plank was slid out along the snow to the group of savages.

"Do not step off the plank," the eagle-masked man told his captives. "Although the snow looks solid there is just a thin piece of plywood that will break under your weight. Underneath is a twenty-foot pit filled with spikes."

Stu understood the wooden plank was a makeshift drawbridge and the savages had turned the shopping mall into a castle of sorts.

"How medieval," Stu commented, dryly.

"But effective against the Creatures."

The savages walked single file along the extended plank and into the shopping mall. Stu, Graham and Krista were led across by the man with the eagle mask. When everybody was across, the savages withdrew the plank and barricaded the entrance with a couple of wooden shelves.

Inside the shopping mall, Stu was astounded. There were hundreds of people walking around just like before the Outbreak. A few stopped to stare at the prisoners but most just ignored them and went on their way, for what purpose Stu couldn't surmise. Against one wall was a row of fifty or more spears and next to that a row of crossbows.

The savages were ready for war, alright.

"Do we get to see the White Chief now?" Stu asked.

"Not yet," the man with the Eagle mask said. "Maybe tomorrow."

"What will he do with us?" Krista asked.

"He is a just ruler. He will do with you what is right for the community."

Just not what is right for us, Stu thought.

That night, Stu tried to sleep but found it all but impossible because he was full of rage. He was angry he allowed the savages to capture him so easily but most of all he was angry the stupid black man in a mask had taken his sword. He swore he would get it back no matter what, even if it was with his dying breath.

The captives had found themselves tethered to a large support beam in the northeast corner of Wal-Mart.

How stupid, Stu thought. *I'm going to die in a Wal-Mart.*

Through the night Stu could hear the footsteps of the Creatures outside. Some screamed as they fell to their death onto the spikes. Some seemed to scream almost in frustration. Of course it wasn't a new sound but at the zoo he felt safe, knowing the Creatures couldn't touch him. He also had his sword by his side. Here if the Creatures somehow broke through the moat and the barricade then there wasn't much he could do. He would be like one of the people Stu had tied up and left for the Creatures. Almost ironic, really.

When Stu did manage to fall asleep he dreamt of his father, a person he almost never thought of or dreamt of. In his dream, Stu must have been about ten or eleven which would have been impossible because his father would have killed him by then.

Stu was playing with some action figures in the family living room when he heard his father noisily enter the apartment.

"Stuart!" His father yelled. "Where the fuck are you Stuart!"

"What do you want with him?" his mother yelled. Although she was afraid of her husband, she could put up a good fight when it came to protecting Stu.

"Can't I fucking talk to my son if I want to?"

Stu's dad entered the room. He cast a large looming shadow on the old floorboards. Stu's old man had been an electrician and Stu remembered he always wore grubby brown overalls wherever he went.

Young Stu looked up his at father in fear. From where Stu knelt he could smell a mixture of sweat and alcohol. Stu knew it was never a good combination and usually meant a beating was coming.

When the old man came near, Stu stood up and braced himself for what was to come next. Stu's old man grabbed his arm roughly and brought him close to his chest. Stu wanted to cry but he knew it would only make things worse.

"You're still skin and bones, Stuart. When will you get some fucking muscle?"

Stu's mother appeared in the doorway. She was petite and fragile-looking, especially when she stood next to her brutish husband. Her face was not pretty, ravaged by the drugs that controlled her.

"Don't call him Stuart," she said. "He prefers Stu."

Stu cringed inwardly. Saying that would only make his temper worse. But maybe that was the point. Stu couldn't tell with his mother sometimes. His mother would sometimes try to provoke his dad to break a bone or two and it would give her cause to leave him for a couple days.

Stu's old man released Stu and flung at rage towards his mother, hitting her with a strong backhand. She fell back against the doorframe but managed to put her hand out before she fell. She bit back a cry, a look of agony flashed across her face.

Stu just watched in horror, unable to move or say anything. He felt his whole body had been frozen.

Stu's mother straightened herself, smoothing out her dress. "That the best you can do bastard?"

Stu's father took her and shoved her against the wall, wrapping his large hand around her tiny neck. He stood there squeezing as Stu's mother's face went purple.

And still Stu was unable to move. His father was going to kill his mother. He knew it. But what would he have done anyways? His father was right: he had no muscles, no strength to protect her with. He felt helpless, unable to stop him.

Stu woke with a start. He shivered as he looked around but he couldn't see anything in the darkness. His ribs and chin were excruciatingly painful from where the savages had beaten him. He wasn't sure if anything was broken or not and wished he had his hands free so he could check the extent of his injuries.

Stu closed his eyes and opened them again, trying to adjust to the dark. He wondered if there were guards watching them somewhere. He could still hear the Creatures outside the mall but even they seemed to have subsided.

"Graham, you awake?" Stu whispered. He heard snoring but he couldn't tell if it was Graham or Krista.

The figure to his left stirred, indicating he was awake.

"You think you can untie your hands?"

Graham struggled for awhile but shook his head. "No, they are too tight."

Stu sighed. He felt angry that he had been bested, out maneuvered by the savages. "We should have gone back."

"What?"

"You were right. I lead us into a trap."

Graham didn't say anything and Stu rested his head against the beam. They didn't say anything for awhile. There was almost no sound and the darkness felt stifling.

It was painful to move but Stu managed to rotate his neck and in the corner of his vision he could see stars giving off a soft, dim light. Stu stared at them, appreciating their beauty.

Finally Stu said, "You know my aunt worked for Perpetuum Industries. She didn't have any fancy titles like you. She just worked in one of the warehouses."

"Really? Which one?"

"Rexdale, northern Etobicoke . . . After my parents died I went to live with her. She was my mother's sister and she was one of the kindest, gentlest people I had ever known. She would come home about seven or eight on the bus and I would prepare her some tea and massage her hands."

"I don't understand. Why are you telling me this?"

Stu shrugged in the darkness. "I don't know . . . I guess I wanted to tell somebody about my aunt before they kill and eat us"

"They aren't going to kill us."

Stu turned to try and peer at Graham in the darkness but he couldn't see anything. "You don't think the White Chief will kill us?"

"No. If they wanted us dead they would have done it already."

Stu shook his head. "What possible reason could they have to keep us alive? They're just waiting for dinner, that's all."

Graham said. "They want the gas. They saw us driving the car and they want to know how we got it."

Stu couldn't help but laugh for relief. He felt foolish. Of course Graham was right. Of course they wanted to know where they got the gas.

"We have bargaining power," Stu said.

"Yes and I suggest we think about how we want to use it."

Stu could see the morning sunrise through a window in the corner of the store. He could now see the small shape of Krista huddled in the corner.

After Stu's conversation with Graham he had only managed to get a few minutes of sleep, interrupted by hiccups of consciousness. He wished he had some drugs to help with the pain but he hadn't seen any painkillers in years. He wondered if such things existed in the world anymore.

Stu judged the sun had been up for two hours before the man with the eagle mask came to get him with a horde of savages and by then he had a plan. His confidence was restored.

"Why don't you show your face?" Stu asked. "Is it because it's so ugly your precious White Chief might cast you out of your commune?"

The eagle man said nothing as he untied his three captives. Stu stretched his arms and rubbed his wrists, trying to get the circulation back into his fingers.

"You will see the White Chief now," the eagle man said.

"About time," Stu said.

The savages pointed spears at them and motioned them to start walking.

Stu turned to Krista. "How did you manage to sleep through the entire night?"

"No talking," one of the savages said, jabbing his spear into Stu's back. Stu quickly spun around and grabbed the spear by the shaft and flung a kick, hitting the savage in the chest. The savage released the spear and sprawled backwards.

Stu quickly flipped the spear outwards and crouched in a fighting stance, ready for the savages but none of them moved. They too readied themselves, waiting for Stu to attack.

Stu smiled inwardly. Perhaps they weren't so naive after all in the ways of the warrior.

The eagle man was the first to step forward. "What do you think you're doing?"

"I challenge you again to fight in single combat. To turn me down once is shameful but twice is utter cowardness . . ."

"There is nothing I would like better than to fight you, samurai, but I have my orders from the White Chief."

Stu didn't move, didn't say anything. He concentrated on his captors. None of them looked like real fighters. He could tell in their eyes they were afraid even though they outnumbered Stu ten to one. They were just savages given spears and told to stick them into the Creatures. But Stu was no Creature. He knew how to fight.

Graham took a step forward in front of Stu. "Enough of this, Stu . . . Let's go meet the White Chief."

Graham tilted his head forward his eyes moving across Stu as if he was ploying him to remember the conversation from last night.

Stu stared back, taking a deep breath, trying to expel all the adrenaline that was seeping up through his body. He stood up, turned the spear upright and held it out. A savage snatched it from him and another hit him in the back of the head.

Stu fell to the ground on all fours. He tilted his head to look up at Graham but he was just standing passively, his hands across his chest. Another blow came from a savage's kick but Stu managed to block this one with his forearms.

The eagle man shouted for the savages to stop and immediately they stepped back. The eagle man picked Stu up as if he weighted as much as a pillow and put him back on his feet. He then took a piece of rope and bound his wrists together.

"You want to do this the hard way so be it," he said.

They walked down the escalator along the center court and then back up another escalator to the second floor where they passed through a doorway leading to the movie theaters. There they went along a long dark hallway still with movie posters of old movies on the wall. They stopped at the first auditorium.

The eagle man cut the ropes to Stu's hands. "You must respect the White Chief," he said, looking at Stu. "If you don't I will cut off your head and dine on your brain."

"That's why you're a savage," Stu said.

"You must address him as 'chief' and only speak when you're spoken to."

The eagle man opened the door and the captives stepped in. The auditorium was big with high ceiling. A large camp fire was burning on the stage, lighting the red-carpeted steps. They looked around but the auditorium seemed empty.

The savages lead the three captives down to the front row and told them to sit. Once they did so, the savages turned and left. They listened to their soft footsteps and then the closing of the door.

Sitting hurt Stu's ribs but he tried to hide it as best as possible.

"I don't like this," Krista said, speaking for the first time since they woke.

Graham looked around. "Okay, we don't have much time. Krista, don't mention anything about the gas. That's the only thing that is keeping us alive at the moment. Whatever they say, don't trust them. They will find the train car and then burn us alive. You understand?"

"Why should I trust you?"

"They are savages," Stu said.

"Stu shut up for a moment," Graham said in a fierce whisper. "Krista, they are cannibals. They eat each other. That's the only way they can sustain this population."

"You're lying."

Graham bent closer to Krista. "Look around us. Do you see any large food supply? It's simple macroeconomics—"

Graham stopped talking when he heard the doors open again and footsteps approach. Stu turned his head to look at the approaching savages. He expected to see the White Chief but instead he saw three women holding plates of food. The women were all tall, slender; their hair long and ropey.

Stu immediately started to salivate. He hadn't realized how hungry he was. He couldn't remember the last time he had anything to eat.

The three women sauntered in almost military fashion down the aisle until they were in front of the three captives. They placed the plates on their laps.

"We are sorry we cannot provide more," one of the women said with a sad smile.

The plates only contained roots and a couple of berries but it didn't matter. The captives started to stuff the food into their mouths and the women turned around and disappeared up the aisle. Stu was finished by the time the women disappeared through the door.

A voice came from behind the curtains, "I hope you've enjoyed your stay here."

Stu looked up and saw a small man step out on stage, next to the fire. He was dressed in spotless white jeans and a large white shawl covered his narrow shoulders. He had deep features, large intelligent creases around his large, dark eyes. His face was covered with a white chalk and on top of his head he had a headdress with entirely white feathers.

"The White Chief," Stu said.

The White Chief nodded and sat cross-legged by the fire. "That is I. Thank you for seeing me today."

"As if we had a choice," Stu said.

The White Chief looked at Stu with dark, piercing eyes. "You had a chance to meet the Great Spirit but instead you chose me. I am humbled my friend."

Confused, Stu looked at Graham and Krista but they didn't offer any answer. "I'm sorry but how did I have a choice?"

"You call yourself a samurai, do you not?"

"Yes, that is correct."

"Then forgive my ignorance but isn't it customary for samurai to commit suicide to prevent from being captured. I gather from my tribe that you had several chances to do this."

Stu opened his mouth to say something, working his jaw around but he couldn't find a suitable retort.

The White Chief smiled kindly. "For my part I'm glad to have you as my guests."

"What do you want with us?" Graham asked.

The White Chief got up and walked down the stairs that lead up to the stage and came around so he was standing right in front of them in the front aisle.

Close up Stu could tell the man really was a Native American. He had a leathery face, sharp cheekbones and sagging eyelids.

Stu could jump the old Indian and kill him with hardly a sound. It would be over in barely a minute and the old man would barely know what hit him. But then the White Chief locked gaze with Stu, his mouth frowned and he seemed to know exactly what Stu was thinking and almost dare him to do it.

"Were you really a chief?" Krista asked.

The White Chief smiled. "I was and will always be chief of my tribe."

"White Chief, we are willing to bargain for our freedom," Graham said.

"What makes you think I want to bargain?"

"You want the gas that fuels our cars. We will trade that for our lives."

Stu turned to Graham. "No, Graham. We're not giving that up."

The White Chief turned and walked down the aisle. "For centuries the white man has raped the planet with your fossil fuel and your pollution. Now the Great Spirit sent the plague to rid the world of such evils and you want to return the world to the way it was."

"So you don't want the fuel?" Stu asked. "Why are we here then?"

The White Chief sighed. "You think I enjoy killing the whites? My ancestors did it only out of necessity as I do now. I would like to see if you are fit to join us." The White Chief paused. "Do you think you can learn the ways of my ancestors?"

Nobody answered for a long time but then Stu spoke up: "I think you underestimate us, chief. You set us free now or face the consequences."

The White Chief laughed and made a motion with his wrist and suddenly a dozen savages appeared from behind the curtains. They quickly walked down the steps and grabbed the prisoners and forced them to their feet. Stu tried to shrug off the dirty fingers but they grabbed him tightly.

"Thank you for seeing me," The White Chief said. "I think I understand you much better now."

Stu, Graham and Krista were taken back to their column in Wal-Mart and tied back up. The savages tested their bonds, muttering insults under their breath before turning and leaving them.

"What do you think they're going to do with us?" Krista asked.

"I guess try and assimilate us," Stu said.

But Graham shook his head. "No, he has no plans to assimilate us. He wants the gas, believe me. He's a cunning old man for sure but I dealt with Wall Street for years and I can tell when somebody wants something."

The Hospital

"You know I have the ability to control minds," Albert told Ewan as they were walking along Mount Pleasant Road. Dilapidated brick houses appeared on either side of them, surrounded by broken wooden fences.

Ewan's fears had proven correct. He didn't know what exactly happened to the car but he assumed he had left it out in the cold too long and now it wouldn't start. They had syphoned the gas and tried it on a different car but that hadn't helped. The new car only made it a couple of feet before it choked and died. They concluded that the gas was too old and was now useless.

Ewan cursed himself for not taking better care of the little resources he had. He had mourned Tim and hadn't thought about anything else.

They decided they would just have to travel by foot, and so, early at dawn they had set off.

They had travelled for a couple of hours now through the empty brick buildings and glass apartment complexes. They were moving slower than Ewan would have liked but it was exhausting work even with snow shoes and skiing polls. Ashley, the most athletic of the three, was several meters up ahead.

"What are you talking about, Doctor Winkler," Ewan said, although he wasn't sure he wanted to hear the answer.

The cold temperature had eased up a bit and it was hovering around zero but it still would chill Ewan to the bones even with his many layers of clothing. There wasn't a sound but the squeaking of snow underneath their feet and Ewan imagined their voices would travel for miles in the still air.

Albert laughed. "You know chap, if I yawn or talk about yawning it will make you yawn. It's a weird physiological response that, according to specialists, indicates some sort of social bonding."

"Okay, stop it, old man," Ewan said. He could already feel the urge to yawn but he wasn't going to give into Albert's tricks.

"You already want to yawn, I know it," Albert said, yawning as he spoke.

"Stop it," Ewan said, trying to quicken his pace to get away from Albert but the doctor managed to keep up.

"It's strange that just by the mere suggestion of yawning it makes you want to, isn't it? Nobody really understands why seeing a yawn will make another person yawn as well."

Ewan couldn't help it. He let out a long yawn. "Please, Albert, just stop talking for awhile."

Albert shrugged. "All I'm saying is maybe this Outbreak was contagious like the yawn is contagious. Maybe we'll never figure out the reason."

Ewan shook his head. He was regretting bringing Albert along on their journey even though they would probably need him.

"What are you two talking about?" Ashley asked, stopping and waiting for them.

"Nothing, forget it."

"My mind control abilities," Albert said.

Ashley frowned at Ewan who just shook his head. "Don't ask."

They travelled in silence for awhile, crossing train tracks. Ewan glanced down the tracks, knowing no train would ever run across them ever again.

They only had maybe four or five hours of sunlight left and they would have to find some place that would be safe from the Creatures. They didn't know how exactly they would protect themselves but they would have to dedicate some time to finding some wood and building a fire.

Ashley stopped suddenly.

"What?" Ewan said, pulling his homemade spear out from his backpack.

"Do you smell that?"

"Is it a Creature?" Ewan asked, sniffing the air.

"I don't think so."

Albert stopped and sniffed the air but shrugged.

They skied cautiously down the road until they could see the cemetery in the distance and again Ashley stopped. By this time Ewan could smell it too.

"Ewan . . . I think this was a bad idea."

"We can't go back."

179

Ashley pointed to the cross street ahead. "What if we take that?"

Ewan shook his head. "I don't want to get lost and if we start taking side streets who knows where we'll end up."

"Can I see the map?"

Ewan sighed but put down his backpack and unzipped the front pocket. "We're wasting time."

Ewan handed Ashley the map. She unfolded it and quickly located their position. "If we take Moore Street we can pass around the edge of the cemetery."

"Why are you afraid of the cemetery? You're just smelling rotten bodies. I'm worried if we get stuck by the cemetery during night then we'll really be in trouble."

Ashley turned to Albert. "Doctor Winkler, what do you think?"

"It's just decaying matter, lass. Nothing to be afraid of. Besides I brought some of my soda pop!"

Ewan groaned. "Why do you even bother asking him?"

Ashley gave Ewan back the map and he shoved it back into his backpack. "Alright, let's go."

As they got closer to the cemetery the smell intensified and then became overwhelming. Ewan was thankful he had a balaclava that came up over his nose but even that couldn't prevent the smell from seeping up his nostrils.

To the left was the chapel, which, strangely enough, seemed reasonably intact. There was a wrought-iron chain link surrounding the cemetery and clusters of old headstones stretching off into the distance. In front there was a green sign that welcomed them to Mount Saint Pleasant Cemetery. As they got closer, Ewan saw the sign had been smeared with dried-on blood. It was copper-coloured and looked like it had been there for awhile.

"Let's just get through as quickly as possible," Ashley said.

Ewan nodded. Now his stomach was turning and he didn't think it was just the smell. The silence had gone from eerie to maddening. Ewan wanted to run screaming through the graveyard just to create some sort of noise.

Ewan looked at Ashley. Her cheeks had gone pale but she nodded resolutely.

I need to be strong for her, Ewan thought.

Ewan took the lead into the cemetery. Albert and Ashley followed. They had only taken a few steps when they saw a pile of human skulls in the middle of the road. Parts of brain and flesh were still stuck to them.

Ashley bent over and heaved but didn't puke. Ewan went over and put his arms around her.

"It's okay. Let's keep moving," he said.

Ashley straightened up, wiped her mouth with the back of her hand and nodded.

They stepped around the pile of skulls and kept walking. Every couple of meters they would come across a scattered bone.

Ewan felt something catch in his throat like a hairball. Was it being surrounded by the dead? He tried to concentrate on the sound of the snow underneath their feet.

"We should never have come this way," Ewan said, after seeing a disintegrated hand sticking up from the snow as if the rest of the body had been swallowed underneath and was crying out for help.

"Millions of people were buried here," Albert said.

"Millions?" Ewan said. "Surely you are exaggerating old man."

But Albert shook his head. "After the Outbreak, the graveyards overflowed with bodies, so much so that the gravediggers stopped keeping records and just digging deeper holes to bury people in."

"Now is a fine time to tell us," Ewan muttered.

To their left they saw a couple of graves scattered by the trees but the snow didn't seem as deep next to the graves as it did in other places. Ewan pointed it out to Ashley.

"Why do you think that is?"

Ashley shivered but didn't say anything.

Ewan couldn't resist stopping. He went over to the side of the road and bent down to examine the snow. It was mixed with gravel and dirt.

"Ewan, be careful. We should stick to the middle of the road," Ashley said.

Albert came up beside him. Ewan showed him the mixture of dirt and snow.

"The Creatures are digging the graves up and eating the remains," Albert said softly.

Ewan stood up quickly and a felt a wave of nausea come over him. He looked at Albert for a long time without saying anything. Albert just stared back, his face stern and serious now. The wild look he often gave Ewan was gone which made Ewan wonder, not for the first time, if Albert was putting on the dementia act a little bit for their benefit.

"Let's go," Ewan said, finally.

They walked further. Each step seemed to be more of an effort as if their feet were carrying greater and greater weight. Ewan scanned the trees for any movement, for any threats.

They came across an opening of trees to their left. When Ewan looked, what he saw made him gag.

"Don't look," he told Ashley but it was too late. Her whole body was trembling. Albert seemed to be the only one not affected by the sight.

Strung up between the trees was a thick chain and dangling from the chain were three bodies of the Creatures, hung there by a meat hook that pierced their bodies. Their eyes had been gouged out and black bile had poured from their bodies and melted the snow beneath them.

"What on Earth?" Ewan muttered. The Creatures looked like they had been tortured, but for what reason he couldn't think of.

"No humans did that," Albert said.

"If humans didn't do that then what did?" Ashley asked.

"Something else."

"Let's keep going," Ewan said.

But Albert took a couple steps closer. He stared up at the bodies with a thoughtful expression.

"Let's go, doctor."

"Just a minute."

Ewan couldn't stand the cemetery one minute longer. He turned and continued along the path, not looking back. He could hear the soft footsteps of Ashley following him. He didn't care about what happened to Albert. He just knew if he didn't escape the cemetery he would do something he regretted.

They made it through the cemetery without saying another word. Ewan paused and saw Albert was only a few paces behind him.

"Why are you still here, old man?" Ewan asked. "You could go home, back to your funhouse."

"Somebody has to help you, chap."

About ten minutes later they found an overturned army Humvee with the gun still attached. It was lying in the middle of the road, abandoned long ago.

"Let's go see if we can find anything," Ashley said. She seemed to have recovered from the cemetery.

She approached the Humvee carefully, circling it at first. Once it seemed there were no Creatures hiding anywhere Ewan looked into the cracked windshield. He could see blood was all over the front two seats but the bodies had long disappeared, probably devoured by the Creatures. There was a strong rotting metallic odor that made Ewan gag. He scanned the floor but he couldn't see anything lying around that they could use so he turned to Ashley.

She was checking out the machine gun turret and didn't seem to notice the repugnant smell. Ashley looked up at Ewan and shook her head. There was no ammunition left.

She then wiped away the snow and tried to open the side door but it was rusted shut.

"Can you help me?" she asked.

Ewan nodded and together they pulled on the door. It slowly came open.

Ashley climbed in. She bent down and crawled around on all fours. Ewan waited for her and when she climbed back out she just shook her head.

Ewan shrugged, trying not to feel disappointed. The empty Humvee had probably been searched a hundred times before.

They continued on Mount Pleasant Road until they reached Eglinton which was where they had agreed on the day before to look for shelter.

The sky was turning a deep blue and Ewan calculated that they had at least an hour before it got dark, but they would need that hour to barricade themselves.

The buildings had turned into skyscrapers and they all agreed they needed to find a small house so they went east until they found a row of brick houses.

They picked a small house on the block which had all of its windows boarded up.

Ashley tried the front door and found it was unlocked. The rusted hinges creaked as the door swung open. She entered first, her spear searching for targets in the darkness. Ewan went behind her and Albert followed in the rear with a flashlight.

They found their first Creature in the living room. It came from underneath the couch and attacked Albert's ankle. Albert gave out a low yelp and shone the flashlight on the Creature before it could do any damage. The bright light made it retreat back under the couch for safety.

Ashley turned to Ewan. "Stand up on top of the couch and protect me. I'm going after it."

Ashley put the flashlight on the floor facing crouched. Ewan knew she was in an extremely vulnerable position and if things went wrong it would be his job to protect her. He held his breath as Ashley slid her body forward, her spear was on the ground. Then she flicked on the light and thrust her spear. Ewan heard a loud roar and the sound of the spear sinking into the flesh of the Creature. Ashley pulled the spear out and thrust it at the Creature again.

The Creature slid out the unprotected side of the couch and stood up quickly. Ewan tracked its movements and stabbed the Creature repeatedly. The Creature staggered, allowing Ashley time to get into a crouch and launch herself at the Creature with a force Ewan didn't think possible.

She thrust her spear deep into the body of the Creature. The Creature gave a hideous scream and grabbed the shaft of the spear and tore it out of Ashley's hands. Ewan reacted quickly, tossing Ashley his spear and taking out a cleaver from his belt. Ewan jumped onto the Creature and brought the cleaver down onto its head. From the shear force the cleaver cut deep into the skull and brain. The Creature brought its arms up but then its eyes rolled into the back of its sockets and it fell over dead.

Ashley walked over and pulled her spear from the Creature's body.

"If it's that hard for us to kill one Creature we're going to be in trouble tonight," she said.

Ewan nodded, wiping his spear off on the Persian carpet. "Then we better get started."

They went upstairs together. The floorboards of the stairs creaked heavily under their footsteps. They entered a long narrow hallway with a wrought-iron banister and a deep-blue carpet. Lying on the floor was a teddy bear with an eye and an arm missing and most of its stuffing gone.

Ashley bent down and picked it up. She held it at arm's length, examining it. Ewan couldn't tell for sure in the darkness but he thought he saw a tear roll down her face. She propped the teddy bear up on the banister.

There were three closed doorways and here they hesitated. Ashley pointed to the door to their left. Ewan nodded. They closed in on the door. Ashley kicked it open, their spears at the ready.

The room was a bathroom. The sink was moldy and the pipes rusted away. Ashley checked the bathtub but found nothing. There was an open medicine bottle on the counter but no pills.

They exited the bathroom, back into the hallway and chose a different door. They were in a small room, orange-painted and with a bunk bed in the corner. A bookcase was in the corner full of picture books. They checked underneath the bed but there were no Creatures.

"What sort of social unit do you think the Creatures have?" Ewan asked.

"What do you mean?" Ashley asked.

"Well, humans naturally form pairs while most other animals are either alone or form some sort of pack. For example, chimpanzees are 98% human but they don't have mates in the human sense."

"This is disgusting," Ashley said, making a face. "I don't want to even think about it."

"What?"

"You're talking about if the Creatures having sex!"

"No, that's not what I mean," Ewan protested.

"The Walder guy poses an interesting question," Albert said. "It would be interesting to know more about the social behaviours of the Creatures. Are they territorial? Did the Creature you chaps killed

185

down there own the house – in a manner of speaking – or is the social hierarchy flat?"

Ashley just shook her head and walked back out into the hallway. Ewan smiled at Albert and followed her.

They entered the last room on the second floor. It was obviously the master bedroom and had a large queen-size bed and a painting of Toronto with a thin black frame overtop.

They opened the closet and found a Creature waiting for them. The Creature tried to launch itself at its attackers but Ashley stabbed it first, driving it back against the wall. Ewan stabbed it in the throat. Black bile poured out onto the floor and the Creature twitched and fell to the floor.

Ashley stared at the body. "So you think this was the papa Creature and the one downstairs was the mother Creature?"

Ewan couldn't help but laugh.

"I'm not trying to be funny," Ashley said.

After they made sure the rest of the house didn't have any more Creatures lurking, they went outside to collect firewood.

The clouds had disappeared and overhead there was nothing but blue sky. It would have been very beautiful under different circumstances.

"Should we split up or stay together?" Ashley asked.

"I think we should stay together," Ewan replied.

"It will take longer and we will need lots of wood."

Ewan frowned and stared across the street towards the wooded area. "Let's stick together for now and if there doesn't seem any danger perhaps we could split up.

They worked diligently for about thirty minutes until they had a good stock of wood and by the end Ewan was exhausted.

"We should rest a bit before night falls," Ewan said, breathing heavily.

Ashley nodded. She was also out of breath.

They went back inside the house and collapsed on the couch. Ashley passed around a couple roots and they all ate in silence.

Ewan stared up at the family portrait hanging on the wall. It was of a mother and father with two boys. It made him think of Amy and his family before the Outbreak and how the Creatures had attacked them in the middle of the night. He wondered what had happened to the family that had used to live in this house. Had they been taken by the Creatures? Had they been killed by looters?

Albert muttered something that Ewan didn't catch.

"What was that, doctor?"

"Those Creatures hanging in the cemetery."

"What about it?"

"Very peculiar, is all."

"More Creatures dead the better if you ask me," Ewan said.

"I wouldn't wish that if I were you."

Ewan had more than enough of the doctor. He needed something to take his mind off of everything. "Did you bring Gatsby with you?" Ewan asked, turning to Ashley.

"Of course."

Ewan nodded. He was still staring up at the portrait. "Doctor Winkler, do you like the Great Gatsby?"

"I always enjoy classical literature, chap."

Ashley brought the book out, took the bookmark out and placed it on the coffee table and started reading.

The truth was Ewan didn't really care about the story. It was about some spoiled rich guy who was in love. It took place during the roaring twenties. The Great War and the H1N1 flu pandemic, commonly called the Spanish flu, had faded from the collective consciousness and everyone was getting wealthier from real estate and stocks.

Ewan found it hard to relate to someone who owned an airplane and threw lavish parties and owned a large mansion just outside of New York. He was supposed to be the tragic hero?

Ewan just loved to listen to Ashley speak. She had a good reading voice that was soothing and it made Ewan forget all about the Creatures or the Outbreak.

Ewan closed his eyes and listened to the words she spoke. This time, for whatever reason, Ewan didn't feel comforted and Ashley's voice morphed into Amy.

Save the kids.

But how? Ewan wondered.

Find them.

But where are they?

Ashley stopped talking and Albert said something. Ewan opened his eyes. "What?"

"We should get back to work," Albert said.

Ewan nodded and stood up. His entire body ached. Most of Ewan's injuries had healed but Ewan didn't think he would be ever rid of the Creature's wounds. "We'll put the furniture up against the door."

Together they pushed the couch up against the door and then piled a table and chairs up on top of that. Afterwards they surveyed their handy work.

"What do you think, doctor?" Ewan asked. "You think it will hold them?"

Albert shrugged. "I hope so."

For some reason this made Ewan laugh. "I hope so too, doctor."

Next they put the wood in the center of the room and built the perimeter of the fire with large rocks. It would contain the fire to a small circle in the middle of the room. Next they piled logs into the middle of their makeshift fireplace.

"You know, we may all die of carbon dioxide poisoning," Ashley said.

"It's a better death than being eaten alive."

Ewan went back upstairs to check for any holes or gaps in their defence that the Creatures could possibly sneak through. He found none. Whoever used to live in the house had obviously survived the Outbreak long enough to be able to defend themselves against the Creatures.

He went back downstairs and found Ashley had gotten the fire going. It was a small fire and he doubted they would ever be able to get it big enough to scare away any Creatures but in a worst-case scenario they would be able to use it as a weapon.

Ewan sat down beside Ashley. The fire felt warm and safe. Beside them Albert was snoring.

"How can he sleep in a time like this?" Ashley asked.

Ewan shrugged. "I guess that means one of us has to take the first watch."

"Ewan?"

Ewan turned to look at Ashley. Her large brown eyes stared at him worriedly. "Don't worry, we'll be fine."

"You really believe that?"

"No."

Ashley put her head on Ewan's shoulder. Ewan watched as the flames danced around the logs, cracking and popping. It felt good to have her body close to his but he could still hear Amy's voice in his head.

Ashley shifted slightly, turning her head and pressing her lips onto Ewan's neck, digging her teeth into his skin. Ewan closed his eyes. What would Amy think? Would she judge him? Would she want him to be happy?

She's too young, Ewan thought. *This isn't right.*

But Ewan didn't stop her. He pretended it was Amy who was kissing him. But he couldn't remember Amy ever kissing him like that before. He felt her hands lower to his crotch but he caught her before it got there.

"We have a few minutes before night," Ashley whispered.

Ewan opened his eyes. "I'm sorry, I can't."

Ashley sat back upright quickly. "What's wrong? I doubt Doctor Winkler will wake up."

"It's nothing — I don't know."

"You don't like me?"

Ewan turned and looked at Ashley. "You ever think you'd still be with Lucas if it wasn't for the Outbreak?"

Ashley shrugged. "I don't know. Maybe. I was in love with him, if that's what you mean."

"Did you want to marry him?"

"I thought you said you didn't give a shit."

"I told you I was sorry, remember?"

Ashley bowed her head and didn't say anything for awhile. "Does marriage mean anything?"

"I guess it doesn't now."

"But even before the Outbreak. Nobody got married."

"I was married."

"But you come from an older generation."

Ewan forced a smile. "If this is how you try to get into a guy's pants. . ."

Ashley playfully nudged Ewan with her shoulder. "You don't want to mess with me, Ewan."

"You know you do an awfully good job of avoiding questions you don't want to answer," Ewan said.

Ashley opened her mouth to say something but she was cut off by a loud scrapping at the doorway.
"They are here," Ewan said, reaching for his spear.

Revival

Stu woke up from a dreamless sleep to find that Krista was gone. He kicked at Graham until he woke as well.

"What?" Graham asked, grumpily.

"What happened to Krista?"

Graham looked around before shrugging.

"Those bastards better not harm her," Stu said.

Stu struggled with the rope but it was bound tight. His throat was parched and he felt weak. The berries and roots the savages fed them didn't do anything to help his body heal.

Graham closed his eyes again and seemed to go back to sleep.

"How can you be so relaxed?"

"Because we still have the upper hand."

Stu opened his mouth but then closed it again. "Excuse me? Don't you see we are their captives? Am I missing something?"

Graham opened his eyes again and stared at his fellow captive. "Stu, do you know how I became the largest stock holder of Perpetuum Industries?"

Stu sighed. "I suppose you're going to tell me whether I want to know or not."

Graham smiled faintly. "The company was full of the brightest minds in the world. These people are the type who got two doctorates from Harvard, MIT, Princeton. I got my degree from Concordia in Montreal, not exactly Ivy League material but I outsmarted them all. I could analyse people and figure out how to play them. This White Chief talks about sacred land and all that bullshit but what he wants is power. And we hold the key to that power and as long as we have that we hold the upper hand."

"How do you know that Krista isn't spilling her guts out to them right now?"

"Because she knows if she does that she's dead."

"They are probably torturing her. You think she'll withstand torture?"

Graham shook his head. "Not everybody is as blunt as you."

Stu shook his head. Maybe Graham was right, maybe they had a bargaining chip but to say they had the upper hand . . . that just seemed preposterous.

"We just have to outsmart them," Graham said.

"How do we do that?"

"I don't know yet but we will. We're smarter than the White Chief."

Stu tried to get back to sleep but the pain kept him awake.

Eventually they heard the sound of footsteps from the escalator and three women appeared carrying platefuls of food and water. They were the same three women that had served them in the movie theatre the previous night.

The women placed the food down on the floor and untied Stu and Graham's hands. The food was the same roots as they had before but Stu didn't care. He ate hungrily.

The women stood at a safe distance watching in silence. There didn't seem to be any guards around just in case Stu and Graham did manage to slip out of the bonds that secured their bodies to the post. The women were in their mid-twenties, all pretty, despite their malfunction. The woman who seemed to be in charge had long dark-red hair braided that reached down to the small of her back. She wore a white blouse and a tied-dyed shirt. Her cheeks were high, rosy and her eyes were clear-blue.

"What are your names?" Graham asked.

The women smiled. The woman with the red hair answered. "My name is Chenoa, this is Kasa and Tanis."

"Very pretty names."

Chenoa smiled. "Thank you. They are the names the White Chief gave us when we joined the tribe."

"What was your original name?"

Chenoa frowned and glanced at the two women beside her. "I do not repeat it. It died when I became part of the tribe."

Graham nodded as if he understood. "How does one go about joining the tribe? Does the White Chief decide?"

Chenoa smiled again. "You have to have a vision sent to you by your ancestors"

"Did you have such a vision?"

Chenoa nodded. "Yes. My grandmother came to me in the form of a white wolf and told me I would one day save humanity."

Graham nodded as if in deep thought. "Did your vision come true?"

"Not yet, but Gods be good it will."

"When will the White Chief see us again?"

Chenoa shrugged. "I am not privy to the White Chief's council."

Once Stu and Graham finished their food and drink, the women took the trays. "We need to tie up your hands again," Chenoa said.

"Can't you just leave our hands free? Where are we going to go?" Stu asked.

Chenoa shook her head. "I'm afraid not."

"It's okay," Graham said. "Maybe we can ask the White Chief for better conditions when we talk to him next."

Chenoa bent down and bound their hands back to the post.

"What happened to Krista?" Graham asked.

"We gave her a room."

"Why?" Stu asked.

Chenoa looked down at Stu. Her lips were pressed together. "You don't know, do you?"

"Know what?"

"She says she is with child, your child. It is not proper to leave a pregnant woman tied up in this manner."

Stu looked up. A small smile crossed his face. "You have to let me see her."

But Chenoa shook her head. "That is not possible. We are taking care of her now."

The three women turned around and walked towards the escalator. Once again Stu tried to escape the rope. He twisted and turned but he was bound too tight.

After exhausting himself, Stu turned to Graham. "You still think she won't tell them anything?"

Graham frowned thoughtfully. "It is too soon to know if she is with child or not. She is using it as an excuse to get more favourable conditions."

This made Stu strangely happy. "I'm surprised she could be so cunning."

"Anybody who survived this long is not stupid."

The hours went by like days, and the minutes like hours. Time seemed to slow down like a large locomotive chug, chug, chugging along, the large iron wheels turning over and over, again and again.

Stu tried to sleep but his body hurt and he couldn't get comfortable. He thought about his mother who had for years tried and failed to save him from his abusive father. Truth be told he was relieved when his father killed himself and his mother died shortly after. Of course, at the time, he didn't know he was trading one hell for another.

When he had turned eighteen he joined the air force to get out of Toronto. Of course by then he had trained to become a fierce fighter and hadn't lost a fight in years, even against bigger, stronger opponents. His lack of formal training had actually helped in street fights. His unconventional style threw his opponents off and nothing was off limits.

Stu turned and looked at Graham. "Tell me how you killed your father."

"There really isn't much to tell."

"How old were you?"

"It was during the 39 riots. Those days were madness. I was already successful and rich by then. I told myself I went over there to check on him. I told my bodyguards to stay in the car. They protested but of course they relented," Graham said. "Part of me, you know, wanted to make sure he was okay but I don't think that was the complete truth. I let myself in. I had a key. He came at me with the knife in the dark. I'm not really sure he knew who I was. He reeked of sweat and alcohol. I kept yelling, 'I'm your son. It's me Graham.' But I'm not sure he heard, or maybe he just didn't care. . . I don't know."

Graham stopped talking. He was breathing rapidly, as if all this talking took great strain. But Stu understood and waited for him to continue. Sometimes the past took up a lot of space.

"It wasn't hard to disarm him. I sat him down and put the knife on the counter. I went to get him some water and food from the fridge. He yelled from the living room . . . I still remember his words. He said, 'I wish your whore mother had strangled you at birth.' Well . . . after that something inside me just snapped. I picked up the knife and stabbed him over and over again. Blood sprayed everywhere"

Graham stopped abruptly and Stu had to ask, "What happened next?"

"In a daze, I called 911 but it had been disconnected. I called the local police line but there was no answer. Martial law had been ordered and the army was in charge . . . but it wasn't like I could just call them up . . . So I left him there and got into my limousine and never looked back. The bodyguards saw the blood on my clothes and asked if I was okay. I wasn't hurt and told them to take me home."

For a long time afterwards neither Stu nor Graham spoke. Graham spent the next hour with his eyes closed, but whether he was sleeping or not, Stu didn't know.

"You think Krista told them?" Stu asked, when he heard Graham shift his body.

"I don't know," Graham said.

"They will kill us."

"I think they would have done it by now if they were going to."

"So if The White Chief has the oil, what do you think he plans to do with us?"

"I don't know. Maybe Krista didn't tell him about the oil yet. Maybe they're using old police techniques on us."

"Divide and conquer?" Stu asked. That did make sense. Krista was too scared to say anything. *Yes, fear will rule over charm any day*, Stu thought.

"You think she could be pregnant?" Stu asked.

"One thing is certain. I don't take their word for it."

"Graham, I'm glad I didn't kill you when we first met."

Graham let out a soft, low chuckle. "I didn't ever give you a chance."

Stu smiled, thinking back. "Very true."

That evening the man in the eagle mask came with a bunch of savages and untied Graham and Stu.

"The White Chief honours you by asking you to dine with him," the eagle man said.

Stu and Graham were led to the other side of the mall to the same movie auditorium they had been before. The White Chief was sitting on the stage with a fire burning. He was wearing the same outfit as before, dressed from head to toe in white.

The three women came and served them some type of vermin for dinner. Stu supposed it was better than just eating roots all the time. A fourth woman came and served The White Chief. He ate the same meal that Stu and Graham had.

Midway through their meal, The White Chief turned to Graham. "Krista tells me you were the chief technology officer of Perpetuum Industries before the Outbreak."

Graham nodded. "That's right."

"You were in charge of new inventions at the company?"

Graham's eyes narrowed and concentrated on the White Chief. "I was in charge of a lot of things."

"I once heard you had a prototype of a Perpetuum car. Is that correct?"

Graham nodded. "We were good at making the motor but unfortunately we had no experience in the other parts of car manufacturing and we were having a hard time trying to team up with major car manufacturers."

The White Chief nodded. "You white men never think about what is good for anybody but yourself."

Stu couldn't stop himself any longer. "You have white men in your so-called tribe."

The White Chief stared at him with his large intelligent eyes. "They are no longer white men. They have accepted new names and have new identities."

"That's complete bullshit."

The White Chief smiled thinly. He didn't seem to take offence. "Krista told us everything. She told us where you got the oil and how you make the oil."

Stu looked at Graham who looked as if he was struggling to keep his face neutral. "You're lying. You would have killed us already," Stu said.

The White chief folded his fingers together. "I already told you. I don't want white man's poison. What I want is the Perpetuum generator."

"You're willing to trade our freedom for the generator?" Graham asked.

The White Chief nodded. "I will let you go if you teach us how to make a generator."

Stu turned to Graham. "Don't do it. Don't trust him!"

The White Chief brought a hand up in the air and a dozen men with spears appeared from behind the curtains. They grabbed Stu and shoved his body against the stage. The half-finished plate of food went sprawling on the ground. Stu struggled against the savages but there were too many of them and they were too strong.

"I need the smart white man, not the warrior white man," the White Chief said.

A savage unsheathed a large curved sword and took a step towards Stu.

"No wait," Graham said. "The deal is for all three of our lives."

The White Chief turned slowly towards Graham and studied him. Stu was still struggling but to no avail.

The White Chief slowly rose to his feet and walked up to Graham. Graham likewise rose from his seat so he could study the chief. Graham was about six inches taller than the chief but the Native American didn't back down. His large dark-brown eyes glared at Graham, his large lips formed a crease across his old, wrinkled face.

"Why do you want this small-brained foreigner?" The White Chief asked.

"Because he's my friend and he saved my life against the Creatures."

The White Chief seemed to except this with a nod. "Very well. If you give us the generator then we will give you three lives."

The White Chief nodded and the savages took Stu and shoved him back in his seat next to Graham.

"I want to see Krista, to make sure she's okay," Graham said.

"You are in no place to make demands," The White Chief said, curtly.

Graham smiled. "But I think I am. I won't cooperate until after I see her."

The White Chief again gave Graham a hard stare. "You know I could just torture you until you do as you're told. Or I could torture the white female."

"But I know you won't. You have other considerations."

The White Chief snorted. "What other considerations do you think I have?"

"The considerations of your people, of your tribe. You need to appear better than us," Graham said. "All I want to know is if she's alright."

"You can take my word for it. She is being well taken care of despite her mistreatment at your hands. She told me what you did to her," The White Chief said, glancing at Stu. "I should cut your balls off for what you did to her."

Graham nodded. "You're a good ruler and you're also fair. But forgive me chief. I just need to see her with my own eyes."

The White Chief didn't say anything for awhile, then he clapped his hands and a man appeared from the curtains and the White Chief whispered in his ear. The man nodded and quickly disappeared into the darkness.

"Alright I will permit you to see her."

They finished eating. Stu refused to eat the rest of his food that had been tossed onto the floor so Graham picked it up and ate it.

Just as the women came to take away their plates, the door opened and two savages appeared on either side of Krista. She walked freely down the stairs towards the stage. She held her head up, not looking at either Stu or Graham but instead stared straight ahead at the White Chief. She was wearing a dirty white blouse and jeans but her cheeks seemed fuller and a little colour had appeared on her face.

"You called me, White Chief?"

The old chief nodded. His voice changed into a soothing low purr. "Yes child. These foreigners have requested to see you, to make sure I'm not mistreating you in anyway."

Krista frowned, still staring straight ahead. "I don't understand. What would the purpose of mistreating me be?"

The White Chief opened his arms, palms upwards. "You will have to ask your companions."

Krista opened her mouth as if startled. "Chief, they are not my companions. More like my captors."

198

"Nevertheless, they requested your presence."

Stu got up and stepped forward. "Krista, is it true? Are you with my child?"

"My name is not Krista it is Makawee."

Stu slapped her. "Don't be stupid, girl."

One of the savages stepped up and hit Stu across the head with the shaft of his spear. Stu felt a hot pain and fell to the floor.

"Don't disrespect Makawee," the savage said.

Stu got to his feet, dusted his pants off and stepped up to the savage. "You know if you ever hit me again, you better knock me out."

Stu grabbed the spear, leaned his head back and brought his head forward, smashing it into the bridge of the savage's nose. The savage let go of his spear and dropped to the ground, screaming.

Stu stood over him and threw his spear to the ground, and, before the other savages could attack him, he sat down.

"Enough of this foolishness," the White Chief said, holding up his hand.

"You still haven't answered the question," Stu said, looking at Krista.

"Yes . . . I am with your child." She then turned to The White Chief. "Can I go now?"

"In a moment. Tell them how we treat you."

Krista reluctantly turned to Stu and Graham. "The tribe treats me as one of their own even though I have not gone through the official ceremony yet. They realize I have suffered a lot."

Graham got up and walked over to Krista but the savages stepped in his way.

"It's okay. I'm not going to hurt her."

The savages looked over to The White Chief who again nodded. The savages gave way and Graham walked so his face was only inches away from Krista's. Krista met his gaze.

"Do you like the name Makawee? Did you choose it?"

"No, the healer gave me the name but it fits me very well. She said it would bring luck."

Graham nodded and then bent closer to Krista and whispered something into her ear that nobody could hear. Krista brought her hand up and touched Graham on the cheek.

Graham then turned to The White Chief. "Thank you. I am now satisfied."

The White Chief nodded towards Krista who bowed slightly and turned around with her guards. Stu and Graham watched her leave.

When she was gone, The White Chief turned to his two captives. "What happened to the Perpetuum cars you built?"

Graham shrugged. "When the military declared martial law they took the cars. Chaos broke out and we never got them back. I don't know what happened to them. They could be in the north pole for all I know."

"Now many generators are there in the city?"

Graham shrugged. "Maybe a few thousand but I haven't found any that still work. And I have been looking.

The White Chief stared pensively at Graham for a long time. Stu observed the chief for a long time.

He's not a man to be rash in his actions, Stu thought. *He has thought about this a long time.*

"Did you smoke?" the chief asked after a while.

Graham shook his head. "I gave it up after I graduated."

The White Chief turned to Stu. "How about you, white man?"

Stu nodded. "I was up to a pack a day before the Outbreak." He paused. "I guess the Outbreak probably saved my life in a way."

"I wish I could offer you tobacco," the chief said. "It was what my ancestors would have given visiting white men and you brought us alcohol which we don't have either."

Neither Stu nor Graham said anything for a while. The White Chief stirred restlessly and Stu felt he wasn't finished speaking.

"My ancestors had the perfect way of life, nomadic, free, one with nature, a close connection with the Great Spirit, but white men took it all from us."

"If you are going to make us feel guilty for something that happened a hundred years ago you've got the wrong audience," Stu said.

The White Chief frowned at Stu. "No, white man. I am not. What the death of my ancestors taught me was that we always have to evolve even if it's away from perfection. And so too we must change as well if we are not to be wiped out."

"You think the Creatures will eventually kill us?" Graham said.

The White Chief shrugged. "I don't know. Maybe. Maybe it will be another tribe. But most likely the threat will be from something we never saw coming."

"It will be very difficult to make the generator with what you have," Graham said. "I don't know if it can be done without electricity."

"Well let's just say your life depends on it," The White Chief said.

The House in the Night

Ewan's eyes snapped open when Albert woke up with a loud gasp.

"What's that noise?" Albert asked, sitting up.

The thumping grew louder at the door and the windows and the whole house seemed to rock. It was almost rhythmic, a slow, constant, terrible drum beating again at the doorway, bidding them to come out.

Ewan turned to Ashley and said the words everybody was thinking: "It's not going to hold them."

Ashley didn't say anything but Ewan could almost read her thoughts: *We're not going to get much sleep tonight.*

"How many are out there?" Ewan asked.

"I would say somewhere between three to four hundred. But I suspect more will come as we get further into the night."

"More?" Ashley said.

Albert nodded. "Yes. I'm not sure how they communicate but I suspect they do somehow and will call for help."

"How do they know we're in here?" Ewan said. "Did they hear us?"

"Smell probably, chap," Albert replied.

They listened to the loud thudding of the Creatures and their roaring. It was awful to listen to. Over the years Ewan had managed to block out the noise but it was much harder when they were only about twenty feet away and the only thing that separated him from them was a thin stone wall.

"Albert, did you have any family?" Ashley asked.

Albert knitted his forehead. "A wife . . . and a daughter, I think, lass."

"His wife was named Lydia," Ewan said. "Their daughter's name was Hope."

Albert smiled, his face lighting up. "Yes Lydia, I remember her now."

202

Ewan nodded, trying to smile but he found it difficult. For the first time he considered maybe being torn apart by the Creatures wasn't the most terrible fate. How many years had Albert spent alone with nothing but his crumpled memory for company? What if he couldn't remember Amy? Sure, the dreams were a certain type of torture but to forget? Ewan wouldn't want that either.

"Lydia and Amy were friends. Sophie was three years younger than Hope and so we would get them together for playdates."

Ewan remembered Sophie never wanted to go. It had been more Amy's insistence that they be friends, although why Ewan never understood.

The sound of the Creatures interrupted his thoughts.

This was a dumb idea, Ewan thought. *What made them think they could last an entire night out in the open?*

Nobody said anything for a long time. Miraculously the furniture against the door seemed to hold. Ewan tried to distract his mind as the hours slowly went by but nothing seemed to work, not even thinking of Amy, Timmy, and Sophie.

After some time, Ewan glanced at Ashley who was staring into the flames of the fire, feeding the logs when necessary. Ewan stared into the small flames with her. The warmth was good after a day in the cold weather.

"You should get some sleep," he told Ashley.

"How can I sleep with this noise?"

Ewan shrugged, knowing she was right. Everybody was on edge; even Albert was looking around wide-eyed.

Suddenly the banging noise stopped, and except for the sound of the soft crackling of the fire and from outside feet hitting cement and dirt, everything was silent.

"They must be inside," Ewan said. He stood up, grabbed his spear and stuck a piece of wood in the fire. Ashley did the same and followed Ewan up the stairs.

They checked the master bedroom first but didn't see anything. The bathroom was empty as well. Then they heard a noise from across the hallway. It came from the kid's room, the slow thud of footsteps.

Ewan glanced at Ashley. "We need to plug the hole quickly."

They raced forward. Ewan swung open the door. He quickly rotated his torch around the room, illuminating the small room. Two Creatures stared back at them. They roared when they saw the fire.

Ewan saw there was a hole about four feet in diameter in the ceiling. It looked like somehow the Creatures had dug their way in through a weak spot in the roof. Ewan cursed himself for not noticing it before.

Ashley stepped up and stabbed the first Creature with her spear in the chest. The Creature let out a hideous cry but didn't falter. The other Creature charged towards Ewan. With his right hand, he thrust his spear towards the Creature, hitting him in the shoulder. The Creature grabbed the shaft but Ewan dug it deeper into its rotting flesh. Still the Creature stepped towards Ewan, its gigantic claws stretching outwards, swiping at Ewan's face.

Ewan dropped the spear and hit the creature with his torch. The flame leapt onto the Creature and it started to flail in agony as the flames burned its body. The Creature tried to back away but its body was caught on the spear and it couldn't move.

Ewan grabbed the spear again and pushed the Creature against the wall. He then turned and attacked the other Creature with his torch. The Creature went up in flames. It took a couple of steps before falling to the ground.

Ashley took the sheets off the bed and started beating the flames, trying to smother them. Ewan took her arm and shook his head.

"What?" Ashley asked.

"Don't bother."

Two then three Creatures crawled down from the hole in the ceiling.

"But we'll burn the house down."

"Might as well take as many of them as we can," Ewan said.

Ewan and Ashley picked up their spears and back towards the door to the hallway. The Creatures approached slowly, as if they knew they could take their time. A fourth Creature crawled from the hole in the ceiling.

They attacked together, stabbing the Creatures repeatedly but their attacks didn't deter the Creatures.

Ewan heard footsteps from behind him. He thought a Creature had gotten in from behind them and surrounded them. He turned to attack but instead of a Creature he saw Albert. He was holding a small red water gun in his hand.

What was he doing?

"Get back, old man," Ewan shouted. "Stay by the fire."

Albert raised his water gun and fired it at the Creatures in quick succession. The water hit the Creatures and seemed to melt their flesh. All four Creatures backed away, tearing at the burned areas.

The retreat of the Creatures allowed Ewan and Ashley to move forward. The Creatures now seemed afraid of the humans and backed up against the wall. One Creature tripped and fell into the flames. Ashley and Ewan stabbed the others repeatedly until they too collapsed.

Another Creature jumped down from the ceiling and Albert squirted it in the face. The Creature covered its eyes, letting out a horrible scream as Ewan ran and thrust his spear into its neck. He then turned, expecting other Creatures to come but there was nothing. Ewan wondered if it was the burning fire or Albert's water gun that they were afraid of.

Breathing heavily, Ewan asked, "What do you have there?"

"Soda pop," Albert said, happily.

"I thought you were working on the cure."

"It's not perfected yet," Albert said, defensively.

Ewan knew he didn't have time for a full explanation. He had to turn his attention to the fire. He took the second blanket from the bunk bed and started to help Ashley beat the flames. Ewan was exhausted but somehow he kept going. But the fire was spreading too fast, jumping from object to object.

"Let's get out of here," Ashley said, pulling Albert through the doorway to the hall. Ewan followed and closed the door behind him.

"What are we going to do?" he asked. If they went outside they would be eaten alive but they couldn't stay in the building either.

Ashley stared helplessly back.

"Come with me," Ewan said. "I've got an idea."

Ewan ran past Albert and Ashley to the master bedroom. He took a lampshade from the corner and smashed it against the plywood that was nailed across the window. Ewan swung a couple of times and managed to smash a hole through the wood. He dropped the lampshade and pried a hole so it was big enough to climb through. He looked outside where there was a foot-wide tile ledge that circled the perimeter of the second-story of the house.

He turned back to Albert and Ashley. "Stay here." He paused. "Albert, get your gear out, now!"

Ewan climbed through the hole and onto the ledge, straightening his back so it was flat against the tile siding. He stared below him in the darkness. Albert had been right. The street was crowded with hundreds of Creatures staring up at him with small black eyes.

Desperately he looked around him. The adjacent house was only about two meters away and had a similar ledge that he was standing on. They could jump across but he could see inside the window that the house was packed with Creatures. The previous owners obviously hadn't thought to board up their windows — or hadn't lived long enough to do so.

Ewan could hear footsteps above him as the Creatures ran across the roof. He looked up just to see a Creature jump down on him. Ewan managed to sidestep the Creature which hit the ledge, did a half spin before falling to the ground. Ewan watch it hit a small shrubbery and then get up, seemingly unharmed.

While Ewan was looking down he felt something heavy knock the side of his head. He stumbled but the window frame prevented him from falling. He turned to see what had hit him and saw a Creature crouching low on the roof. Ewan grabbed his spear and stabbed the Creature through the eye. The spear dug deep into the Creature's brain and when Ewan pulled it out the Creature flopped over dead.

Ewan crouched and spoke to Ashley through the hole he had created. "Can you get me a couple of torches?"

"I will try."

"Actually, wait. Doctor Winkler, can I borrow your water gun?"

"Sure thing, chap," he said, handing Ewan his water gun through the hole. Ewan took it and squirted it against the window. Ewan expected the window to melt just as the Creatures had, but nothing happened.

"Albert, your soda pop isn't working against the window."

"Of course not, it only works against the Creatures' DNA structure."

"Ewan, please hurry," Ashley said. "The fire is spreading."

"I'm thinking."

Ewan wished he had ol' Bessy with him and a round of bullets. He turned to fire at a Creature that was approaching from above him, on the roof. Ewan got the Creature in the leg. The Creature fell, clutching its leg and slid off the roof.

Whatever Albert had in the water gun really worked against the Creatures, Ewan thought.

Ewan bent down to the hole again. "Alright let's go."

He helped Ashley and Albert out onto the ledge. He looked down into the darkness. Hundreds of heads were swaying, trying to get at them. The wind picked up and brushed against Ewan's face.

Ewan felt a sudden acute pang in his stomach, wishing Amy was with them. She was always the fearless one, the headstrong one. She would jump across without a problem. He thought about how Tim had gone into the forest without hesitation.

Amy, where did you get your courage?

You have no choice, my love, she told him. *You need to jump.*

Ewan took a deep breath and leapt. For a moment he felt weightless and then he landed on the opposite ledge.

He heard a smash as the window broke, sending shards of glass down to the ground below. Ewan fired the water gun into the room, pressing the trigger repeatedly.

The Creatures were packed so closely together that when they were hit they couldn't move.

Ewan turned to Albert and Ashley and motioned them to jump. Ashley looked down and then back at Ewan.

"Just do it. You have no choice."

Ashley nodded and jumped. She cleared the distance easily. Ewan grabbed her just in case she lost her balance. She leaned into him and smiled faintly.

"Thank you," she murmured.

Ewan turned to Albert who was looking around him, his eyes wide in fear.

"Doctor, you have to jump," Ewan said. "Albert, please jump."

But Albert shook his head. "I can't chap. I'm not as young as you are."

The Creatures in the upstairs room were scattered but they were beginning to regroup. One came through the broken window, and before it could sink its teeth into Ewan, he grabbed it and hurled it to the ground below. It didn't even scream as it fell.

"Go on without me, chap," Albert said.

"But we need you," Ashley said. "We can't find the cure without you!"

"There is no cure, lassie," Albert said, shaking his head.

Ewan wanted to turn and escape but he knew if they left Albert behind he would never find Tim and Amy would never forgive him for leaving her old boss behind.

Ewan gave Ashley the water gun and looked back to the building Albert was stranded on. He could see the smoke and the flames rising. Ewan sucked in a deep breath and jumped back across to the burning building.

His feet landed partly off the ledge and he struggled to regain his balance. Luckily Albert held out his hand and Ewan grabbed it, stabilizing himself.

"Thanks."

"No worries, chap."

"Doctor Albert Winkler, you need to jump. If you have trouble we'll help you, but I'm not going to let you burn alive."

"I'm a crazy old man. I'm not a doctor. Not anymore."

"Don't be an idiot. Of course you are," Ewan said. He couldn't believe he was having this conversation on top of a burning building.

Albert shook his head. "You need schools for doctors. We have no schools."

"But you graduated with all the honours. It doesn't matter what we have now."

Albert bit his lip and then nodded. "What did you say my wife's name was?"

"Lydia."

"Walder," he said, his eyes narrowed. "What's the point of living if you can't remember who your wife was?"

Ewan looked on the other side at Ashley. She was squirting the Creatures through the window, but he knew soon the water gun would run out. That moment he felt something inside his stomach tighten.

"I don't know Albert," he said finally. "But I need your help. I know without your help we'll all die. And I don't want to sound drastic but if we die then what hope is there for anything?"

Albert hesitated and then nodded.

"Will you jump with me then? We'll do it together."

Albert nodded again and Ewan took the old man's hand. It was scaly and soft and fragile. Ewan felt if he held it too hard he would crush the bones.

"Okay, on the count of three . . . one. . . two . . . three."

Albert and Ewan leapt across the small gap between the houses and landed on the ledge. This time they both landed squarely on the tile. Albert spread his arms out for balance but he didn't even wobble.

"We got to move," Ashley said.

Using one of the gables as leverage, Ashley climbed up on top of the roof and made her way along the seam of the roof. Ewan helped Albert up and together they walked on the point of the roof like they were tightrope walking.

The next house along the row was only a short jump away. Ashley bent down and vaulted across without much difficulty. Albert turned and looked back at Ewan who nodded. A few of the Creatures had managed to follow them up on the roof but they were having trouble balancing on the slanted roof and kept sliding down.

"Jump, doctor," Ewan said. "You can do it."

It seemed to be all the encouragement he needed. Albert jumped and landed next to Ashley. Next Ewan cleared the distance no problem. They kept walking along the roof tops for the next couple of hours. Ewan was exhausted and he could tell his two companions were tired as well. They moved slowly, stopping whenever they found a flat roof to rest for awhile. But they knew they couldn't stop for long. The Creatures evidently found it difficult to track them on top of the roofs but they had no illusion that if they stopped for more than a couple of minutes the Creatures would track them down. So as exhausted as they were, they kept moving.

A couple of times they found themselves trapped by a house at end of a street with nowhere to go but they backtracked and found a garage or a lane house they could jump onto and another row of houses they could follow.

Thank God for old Victorian houses, Ewan thought.

Ewan had no idea which way they were going but it didn't matter. In the morning they would adjust and find out which way to the hospital. Right now they just had to stay alive.

Chenoa

Graham had managed to negotiate Stu and his release. The White Chief allowed them freedom to move around the mall but they were forbidden to wander outside.

Forbids me? Stu thought as they left the movie theatre. *Nobody forbids me anything.*

The White Chief had given them Chenoa to help them find their way around but Stu had no illusions that she was there to keep them from escaping.

"You really think I can prevent you from escaping?" Chenoa said, when Stu told her of his suspicions.

"The White Chief doesn't strike me as a stupid person," Stu said. "I'm sure this is some sort of test."

Chenoa smiled. "Yes, the White Chief is wise."

"So you don't deny it?"

Chenoa shrugged. "I do not know the Chief's thoughts but I'm sure he has good reason to do what he does."

Chenoa showed them around the mall. The shops had been all converted into tiny apartment-like housing. Stu looked in astonishment. The shelves were still visible from where the merchandise had once been but the stores had obviously been personalized. In some of the former stores there was artwork hanging on the wall or a set of knives or other utensils. In most of the stores there was a mattress of some kind or a blanket.

Stu saw a young man of about fifteen or sixteen open up the gate to an old shoe store and then close it as he went inside. In the next store, a naked woman was bathing in a small bucket of water. She stared out at Graham and Stu, seemingly unashamed of her nakedness.

"I guess most don't have much privacy," Graham said.

Chenoa shook her head. "No. We don't even have any keys or locks. I suppose anybody could go into any pod," Chenoa said. "It's only a matter of custom that each family only goes into the pod they are assigned.

"Family?" Stu asked.

Chenoa nodded. "Yes, in the beginning people sort of just gravitated towards certain people and formed – for a lack of a better word – families. Some have children, some do not."

"How do you decide which family gets which store?" Graham asked.

"The White Chief grants families their homes based on their actions. If a family provides a great service to the tribe then they are granted a better pod."

"Do you have elections?" Stu asked, a bit sarcastically. "Did somebody vote the mighty White Chief leader into power?"

Chenoa shook her head. "He was the natural choice. The White Chief decreed once he dies then we'll be able to elect a new leader, but nobody can challenge the chief."

They walked down the escalator and from there they could see down the hallway towards the main entrance. Just outside of the moat, Stu saw a savage get into a car, start the engine and drive through the parking lot and onto the road.

Furious, Stu turned to Chenoa. "I thought the chief didn't want to kill Mother Earth."

"He didn't but the council persuaded him that it was only temporary."

"We will need the cars if we are to get a generator up and running," Graham said.

Stu glared at Graham but he didn't seem to notice. "So the White Chief isn't all powerful, after all?"

"Nobody said he was."

They turned left and went to the food court. They passed both men and women who greeted Chenoa by name and she greeted them in return calling them Elki, or Sahale, or Bemossed, or Pallaton. The savages seemed to have nothing in common with each other. There were some who were white, black, Hispanic or Asian and, to Stu, it seemed strange that they all took Native American names.

At the food court, the rows of colourful plastic tables and chairs were mostly empty except for a group of savages cleaning and a few carrying white buckets that disappeared through a doorway. Overhead were the signs of once-famous fast food chains that had dominated every mall in North America.

"This is where we all eat. We have two meals a day, one in the morning and one in the evening. We have a group of cooks and helpers who prepare the food for the entire tribe."

Stu looked around at the savages. Nobody carried any weapons — at least none that he could see. To Stu, who had gotten used to always carrying his samurai sword, he found it strange.

"How come nobody is armed?" Stu asked.

"Weapons are forbidden here unless you have a written exemption from the White Chief himself."

Stu smiled and glanced towards the exit. He could just walk out. Nobody would stop him.

Chenoa seemed to know what he was thinking. "Like I said, this is a test. Do not fail it."

"Or what?"

"The White Chief will find you. You cannot hide from him."

"What happens if somebody steals something from another person?" Graham asked. He seemed extremely interested in the savage's ways.

"We share everything," Chenoa answered. "If you steal you only steal from yourself."

"A bunch of fucking commies," Stu said, and spit on the ground.

Chenoa eyed him distastefully. "That's a disgusting habit."

Stu spit on the ground again.

"What if somebody wants a bigger pod and takes it for himself?" Graham asked.

"Then they have to share, but generally people stick to the pods they are assigned. Of course there is always some shuffling around."

"So where do you live, Chenoa?" Graham said.

"Would you like me to show you?"

"We would be greatly honoured."

They backtracked along the hallway, past a former restaurant and a former clothing store to the back of the mall to where a salon had once been. Chenoa pulled the gate back.

"Please step into my humble pod," she said.

Graham smiled. "It looks very spacious. You must be an important member of the community."

"You do honour me, white man, but it's my partner who is the important one."

Graham and Stu stepped in. There was a large white counter with an old computer still sitting in the middle. Next to it was a broken lamp. Pictures of skinny models with fancy dresses and strange hairstyles hung on the wall.

A large black man stepped out from one of the doorways. He was handsome with a square jaw, round cheeks and a high forehead. He was wearing a pink dress shirt and an old pair of jeans. He seemed to be expecting them and bowed his head.

"Welcome, white men, to my house."

Stu suddenly recognized the man. It was the man who wore the eagle mask.

"You son of a bitch," Stu said, stepping forward, but Graham put an arm across his chest, stopping him.

The man laughed. "Trust me white men, I like this situation no better than you do, but the White Chief has commanded it so and I obey. You are guests in my pod."

"Otakay, please," Chenoa said.

"I am sorry, my darling. But these white men have no place in the tribe. We both know that."

Chenoa went over to her partner and leaned against him. "Maybe so, Otakay, but the White Chief says these men can help us."

Otakay looked at Graham and Stu, his mouth creased into a frown. "I hope so."

Graham stepped forward. "Otakay, my name is Graham Meyer. We meant no harm to anyone, least of all your men. We very much hope we can assist the tribe with Perpetuum energy."

"Falcon says this Perpetuum energy is a pipedream," Otakay said.

Graham nodded. "Maybe so, but isn't it worth trying? A clean, practically unlimited energy source? Everything could be rebuilt."

Otakay shook his head. "Some things weren't meant to be rebuilt." He turned to Chenoa. Excuse me, my darling but I need to go get ready."

Otakay walked out of the room and into the hallway. Chenoa watched him go, a pensive look was on her face.

214

She sighed and turned to face her guests. "Before the Outbreak, Otakay drove a cab during the day and worked as a school janitor at night. Do you know what Otakay means?"

Both Graham and Stu shook their heads.

"It means killer. He is the best hunter in the entire tribe. Here he's practically treated as an emperor."

"And what do you think?" Graham asked. "Should we try and rebuild society?"

Chenoa didn't answer for awhile. "Why does it matter what I think?"

"Surely you have an opinion."

Chenoa smiled thinly. "Let me show you the rest of our pod."

They stepped through a doorway and found the salon had been converted into a comfortable-looking living room. There were a stack of books and magazines piled in the corner. A rack of clothes was hanging on the far wall and next to it was a rough sketch of a man and a woman, presumably it was supposed to be Chenoa and Otakay.

"Please have a seat," Chenoa said. "Can I offer you something to drink?"

"It depends on what you have," Stu said. "I would prefer a cold beer myself."

Chenoa gave a pretty smile. "We have tea or water."

"I guess tea will have to do," Stu said.

Chenoa took some logs from the corner and put them in a sink in the corner of the room. She then took two pieces of flint from the cupboard and with little effort was able to strike them together and spark up the fire.

She then took some petals and roots and placed them in a pot of water which she then placed over the fire.

She then turned to her guests. "Can I make a confession?" she asked, but before waiting for an answer she said: "There's really only one thing I miss. Coffee. Isn't that terrible? All the luxuries we had, the technology. With a touch of a button we could talk to anybody across the world. We could jump on a plane and fly to Hong Kong or Australia, or Timbuktu. Now we can't do any of that and I'm actually glad."

Chenoa sat down across from Graham and Stu. "Is that horrible? What does that say about me?"

Neither Graham nor Stu said anything for a long time. Stu felt strange in this woman's presence. He couldn't explain it exactly. The pain and hatred he seemed to perpetually feel was slowly draining away from him. What would have happened if he had met her a long time ago?

"What I miss is the music," Stu said. He felt surprised to be talking about it. He hadn't told anybody about his love for classical music. Certainly not when he had been in the air force and not when he was an ambulance driver. "Not the junk on the radio but the real thing. The type of music you'd get dressed up for and go see the orchestra play. I only went once but it's an experience I'll never forget. I sat there around other people who were dressed in fancy suits and dresses and we all listened to the string instruments and together they made this perfect harmony."

Chenoa turned to Graham. "And how about you Graham? What do you miss most?"

Graham shrugged. "It's useless feeling nostalgic about the past."

Chenoa smiled. "I find people who say that are the most nostalgic."

Graham leaned forward. "So what do you think about the White Chief's plan? For energy and Perpetuum power?"

Chenoa bit her bottom lip and her eyebrows creased. "It's not my place to question the White Chief. He brought us together when we had nothing. He stopped us killing each other. He made us civilized."

"But you don't think Perpetuum power is good for the tribe?" Graham asked.

Chenoa got up and went over to the sink where the tea was boiling. Using a strainer she poured the tea into three cups. "I think it would be good to have more light and fuel to cook with and maybe do laundry."

She handed Stu and Graham each a mug of tea. Stu took a sip. It was strong and bitter but he enjoyed the taste. It was better than drinking murky water all day long.

"I remember when I first met Doctor Albert Winkler. He first brought me the concept of the Perpetuum generator on a scrap piece of paper. I remember he wanted to give it away to the top minds at the universities so they could solve the problem and reap all the benefits but I persuaded him not to. Doctor Winkler was the smartest man I ever knew and if anybody could build the generator it was him, not some university hack. So we kept the plans secret and developed them on our own. Finally after years we had a breakthrough and developed a prototype."

"Do you think you could do it again?" Chenoa asked.

Graham shrugged. "I don't know. On one hand I have the experience and the knowhow but back then we had a particle accelerator to test our theories on."

"Can't you just build it again using the same specifications," Stu wondered.

Graham shook his head. "Some of the parts are very specific. For example part of the coils were made up of a completely artificially manufactured aluminum-sandium alloy. Without whole factories producing the parts from across the world I have to say Otakay is correct in saying Perpetuum energy is only a pipedream."

"Can't you find the parts?" Stu said. "Are you sure that there are none still working?"

"I don't know. Maybe with the efforts of the whole tribe we might be able to find what we're looking for."

Daylight

The travellers slept until midday. The fire they had built at dawn had burnt down and Ewan woke up shivering. He didn't know where they were or how to get to the hospital. They had been on the move all night, afraid to stop until the Creatures had disappeared back into their dark holes.

Ewan dreamt of the samurai again. He didn't know how he could remember his dreams so vividly when he was so exhausted but he had.

He had dreamt he was at the ROM chasing Anthony and Justin, telling them to be quiet because Tim was trying to sleep but they kept laughing and playing with the old Roman swords.

When Ewan finally caught up to the boys the samurai appeared and attacked them. Ewan grabbed the boys and dragged them away from the samurai, down a flight of steps towards the doorway. But just as they reached the door, pushing it open into the sunlight, the samurai appeared in front of them and brought his sword down on Ewan just as was when he awoke.

Ewan stood up, stretching his legs, wondering what the dream meant. If Tim was asleep in the dream, did it mean he was dead? Did the samurai represent the Creatures?

Ewan shook Albert and Ashley awake.

"Come on," he said. "We don't have much time."

They had already spent the first five hours of daylight asleep and they needed to get to the health center before nighttime if they were able to search it properly. Even then, Ewan didn't know if they would have enough time. It was a big complex and he didn't know exactly what they were looking for. Only Albert would be able to tell them for sure.

Ashley opened her backpack. "We should eat something before we go."

But Ewan shook his head. "We only have half a day. We need to get moving."

"If we don't eat something we won't make it very far."

Ewan took in a deep breath and slowly released it. He looked at Albert who was staring at the trees across the street, seemingly oblivious to the conversation. Was this man truly their only hope?

She's right. We can't walk very far without some nourishment, Ewan thought.

"Okay," he said. "But we need to do it quickly."

Ewan and Ashley each took a can of baby food from their knapsacks and ate it quickly. When Ewan realized Albert wasn't doing the same he asked, "Aren't you hungry, doctor?"

"But it's not dinner time yet," he said, sounding uneasy.

"It's okay, I think we can make an exception this time."

But Albert shook his head. "The egg timer hasn't gone off yet."

Ashley put an arm on Albert's shoulder. He flinched at first but then relaxed.

"Doctor Winkler," Ashley said, as if he was talking to one of the boys. "You're not at home. There is no egg timer to signal dinner."

"You didn't need a timer yesterday," Ewan complained. "Why now?"

"Because eating meals at regular times aids the digestion," Albert said. "Did your wife not teach you anything?"

"Oh so you remember my wife now?" Ewan said, feeling his temper rise.

It was Ashley's turn to put a hand on Ewan's shoulder. "Ewan, don't make the situation worse."

Ewan nodded and packed up his things and then took out the map. He found the street sign and saw they were on Hillhurst Boulevard and Chaplin Crescent, far away from their destination. Ewan groaned. He doubted they would be able to make it to Sunnybrook Health Science Center by nightfall which meant they would have to find somewhere else to stay for the night.

Could they survive another night with the Creatures chasing them down? They couldn't walk on top of the rooftops again like last night until they collapsed from exhaustion.

Ewan scanned the area on the map between where they were and Sunnybrook Health Science Center, hoping he could see some natural hiding place for them but all he saw were endless stretches of roads and buildings.

They didn't talk much while they walked. They passed by houses and buildings made of brick and clay. They passed signposts and evergreen trees. They passed rusted swing sets, covered in sparkling white snow. They passed wrought-iron fences, and basketball courts with the hoops warped. They passed a wall filled with hundreds of bullet holes and Ewan wondered what had happed and who had shot whom. Men shot at Creatures, men shot at men?

The violence seemed so out of place in the tranquil streets, as if it was a dream or a mirage.

They travelled for several hours with the only sound being the soft squishing of snow underneath their feet. They had lost their skis in the fire and that made their progress even harder.

Ewan wondered how many Creatures would be at the hospital. He remembered in the early stages of the Outbreak people had been brought to the hospital by the thousands and there they slowly mutated into Creatures.

The night staff would have been the first ones to be killed but quickly the Creatures took over the entire hospital. Doctors had been in high demand yet most of them had been infected or eaten by the Creatures.

It wasn't long before people stayed away from hospitals and died horribly at home or mutated into Creatures.

Occasionally Albert would point out something along the way about the behaviour of the Creatures. He noticed a concentration of tracks circling a particular house and stopped to examine them.

"Come on, old man," Ewan said. "We need to keep moving."
"Do you think people were inside this house?" Ashley asked.
"If there were then they're long gone," Ewan said.
"The tracks are fresh," Albert said. "Maybe they could use some help, or maybe they could help us."
"I doubt that very much," Ewan said, turning and walking away but when he noticed neither Albert nor Ashley were following him he stopped and glanced backwards. He saw Ashley open the door and then Albert follow shortly afterwards.

Ewan cursed underneath his breath. He thought about going forward without them but knew it would be impossible without either of them and so he turned and walked back. He took his spear out from the loop in his backpack and followed them through the front door.

The air was so thick with flies he could barely see what was in front of him. The smell of copper and rotten flesh was overwhelming and he knew whatever they found, it wouldn't be good.

Let's get out of here, Ewan thought. *Far from here. I don't care if we ever reach the hospital. Let's just keep walking until we reach the ocean.*

But he knew he couldn't continue unless he had a hope of finding Tim. He had to get Ashley and Albert out before they could continue.

He swatted away the flies and took another step into the room, trying not to gag and keep down what little food he had in his stomach.

The room was dark, painted a deep red. The heavy drapes blocked out the light, making the whole room seem an endless, bottomless pit.

In the middle of the room was the most unspeakable horror Ewan had ever seen. There was a black leather couch, torn on the side with bits of white stuffing on the shag carpet. A lampshade stood next to it covered in a thick layer of dust.

On the couch was a human, only after Ewan's eyes focused in the darkness did he recognize it as a woman, covered in blood. Her face, pale, her jaw open, the lips stretched back, showing a row of white teeth in a state of Rigor mortis, screaming eternally.

She had probably been dead only since last night.

Ewan had seen this sort of thing at the beginning of the Outbreak but to have survived for so long and to just give up like that? The way her body was sprawled out on the couch it looked like she hadn't even bothered to run or defend herself.

Ewan couldn't look away. She had long, curly blonde hair that fell over her face. Her chin was round and her cheeks were hollow, probably from a lack of food.

In her arms was a bundle of white cloth soaked with blood. Only when Ewan took a step closer did he realize what was in the bundle of cloth.

"My God," Albert said, although those words were terribly inaccurate. There were no words.

The bundle was a mutilated little body, a baby, only it was just a body. The head was gone, torn off from the neck. Its arms and legs had been hacked off. Below the dead baby, on the mother's lap the woman's intestines and guts had been savagely torn out.

Ewan looked over at Ashley who was just standing, mesmerized by the gore, her neck muscles tense, her arms, flat against her side.

Albert was holding his water gun out, sniffing the air and scowling.

Ewan took Ashley by the shoulder and forced her to move closer to the door.

"Come, I'm sure they will be back."

"We should bury them," Ashley said.

"With what? We don't have any shovels."

"Let's just take them out into the snow and dig a hole in the snow."

Ewan sighed. "The Creatures will find them and dig them up again."

"You just want to leave them?" Ashley said, her voice rising.

"Ashley, we need to keep moving, otherwise we will end up like the woman and the poor baby."

"That poor baby," Ashley said. "I should never have left the boys alone."

"They'll be fine. They have the generator and some extra coils to keep them going."

Ewan didn't want to tell Ashley about his dream, for fear of worrying her. It was silly to think too much about them.

"We should give them a proper burial," Albert said, looking at the dead bodies.

Ewan shook his head and sighed. "Ashley, this isn't like you. What happened to the strong, confident Ashley I knew when I first met you?"

"Do this for me, Ewan. I know it doesn't make much sense . . . I just feel it will keep me sane, you know?"

Ewan walked back outside, into the light and the cold, dry air. He couldn't take the smell anymore. He felt it was clouding his judgement.

Ashley and Albert followed Ewan outside.

"Albert, this is craziness."

Albert nodded. "People think chemistry, biology, physics are all logical – laid out mathematically but true genius takes creativity and creativity often looks like craziness."

Ewan looked from Albert to Ashley. Her eyes were large and puffy and pleaded with him.

Ewan took in a deep breath. "Alright, let's do it quickly."

They went inside. The force of the smell made Ewan's eyes water. Ashley grabbed the decapitated baby and Albert and Ewan each took an end of the woman. Her limbs were white and cold and she was heavy and hard to move. They lifted her up and half dragged, half carried her outside.

They laid her down on the snow, her body curled up as if in the fetal position. Ashley laid the child down beside the mother.

"Help me dig a hole," Ewan said.

Together the three of them bent down and with their hands dug until they hit pavement. They dragged the bodies in and then covered them with the snow. By the end Ewan's hands were freezing. Even with the large insulated gloves he was wearing he felt his fingers go numb.

He stared down at his hands and then he saw droplets of water fall onto his big gloves and then roll down his fingers. He was confused. Where was the water coming from? It wasn't until after he realized he was crying.

Was he crying for the woman and her child? Was he crying for the entire human race? No, he was crying because of Tim. He had never had the chance to say goodbye. He had never had the chance to bury his own son and daughter.

Amy's funeral had been a small, simple one. Her sister and her husband had come. Timmy of course. Ewan's father. They dressed casually in jeans and sweatshirts. It was how Amy would have wanted it.

They were all dead now. Killed when the Outbreak had gotten worse but that would have come later.

It was all a blur, even now. When she first learned she was pregnant with Tim, she made Ewan and herself draw up a will. She was practical like that.

Ewan had gone to the lawyer's office, complaining all the way he was missing something on the Learning Channel – he couldn't remember what show now. They were pregnant. Why think of death when they were bringing life into the world? But of course, she wouldn't hear of it. She argued logically with him and of course logic always won out. They were both scientists.

She had requested her ashes be spread down by the water. She wasn't religious so didn't want a priest. It had been a cold, wet March day. The sky was grey and overcast and the CN Tower loomed like the Tower of Babel in the distance, its tip clouded in darkness.

Her urn was a simple white box. They had all picked it out and decided it fitted Amy the best — everybody except for Tim who had wanted a golden one with a carved pattern in it. He threw a small tantrum but hardly anybody paid attention to him.

Ewan had said some meaningless words — he couldn't even remember what they were. Her sister had said something similar and then Ewan opened the urn and let the ashes spill out.

Together they watched in silence as the bits and pieces that had been Amy leapt into the wind. The wife, who had never been a dancer in life, now danced across the lake.

They watched for a long time. The sound of the wind murmured from the city, as if it was praying for Amy's soul. They then turned and walked back to their cars.

Ewan closed his eyes, coming back to reality. He could feel his eyes now swollen, burning, and liquid. He turned to Ashley who was staring at him. He walked over and kissed her, pressing her against his body. Her warmth felt good; her lips were moist and perfect.

They leaned back and looked at each other, searchingly. Their awkwardness had disappeared and had been replaced by something deeper, something meaningful.

They bent in and kissed again. Ewan felt his teeth hit the back of his lips. Her fingers wrapped around the back of his neck and dug into his flesh. He welcomed the pain, the taste of her, her breath.

"Don't let me go," Ashley whispered.

Ewan replied by kissing her again, biting her lip, digging his teeth into her. Their movements became almost wild. Ewan wondered what had happened. He had always been a gentle lover, making love sweetly, kindly, even when his past girlfriends had begged him to get rougher.

"Okay, I know you're young and have an overwhelming amount of oxytocin," Albert said. "But really, the middle of the street?"

Ewan and Ashley looked at Albert and started to laugh, breaking their trance-like state. Albert smiled and that only made them laugh harder. They laughed and couldn't stop, even when they didn't know what they were laughing at.

They continued to walk, making their way towards the hospital, but perhaps they were really trying to get away from the grave and the woman and her child.

The sun was sinking quickly and they had to seek shelter somewhere, but where would they be safe from the Creatures. Was anywhere safe?

Nobody said anything. They just continued to walk slowly down the street, lost in their own thoughts. Ewan tried to think of where they could be safe, but instead he just thought of Ashley's lips.

I'm sorry Amy. Will you forgive me?

On one street they saw several dead Creatures that looked like they had been disembowelled and that made Ewan think about the mother. Was this some type of revenge?

Only humans could have done that, Ewan thought. *Did the Creatures understand it for what it was? A signal to stay away from humans?*

Ewan doubted it. The Creatures only understand food and sunlight.

"You think there are more humans around?" Ewan asked Albert.

Albert shook his head but didn't elaborate and Ewan didn't press him.

They continued to walk. Their progress was slower than ever but even Ewan didn't say anything. His legs were burning and he was breathing heavily.

Albert begged them to stop a couple of times and they rested, sitting on a park bench or a trash can. In truth, Ewan was grateful for the excuse to stop. The third time Albert asked them for a break Ewan looked over and saw he wasn't doing very well. His face was pale and once or twice he clutched his chest and Ewan preyed he wasn't having a heart attack. Ashley put her arm around Albert and his breathing stabilized.

"We better find someplace to spend the night quick," she said.

Ewan just nodded.

Attack at the ROM

It was nearly dark and the savages in large convoys had been collecting parts from various factories and buildings all day. Graham had given them a long list of parts they needed and they had taken the ones that looked to be in the most working order.

For most of the day Otakay had driven Stu around with various other savages while Graham had remained in another car. Stu wanted to be in the same car but Otakay wouldn't allow it.

For the entire morning Stu didn't say a word to Otakay and Otakay only spoke when he needed Stu to do something.

Rummaging through the destroyed factories was exhausting work and for the most part the savages did it in silence, concentrating on the task at hand.

When they stopped midday for a snack, Otakay gave Stu some root and a bit of meat.

Stu sniffed the meat suspiciously, recalling what Graham had said about them being cannibals. "What is this?"

"Just eat it," Otakay said.

Although he was hungry, he gave it back to Otakay and bit into the tasteless root.

"You need iron to keep you alive," Otakay said.

"Why do you care what happens to me?"

Otakay shrugged. "I need you to complete the work the White Chief has charged me with."

"But you don't believe in it."

Otakay shrugged again. "It doesn't matter what I think."

"Why does everybody in your tribe say the exact same thing? Why shouldn't it matter what you think?"

"I think this energy sounds very amazing. I would like to have lights and ovens again. But I don't think your friend can build it by himself."

"Tell me Otakay," Stu said. "What would you do if you were chief?"

"But I'm not chief so it doesn't matter."

Stu ate the last of the root. "Do you know what a theoretical question is?"

"Don't insult me, white man."

Stu smiled. "Then what would you do if you were chief?"

Otakay took the meat he had given Stu and ate it. "I would have killed you long ago."

Stu smiled widened and nodded. "It was a mistake to keep us alive."

Otakay jumped up quickly and backhanded Stu in the mouth. "You question The White Chief again and I will kill you."

Stu stepped back, taken by surprise but then he laughed. "What sort of man backhands another?" he said. "You want to hurt me then punch me."

Stu crouched into a fighting stance but Otakay didn't move.

"I'm not going to waste time fighting you now," he said. "We have one more stop before we head back home."

Their last stop was going to be the Royal Ontario Museum.

Graham had said it was one of the original Perpetuum generators and so would likely have broken down by now and would be of little use, but they were still missing several crucial parts.

The convoy got back into their cars and started the long drive downtown. Again Stu sat by Otakay and watched as the industrial warehousing became buildings and then buildings became skyscrapers.

It was slow going through downtown as cars and debris covered the streets, causing the convoy to take several detours but eventually they made it to the ROM.

The convoy parked on Bloor Street and everybody got out.

Stu entered the building after Graham and Otakay. There were toys and books scattered across the lobby which seemed a bit odd but Stu had seen stranger things.

"The generator would be in the basement," Graham said. "Careful because there will mostly likely be Creatures down there."

Stu and the group of savages followed Graham into the basement where they were surprised not to find any Creatures or even any trace of them. They found the generator down a passageway. It was humming and vibrating.

Graham let out an exclamation of surprise, reaching his hand out to touch it.

"What?" Otakay asked.

"It's still running," he said. "And not only that but it looks like the coils have been changed recently."

Otakay thought for a moment. "You think there could still be somebody living in the museum?"

Graham shrugged. "It would make sense. This would usually be a perfect place for Creatures to sleep."

"We don't have time to search the entire museum," Otakay said.

"With this generator running we can stay here the night," Graham said. "We will be absolutely safe. We don't need to go back."

Otakay seemed to hesitate.

He probably just doesn't want to keep that pretty girlfriend of his waiting, Stu thought.

"Alright," Otakay said, finally.

"If we find out who has been keeping it running perhaps they know where to find some extra coils," Graham said.

For the next hour they systematically searched the museum. Whoever had been living there had been doing so for a long time. There were several rooms that had been converted to bedrooms. The trashcans were full of garbage and there were several changes of clothes.

"By my calculations five people have been living here," said Graham.

"They obviously have some children here," Stu said. They had found kids toys and books next to several of the beds.

"Perhaps they are out trying to find food," Otakay said. They had gathered on the third level in the Egypt gallery. Stu was surprised that most of the displays were intact and still held ancient artifacts.

Just then Stu heard something come from the ceiling. He motioned everybody to be silent but the sound never came again. They stood there staring up at the ceiling. Stu closed his eyes and tuned his ears to his surroundings. He never heard the sound from the ceiling again but he was sure he had heard the shifting of something heavy in the vents. Using hand signals he motioned to Otakay and Graham to communicate his thoughts.

They were confused at first but after several motions he made them understand. The inhabitants of the museum were hiding in the vents.

"Well let's pack up and get out of here," Graham said, but as he did so he leaned towards Otakay and whispered something in his ear, pointing upwards. Otakay nodded and in return whispered something in one of his subordinates who turned and disappeared from the gallery.

They waited for several moments until they heard the savages enter the vents and then the scraping of something against metal and then everything was silent.

The savages returned a couple of minutes later holding two boys about ten or eleven years old covered in dust and dirt. They were boney but they didn't look unhealthy.

Was it possible they lived here alone? Stu wondered. *No, their parents or guardian must still be around.*

Otakay took the two boys by the throats and dragged them to the center of the gallery.

"What are your names?"

"Justin and Anthony," they whimpered.

"Who else lives here?"

The boys looked at each other but didn't say anything.

Otakay grabbed each of them by the necks with his large, powerful hands and started to squeeze. "I won't ask a question twice."

"Ewan and Ashley," one of them said and Otakay released them.

"They're your parents?"

They shook their heads. "No. They just take care of us."

"Where are they now?"

"They went on a journey."

"You're lying."

The boys started to whimper. "We're telling the truth, we swear."

"A journey to where?"

"To a hospital to find the cure."

Otakay looked up at Graham. "A cure?"

"Yes, they believe it was hidden or something," one of the boys said. "We don't know. Please don't hurt us again."

"There is no cure, white boy. They are fools to believe so."

"When will they be back?" Graham asked.

"They said they would be back tomorrow."

Otakay leaned down towards the boys. His eagle mask must have been terrifying to the boys. "You better not be lying to me, white boy."

"We . . . not. . . lying," one of the boys stammered.

Otakay turned to one of the savages. "See if you can find something to tie him up with. We'll take him back to the White Chief and see what he wants to do with him."

The savage nodded and turned and disappeared through the doorway.

Graham bent down so he was eye level with the kids.

"Don't be scared, I'm not going to hurt you," he said. "I just have one question for you. Do you know where you got the coils for the generator?"

The boys looked confused for a moment. "Sorry," the braver one stammered. "We don't know anything about coils."

Graham nodded, smiling. "Okay. Thank you for being honest."

Graham stood up. "I don't think you need to tie the boys up. They'll behave."

"We tie them up until we present them to the White Chief."

"And what will he do with them?" Graham asked.

"I cannot say what the White Chief will do. Perhaps he'll let them join the tribe, perhaps he'll sacrifice them."

"Sacrifice?" Graham said. His normally neutral demeanour couldn't hide the revolt from his voice.

Stu glanced at the two boys who shifted nervously.

"I'm only offering a possibility," Otakay said. "Like I said, I do not know what the White Chief will decide."

That night Stu couldn't sleep and so he got up and wandered the museum, looking at the various displays. The lights were dim yet clearly functioning. It seemed weird to be looking at all the exhibits from other civilizations and other times. He wondered if somebody would one day look at a display of present time and wonder how the Creatures had almost destroyed humanity.

He knew if humanity were to survive it wouldn't be because of the White Chief. He had a noble heart but not a practical one and that is why he had to be replaced.

Stu stopped in the Asian section of the museum and looked at a samurai sword in a display case. It would be easy to smash the case and take the sword. It would be blunt but he would still be able to kill Otakay in his sleep.

But . . . no, Graham had told him to be patient and he would heed his advice for now.

Graham saved my life, Stu thought. *Perhaps he knows what he's doing.*

The savages already trusted them too much. Give it a couple more weeks and if Graham got the Perpetuum generator up and running they would all be dependent on them.

Stu stared at the mannequin of the samurai warrior and thought it strange that while most of the city had been destroyed and looted; the museum had remained undamaged, untouched by the Outbreak.

Stu didn't know why some of these priceless artifacts hadn't been relocated or stolen. He supposed once the Outbreak had peeked, all these valuable artifacts were useless and nobody would even bargain them for food or water.

Perhaps Ewan and Ashley had been protecting the museum all along, Stu thought.

Stu heard a sound from another room. It could just be somebody rolling over in their sleep or maybe it was one of the guards Otakay had posted or maybe a Creature had somehow gotten into the vents.

Stu went to investigate and found Otakay kneeling in the middle of the room, his hands pressed together and his mouth mumbling words from a prayer.

Stu watched him finish and then said, "After all that you've seen how can you still believe in a God?"

Otakay turned startled by Stu's presence. "What are you doing here?"

"I couldn't sleep." Stu entered the room noiselessly. "Are you avoiding my question?"

Otakay shrugged. "I always believed in God. I figure why stop now?"

"That seems like a nonsensical answer."

"Maybe so, but how can you just stop believing something you've believed in your entire life?"

Stu shrugged. He had always thought people who believed in a higher being were fools but he was too tired to antagonize Otakay now. "What do you pray for?"

"For him to forgive my sins."

"You think you've sinned?"

"Everybody sins," Otakay replied.

"You seem like a just, fair man," Stu said. "One day you will be chief of the tribe."

"I told you not to say that."

"What? The White Chief isn't a young man. I haven't seen a man that age for many years. Surely you've thought of succeeding him?"

Otakay stayed silent for a long time. "Did Chenoa tell you that everybody who joins the tribe must have a vision?"

"Sure."

"I fasted for seven days and then went outside. At first I didn't see anything and I was afraid if I went back they would know I didn't have a vision but then a couple of hours later I saw a large black snake, about ten feet long and as big as your fist. It looked at me and then turned and slithered away so I followed it. I followed it as it made its way down the street, disappearing into this tall pasture of grass."

Otakay paused and looked over at Stu who remained silent and waited.

"I was afraid of going into the grass. What if the snake turned and bit me? But I knew that it was my destiny to follow the snake and so I walked through the grass. The pasture dipped and came to a little dirt clearing and in this clearing was this large white tiger. It was pacing around the dirt but it too seemed afraid to venture into the grass. I managed to coax it towards me. The tiger wasn't dangerous and reached out to nuzzle me and I petted it. But just as I dug my fingers into its white fur the snake struck and wrapped its body around, suffocating the beautiful beast. I just stood there helpless."

Otakay paused; his eyes stared into the distance.

"What do you think it means?" Stu asked.

"I told the White Chief it meant I would be a great hunter."

"But you believe it means something different?"

"I think it means I will kill the White Chief and take his place as leader."

Timmy

Ashley tripped over something in the snow and when she brushed it off she found it was an army helmet.

Several blocks up they found a tank. It was brown with rust and covered in snow, an old relic from when martial law had gripped the city.

"We're going to stop here for the night," Ashley said.

It took all three of them to swing the hatch open. The gasses and stench that were released were almost unbearable.

Albert made a face. "We should have stayed in my funhouse."

"Well you had your chance, old man," Ewan said.

Ashley was the first one to climb in; Ewan second and then Albert. They found a dead soldier inside, killed by what looked like a single gunshot wound. Ewan couldn't help but wonder what had happened. Under what circumstance had he died? The bullet hole had gone through his chin and had exited the top of his skull.

Had it been self-inflicted? Ewan searched the tank's floor for a gun but it was empty. It was possible the soldier had chosen to end his life but if that was the case the gun was long gone.

They hoisted the body up and dumped him over the side. He looked ghastly in the fading sunlight. His hair was mostly gone and his skin was rotten and chunks of white bone were visible. He looked like he had died a teenager, a mere boy.

But Ewan couldn't bring himself to feel any emotion for him as much as he willed his body. Perhaps all his tears had been wasted on the mother and her child.

"We're just going to leave him for the Creatures?" Ashley asked.

"You want to bury him too?"

Ashley looked at Ewan. "Can we? We need to let the tank air out anyways."

Ewan shrugged and they buried the solder just as the sun faded slowly behind the buildings. It would have been beautiful if it didn't bring the night.

They quickly scrambled into the tank but the hatch wouldn't close. Ewan took the handle with both hands and yanked it closed. It groaned and closed with a resounding clank.

They waited and although they were exhausted none of them could sleep. It didn't take long before they heard of the soft pitter-patter of the Creatures as they made their way down the street. Their heavy breathing and sniffing. It got closer until it was right outside the tank.

Ewan could only make out the vague outlines of Ashley and Albert in the dark. He wondered what they were thinking and if they were scared.

There was a furious noise and a loud scraping sound. Then a roar of excitement that seemed to echo inside the tank's chamber. Ewan closed his eyes but of course that didn't help in the darkness. He heard the hideous sound, almost like paper tearing but Ewan knew it wasn't. It was flesh tearing off the bone. The Creatures had found the soldier. Ewan pressed his hands up against his ears but he couldn't block out the eating frenzy.

Afterwards the Creatures made loud, high-pitched screeching sounds. Evidently the meat had caused some sort of excitement.

The screeching continued and there was a loud thumping against the side of the tank. The thick steel plates that armoured the tank would hold against the Creatures.

But what if they don't, Ewan thought. *We would be easy prey.*

For the millionth time, Ewan told himself he didn't care. If he died, he would join Amy, wherever she was and how could that be bad?

One day I will be with you, Amy.

The Creatures sounded like injured hyenas as they continued their barrage on the tank. Scaly deformed hands grasped blindly through the sight hole, searching for them. Ewan wondered again if it would hold the entire night. He hoped the Creatures would eventually give up and leave them in peace. He wasn't sure if he was imagining it but the Creatures' sounds seemed to intensify in the small metallic cabin.

"Ashley?" Ewan called out in the darkness, not caring if he woke anybody.

"Yeah?"

"Can you read something to me?"

Ashley laughed softly in the darkness. It was a light airy laugh that was unusual for her. "I can't see a thing," she said.

"Well just make it up. I won't know the difference."

So Ashley started talking about Jay Gatsby and Tom and Daisy and it helped to block out the whining and the screaming from the night.

"What happens to Daisy?"

"That would be giving away the ending," Ashley said.

They could hear the loud snores of Albert and it made them both laugh. It was a light-hearted moment in an otherwise bleak situation.

"That guy can sleep through anything, can't he?" Ewan said.

"I wish I had that gift."

"You know, I used to be envious of him. He made millions, perhaps billions of dollars when he invented the Perpetuum generator."

"I didn't know he was that rich."

"Well he lost most of it a couple of years later through bad investments . . . he was never a business guy, but still he was a wealthy man," Ewan said. "And I was just a biology teacher. Not really that smart but pretending to be. I would hang out with pretentious scientists pretending to be one of them."

"Oh baby, you're smart. I don't understand half the stuff you know. That stuff about the hydra. . . That's really cool."

Ewan grew uncomfortable. "Does Daisy come to a tragic ending?"

"No, she gets off just fine I suppose. But it's not really the life she wanted . . . so in a way it is tragic."

"Strange." Ewan blinked in the darkness but there wasn't much difference from having his eyes open or shut. "I always thought she would die in the end."

"What do you think will happen to us?"

"I suppose we'll die, whether it's because of the Creatures or something else. . . who can say? I don't suppose we'll die in our deathbeds like our parents."

"That's funny."

"Why's that funny."

"I always told my parents I would rather go out skydiving or swimming with the sharks or something."

"Sharks don't actually eat people. It's a common misconception. The only reason sharks attack—"

Ashley cut Ewan off. "You know what I mean."

"Oh. . .Sorry."

"Anyway now there is a very real possibility that we won't make it past tomorrow and if we do, the day after that, and the day after that and so on."

"You wish you hadn't said that to your parents?"

"I suppose we all lose our nerve for death."

Ewan thought of Tim and how kids changed everything: your whole outlook on life. "Yeah, I suppose so."

"I know we're going to die, sooner rather than later but what about the boys? Justin and Anthony? And Tim? Do you think the human race will survive?"

Ewan didn't say anything for a long time. The Creatures weren't giving up and still bashing against the unmoveable tank.

"I suppose the human race is just like everything else and has it's beginning and ending. Maybe it's our time to become extinct, just like the dinosaurs."

Now it was Ashley's turn to be quiet. "I hope we find Tim," she said. "I miss him."

Ewan thought of when he had been born. Sophia was the firstborn and would always be special because of it, but Tim was special too because he was his son. "I miss him too."

Suddenly Ewan felt a pressure against his legs and saw Ashley's shadow in front of him. Ewan drew her close and kissed her. Somehow it helped to block out the outside distraction, muted the attacking Creatures.

He felt her hand lower on his body and dig into his pants. She unzipped his fly, lowered her head and put her mouth on him. Ewan bit his lower lip, a tingle of pleasure ran through his spine, a sensation he couldn't remember when he had felt last. He wondered if the old pervert was asleep or if he was watching in the darkness and he found he didn't care.

Ewan pulled Ashley upright and unbuckled her belt and slid her pants down to her ankles. He ran his fingers up her cold thighs feeling her smooth buttocks. He barely could see her body, just the contours of her shape in the blackness.

Ashley inserted him into her and he slid easily in. Ashley let out a low moan that counteracted the scraping of claws on metal and the thumping against the steel walls.

Ashley moved rhythmically over top of Ewan. His hands guiding her hips, her hands wrapped around his body, clasping him tight as if he would slide through her fingers and disappear. Her eyes black and shrouded in darkness.

Her body started pumping faster and he bit into her shoulder, tasting gortex. At the last moment Ewan pulled out and Ashley finished him off with her hands.

"Great, we've made a mess," Ewan whispered.

"What do you mean we?" Ashley giggled, pressing her body against Ewan.

It was only then Ewan realized he hadn't thought about Amy the entire time.

Ewan woke with a start. Ashley was curled up in the seat next to him. Albert was snoring softly up front.

Ewan couldn't remember falling into a dreamless sleep. The samurai hadn't haunted him and he wondered if that was a good sign. He stared at Ashley as she slept, her chest rising and falling with her breath and he thought how beautiful she looked.

A small ray of light shone through the sight hole and lit up the inside of the tank.

The whole cabin stank of sex and it made Ewan embarrassed. He scrambled to open the hatch and escape.

The cold air was refreshing as it hit his face but then the smell of decay quickly followed. He looked down and saw hundreds of footprints in the snow and the shredded up body of the soldier.

There was surprisingly little blood but he supposed that was to be expected from a half-decayed body. The limbs had been torn from the body and were now only bits of cloth and bone. The skull still had bits of flesh on it and Ewan could see spinal cord was still attached.

Ewan went back below and woke up Ashley and Albert.

"Come on, we need to get going," he said.

The walk was a mostly silent one but for a change Ewan was glad for the quietness. They were better rested and were able to move quicker than the previous day.

"Why did you pull out?" Ashley asked Ewan when Albert had fallen a couple of meters behind them.

"What?"

"Last night . . . why did you pull out?"

"I didn't know," Ewan stammered. "What are you saying?"

"I don't know," Ashley said, thoughtfully. "I just have this feeling, I'm not sure if I can explain it."

"You want to get pregnant? Bring life into this world? Are you nuts?" Ewan said, a little louder than he meant.

"It's not that I want to, it's just . . . shouldn't we?"

"So we can feed it to the Creatures?"

Ashley turned away and Ewan immediately regretted saying it.

"Our ancestors brought life into the world even when life was harsh and as terrible as this. They felt the need to carry on their family or the human race or whatever."

"Don't you feel that maybe our time is up? That maybe we should just let it all go."

Ashley didn't reply and they elapsed into another long silence.

They walked for about an hour and when they were tired they rested on a porch. They scooped up a handful of snow and started sucking on it. It was cold but at least it quenched their thrust.

Ewan noticed a fly as it buzzed around, doing loops in the air before settling on Ashley's shoulder. She brushed it off but it just buzzed and settled back down. It seemed unafraid of the humans. Perhaps it had never encountered one before and so didn't know to be afraid.

"Perhaps we should try and catch it," Ewan said.

Ashley just shrugged. "I'm not that hungry."

Ashley brushed it off again and this time it flew away. Ewan watched it until he lost it in the blue sky.

"Do insects feel pain?" Ashley asked.

"Nobody really knows," Ewan replied. "They don't have the neurological sensors we do that translates a negative stimulus into an emotional one."

"Yet we know insects can learn," Albert interjected. "Even if they can't feel or think."

"I think I would like to be an insect," Ashley said. "Not to have to feel pain or to think. Just go on looking for food, following my programing."

They came on Sunnybrooke about midday. It was a large complex, several blocks wide and consisted of rows of buildings. It was the largest medical center in the country but now stood vacant.

"I don't even know where to start," Ewan said. "We'll never be able to search the entire facility."

"It's knowing where to look," Albert said, cheerfully.

Ewan scowled at the doctor. "Do you know something you're not telling us?"

Albert shook his head. "But the research facility would be a good start."

"Do you know where that is?"

Albert led the way through the streets, the tall medical buildings on either side and onto the aptly named Wellness Way where they turned right and got to a large modern-looking building.

"If memory serves," Ewan started, "There were significant advancements in cancer treatment here."

Albert nodded. "They discovered that with increased dosage of antiangiogentic drugs they could decrease chemo treatment."

"You think there will be Creatures inside?" Ashley said.

"I would bet my bottom dollar," Ewan said.

They entered the wide, spacious main lobby. There was a front desk with a white linoleum countertop; behind that was an elevator with its door slightly ajar.

"Do we divide the floors up or stay together?" Ewan asked.

"We stay together, chap."

"Do you know where to go?"

Albert consulted the directory. "Let's start at the center for disease control."

Ewan nodded. "Sounds reasonable. What floor is that on?"

The disease center was on the fifth floor. The emergency stairwell was in the back right hand corner of the lobby.

Ewan and Ashley went first up the stairs followed by Albert and his water gun.

They climbed the stairs slowly and carefully. Their steps echoed from the ceiling and the walls. Everyone knew the stairs were potentially the most dangerous portion of their trip through the building. Stairs were always dark and they lacked clear visibility.

However they managed to make it to the third floor without encountering any Creatures. They entered a long hallway that was similar to the lobby with bleak white walls and tube lighting, long extinguished. The floor was tiled in linoleum and was thick with dried blood. At the end of the hallway was a large red sign that read, "Center for Disease Control.'

Ewan looked at Ashley and Albert but their faces gave away nothing. He started walking and Ashley and Albert followed.

Ewan pushed the door open and saw something stir in the corner. He held out his spear and waited.

The Creature uncurled its body and lunged at Ewan who stabbed it multiple times. Ashley brought her spear up and attacked also. The Creature retreated from the spears and Ewan and Ashley backed it into a corner where they were able to finish it off.

Apart from that one Creature the room seemed to be clean.

The room was large with rows of work benches. Equipment and computer monitors had been tossed on the floor. Chairs had been upended and blood stains were everywhere.

Ewan turned to Albert. "What are we looking for, doctor?"

"We'll know it when we find it."

They searched for two hours through the wreckage without finding anything that looked even remotely promising.

"If there was some sort of super lab, I don't think it would be labeled on a CD," Ewan complained. He thought back to when he and Ashley had searched the lab in the University of Toronto building. He hadn't been hopeful back then but somehow having Albert Winkler along made him more hopeful this time around, but had he been wrong to trust the doctor? Perhaps they were relying too heavily on him.

Ewan leaned his body against a table.

"I found something," Albert called out, excitedly. Both Ashley and Ewan moved over to where Albert was to see what he had found.

Albert held up a test tube with a blood sample on it. Written in fine ball-point marker were the words Magnetar Virus.

"I do recall this had something to do with the Outbreak," Albert said. "Although what exactly I don't remember.

"Magnetar was the early name given to the mutation that resulted in the Outbreak," Ewan said, remembering reading the early news reports.

Ashley stared at the red liquid closely. "It's so strange to think that the Outbreak was caused by something in this small tube."

"The Outbreak was caused by a mutation, more along the lines of cancer than a bacteria or a virus," Albert said. "What caused the mutation always baffled scientists but I have theory that it was something genetic in the food."

"Alright we have a sample but we are no closer to discovering the source or the lab," Ewan said.

They searched the pile of hardware in which Albert had found the sample. Albert picked up a hard drive that had been next to the sample and put it into his backpack.

"Are you sure you want to carry that around?" Ashley asked. "It looks awfully heavy."

"It might have some useful information on it that will help me," he said.

Ewan found underneath the side of a broken shelf a few pieces of paper. They were computer read outs and written over them in black sharpie were the words "God save us all."

Ewan shivered thinking about the person who had written the words out and the unequivocal sense of doom the person must have felt as he scribbled in large block letters. He tried to study the chart but couldn't make sense of it without some sort of context.

He handed them to Albert. "Do you know what these are?"

Albert scanned the pages. "Looks like whomever did this was charting the levels of some chemical makeup in a human subject, chap." Albert scanned through the pages. "It doesn't say what the chemical is or the effects it had on the subject."

"Whatever the chemical is, I bet it wasn't good," Ewan said.

Ewan folded the papers up and put them in his backpack. They search for thirty more minutes but didn't find anything more that they thought was useful.

"We need to go to the general hospital," Ewan said.

"You realize that there will be a lot of Creatures there, maybe thousands," Ashley said.

Ewan nodded grimly. "If I don't do everything in my power to find Timmy then I won't be able to live with myself."

"Maybe the doctor can find something useful off the hard drive," Ashley said. "At least let's come back another time."

Ewan shook his head. "Every moment we delay the less chance I have of finding him."

Ashley looked over to Albert who as usual refrained from speaking out when it came to making decisions.

"Okay, but we need a plan."

Ewan stepped into the front entrance of the hospital carrying only a torch and a spear. The torch he had made out of a tree branch and some cloth he had taken from the research center.

The lobby of the hospital was empty. It smelled of decay and rot. His torch flickered and danced in the darkness. He knew it wouldn't last long and he had to get deep within the hospital so he hurried along into the hallway, past the reception and waiting area.

It wasn't long before he heard a low growl and the sound of feet.

Here they come, he thought.

He ducked into a patient's room. A Creature was just getting up from the bed. Ewan swung his torch at it, lighting it up. The Creature screamed and ran towards Ewan who turned and ran.

His job was to create a diversion so hopefully Ashley and Albert could sneak in the back way. He had ten minutes to do so.

Ewan ran down the hallway. He could hear the Creatures behind him. He turned right and went up the stairwell, taking two steps at a time.

He entered the second floor and saw fifteen or twenty Creatures in front of him. The hallway was narrow which provided Ewan with an advantage.

The Creatures hesitated with Ewan's torch and some even averted their eyes from the light. Ewan attacked them at full speed, swinging the fire at them. They took several steps back allowing Ewan to step in a room.

Ewan swung the door closed and put his weight against it to prevent the Creatures from entering. The Creatures bashed at the door but it held firm. Ewan looked around. There were several beds in the room, each with a Creature in it. To Ewan's right was a chair. While the Creatures rose, Ewan hooked his right foot around the leg of the chair and dragged it closer to him. He wedged the chair underneath the door handle and turned to face the Creatures.

Ashley and Albert walked silently through the hallway. They could hear the calamity Ewan was making at the front of the hospital and Ashley hoped Ewan would be alright. She thought about the night they had spent in the tank, their bodies pressed together — the warmth she had felt not just on her skin but deep in her bones.
You can do it, Ewan, she thought. *I have faith.*
The distraction seemed to be working as they made their way to the triage center which was next to the ER. There were several broken computer monitors and nothing of value. The stairs were covered in dried blood.
"You want to take them?" Ashley whispered to Albert.
Albert explained the triage center was where the patient's priority was determined and could potentially have valuable information about how the Outbreak had spread.
Albert shook his head and they moved on into the ER which still stank of rich metallic blood. The room was covered in blood, now soaked into the bed sheets, on the floor and even on the ceiling.
The Creatures must have had a feast here, Ashley thought, as she stepped into the room, trying in vain to avoid the blood.
Here at last they found some paper charts written by long dead doctors. The charts were scattered across room but most of them said the same thing.
Patient complains of stomach pains, severe acne, eyes react to bright lights . . .
"Let's collect as many charts as possible," Albert whispered.
They spent several minutes collecting any scattered paper they could find. The charts were all disorganized so it was impossible to track a single person's mutation.
Underneath one of the charts Ashley found a book, Catcher in the Rye by J.D. Salinger. The front cover was from an older version and the book itself looked well read. She picked it up out of habit and leafed through it, stopping on the front page and felt her throat constrict.

It had an inscription from her dad, given to her on her thirteenth birthday. Ashley had given it back to her dad when he had first entered the hospital to pass the monotony.

How had it gotten here? Her dad had died at Credit Valley Hospital shortly after her mother. It had been early in the Outbreak, before martial law had been declared. Had somebody taken the book and passed it on to somebody else?

Ashley slipped the book into her backpack and as she did so she could hear a lot crash and the sound of hundreds of feet.

Ewan attacked the Creature on the right first with his spear and then lunged at the middle Creature with his torch. The Creature managed to dodge the spear but Ewan got the center Creature with his torch. The Creature fell backwards, trying to beat the flames from its burning chest. Ewan spun to his left and smashed the other Creature with the shaft of the spear. The spear broke in his hands but seemed to stun the Creature.

Ewan took out his cleaver and buried it into the Creature. The Creature screamed and dug its fingers into Ewan's face. Ewan took the cleaver out and swung it again, this time slicing at the Creature's throat.

The Creature fell but Ewan felt teeth sink into the back of his shoulder. Pain spread across to his spine. Ewan dropped to his knees and rolled the Creature over. He then took the splintered end of his spear and with all his force he dug it into the Creature's eye. The Creature's eye popped like a balloon and Ewan drove it all the way down through its brain.

Ewan crawled to the bed and pulled himself upright. The room was on fire from the torch, smoke rose to the ceiling.

Ewan turned towards the door. The door shook, knocking the chair down. The Creatures burst through. Ewan turned, took a television stand and smashed the window. The Creatures stopped just short of the light that now shone through the room, screaming with outrage.

Ewan faced them. He was trapped with nowhere to go but out the window. He turned just as one Creature lunged clumsily at him into the light.

Ewan managed to sidestep the Creature and climb out onto the ledge. It had begun to snow again and the wind half blinded him as he searched for a landing spot below. He was about forty-five feet above the ground and realized he could possibly break something if he jumped but it seemed the only alternative. But then he realized there was a pipe several ledges over. If he could just make it to the pipe he might be able to climb down safely.

Ewan took a deep breath, and measured the distance. It was about five feet away. The trick would be landing on the two-foot ledge. Ewan stepped back and then ran and leapt. He felt a gush of wind and realized he was going to miss the ledge. Desperately he reached out with his hands and caught onto the ledge with his hands. His body swung but he managed to find the ledge below with his feet. When he did so, he let go of the ledge and spread his arms out for balance.

He jumped the next two ledges without any problems and then took hold of the pipe and half slid, half climbed his way to the bottom.

Ashley thought about her father reading Catcher in the Rye as his skin peeled away and his eyes slowly disintegrated.

She should have been there with him more but the doctors told her he might be contagious. She should have insisted. They kept him in an isolated room without any human contact and just that one stupid book.

She followed Albert as they climbed the stairs pushing the door open to the fifth floor. They hadn't encountered any Creatures along the way and that made her wonder where Ewan was. Was he even still alive? She didn't think she could bear losing him as well.

Her thoughts turned to Amy. She must have been special. She hadn't known many couples that cared for each other like Ewan cared for Amy. Was it fair that she was trying to replace her? Should she just leave Ewan with her memories?

She certainly had loved Lucas and she had mourned for him but, truth be told, she could barely remember his face. If she closed her eyes she saw a fuzzy outline: his curly hair, his strong cheeks, his thick neck and blue-grey eyes. She wondered if one day he would fade from her memory completely and she would only be able to clutch to a couple of syllables. Lucas Goldsmith . . . Lucas Goldsmith . . . Lucas Goldsmith. It didn't represent anything, just meaningless words.

Whether the human race survived or not, she supposed one day they would all be forgotten. What did it matter?

They made their way along the hallway until they came to a room that said "Chemotherapy and X-Rays."

Ashley pushed the double doors open. They groaned a little too loudly. This room was dark and reeked of mold and decay but looked no different than the others with its counters and ominous white walls.

Ashley gripped her spear tightly and moved forward cautiously. Albert stood behind her, his water gun poised.

They heard a sound come from far back in the room.

"I think we should get out of here, lass," Albert said.

Ashley nodded and they backed up. The sound grew louder. It was almost like the roar of a water dam.

"Run!" Ashley whispered.

Suddenly there were hundreds of Creatures in front of them, running towards them. Ashley and Albert turned and ran back down the hallway. Ashley headed towards the stairwell but Creatures started pouring out into the hallway.

They were trapped. She looked for an escape and saw a door on their right. She crashed her shoulder into it. The door swung open and she tumbled in, almost losing her balance.

The room was dark and silent. She didn't know where she was, some sort of waiting room.

"Quick, bar the door," she told Albert.

They tried to move a desk in front of the door but they were too late. The door burst open and Creatures flooded into the room.

Ashley looked around for an escape route, a door, a window — something. But there was nothing. She bit her bottom lip, thinking of Ewan, thinking of the twins.

Well, if I'm to die today, she thought, as she charged them with her spear. She impaled the first Creature with such force the spear went clear through it. She tried to pull it out but it was stuck and so she dropped it. Albert ran up beside her and squirted them with his water gun, giving her time to take out two knives she was carrying.

She blindly slashed and hacked at the Creatures, feeling nothing as she did so. The black bile squirted everywhere but finally a Creature got through her defences and pounced on her. She dropped her knives and grabbed its throat as it tried to bring its teeth down onto her face.

Albert squirted it with its gun but it didn't seem to feel anything. Albert kicked it but it still didn't move.

The Creature was incredibly strong and Ashley, exhausted, could feel its strength wane. She was going to lose, she realized. Her arms shook with effort and she could no longer feel pain in them. The Creature's face came closer. Ashley could smell it's rotten breath.

In her peripheral vision she could see Albert turn and squirt his gun at another Creature who was only inches away from him.

She closed her eyes, bracing for what would happen next. Again she thought of everything she lost. But now it wouldn't be lost anymore. Wherever her parents were and her family and all her friends she would go there too and it gave her this incredible sense of peace.

But it never came. She felt the pressure on top of her suddenly disappear and for a brief moment she thought she was dead but there hadn't been any pain and then sensation returned to her body. Her chest was heaving and her arms were burning.

She opened her eyes and looked around. She was alone with Albert. Where had the Creatures gone?

Then something came through the darkness. It was a Creature, only stunted.

With her last remaining reserve, Ashley grabbed her knives and threw herself at the Creature but the Creature just put up its hands as if to tell Ashley to stop. Or maybe it was a greeting.

Confused, Ashley stopped and lowered her knives. She glanced at Albert who too was motionless, his face a mask of confusion.

The Creature stepped closer. It didn't move like a Creature. It was almost human. Ashley too took a step closer, focusing her eyes on the Creature.

Only it wasn't a Creature, not really. Then she let out a low gasp.

"Tim?" she said.

"Hello Ley-ley," Tim said, smiling, using the nickname he had given her.

"My God," she said, dropping her knives and covering her mouth.

He was midway through transformation. His skin had turned to a greyish colour and his head seemed more oval, his hair was all but gone. But it was Tim, his brown eyes were still there, his small rosy cheeks and thin mouth.

"We don't have much time before they discover I'm gone," Tim said.

"Who? What are you talking about?"

"I need to warn you, warn Dad to get out of here, get out of the city. Go far from here."

Ashley shook his head. "He won't leave without you."

"No, it's too late for me, but you can save yourself. You'll have to convince him. Tell him you saw my dead body."

"It'll kill him, Tim."

Tim held up his hands. His fingers didn't look human. They were long and curled and sharp.

Ashley fought back the tears. "Come with us, Tim. Doctor Winkler will find a cure and reverse the effects."

"You know what happens when I'm fully transformed."

Ashley turned to Albert. "Tell him, doctor. You'll find a cure. Tell him there's hope."

Albert took a step closer to Tim and studied him. He ran his fingers through Tim's hair and a clump came off in his hand. "I'm sorry, lassie but the boy is right."

"What happened to you in the forest," Ashley asked. "When you were with your dad?"

"There's no time," Tim said, shaking his head. "The Creatures will be back. You have to follow me if you want to get out."

Tim turned and ran towards the door. Ashley looked at Albert and then they followed him into the hallway and then down the stairs. They didn't encounter one Creature along the way.

In the lobby, Tim stopped. "This is where I leave you. Remember what I said and take care of my father for me."

"No, Timmy," Ashley pleaded. "Come with us. Let us help you."

"If you've seen the things I have you'll know there is no hope for us. The days of humans have come to an end."

"I can't believe that, Tim," Ashley said. Tears were falling freely down her cheek.

"I'm sorry Ley-ley."

Ashley pulled Catcher in the Rye from her backpack and handed it to Tim. "I want you to have this," she said. "I gave it to my father who was one of the first to die. I hope it brings you better luck."

At first Ashley didn't think he was going to take it but then he held out his hands, palms stretched upward. He could barely grasp it with his awkward claw-like hands but he managed to half close his fingers around the book and he pressed it to his chest.

"Thank you Ley-ley."

Ashley tried to say something more but she felt something press in her throat.

Tim turned and disappeared back into the darkness. Ashley ran to stop him but Albert grabbed her and stopped her.

"He's right, let's go, lass."

"Why didn't you say you could help him?"

"Because I can't."

"You could have at least tried you coward."

Albert stared at Ashley, his eyes small and intelligent. "Because I keep telling you it's not a disease and I cannot cure something that isn't sick."

"If that isn't a sickness then I don't know what is," Ashley screamed.

Outside Ewan waited hopefully watching as the light slowly faded, wondering how long he should stay. He didn't know how long he was there, not even feeling the cold. He felt certain they were fine, that they had accomplished their mission. He listened for their voices, knowing he wouldn't hear them. He listened for their footsteps, knowing he wouldn't be able to distinguish them.

He started pacing outside on the pathway, his mind going to dark places. What if they were both dead and he was really and truly alone? The last man alive?

Eventually he heard something from the building. Was it a scream? It sounded like Ashley. Ewan rushed into the building and saw Albert clutching Ashley. They were both covered in black bile but seemed relatively unharmed.

"What happened?" Ewan asked.

Ashley and Albert looked back at Ewan but neither said anything for awhile. After a while Albert said, "You're alive Walder. Always a good sign to meet a member of the living."

Ewan looked at Ashley. Her eyes were red and wide but she said nothing.

"We need to get back home," Albert said.

"You okay, Ashley?"

"Yeah . . . I just found a book . . . belonging to my dad, is all."

Ewan felt something wasn't right, they weren't telling him everything but they needed to get back to the tank before the sun set and he didn't have time to debate.

The White Tiger

As Graham taught the savages about the Perpetuum generator, Stu spent the time meditating. He couldn't remember the last time he was able to mediate so well. Perhaps it was because his worries had decreased and he didn't have to worry about where his next meal would come from.

He had even been able to have a hot bath. Although they had no running water he was able to place buckets of water next to the pipes that fed the electricity to the building. Stu couldn't remember when he had felt the sensation of warm liquid on his body. He had forgotten how good it had felt. It really was the little things.

The White Chief was supposed to arrive that afternoon to inspect the museum and there was nothing to do but wait.

Ever since they had discovered the oil he hadn't had much chance to meditate – there had been so much to do – and so he was slightly out of practice but he was glad to be able to use the time productively.

He usually found a secluded part of the museum where he couldn't be disturbed and would mediate for hours. It helped him feel calm and less angry. It also helped him plan his strategy.

Stu sat cross-legged, his hands rested on his palms and his eyes closed. He was jolted back into reality when he heard heavy footsteps approach.

Stu called out. "You know for somebody who is reputed to be the best hunter in the tribe, you'd think you would learn how to approach your target without so much noise."

"Who says you're my target," Otakay said.

Stu opened his eyes and turned to see Otakay standing next to a pillar. "Forgive me but I thought you wished me dead."

Otakay shook his head. "The White Chief has deemed your life worthy enough for you to be hold onto. . . for now."

Stu smiled and stood up. "My proximity to Graham has made me a valuable commodity, it seems. But you are wrong if you think the White Chief will one day grow tired of me and have me killed."

"I don't understand why you haven't run away yet. Nobody is guarding you."

"You wanted me to escape, didn't you?"

Otakay said nothing. He just stood and stared at Stu.

Stu's smile widened. "And that is why I haven't escaped. Appear weak when you are strong and strong when you are weak. Here we have endless energy and warmth."

Otakay kept staring at Stu. "You know, I can't figure you out and that bothers me. What do you want, Stuart?"

"Don't call me Stuart. I hate it."

"I'll call you whatever I want."

Stu forced his body to relax. "Have you ever read the *Art of War* by Sun Tzu?"

"I can't say I have."

"In it, Sun Tzu said: 'The supreme art of war is to subdue your enemy without fighting'."

Otakay looked puzzled. "Good advice, I suppose."

"What I'm trying to say is meditation has been good for me. It's made me see things clearer." Stu lowered his voice just in case somebody was listening. "I can't defeat you and I've realized I don't want to defeat you. I know I'll never be your friend. I realize that, but maybe we can come to a mutual understanding."

"What type of mutual understanding?"

"That you should be the next chief of the tribe."

"What you are suggesting is . . . treasonous."

"I call it being practical. The White Chief is an old man. You are young, strong and powerful. Nobody else in the tribe has the qualities you have."

Otakay laughed. "And you've met everybody else? You feel qualified to make that assumption?"

Stu spread his arms out, his palms upward. "Tell me I'm wrong."

Otakay bent his head down, thoughtfully.

Stu continued. "I'm not saying you make a move against the chief, but it's only a matter of time. I will get Graham to support your leadership claim and then you'll have Perpetuum energy. Nobody from the council will dare oppose you."

"But what about the free elections that the White Chief promised?"

"You think the tribe is ready for free elections? We are in our infancy. One day, yes, we will have them but if we make one misstep it could mean all our deaths."

"You are talking 'we' but you're not part of the tribe yet. You haven't gotten through your right of passage yet."

"I want to become a part of the tribe. I want to see my destiny."

Otakay didn't say anything for awhile but stared past Stu out the window. The sun was out and shone onto the carpeted floor. "You know, on days like this you could be forgiven to forget we are at war."

Stu watched the White Chief pull up to the front of the museum in a Lincoln Town Car. It seemed fitting somehow that the chief would choose such a vehicle. Another Jeep pulled up behind the chief's vehicle. The Jeep's doors opened first, and a group of armed men got out.

The driver in the Town Car cut the engine and two savages armed with large swords got out. Stu presumed they were all bodyguards. They opened the door and the White Chief stepped out onto the curb. He was wearing leather pants and a leather vest. His face was powdered white just as it had been when Stu had last seen him.

Otakay went out to greet him. He bowed slightly and the chief bowed back. They smiled at each other and the White Chief said something to Otakay that Stu couldn't hear. They continued to the doorway, the bodyguards trailed after them.

The White Chief didn't look at Stu but talked to Graham about the generator. Graham explained to the White Chief how it worked but Stu got the impression he didn't understand a word he was saying.

At one point the chief turned to Otakay. "Do you think you could operate it?"

"Operate it? Yes, but when it breaks it's hard to say if we would be able to fix it. Having said that, some of our smartest people have been working with the white man to understand it."

The White Chief nodded. "Bring me to the two boys."

They went up a flight of stairs to the dinosaur exhibit. There the two boys were brought before the White Chief. They looked frightened but when the White Chief smiled kindly at them they seemed to relax a little.

"They really are just boys, aren't they?" the White Chief said. "Please tell me your names? I promise we won't hurt you."

"Justin and Anthony."

"Where are the adults you told Otakay about?"

The boys looked at each other. "We . . . don't know . . . We're worried."

The White Chief looked at Otakay.

"I've sent out a small search party but there has been no sign of them. We doubt they're still alive."

The boys tried to hold back their tears.

The White Chief nodded and turned to the boys. "I'm sorry, Justin and . . . Anthony." He spoke as if he had a hard time pronouncing the names.

"I want to give you a choice. It's not often you're given a choice. I know Otakay was rough on you but that's the world as it is right now. It used to be soft and easy. You used to be able to get whatever you wanted, but that's not the case anymore."

The two boys looked up at the White Chief, tears rolling down their faces. "We are a civilized people. We are a fair people. We are the only hope for humanity. If you join us you'll be taught, have food and a safe place to sleep at night. What do you say?"

The boys didn't say anything for a long time.

"What is that white stuff on your face?" the quiet one blurted out. The other boy covered his mouth trying to hide his laughter.

Otakay stepped up and raise his fist. "Insolent bastards!"

The two boys tried to run but were caught by two of the savages and held around the waist.

"It's okay," The White Chief said, raising his hands and Otakay stepped back and the two savages released the boys who stopped struggling.

"The boys are just curious," The White Chief said. He turned to the boys. "Before the Outbreak I had a vision in which one of my ancestors came to me in the form of a white tiger and spoke. He said I would be called The White Chief and would be very powerful but only if I became one with the white tiger. "

Stu glanced at Otakay at the mention of the white tiger and thought of Otakay's vision. Otakay did not show any sign of recognition. Surely Otakay must have heard this story. Did the big black man really have a vision involving the white tiger? Or was it just made up, a fanciful wish after lack of sustenance?

"The white tiger told me the white man would pay for raping Mother Earth and ignoring her warning signs," The White Chief continued. "And that since I had always listened to Mother Earth and had never taken more than necessary I was chosen as I would be rewarded."

The twin boys listened and didn't say anything.

"So you can choose to join us, if you so desire."

"What happens if we don't want to?"

The White Chief smiled. "We can live in harmony but we're taking the museum and I don't suspect you will live very long out in the wilderness."

"And what about Ewan and Ashley?"

The White Chief frowned and looked over at Otakay.

"Those are the names of the two adults that were with them."

The White Chief nodded and turned back to the boys. "Well that depends on them. If they deem worthy they might be able to join the tribe, but it's much harder to join as an adult than a child."

The boys looked at each other. One whispered in the other's ear.

"We want to stay here."

"Excellent," The White Chief smiled.

The boys were lead back to their room and the White Chief toured the rest of the museum.

He frowned when he saw the First People exhibition on the first floor. There was a hollowed out canoe behind plexi glass, Native art hanging on the wall and paintings of Europeans encountering the Natives. The White Chief stopped in front of one oil painting of a bare-breasted Native welcoming a boatload of Englishmen. "I never understood why the white man always celebrated their conquest of our land. Columbus Day is a travesty."

"I don't think they feel any shame," Otakay said.

The White Chief took the painting off the wall and held it at arms distance. "This painting is shameful. The white man always thought we were a bunch of cloth-less savages."

Stu thought of the woman he saw changing in the shopping mall.

Because you are a bunch of savages, he thought. *You are the ones without shame.*

The White Chief tossed the painting on the ground. "I want all these paintings burned."

Otakay bowed in obedience.

They moved into the Korean exhibition where there was pottery and statues. Some of the pieces made of gold had been stolen but most of the artwork was still there.

"We need to start moving part of the tribe here," The White Chief said.

"Yes, chief."

The White Chief stopped walking and turned to Otakay. "You did well, Otakay. For that I will reward you with the first pick of pods in our new home."

"Thank you, chief," Otakay said, smiling. "Forgive me for asking this but will we move the entire tribe here?"

"That will be a matter for the council to decide." The White Chief looked around the museum. "There will certainly be challenges to moving everybody here."

The White Chief finished his inspection and went back outside before it got too dark. Otakay stood and saw him off.

"Don't forget our priority is the Perpetuum generator," The White Chief told Otakay as he got into his town car.

Stu noted that half of the chief's bodyguards stayed with Otakay.

When the chief was gone, Stu walked casually up to Otakay. The bodyguards didn't even seem to notice his presence anymore.

"Don't forget it was the horrible white men who brought you the generator," Stu said.

Otakay scoffed. "Don't pretend you did me a favour. You had no choice."

"Just remember that you need us."

Homeless

The wind blew across the frozen city, picking up ash and snow and particles, displaying them across the parks and streets and sidewalks.

Ewan, Ashley and Albert walked on. After awhile they turned the corner and Ewan saw a building he recognized which meant they were almost back home.

They hadn't said anything since they had left the tank that morning. Ewan glanced over at Ashley who seemed more pensive than normal. He wanted to ask her if everything was alright but for some reason he didn't.

She's just upset over the book she found, Ewan thought. But he wondered if there was something more than that. Was there something she wasn't telling him? He pushed the thought quickly out of his mind.

They stopped briefly underneath a spruce tree, wishing there was a way to build a fire but the snow had made it all but impossible. They knew they should continue but Ewan could tell nobody had the energy to move on, even though they were so close. They would rather suffer the cold than continue to walk.

Ashley folded her arms against her chest and said, "I am Ozymandias, king of kings. Look on my works, ye mighty and despair!"

"What's that?" Ewan asked, his teeth beginning to chatter.

Ashley half shrugged and shook her head. "Forget it."

"Is that Shakespeare?"

"I said just forget it," Ashely snapped. "What does it matter if it's Shakespeare or Blake or Wordsworth?"

Ewan frowned, puzzled at Ashley's hostility. "What happened in the hospital?"

Ashley tilted her head forward, glancing down at the snow. Ewan looked at her, waiting, her chest heaving.

"Some things are best forgotten," she said after some time.

"Come on," Ewan said. "We should keep moving, otherwise we'll freeze to death."

"Just let us rest a little longer," Ashley said.

Ewan was about to protest but something about the pensive, sad tone in Ashley's voice stopped him. Instead he rested his head against her leg and closed his eyes. He thought about just going to sleep. It would be so easy. And maybe they wouldn't wake up. The twin boys might miss them, might morn them but they would move on. He could be with Amy, Sophia and Tim again and that thought filled him with joy. He wouldn't have to fight the Creatures anymore.

Ewan was dozing when he heard the sound of many footsteps running. The sound was coming closer and Ewan snapped out of doziness. He got up and grabbed his spear. The sound was a soft padded thump, thump of many feet hitting the snow, like a small army was approaching.

"Get behind the trees," Ewan said.

Each of them crouched behind a tree. Ewan grabbed his spear tightly, now feeling the adrenaline course through his body. As they waited for the footsteps to approach, Ewan looked over at Ashley. Her eyes were glazed over with a film of sadness. He tried to make eye contact with her but she wouldn't look in his direction.

It turned out it wasn't an army approaching, or even a human. Instead a large chestnut-coloured horse appeared from the distance. It was galloping at full speed towards them. Its head stretched forward and its mane flapped in the wind.

It seemed to sense or smell the humans behind the trees and stop about twenty meters away. It turned ninety degrees, its strong sleek muscles glistened in the wind.

Ewan couldn't believe it. He couldn't remember the last time he had seen an animal, let alone a beautiful horse. How had it survived for so long? It seemed all but impossible.

Ewan watched the horse, mesmerized by its beauty and prowess. It let out a low, fluttering whiny and trotted closer to the trees. As it did so, Albert stepped out from behind his hiding spot and took a couple of hesitant steps towards the horse, holding out his hand, clicking his tongue to the roof of his mouth.

Ewan wondered where the horse had come from. It had no saddle, yet he knew there were no wild horses anywhere near so it must have somehow come from somebody's barn, escaped somehow. It must have a good hiding spot somewhere, sensing the night's danger and staying put until morning.

Ewan didn't believe in miracles, but he couldn't think of any other way of describing it. Was it a miracle?

Everything seemed to slow down in time. Albert slowly moved closer, the horse threw its strong neck up. It's large dark eyes seemed friendly and inviting. Maybe it needed companionship and sensing Albert wasn't a threat, stepped closer.

Albert stretched out his fingers and slowly held them under the horse's large nostrils. The horse smelled Albert and then nudged him. Albert smiled and ran his hand through the horse's thick mane. Its neck muscles pulsed with its breath.

Albert looked back at Ashley and Ewan who were just staring in bewilderment. Was this real or was this just a dream?

Suddenly, the horse whinnied, threw its head upwards and galloped off, kicking up snow as it went. Ewan watched as it disappeared into the distance. The sound of its strong hoofs echoed from the cement and glass long after the horse had disappeared.

"Well, you look at that?" Ewan mumbled.

They decided to continue on. Their mood was more jovial than an hour before. Ashley was smiling now and Albert was walking quicker, his head held up. A sense of hope seemed to hang over the travellers. If a horse could appear to them like a mirage then what else was possible?

Soon they saw the ROM in the distance, the jagged glass edges against the old brick siding. It looked like a spaceship had crash-landed right on Bloor Street. Ewan hadn't been away from the museum for so long in years and although he was happy to get away from it, he was equally as happy to return to it.

But wait . . . Something was wrong. He saw people walking in and out of the front door. How was it possible? Was he imagining it? No. There was a Lincoln town car parked in the front that hadn't been there before. How had it gotten there? They must have gas somehow.

"Stop," he told Ashley and Albert. He directed them behind a parked car and together they crouched.

"What's wrong, chap?"

Ashley looked at Ewan, a frown on her face. She had seen the people too.

"My God, Justin and Anthony," she said.

She started to run but Ewan caught her. "We don't know who they are or what their purpose is."

"They better not have harmed the boys," she said, struggling to get away from Ewan. She was strong and Ewan was faint from hunger and the long trek and she slipped from his grasp. She started to run.

"Doctor, you have to stop her," Ewan said, unable to breathe.

"Lass," he called out. "Lass!"

"Not so loud, they'll hear you."

But Ashley did stop. She looked towards the museum and then back towards Albert and Ewan. She turned and walked back to where Albert and Ewan were.

"What do we do now?" she asked.

"Good question," Ewan said, looking towards Albert.

"What's going on? Are their Creatures up there?"

Ewan shook his head. "No, humans."

"Well they can't be so bad then."

"I don't know," Ewan said, hesitating. He still remembered all the looting and the murders before martial law was declared. They probably did as much as or more damage than the Creatures had done. Had anything changed now?

"I guess we go to my funhouse."

Ashley shook her head. "No, I'm not leaving the boys. I need to know where they are."

"Perhaps they are in hiding," Ewan said, hopefully.

"But what if they're not," Ashley said. "What happens if they have them locked up somewhere? We need to free them."

He thought about how they would do anything to help Tim. Ewan had grown fond of the boys. They watched for awhile, crouched behind the car, shifting their weight trying to stay warm. The sun was sinking low on the horizon. It wouldn't be long before the Creatures would be stirring.

After about thirty minutes they saw several people exit the ROM and get into the Town Car and start the engine. Then this tiny figure with a Native American chief's headdress came out of the ROM. One of the other men opened the door for the chief and helped the chief into the car.

The town car pulled out, went around an over turned car and drove off in the opposite direction. Ewan watched it until it disappeared from the landscape.

He turned to Ashley and Albert. "What do you think?"

"I think we should just present ourselves. Come in peace, so to speak," Ashley said.

"They don't look very friendly," Ewan commented.

"We are surrounded by those Creatures. Nobody looks very friendly."

Ewan looked at Albert who up to this point hadn't said anything. "Doctor Winkler? What are your thoughts?"

"The way I see it, we have several choices. We could, as the lass suggests, throw ourselves at their mercy. But the outcome will be unknown. We could attack them but then it would most likely result in our deaths. My vote is we regroup at the funhouse and see if we can learn more about these people."

"But what about Anthony and Justin?"

"If they are alive then they will be alive for another day."

"The doctor is right," Ewan said. "We can't do anything for them now."

Back at the funhouse they collapsed from exhaustion. They slept uninterrupted for eight hours and woke the next morning and Albert made them all eat cereal with yogurt — in the form of baby food.

Once they had finished eating, Albert plugged in the hard drive to an outlet that was hooked up to the generator. He then took an old monitor from a junk pile.

"Doctor Winkler, we need to go get the boys," Ashley said.

"Let me look at what's on this drive first."

Ashley tried to convince Albert that whatever on the hard drive could wait but once he was at the computer Albert became almost unresponsive.

"It's okay," Ewan told Ashley. "He's not going to be very useful in any rescue operation anyway."

Ewan searched through Albert's things and found an old pair of binoculars.

"Come on, let's do a little scouting."

Ewan and Ashley found a good vantage point behind a burnt out Honda on Queen Street where they could stake out the museum. Trees lined both sides of the streets, casting small shadows on the snow. Icicles had formed on the abandoned vehicles.

They had brought a couple of sleeping bags and a lawn chair so they could stay warm but even with them they had a hard time keeping their minds from the possibility of freezing to death.

Ewan didn't know how long they watched but there seemed to be lots of activity from the museum as people came in and went.

"What do you think they are doing?" Ewan asked.

Ashley shrugged. "Probably moving in. They think they've hit the jackpot. Large space free of Creatures with all the light and energy they could want."

"Really . . . you think they're friendly?" Ewan asked. "You think we can go up and just ask them to give the boys back?"

"I don't know."

Ewan looked at Ashley. He thought about how she had taken care of him when he had first lost Tim. He probably would have died of starvation if it hadn't been for her.

"How about I go up there and talk to them. You wait here and if I don't return before sundown you have your answer."

Ashley didn't say anything for a long time but eventually she shook her head. "No, I don't want you to do that."

"At least we'll know for sure."

"What do you think Doctor Winkler will find on that hard drive? You figure anything useful after so much time?"

"If anybody can do anything with that hard drive it's Doctor Winkler."

They lapsed into silence for a long time. They took turns watching the ROM with the binoculars but the activity seemed to have stopped. Ashley had brought a book to read but hadn't touched it.

"Why don't you want kids?" Ashley asked.

"Look what happened to the ones we were put in charge of."

Ashley looked at Ewan as if she had been slapped.

"I'm sorry," Ewan said. "But it's true. This world is not fit for children."

"You've wanted to quit the moment I met you. Even with Tim, you've always wanted to lie down and just die."

Ewan felt anger swelling up inside of him. "That's not true. I'm here, aren't I? I just offered to risk my own life to get Justin and Anthony back."

"That's just another way for you to quit and not feel horrible about it."

Ewan wondered if Ashley was trying to hurt him on purpose. "What is happened to you?"

"What do you mean? Justin and Anthony may be dead. I can't bear to think of it."

"No, I meant before that. What happened in the hospital? You haven't been yourself."

"Nothing happened. It was just the thought of how my parents died. My dad and that stupid book."

Ewan could tell Ashley was lying but he couldn't understand why. What had she seen there for her to lose her optimism? "I'm sorry about that but I don't think that's the reason," Ewan said.

"Why does there need to be a reason?"

"Okay, you don't have to tell me," Ewan said in frustration.

"What do you think would have happened if we had met before the Outbreak?"

"What do you mean?"

"Well, do you think we would have gotten together?"

"I would have been married for starters. I loved Amy more than anything."

"You don't think you could learn to love me as you loved Amy?"

"I don't know Ashley. That's like asking…"

"Sometimes I think if I had a baby, you know, of my very own then things wouldn't seem so bad."

Before Ewan could say anything, a group of men carrying boxes exited the ROM and headed up Queens Street, directly towards them.

Ewan quickly glanced around, looking for someplace to hide but there was no obvious spot where they wouldn't be seen. If they crawled into the trees they would have to contend with the Creatures and …

"Quick," he said. "Into the car."

They opened the car door and crawled in. Ashley hid out in the back while Ewan hid in the front, his body pressed against the floor.

Soon he heard the soft footsteps crunching in the snow. Ewan held his breath, praying they would pass them by without notice.

"I don't see why we should be looking for them," a voice said.

"Because Otakay told us to, dimwit. Who are you to question orders?" a deep voice said.

"They're dead by now. The Creatures got them."

"I hope we catch them and cook them up nicely. I haven't had a good meal in months."

"We're not going to find anything. Let's just make this quick."

Ewan listened but the footsteps dissipated down the street. Ewan didn't dare to breathe for a long time. After awhile Ashley got up the courage to lift her head and look through the broken window.

She motioned Ewan to get up. He lifted his head. The search party was nowhere to be seen.

"Cannibals," he said. Back in the early days of the Outbreak he had heard rumours that some people had turned to cannibalism but he had never actually witnessed it.

He looked at Ashley who had become pale.

"We need to get Justin and Anthony out of there," she said.

Ewan nodded. *If they are still alive*, he thought.

"What do you suggest?"

"We get Doctor Winkler to help us."

They returned to the funhouse where they went through the maze of mirrors and found Albert pacing excitedly back and forth in his lab room.

"You wouldn't believe what I've found," he said. "I have all the early information about H-Strain. The first man to contract it was indeed an Employee for Albros named Sandy Middleton. He worked in one of the factories in North York. Apparently he killed four other patients, five nurses and two doctors before he was killed with a scalpel by an old lady in a wheel chair who was in the geriatrics ward."

Ewan raised his eyebrows and Albert just shrugged. "I couldn't make that up if I tried."

"That's great but is that going to help us find a cure?"

Albert walked over to his desk and picked up the tube of blood he had found at the hospital. "If you're asking can I reverse the effects of the H-Strain, the answer is no, but I might, with some more studying and the right resources, be able to prevent somebody else contracting it."

"You said the H-Strain worked like cancer with the body's own cells attacking each other?" Ashley said.

"Yes, fast forward through the early tests and stages, the doctors realized it worked much like cancer, in fact could probably be classified as a form of cancer, except, according to the studies done, it seems to attack the body more aggressively."

Ashley looked at Ewan who rubbed his head.

"Doctor Winkler, I think that's all fantastic but we have a bit of a problem."

"A problem bigger than the Outbreak, lass?"

Ewan wondered if Albert was trying to be sarcastic but he wasn't sure if he was capable of such things.

"No," Ewan said. "It's a different type of problem. The people who have Justin and Anthony are cannibals."

Albert frowned, looking from Ewan to Ashley. "I'm not sure I'm following you folks."

"You really want me to say it? We think they're going to kill and eat the boys," Ewan said, his stomach was queasy just thinking about it.

To Ewan's surprise Albert shook his head. "You don't have very good logic, Walder."

Ewan frowned. "The boys are outsiders. I'm sure they'll see them as captives."

"Just because those people are cannibals doesn't make the boys in more or less danger. Cannibalism is an extremely natural condition in ecosystems and has been recorded in more than fifteen hundred species. As a biologist, I'm surprised you don't know that."

Ewan closed his eyes and rubbed his forehead, trying to remain calm. "Surely you don't agree with it?" He then opened his eyes, thinking of something. "Albert . . . you haven't. . ." He couldn't finish the sentence, his voice full of revolution.

"Of course not chap, I told you, I'm a vegan but that doesn't mean I let a sense of inconsistent morals govern my thought process."

"Doctor," Ashley said. "Regardless of what you think of cannibalism my boys are in danger and we need to form a plan to get them out."

"I'm afraid I have limited experience in this field. Perhaps if I had been in the military you might find my advice useful but since my realm of expertise is purely scientific I don't think I can help."

"But surely you can think of something," Ewan said, desperately.

Albert sighed and fell silent for some while. "I think we need to attack them at night when they least expect it."

"But how do we do that?" Ewan said. "We'll never be able to get past the Creatures."

"Lassie, I seem to remember you like classic literature."

Ashley nodded hesitantly.

"Are you familiar with the Trojan horse?" Albert said.

Ashley suddenly smiled brighter than she had in a long time. "Doctor Albert Winkler, you are a genius!"

"What do horses have to do with anything?" Ewan asked.

Ashley looked at Ewan, smiling but with her forehead creased. "You're telling me you've never heard of the Trojan horse?"

The Plot

Stu found Graham in the basement, sitting and staring at the Perpetuum generator. His eyes were red and he was pale. He barely looked up at Stu when he approached. If it was possible, it seemed as if he had even lost more weight than before. His skin was knitted tightly around his cheeks, forehead and chin as if it were saran wrap.

"When was the last time you took a break?" Stu asked.

Graham blinked. "I don't know."

Stu looked around. The light was a tawny-orange and there were various parts scattered around the room. "Where are all your disciples?"

"They're meeting with Otakay."

"About what?"

Graham shrugged. "Reporting to him I guess."

Stu crouched next to Graham so he was no more than a foot away from his ear. He then grasped a clump of his long greasy hair. Graham's eyes went wide in surprise but then narrowed.

Stu stared at him. "You realize the information in your head is the only thing that is keeping us alive. If you give it away freely we're as good as dead."

Graham yanked his head back, trying to escape Stu's grasp. "No, what is keeping us alive is our continued usefulness. As soon as the tap turns off then we're dead."

Stu let go of Graham and sat back. "You need to stall them."

"I am but I can only stall them for so long. We need to come up with an alternate plan."

"I'm working on it."

"Well you better work faster, because I don't know how much more I can teach them about the generator."

Stu got up, dusted off his kimono. "You don't look very well Graham. I think you need some rest."

Graham looked up at Stu, a half smile on his face. "Now you mention it, I think I'm coming down with something."

Stu climbed the stairs back to the main floor where he bumped into Chenoa who was carrying a basket of clothes. She was wearing a white tank top with bellbottom jeans. It was different seeing her in more casual clothes and not bundled up in a thick sweater. She looked more energized, a little healthier.

"Where is Otakay?" Stu asked.

Chenoa shrugged. "He might be in our pod. I haven't seen him since this morning."

Since the White Chief had granted Otakay first pick of the pods, he had commandeered the top floor of the ROM which had once been a restaurant. It was spacious and had a beautiful view of the city. It was certainly a step up from the salon in a shopping mall.

"How's Krista doing?"

"I don't know any Krista."

Stu frowned. "Stop playing games. You know who I'm talking about. Mal something."

"You mean Makawee?"

Stu had to control his frustration. "Yes."

"She's doing fine. She's healthy.'

"I want to see her."

"You will have to ask the White Chief."

"But I'm asking you. I know you're taking care of her. You can make it happen."

"Makawee doesn't want to see you."

"She's carrying my child. Certainly I have a right to my child."

Chenoa frowned. "You raped her. You have no rights. In our tribe that is punishable by death. The White Chief, in his wisdom, sees fit to keep you alive."

"So if you had your way, you would execute me?"

Chenoa looked down at her basket. "I told you, it's not up to me."

"That's right, it's always up to the White Chief."

"Careful. Do not speak against the White Chief."

"Why? You'll kill me twice? I'm a warrior and warriors don't fear death."

270

Once again, Stu climbed the stairs to the top of the ROM. He knocked on the tall double doors but when there was no answer he opened it and looked inside. It seemed they were still in the process of moving in, as furniture and clothes were lying around the floor.

"Otakay?" Stu called out but there was no answer.

He eventually found Otakay in the glass room talking to a group of savages that Stu recognized were working with Graham. The glass room was on the fourth floor and looked out onto the city below. From where they were, Stu could see the waste and destruction from a different perspective. To the south, they could see Queen's Park and past that there was nothing but high rises.

When Otakay noticed Stu enter he told the savages to go back to work. They glared at Stu on their way out but didn't say anything. On the table Otakay had a diagram of the Perpetuum generator.

When they were alone, Stu said: "I'm afraid the White Chief might not keep his end of our bargain."

"And what bargain is that?" Otakay asked.

"The one where he spares our lives in return for the generator."

"The White Chief will either let you live or die. There's nothing I can do about it."

"What if I convinced the council you should be made chief? That the White Chief should resign."

Otakay shook his head. "It doesn't work like that."

"Who says how it should and shouldn't work? The council? The White Chief?"

Otakay scowled. "You couldn't possibly have any sway over the council."

"If I deliver them the generator they will listen to me."

Otakay laughed. "I just spent an hour with the mechanics. They briefed me on everything about the generator."

"You don't think Graham would be foolish enough to teach them everything, do you?"

Otakay paused, his eyes glaring at Stu. "My mechanics know enough to be able to do basic maintenance on the generator."

"You're a fool to think that will be enough. Your so-called mechanics are merely lackeys. Graham is the real genius; he's one of the founding members of Perpetuum. He can build you a generator. It might take time but he'll be able to do it."

"You're just trying to save your own skin."

"Damn right I am."

Otakay leaned his large fingers against the window and stared out at the city. Stu wondered what he was contemplating.

Eventually Otakay turned to Stu. "You ever wonder about things? Wonder where they'll lead you? You wake up each day and make a series of inconsequential choices like one day you'll take your driving test and then the next you decide you can make a living from it. And then one day you get robbed at knife point so you start to carry a gun for protection. But then you figure you have to learn how to shoot that gun so you practice at the shooting range. Then you realize you enjoy shooting guns and go to the range after work to relax.

"Then this crazy Outbreak occurs and all those hours spent at the gun range actually come in handy. Then you meet this old Indian who at first seems batshit crazy but after awhile starts making some sense but you're not sure if it's just because you've listened to him for too long or because you have no alternative. Then you get something you've never ever received you're entire life: some respect. You're not just that dumb nigger that never had enough money to go to college or get a decent job."

Stu nodded. "You and I are not so different. I grew up poor as well. I joined the Air Force to get away from my abusive family. After that I became an ambulance driver."

Otakay's eyes flared. "You and I are very different. I don't rape women."

Stu sighed. "At the time I thought we were possibly the last people on the Earth. I didn't do it because I enjoyed it, believe me. I did it so the human race wouldn't become extinct. I saw the way you hurt those children. You of all people understand we must take extreme measures."

Otakay lowered his large brown eyes. "I shouldn't be talking to you."

"But you are because I understand." Stu said. "What was your name before you joined the tribe?"

Otakay didn't say anything but stood motionless.

"Is it forbidden to talk about the past?"

Otakay shook his head. "No, just frowned upon."

"Then why won't you tell me? I hate all these fucking fake redskin names. People should be called the names they were given at birth."

"Tim," Otakay said. "Timothy Poole."

"Tim. . . I like that name. Timothy Poole. It's a good Aryan name."

Otakay laughed, lifting his massive arms, palms raised. "Do I look like an Aryan to you, you racist bastard?"

Stu smiled. "Don't you think Otakay is just another slave name? Don't you want to be known by the name your mother gave you?"

But before Otakay could say anything else he heard the sharp, loud sound of footsteps coming up the stairs and a man appeared in the doorway. He was a young man with a shallow face and smooth skin.

"Otakay, we have found one."

"Found who?"

"One of the people who occupied the museum."

Otakay smiled. "Thank you, Nakai. I will come see him."

Stu followed Otakay downstairs to the main lobby where the savages surrounded an old man and a large machine. The machine was ten feet high and about six feet across. The metal was rusted and was discoloured in places but there were also parts of the machine made with some sort of strong glass and the glass seemed to be in better shape than the metal. Across the side of the machine in large block letters was "PERPETUUM INDUSTRIES: THE FUTURE IS NOW!"

The old man had a scraggily white beard and deep wrinkles. He was wearing a red snow suit. He had a big gash across his forehead that was bleeding all over the floor.

The savages let Otakay through until he was only a couple of feet from the old man.

"What is this thing?" Otakay asked Nakai.

"The old man says it's an old prototype of the Perpetuum generator. It doesn't seem to be working but we might be able to scrap it for parts."

Otakay seemed pleased. "Good work, Nakai. What's this old man's name?"

273

Nakai frowned. "We couldn't get a straight answer from him. I think he's suffering from some sort of dementia."

"How did you find him?"

"We spotted him only five blocks away and when he came close he ran. He led us into the basement of the old TD building where we found the generator. I tell you, we had a hell of a time getting it out."

Otakay turned to the old man. "What's your name?"

The man touched his forehead with his fingertips and looked at the blood as if he was surprised by it. "What's in a name but a form of control, a false label?"

Stu frowned at the old man. Although it sounded like gibberish, it was strange they had just been talking about names.

Otakay appeared annoyed and stepped closer to the old man. "Do you have a name?"

The old man looked around in confusion. "Probably once did, yes, but why do I need it now? We are the last surviving men on Earth. We know each other by faces. We need no names."

Otakay slapped the old man hard, knocking him backwards. The old man yelped like an injured dog and crawled towards Otakay.

"Please good chap, I don't know my name. It could be Bob or Chris or Nick for all I know."

"Alright," Otakay said. "What do you know of this machine?"

"I know it once gave me warmth and protection from the anomalies that haunt the night."

"It doesn't work anymore?"

"No, good chap. It broke down last year or so. I was out trying to fix it when I saw your band of merry travellers. I cannot remember the last time I saw a human. They gave me such a fright, they did. I thought they were Creatures who had come out in the day time. That is why I ran, good chap."

"How have you survived without the generator?"

"By hook and crook, good chap."

"Why don't you give a straight answer?"

"Straight, crooked? Don't all roads lead to the same path?"

Otakay looked visibly exasperated. He turned to Nakai. "What else did you find in the building?"

Nakai shrugged. "Nothing much. An old sleeping bag, a couple of biology books, and a candle."

Otakay grabbed the old man by the throat and started to choke him. "Last chance, old man."

The old man started to go purple. Cold, wrinkly fingers clawing uselessly against Otakay's. "Don't . . . call . . . me . . . old. I'm . . . young. . . compared . . . to . . . a . . . tree."

Otakay released the old man and threw him down as if he was a rag doll. The old man coughed and gasped for air.

Otakay turned away, crossed his arms and fell silent.

"What do you want us to do with him?" Nakai asked. "Shall we take him to the White Chief?"

Otakay shook his head. "No, put him with the boys. We'll serve him for dinner tomorrow."

"And what would you like us to do with the generator?"

"Let's leave it here for now. We'll have the smart white man look at it. See if it can be repaired or salvaged.

The savages dragged the old man away as he started to sing some sea shanty. Stu watched them as they disappeared into the stairwell.

"You shouldn't kill him yet," Stu told Otakay once they were alone.

"Why not?"

"Because there is something not right."

"What do you mean?"

"That man couldn't have lived out there all by himself."

"You think somebody took care of him?"

"Those two boys never mentioned anything about an old man. But probably the same people who probably lived in this museum also took care of him."

"So what? You think we can use him as collateral? We already have the two boys. I figure they're worth much more than some old man."

"Still," Stu said, thoughtfully. "Sun Tzu said know thy enemy. I don't like unanswered questions."

Otakay nodded. "Perhaps you are right but you think we can learn anything more from the crazy old man?"

Stu shrugged. "I know one thing: you won't be able to learn anything from him if he's dead."

275

The Horse's Mouth

Ewan couldn't remember ever feeling so claustrophobic in his life. Claustrophobic . . . it brought back images of Tim. In the darkness he could almost feel his small body curling up next to his. He could hear his shallow breathing.

Ewan tried closing his eyes. Could he sleep? He tried to relax but pain jolted up his body from the uncomfortable crouch the tight space afforded him.

Perhaps when he was younger he might have been able to fall asleep but now his joints were old and not as malleable as before.

He had nothing to do in the darkness but think. He thought about a lot of things, about Tim, about the twins he was trying to rescue, about Ashley and of course Amy.

They had gotten married at Niagara Falls. It had been a quiet affair with only a few friends and family. The justice of peace made them repeat their vows.

Until death do us part.

But did it mean the death of both man and woman? Was he free from his vows just because she had died and he had lived? They had never explained that part to him. He had never wanted another woman after meeting Amy and after she had died Ewan thought his life as well as love life was over.

So when Ashley had come along after so many years of a dead libido she had stirred something in him that he hadn't thought possible and for the first time in a long while he thought a future was possible. Maybe he was wrong and Ashley was right: having children would be a good thing.

Claustrophobic . . . he could hear Tim's voice in his head saying the word slowly, pronouncing every syllable carefully.

"Claus . . .tro . . . phobic," Tim said, smiling. "Claustrophobic."

Ewan was aroused from his daydreams by the sound of voices. Their first step of the plan seemed to have worked as Albert had led them to the generator Ewan was now hiding in.

After awhile the voices fell silent and he felt the whole generator move and he was shifted around in the small box.

He heard Albert play the crazy old man with perfection and it made him wonder when he had first met Albert how much of it had been an act. When the man with the deep voice started to beat Albert, Ewan wanted to jump out there and kill the cannibals but Albert had warned him they would probably rough him up and not to let emotion get in the way.

And so Ewan waited and waited. He cursed the Trojans and their silly horse. He figured the whole story must have been a myth, that there was no way anybody would fall for such a ploy. But after a long time in the dark, Ewan wondered what those old Greek soldiers must have felt spending hours in the Trojan horse, waiting for nightfall.

After what seemed like an eternity, Albert's egg timer went off and Ewan listened for voices. Despite the cramps, he didn't want to open the door. At least he felt safe in the box. Outside he didn't know what waited for him.

Claustrophobic, scared of small spaces, Timmy told him.
Cannibalphobic, scared of cannibals, Ewan said.
There's no such thing! Timmy said.
I didn't think there were such things as cannibals. No wait . . . the Creatures of course. But these were humans.

"You're stalling," Ewan told himself.

Ewan listened for voices, for footsteps. Hearing none, he opened the lock which they had especially created and pushed the door open. The door creaked open with a low groan.

A low neon light shone across the floor, and even though it wasn't very bright, it hurt Ewan's eyes. He shielded his eyes with the back of his hand and climbed out of the generator. His legs were sore from not being able to stretch them out for so long and he was reminded of the long airplane rides his family used to take.

Ewan had two long knives with him as weapons but he knew if he needed to use both extensively he would be in trouble. He would have to rely on speed and stealth for this mission.

He looked around the large lobby he knew so well and saw nothing. The cannibals were evidently certain the Creatures wouldn't be able to breach the building.

It was a fair assumption, since Ewan had made it many times.

Ewan headed for the walls and walked along the shadows until he got to the stairwell. The generator was working. The lights were on casting long yellowish shadows onto the floors. There he paused and listened again for any sound or indication of movement. When he heard nothing he climbed the stairs, again, hugging the wall.

He wondered what would happened if he was captured or killed. Would they torture him before they ate him? Regardless, he was sure the boys and Albert would die with him.

Ewan knew the museum better than most and he figured if the boys were being held captive they would be held on the third floor bathrooms on the eastern side of the building. That was where he headed. He hoped he wasn't wrong. He doubted he had time to search the entire building. Time was against him.

Ewan climbed the stairs silently, wondering how many cannibals were in the museum and where they would be staying. Would they be together or would they be spread out across the museum?

Most higher primates such as gorillas and monkeys lived and slept in groups. Although humans had similar instincts, he guessed the cannibals would have separate living quarters if possible. In the museum they would feel relatively safe from the Creatures so there would be no need to stay together.

Ewan wasn't sure if this was good or bad news for him. He wondered if he could pick the cannibals off one by one. Take out the guards first and then kill those who were sleeping.

No, Ewan thought. *I should stick to the original plan.*

Ewan reached the third floor when he heard voices whispering softly from Eaton's Court, directly to his right. They were getting closer. Ewan crouched behind a display. As the men entered the room, he could now hear the voices clearly.

"I wish the chief would just get it over with. I don't like that guy who pretends to be a samurai," one of the voices said. "He's nothing but trouble for the tribe."

Ewan's ears perked up at the mention of a samurai. Could it possibly be the samurai he had been dreaming about? Ewan held his breath and peeked over the displace case.

Luckily the two men weren't looking in his direction and didn't seem to be interested in much else other than their conversation.

"Yes but he's friends with Graham and Graham won't let anything happen to him," the other voice said.

"I don't understand. Why does Graham care what happens to the samurai?"

The voices dissipated but Ewan wanted to find out more about the samurai. Should he follow them or head towards the bathrooms?

Against his better judgement he followed the two men, careful not to make any noise. He crawled quietly until he was able to hear them again.

"I wish my wife could move here with me. Sometimes I feel like I'm trapped here."

The other man laughed softly. "If you feel trapped by having all the heat and light you want then I feel sorry for you. As for me, I'm just glad we're not cold all the time."

"I agree but sometimes I don't know if the chief knows what he's doing."

"Careful," the other man warned. "The wrong ears hear that and you'll be next day's dinner."

"It's the samurai's fault. He's corrupting the chief. I just know he is."

"Why do you have such a hard on for the samurai anyway?"

"Do you ever look at him? I mean truly look into his eyes? He's pure evil. I'm sure he's scheming something."

"Whatever it is, I'm sure the White Chief can handle it."

The White Chief? Ewan wondered. *Was that the man they had seen get into the car?*

Ewan decided he had heard enough and made his way towards the Eaton's Court but stopped when the floor groaned underneath him.

"Did you hear that?" the voice said, an octave lower than before.

"It's probably just the air pressure. It can make funny sounds."

"We should probably go check it out anyways."

279

Ewan took out his two knives and crouched, ready for action. The footsteps approached cautiously. Ewan had never killed another human before, not even during the mass hysteria of martial law when neighbours were killing neighbours and leaving them for the Creatures.

He supposed it was just like killing a creature. Ewan braced himself. His hands were shaking badly. He tried to swallow but his mouth was dry.

The footsteps came closer.

Get it together, Ewan . . .

When he saw the two shadows against the wall he forced his body to lunge.

The two men surprised, reacted slowly and weren't able to get their spears up quickly enough. Ewan stabbed each of them in the chest, aiming for their lungs. Simultaneously they both opened their mouths as if to scream, but Ewan dug his knives deeper into their bodies, the sound of metal cutting into flesh seemed loud. Blood poured onto the floor and onto Ewan's hands as he shoved the bodies against the wall. He released the blades, letting the bodies fall to the floor.

He stuck his hands against his chest, trying to control them but they kept quivering. He squeezed his eyes shut and then opened them.

Ewan debated whether he should hide the bodies. He might be able to shove them into the corner but he doubted he could do anything about the blood that was seeping across the carpet.

In the end Ewan decided to leave the bodies. He needed to keep moving. That was the only way he was going to free the twins.

Ewan wiped the blood off of his hands and cleaned the knives on the pants of the cannibals as best as he could and continued to the bathroom.

He found two more guards standing outside the bathroom. Luckily they looked tired and not very alert. He sat down behind a statue, debating what to do. Adrenaline was still pumping through his blood. He no longer felt the cramps in his legs. In fact he couldn't feel much of anything at all. He was completely numb.

What if he just stayed there? Waited until morning or someone to find him? What if he slit his own throat?

The twins and Albert would be dead. Perhaps roasted alive in unspeakable fashion. They were counting on him.

Ewan unlaced his dirty boots and took them off his feet. He had taken them off a dead soldier a couple years ago. The laces were frayed at the ends and the leather worn.

It was time to get new ones anyway, Ewan thought.

He looped one shoe across the room in a high arch, hitting a display case. The two cannibals looked up. They whispered to each other, getting louder as they seemed to be disagreeing with each other.

Eventually one of them slowly moved towards the sound, his spear held out in front of him.

Ewan frowned. Dealing with them separately was going to be more difficult. He realized too late his plan was faulty. Ewan got up into a crouch and watched as the first cannibal made his way towards the display case at the far end of the room. Ewan knew he had to make a move before they found the shoe . . . but what was he going to do?

Ewan wiped the sweat off his brow and took his other shoe and tossed it towards the opposite side of the room. It made a soft thumping sound as it hit the floor.

The cannibal that had remained by the bathroom straightened his back. "Timber?" he said.

The cannibal walked part way towards the sound he had heard but that was close enough for Ewan. Ewan stuck one knife into his belt and, crouching, he shuffled forward until he was behind the first cannibal. He stood up, pulled the cannibal's hair back and brought his knife around, digging the blade into the cannibal's neck. Blood gushed out.

Ewan then dropped himself onto the body of the dead man and started to crawl around the nearest display. He heard the other cannibal calling out to his friend.

"Cloud? What the hell? This some kind of joke?"

Ewan watched from the floor as the cannibal called Timber came closer. Timber stopped, noticing the pool of blood.

"Jesus," Timber said, turning and running.

Ewan knew he had to catch him. He couldn't risk the cannibal alerting the others. He sprinted across the room, almost tripping over the dead body. Ewan knew he wasn't going to catch the cannibal before he reached the stairs. In mid stride he grabbed the blade of his knife and threw it at Timber.

It dug into his shoulder blade and Timber yelled, stopped and turned to face Ewan. The cannibal pulled the knife from his back and threw it on the floor.

"You are a dead man," Timber snarled at Ewan, clutching his spear with both his hands.

Ewan didn't reply. Up close Timber didn't look like much. He was perhaps mid-twenties, with long thick hair and a scraggily beard. His skin was droopy and he looked slightly malnourished. But he had a spear and Ewan only had his single knife.

Timber lunged at Ewan with a quickness Ewan didn't expect. Ewan just managed to jump backwards, away from the spear.

Timber came at him again but this time Ewan easily sidestepped.

Ewan looked around for something he could fight Timber with. Ewan backed up again, not taking his eyes off of the spear point. He knew the other cannibal's spear was on the floor, about fifteen feet behind him. Should he run and pick it up? No, he knew if he exposed his back he would be a dead man. He took another step back. He would take it slow.

Timber smiled menacingly, shuffling sideways. Ewan matched his movements, so he stayed an equal distance away from the spear point. Timber kept shuffling, making a large circle around Ewan forcing him away from the spear.

Ewan frowned. Timber seemed to know what Ewan was thinking and was putting himself between the spear and Ewan. Ewan looked around for another plan. He saw Timber was trailing a thick line of blood behind him.

He had to think quickly.

Ewan knew there was roughly four to five litres of blood in a human and that a person could lose up to fifteen percent without any ill effect. Ewan sized Timber up. With his small stature and thin frame Ewan calculated he probably had no more than four liters but it would be awhile before he lost fifteen percent of that. Could he wait that long?

Ewan concentrated on Timber's movements. If he could somehow increase Timber's heart rate he would start losing blood faster.

Ewan stopped backing away and crouched, his feet wide apart and his knife at the ready.

Timber smiled, moving slowly towards him.

Ewan was ready for the cannibal's lunge this time and this time faked throwing his knife. Timber backed up and jumped sideways. Ewan moved closer, forcing Timber to jab again with his spear.

This dance went on for a few minutes. Ewan defended, just out of Timber's reach. Timber attacked. Ewan conserved his energy, allowing Timber to do most of the work. Even so Ewan was getting tired but he could see Timber was also slowing down. Blood was leaking out his back, forming a large puddle.

Ewan could slowly see confusion and terror form in his eyes. All Ewan had to do was keep it up. Yet he was exhausted and hadn't had anything to eat since the morning. They fought at an increasingly slower pace, like they were rehearsing a stage fight.

Timber swayed, his chest heaving. Ewan faked a thrust with his knife but Timber didn't even move.

If only I had the energy to deliver a killing blow, Ewan thought. But he didn't. His own limbs felt heavy and slow.

Timber cried out between gasps. "Somebody help!"

As Timber's voice echoed off the walls, Ewan listened for sounds of reinforcements. If anybody came he would most likely be dead. He could hardly move, let alone fight or run.

But nobody came. Timber's voice was lost in the darkness.

Ewan turned and concentrated on Timber. This time he concentrated all his effort and lunged at Timber who stepped back and thrust his spear.

Ewan saw the point come towards him but couldn't do anything about it. His muscles refused to respond to his firing electrons. The spearhead dug into the side of his waist. A cord of pain went up Ewan's stomach and into his chest. He staggered back and leaned against a display case, clutching his stomach.

Ewan could see Timber smile in the darkness, probably sensing victory; he lunged at Ewan. Ewan rolled, the spear hitting the glass display. Ewan dropped his knife and grabbed the spear with two hands and held on with all his effort.

Timber tried to pull the spear away, but Ewan wouldn't let go. His hands burned with the effort but he knew if he released his grip, he would be a dead man.

Timber yelled again for help but before he could get the words out of his mouth Ewan pushed off the display case with his back and half fell towards Timber who collapsed underneath Ewan's weight.

Ewan dropped the spear and reached for Timber's neck. Timber grabbed Ewan's wrists and dug his fingers into them. Ewan barely felt the pain, intently focused on using the last of his strength. Timber's face turned pale and he made horrible gasping sounds. Ewan tightened his grasp, using all the fury he could muster.

Timber reached up and dug his thumbs into Ewan's eyes. Ewan pulled his chest back but still kept the pressure on Timber's neck. Timber began to flop around like a fish, his eyes rolling back in his head. Ewan watched as the cannibal struggled with death. His hands went back to Ewan's fingers, trying to pry them off but then they flopped to his side.

Ewan didn't move, keeping his hands tightly around the cannibal's throat. Ewan didn't want to take any chances.

After what seemed like an eternity, Ewan released his grip and fell backwards, his eyesight went fuzzy and then he blacked out.

Ewan opened his eyes. He couldn't have been out for more than a few seconds but it felt like hours. He tried to sit up but a splitting pain pierced his stomach and then he remembered his wound. He felt the exposed flesh with the palm of his hands. He was still bleeding but the wound wasn't deep. It seemed that there hadn't been much power in the thrust. If he had been wounded at the beginning of the fight Ewan didn't doubt that the thrust would have been fatal.

He took off his belt and tied it around his waist, over the wound. He then slowly got up, almost passing out again but managed to steady himself against a glass display case.

He stumbled over to the bathroom. He twisted the knob and found the door was unlocked. Inside Albert and the twins were tied up and their mouths covered with duct tape. Their frightened eyes looked up at Ewan.

Ewan stumbled over and cut the cords that bound the twins' arms and legs and then moved onto Albert.

"What the bloody hell happened to you, old chap?" Albert asked.

Ewan tried to smile but the pain in his stomach worsened. "We need to get out of here," he said, gasping. It hurt to talk.

Albert went first and then the twins with Ewan in the rear. They crossed the large room towards the staircase.

"We're going up," Ewan said.

"Up?" Albert said.

Ewan nodded. He opened his mouth to explain but the pain made him nauseated and he had to reach out and grasp Anthony's shoulder to steady himself.

Luckily Albert didn't say anything else and they followed him as they climbed the stairs until they got to the very top.

They were in a small room with a couple of tables and overturned chairs.

"Now what?" Albert asked.

Ewan looked at the kids who still hadn't said a word. Their eyes were still full of fright and it reminded him of Timmy.

"Take . . . a chair . . ." he said. Ewan couldn't finish his sentence so he instead he motioned with his hands.

"Won't they hear us?" Justin asked.

Ewan reached out with his hand to try and comfort him but Justin recoiled in fear. Ewan frowned, confused until he realized his hand was covered in dried blood.

Albert took a chair and began to swing it against the glass. Albert wasn't very strong and it took him several tries before he even made a small crack in the thick glass. The chair looked like it had taken more damage than the class.

Albert paused, breathing heavily. Below Ewan could hear voices. It wouldn't be long before they figured out what was happening.

"Quickly," Ewan said, barely above a whisper.

Albert picked up another chair and continued his assault against the glass. Anthony and Justin seemed to wake from their shock and helped Albert. Eventually there was a tiny hole, big enough to put a fist through.

This seemed to reenergize them and Anthony grabbed the edge of the glass and pulled out a large chunk of glass. The cold air seeped in through the cracks and slowly filled the room. A few minutes later there was a gap large enough for the twins to get through.

"Get going," Ewan told them.

"Go where?" Anthony asked. His hands were bleeding from cuts from the glass.

"Stay . . . on the . . . roof for now," Ewan said, looking over at Albert who looked exhausted from the effort.

"No, we're not leaving you."

Anthony took up a chair and hit the glass but he wasn't nearly strong enough to make any headway.

"You should go," Ewan said.

The twins looked over at Albert who was looking around the room, seemingly oblivious to what was happened.

The twins made up their minds and crawled through the hole and out onto the roof. Ewan watched them as they slid down to the ledge and made their way around to the flat part of the roof. He hoped they would be safe from the Creatures.

With what little strength Ewan had left he pushed a table close to the glass wall. He then climbed on and laid flat on his back so his feet were facing the glass wall. He grabbed the side of the table with his hands and raised his feet. He could already feel his stomach burning. With as much might as he could muster he kicked his feet forward and smashed the glass. The shock rippled up his feet, past his knees and all the way to his torso but when he looked up a large part of the glass had shattered.

Ewan kicked again until there was a sizable hole they could crawl through. Ewan rolled off the table and clutched his side.

"Go . . . first," he told Albert.

Albert slowly climbed onto the table and through the hole. Ewan watched as Albert slid his way down the side of the roof onto the ledge below.

Ewan heard voices from below and thought he better hurry. He climbed back up on the table and through the hole.

The cold air clung to him, burning his stomach. Ewan took a deep breath and followed Albert down to the ledge. He then walked over to the older roof which was made of stone.

In the darkness he could see the twins shivering in the corner but whether that was from the cold or from fright, Ewan couldn't tell.

Albert was pacing back and forth muttering to himself.

"We need to start climbing," Ewan said. He peered down the side of the building. There were several ledges on each floor that if they were careful would provide footsteps.

Albert stopped suddenly. "You want us to climb down that!"

"It's either that or we get eaten by the cannibals," Ewan said. "I'll go first and then the twins and you go last."

"The twins are too small, chap," Albert said. "They'll never make it."

"They'll be fine. They'll have to be."

Ewan wouldn't allow himself to think about the height. The quicker he did it, the quicker he would get down.

He turned around and went down backwards, feeling the first ledge with his foot. He found it and then lowered his weight down. He looked down and saw the cracked cement road only four floors away.

"I can make it, Amy," Ewan said. "I can make it."

He looked through the window into the gallery but the glare from the window prevented him from seeing much.

Ewan again crouched and clutched the ledge and then lowered his feet to the next ledge below. His hands burned with the effort of holding his body weight until he managed to find the windowsill.

Again he lowered himself slowly. He repeated the process until he was one floor away. He managed to rotate himself on the tiny ledge until he was facing outward. He looked down below for any sign of the Creatures but there was none. He wondered if they were hiding in the alleyways or under the cars or if they had abandoned the museum all together. Ewan figured that was wishful thinking.

Ewan took out the knives from his waist and held them out in front of him. He then leapt to the cement pavement below. He bent his legs hoping they would take most of the shock. When he hit the ground, the shock reverberated painfully through the soles of his feet, up his shins and through to his knees.

Ewan tried to remain upright but he was pitched forward, losing grip of both of his knives. Immediately two Creatures came towards him, incredibly fast. Ewan scrambled in the dark for the knives. He wasn't going to make it.

He turned to face the Creatures who were bearing down on him. But before they reached Ewan a black Audi Q7 e-tron sped out of the alleyway and crashed into them, pinning them against the wall. Ewan could hear a loud crunch as their bones snapped and their bodies crumpled.

Ewan looked behind the wheel and saw Ashley. He smiled and got into the passenger's side and quickly closed the door.

Ashley glanced down at Ewan's blood-soaked shirt. "What happened?"

"Got stabbed."

Ashley bent over and kissed Ewan on the mouth. Ewan smiled and held her tightly. All he could smell was oil and gas and sweat.

"Thank you for saving my life."

"Again."

Ewan smiled ignoring the pain. "Again. Thank you for saving my life again."

Out the window they could see the twins climb down one after the other. Despite what Albert had said, their small hands and feet fit well on the ledges and they were very nimble.

Ashley threw the car in reverse and backed up into a row of Creatures that had appeared from the road. Ewan watched on the dashboard monitor, which displayed the backup camera. The Creatures were being crunched underneath the wheels in a sickening, bone-crunching sound. But Ashley didn't stop. It almost appeared surreal as if it were a video game, something his students used to play.

"Where did you get the car?" Ewan asked.

"I borrowed it."

Ashley then hit the brakes and threw the car back into drive. She pressed down on the gas so hard that all four wheels spun on the sleek surface, creating a cloud of smoke and engulfing the Creatures standing on the side. The SUV launched forward, plowing through Creatures and stopping just short of the twins who had just jumped to the ground.

Ewan pushes the backdoor opening button and while the door opened upward the twins threw the back door open and threw themselves into the SUV and scrambled to shut the door.

Ashley looked around. More Creatures were coming towards them, surrounding them. A Creature jumped up onto the hood of the car and was pounding the window with its fists.

Ewan rolled down the window and grabbed the Creature's foot and pulled. The Creature toppled backwards.

"We need to keep moving," she said, her eyes wide with fear.

"What about the old man?" Ewan asked.

She pressed the gas once again and the Creature slid off the side of the car.

"We'll draw them away and then come back."

Ashley swung the wheel, turning the car down Bloor Street away from the Creatures. Ewan was looking behind them when he saw something come out of an alleyway. He had just enough time to register it was a Lincoln Town Car, the same one they had seen earlier. The car accelerated and smashed into them. The ground shook and Ewan's organs reverberated inside of him.

He tried to press down hard on his stab wound like he had been told to do but it was difficult with gravity pulling his body different directions.

Somewhere he heard the sound of smashing glass and metal but it sounded distant, almost surreal. Their car spun around and Ewan became disoriented until finally they skidded into a light post before coming to rest.

His head was buzzing and his vision went blurry.

"Kids?" he yelled. He couldn't see the twins in the back. He glanced over at Ashley who was bleeding from the forehead, her head rolled back on her neck.

The Creatures quickly swarmed them, jumping up on the roof and reaching through the cracked panoramic sunroof glass. The twins in the back squealed and hid beneath the seats.

"Ashley?" Ewan said, leaning over and touching her arm. He could feel the desperation in his voice. "Time to wake up!"

Luckily Ashley stirred and blinked and looked around her, a puzzled expression on her face as if she didn't quite understand where she was.

A Creature reached through the driver's window and clawed at Ashley. Ewan took a shard of glass and started hacking at the arm until black pile sprayed from the limb. The Creature didn't seem to feel any pain, however, as it kept clawing at Ashley.

Ashley touched the blood on her forehead. But then she seemed to shake the daze and put the car in reverse. The Creatures skidded off the rooftop and fell onto the pavement. She navigated backwards away from the Creatures and the Town Car.

The Town Car followed them as Ashley backtracked towards the ROM. The Lincoln's front end came close to the front end of the reversing SUV. Ashley didn't even look backwards; she used the self-navigating camera to avoid obstacles on the road, but smashed through the Creatures.

Ewan looked up and saw the Lincoln was so close to their front he could see the angry faces of the Cannibals.

Ashley turned a corner and threw the steering wheel around making the SUV skid 180 degrees until they were facing forward. Again she threw the gear lever back into drive. Ewan tried to orient himself and saw the Lincoln Car was beside them.

Ashley swerved the steering wheel bumping the side of the Lincoln. There was a loud smash of metal scraping metal but the Lincoln held steady.

Ashley swerved again and flung her entire body into the steering wheel. The SUV hit the Lincoln with such force that the Lincoln's wheels spun out and the car slid sideways through a handful of Creatures, hitting the curb and coming to a crashing halt, smashing into an advertisement sign.

"Where did you learn to drive like that?" Ewan asked.

"We need to get Albert," Ashley said, touching her forehead where she had been cut. "These Cannibals are persistent and will recover fast from the crash."

They found Albert clinging to the second floor window. A group of Creatures had congregated below him and were trying to reach him but he was just out of their grasp, unable to scale the side of the building. Albert glanced over his shoulder, and Ewan could see a look of fear on his face. It might have been funny under different circumstances.

Ashley straightened the wheel and accelerated into the Creatures, crunching them under her wheels and knocking some of them away. She then hit the break, skidding to a halt underneath Albert.

The old man, with remarkable agility, climbed down one more floor and then jumped onto the panoramic sunroof of the car, miraculously not crashing through the glass. The twins opened the rear sunroof and Albert jumped inside the car.

"Hold on," Ashley said, and then again accelerated away from the Creatures.

Ewan looked behind him to see the half-crumpled Town Car had just turned the corner and was bearing down on them.

They turned east on Bloor Street towards the 404 highway. Ewan reached through the window and pulled Albert through.

"Bloody terrible plan. Who thought that one up," Albert grumbled.

Ewan laughed and squeezed Albert's shoulder.

Ashley tapped the fuel gage. The electric charge indicator was hovering over empty. "We're going to have to ditch this pretty soon."

Ewan glanced over his shoulder. "We're going to have to shake our tail first."

Ashley nodded. "It's still several hours before dawn."

"Let's go back to my place," Albert said.

Ashley shook her head. "No, we can't lead them back there. It's our one safe place."

"Then where do we hide?" Ewan asked. "Can we out run them?"

Nobody spoke. The electric hum of the engine spurted on and the dark shadows blurred on past.

"Do you trust me?" Albert said.

Ewan looked back at him. "Nothing good ever started with that sentence."

"What choice do we have?" Ashley said.

The Town Car was still behind them.

"They must be low on gas too," Ewan said. "I think we should head to the funhouse. It's our only option."

"Head for the subway," Albert said.

"The subway," Ashley exclaimed. "It'll be crawling with Creatures."

"You just have to trust me," Albert said.

Ashley looked at Ewan. "What's the nearest station?"

Ewan thought for a moment. "Sherbourne. It's coming right up."

Ewan pointed to the sign and then turned to Albert. "You're absolutely sure about this?"

"I don't have time to explain and even if I did I'm not sure it would be very comforting."

"You always make me feel better, old man," Ewan said.

Ashley pulled the break and turned the wheel. The car skidded to a stop in front of the subway station.

"Go," she yelled.

Albert was the first out of the car and the twins were next. Ewan looked at Ashley. Ashley gave a forced smile and kissed Ewan and then got out of the car.

Ewan watched her hop the turnstile and disappear into the darkness. Ewan looked around and was surprised that he couldn't see any Creatures, however the Town Car came to a stop just behind them.

Ewan sighed and ran to the station. He glanced behind him to see two cannibals jump out. In the darkness he could see both of them were carrying bows.

Ewan tried to leap the turnstile without slowing but his foot caught the top rung and he fell headfirst onto the cement floor. His immediate response was to brace for the fall with his hands and felt the impact on his wrists but he managed to protect his head.

He got up, dusted his hands off, and continued to run. He ran down a long corridor which came to a set of stairs which he descended. It was warmer down here and no wind. He could hear Ashley's quick light footsteps in front of him and the shouting of the cannibals behind him.

Revolution

Stu felt something move and in an instant he opened his eyes and grabbed his knife from underneath his pillow. Stu found Otakay was standing over him, a look of amusement on his face. His wide shoulders blocked the light.

"If I wanted to kill you, I would have done it already."

Stu sat up, lowering the large knife but not completely. "What do you want?"

"The old man has escaped."

Stu wasn't overly concerned. How much damage could an old man do? "How?" he asked.

"Seemed like he had help. There are four dead guards on the fourth floor."

Stu stood up and stared at Otakay. He was naked, but didn't try to hide his nakedness. He faced Otakay, staring at him. But Otakay didn't blink. He just stared back at him.

"You white men are always trying to make up for your small penis size."

Stu sneered. "Does Chenoa tell you she loves your big dick?"

Otakay sighed. "Put some clothes on. The White Chief wants you."

Stu didn't move. He just stood there. "Why? Because this old man has disappeared?"

"He hasn't disappeared. One of them stole a car. But we've sent a group after them. They won't get far."

"How did they get in in the first place?"

"That's what we are trying to determine."

"Why do I care what happens to them?" Stu was actually happy the old man had disappeared, although he would have liked to have had a chance to question him first.

He believed he wasn't as crazy as he had let on. No, it had been an act from the beginning. He had wanted to get caught. But why? It must have had something to do with the generator. The old man had wanted it to fall into their hands. But again Stu didn't understand why.

Stu was intrigued but he didn't let on. Instead he climbed back under the blanket.

"The White Chief will have to figure it out himself. Goodnight."

"One doesn't refuse a summons from the White Chief."

"Allow me to be the first, Tim" Stu said.

"Don't call me that."

"Why not? It's your name."

"Not anymore, Stuart. I told you. I've been reborn."

"Whatever. I'm going back to sleep and if you ever wake me up again I will kill you."

Stu closed his eyes, sincerely hoping that he wouldn't have to kill Otakay. He had big plans for him.

He heard Otakay's breathing and shifting, as he moved from one foot to the other. Stu remained ready, his body tense, in case Otakay made any sudden movements towards him. But Otakay didn't attack him, didn't make any motion towards him. Instead he turned and his heavy footsteps dissipated. Only then did Stu relax.

For a long while, Stu didn't fall asleep. He lay there motionless thinking about the jailbreak the old man had pulled. He found he was admiring the old man or whoever had engineered the plan.

Of course it wasn't very hard to trick the savages. They were stupid, after all.

Eventually Stu managed to fall back asleep and when he woke he was startled to see the White Chief sitting cross-legged in front of him. He was dressed in the same white jeans and white shawl that Stu had first seen him in. His headdress had been laid down beside him. It was the first time Stu had seen the chief without his headdress; he wore his thin white hair braided back into a ponytail.

Stu stretched, as if unconcerned and sat up. Nobody was able to sneak up on Stu, yet somehow the White Chief had opened the door and sat mere feet away from him.

"Aren't you setting a bad precent?" Stu asked.

The White Chief frowned, puzzled. "What do you mean?"

"When I tell Otakay you came to me after I refused your summons, you're going to lose your authority."

"You think my authority is based upon ordering people around?" The White Chief asked, a small, amused smile on his face.

"If it isn't then you have a problem," Stu said. His skaku knife was under his pillow and easily reachable. In several swift movements he could cut the chief's throat and watch him bleed out. But no, he would leave that to others.

The White Chief nodded as if he understood what Stu was thinking.

"Did you recapture the old man and the kids yet?"

The White Chief didn't answer which was indication enough.

Stu shook his head. "This won't look very good for you, I'm afraid. People will talk."

"I didn't come to talk about the captives."

"What did you come here for then?" Stu asked. "What is so important that you broke custom?"

"Death."

Stu waited for the White Chief to continue but when he didn't, Stu asked, "What about it?"

"Are you afraid of it?"

"No, of course not," Stu said, surprised.

The White Chief smiled. "In my opinion, every white man is afraid of it. You took our land because you were afraid if you didn't possess it, it would kill you. It makes you so predictable."

Stu wondered what the old chief was getting at so he didn't say anything.

The White Chief continued. "The council remind me I'm playing with fire. They say you're scheming to overthrow us, threaten to destroy everything we've built here."

"I'm just ensuring we still remain useful to you."

"You think once we learn everything about the generator then we'll eat you?"

"Give me one reason you wouldn't?"

"Apart from giving my word?"

"Your word doesn't mean much to me."

"Of course not. An immoral man can only have immoral thoughts."

Stu forced a smile on his lips. "You know you can never win."

"Why is that?"

"Because I'm prepared to do things that you're not. Murder, rape, steal. The winner is always the person who is willing to sacrifice the most."

"You are absolutely correct," the White Chief said, nodding. "But our goals aren't the same. You only want power and control. I want prosperity for the tribe and for that I'm willing to sacrifice myself."

Stu laughed. "So you've come here to tell me you're not afraid of death?"

The White Chief shook his head. "No, I know what you're planning and it won't work."

The White Chief stood up, put his headdress on and without saying anything left Stu watching after him puzzled.

When the White Chief left, Stu went downstairs and found Chenoa in the kitchen. She had filled the sink with water and was washing dishes with some homemade disinfectant. He watched her work, her long fingers dipped in and out of the soapy water.

She didn't notice him at first and Stu watched her from the doorway. Stu admitted she was beautiful. He never felt a sexual desire, as most of his old friends had described it but he felt something strange around Chenoa. It wasn't sexual — at least he didn't think so, but it was a desire to possess her.

Once Otakay is out of the way, Stu thought, *I will take her.*

Chenoa turned and saw Stu standing there staring at her. A look of shock spread over her face but she quickly covered it.

"What do you want?" she asked, frowning.

"Where's your husband?"

"He just left with a search party. The hunters who went out after the captives haven't come back yet."

"You think the old man killed them? The hunters, I mean."

Chenoa dried her hands and turned to face Stu. "What do you want with Otakay anyway?"

"I need to talk to him about something important."

Stu wanted Otakay to convince the council to see him. He had meditated after the White Chief had left and had decided a more direct approach would be more appropriate now that the chief knew of his plans.

No use in hiding now, Stu thought.

"I don't know when he'll be back," Chenoa said, returning to the dishes. "But whatever you have on your mind you can forget it."

Stu smiled. "What makes you think I have anything on my mind?"

"Tell me, did you have any friends before the Outbreak?

Stu laughed. "Why would you ask me something like that?"

"I bet you were the weird kid who everybody thought was going to buy a machine gun and kill everybody at school."

Stu shook his head. "No, I was never that obvious."

Chenoa turned her shoulders and looked at Stu with a strange, mild expression.

"What is it?"

"Stuart, I need to tell you something."

"Don't call me that," Stu said sharply.

"Makawee had a miscarriage last night. I'm sorry."

Stu stared at Chenoa, at first not registering what she was saying. It took him awhile to realize Makawee was Krista and she had been carrying his child. After it sunk in, he wasn't sure how he felt. What was he supposed to say? He felt a numbness expand in his chest, a sudden emptiness that he had never known before.

"Thanks for telling me," he said quietly, turning away.

"Stu," Chenoa said.

Stu glanced back at Chenoa. "What?"

"You're not going to try it again, are you?"

"Try what again?"

"Try to rape her again, are you? She's under the White Chief's protection. The last rapist was castrated then executed horribly."

"I will keep that in mind," Stu said.

He made his way to the common area. The building suddenly felt stuffy and cramped. He briefly wondered if the savages would allow him to take a walk by himself. He thought about trying but decided against it so instead he sat down on a bench. The savages stared at him strangely as they walked by, whispering to each other but Stu didn't care.

He turned his thoughts to Krista's child — his child. He didn't care about the death of the child. He was always baffled by parents' sorrow. They had the ability to reproduce infinitely so why cry over one death?

He had never felt much of anything when he had learned his parents were dead and it was the same now. He supposed doctors would have labeled him something but for Stu it was just how it had always been.

However it did ruin his plans of having an heir, at least for the time being. He didn't know how much he had wanted an heir until he had been told about Krista's pregnancy. Someone who could be as cunning and ruthless as he was.

He wondered what ancient kings felt when their heirs died. Did they feel sad or was it just another royal duty, same as sitting on a throne or giving out commandments?

Although Stu had never cared much for television, he had watched a show once about some ancient king or something who had eight wives. None of them would give him an heir and so he killed them all. He couldn't remember if it had been a documentary or some sort of network drama but now he wished he had paid closer attention.

Stu found Graham in the basement with his group of newly minted engineers. Graham seemed tired and unwilling to talk.

"Remember what I said before," Stu said.

Graham nodded vaguely but his eyes were glassy and seemed distant and Stu wasn't sure he got the message.

"Can we talk in private?"

But Graham shook his head. "I don't have time."

"This is important."

"I understand. I get it. What's there to talk about?"

Stu stared at Graham for a long moment before turning and walking away. The Art of War taught he should pick and choose his battles and Stu sensed this was a time to back down so he went upstairs and waited for Otakay to get back.

298

He stared out through the glass at the skyscrapers across the street. A triangle of sunlight had fallen on the cracked pavement in front of the museum. Weeds and wild flowers had sprouted through the snow and intertwined with each other.

Stu waited for about an hour before he saw Otakay and his search party appear from the street. Once back inside, Otakay took off his eagle mask and carried it under his shoulder.

"No luck?" Stu asked.

Otakay shook his head. "They must be dead by now."

"Killed by the old man and the two kids?" Stu asked, incredulously.

"Doubtful. The Creatures must have gotten them."

"Otakay, how can the White Chief allow them to escape?"

Otakay took a step towards Stu. "Don't you dare blame him for this."

"I demand to see the council."

Otakay shook his head. "It's never going to happen."

"Why not?"

"Because you're not a tribe member."

"They have to listen. The White Chief must be held accountable. It was his responsibility."

"You're just using this as an excuse," Otakay said. He then paused, looking at some point in the distance. "What do you hope to gain from this anyway?"

Stu glanced at the other members of the search party. "I think we should talk in private."

Otakay stared at Stu for several moments and then nodded to his hunting party. They looked at each other before reluctantly shuffling along. Stu watched them walk down the hallway, their boots scuffing along the cement surface.

Stu waited until they were along before he spoke. "We need a new chief. I'm going before the council and recommending they appoint you."

Otakay shook his head. "It doesn't work that way."

"Why not? Why do we have to follow everything the chief says?"

"Because he's the White Chief!"

"He let an old man and two kids escape. Four guards dead plus the search party. People will be angry. You need to seize the opportunity and harness their anger."

"He brought us here. He gave us Perpetuum energy."

"No, Graham did that. He can't possibly take credit for that."

Otakay remained silent. Stu took a step closer to him. "You told me you want to be chief."

"And what do you expect in return?"

"Our lives. A guarantee. That's all."

"I don't believe you."

"I know you think I'm a monster, and, I don't know, maybe I am. But even monsters want what others have. Safety. Security. A place to call home."

Otakay still didn't say anything. His large dark eyes staring at Stu.

"Look at it this way," Stu said. "Either way, the council will blame me. You can deny everything."

Otakay took in a deep breath. "Okay. I will see what I can do."

Stu smiled and reached out his hand for Otakay to shake. Otakay hesitated, shifting his spear and helmet into his left hand before taking Stu's.

Otakay gripped Stu's hand firmly but Stu squeezed his own fingers around the black man's hand equally as hard and looked into his eyes.

It was at that moment that Stu knew his plan was going to work. He was going to be the chief and all the power was going to be his. His society would be built.

Part Three: Re.Evolution

The Subway

Ewan covered his face with his shirt but it didn't help much. The stench was awful, putrid, filling his nostrils and choking him. What was that coming from? He had paused, listening for the sound of his pursuers but he couldn't hear anything behind him so he slowed down to a walk.

He was exhausted, to the point of delirium. His head was light and he tried to focus ahead but the thick blackness didn't help his dizziness. He couldn't remember the last time he had slept.

He followed the tracks which went straight on and on without deviation into the blackness ahead.

He wondered where the Creatures were. Why weren't they down here? And how did Albert know about this? But even more worrisome was if Albert knew about the subway why hadn't he mentioned it before?

He's just a crazy old man, Ewan thought. *There is no logical reason.*

But something in the back of Ewan's mind told him there was a reason. Somehow Albert was protecting them. If there weren't Creatures in this tunnel it meant there was something worse. Maybe whatever had killed the Creatures in the park is lurking down here.

Ewan wanted to call out to Albert and Ashley, to see if they were close, but he didn't dare so he continued to keep walking. He wondered about Justin and Anthony and how they were doing.

In the distance he saw something on the tracks, a shadowy structure. When he got closer he realized it was a subway car.

Taking several more steps, he saw there was a thick blood splatter on the back window. Ewan's throat became dry. The passengers had obviously come to some horrific end.

That was fun! Can we ride the subway again? Ewan heard a tiny voice say. It was Tim's. Was he down here too?

Ewan stretched his fingers out in the darkness.

"Timmy?" he whispered, still afraid of the Creatures. "Tim. . . Are you here?"

Come on, Dad. Let's do it again!

Suddenly there was light. Ewan didn't know where it was coming from and Timmy was in front of him. He heard a loud high-pitched squeaking sound of metal braking on metal and loud voices all around him.

Ewan looked around him. People were crowding the station, looking at their cell phones or listening to music on their earbuds.

"The next train will be in two minutes," a female voice spoke over a loud speaker.

"I want to go home," Sophie said.

"You're just claustrophobic," Tim said, crossing his tiny arms across his narrow chest.

"No I'm not," Sophie whined. Her small, liquid eyes looked upwards. "Daddy, tell him I'm not."

"Timmy, be nice to your sister," Ewan said.

"I'm not moving," Timmy said.

"Come on, Mom's waiting for us."

"No I want to go back."

"Fine, Sophie and I will just leave you here."

Sophie's face lit up with the prospect of leaving his brother behind. She stuck out her tongue at him which only made Tim angrier.

"I'm going to get on the next train."

"No you're not, Timmy."

"Don't call me that!"

They could hear the rumbling of the next train as it approached the station.

"Come on Tim. Please. Your mother is waiting for you. She's cooking dinner."

"I hate her meals," Timmy yelled. "Why can't we have hamburgers?"

Ewan looked around, embarrassed. People were starting to take notice of the perpetual child.

"Timmy –Tim, please."

The subway car slowed and stopped as it came to the station. The doors opened and a stream of people came out, shuffling through the crowds.

Tim didn't move and Ewan relaxed a little. He wasn't going anywhere. He was trying to get attention.

303

The commuters got on the train and a chime rung out, signalling the closing of the doors. Ewan looked down at Sophie who was looking bored and then back at Timmy. But Timmy was no longer standing on the platform.

Ewan desperately looked around and saw Timmy running for the doors and sneaking his small body through them just as the doors shut.

"Timmy!"

Ewan sprinted towards the train but it was too late. The train started to roll slowly forward. Ewan banged on the window but Timmy just waved happily back.

"Damn it, Timmy," Ewan yelled. "What are you doing?"

The subway train picked up speed and Ewan helplessly watched as Timmy sped away and disappeared into the darkness of the tunnel.

Ewan once again found himself in darkness on the outside of the stalled train car looking in. The stench was almost unbearable, causing him to gag.

He cupped his hands over the glass windows, trying to look in. He couldn't see much of anything in the darkness but in the seat directly in front of him was a dead body, it's flesh all gone and ash-coloured bone exposed underneath a fleece jacket and an old pair of jeans.

Ewan wondered what had happened. Had a Creature gotten in and killed everybody inside? Or had something else killed them?

I'm going to die here, Ewan thought. I'm going to end up like the corpses in the subway cart for nobody to find, nobody to bury.

Ewan turned away from the subway cart when he heard footsteps from up ahead. It was the cannibals coming for him. But no, he realized the footsteps were coming from the opposite direction.

Ewan crouched in the darkness and waited. Although he couldn't be certain, the footsteps had a certain familiar rhythm that sounded human.

Moments later he could make out the dark shapes of Ashley, Albert and the twins as they appeared.

Ewan got up and ran towards them. He gave Ashley a hug and even gave Albert an awkward embrace.

"Careful there, Walder," Albert said, which made Ewan laugh.

"Why aren't there any Creatures down here?" Ewan asked.

"I've been asking the same question," Ashley said, giving Albert a reproachful look.

"It's easier if I show you," Albert said.

"You've been down here before?"

Albert looked at Ewan as if he was crazy. "Yes, of course."

Albert said, turning around and walking back down the tunnel.

Ewan looked at the twins who looked terrified. "I don't like this at all."

"What choice do we have?" Ashley asked.

"Let's find a way out of here."

"Let's hope that's what the professor is doing," Ashley said, following Albert into the darkness.

They walked for a couple of minutes before Albert stopped in the darkness and motioned to the door.

"Over there is an access door. It's unlocked."

"Why? What's behind the door?"

"You won't believe me unless you see it for yourself," Albert said. "I'll stay here with the boys."

Ewan hesitated but Ashley pressed forward to the area Albert had pointed at. Ewan felt he had no choice but to follow.

Together they searched half-blind in the darkness for a doorway and eventually they found a small hatch – it wasn't really a door but Ewan figured that was what Albert meant. The hatch had a small lever that Ashley pushed down using her full body weight. The lever groaned but then clicked into place. Ashley then pulled and opened the hatch.

Ewan climbed in first and Ashley followed. The passageway was circular only about three feet in diameter which meant they had to crawl on their hands and knees through it.

They crawled for several minutes until gradually Ewan was aware of a powerful smell.

"You think that's rotten sewage?" Ewan asked Ashley.

"I don't know — probably."

They continued to crawl forward. Ewan's hands and knees started to hurt. The stink got worse, so bad, in fact, that it made

Ewan's eyes water and gradually they heard a humming sound that continued to get louder.

"We should turn back," Ewan said.

"How? Crawl backwards?"

"How else?"

"Let's keep going."

The humming got louder. It almost sounded like an old electrical generator but of course none of those were still working.

As they got closer, Ewan saw a soft whitish glow in the distance. Maybe it was a generator after all.

Ewan stopped and whispered back to Ashley.

"Can you see that?"

"No your ass is in the way. What is it?"

Ewan laughed despite himself. "It's an electrical light."

"An electrical light? How is there electricity down here?"

They crawled another fifty meters until they reached an open space. The ceiling was high with bright tube lighting. What was this place? Ewan didn't know. There was no indication what this room had once been used for?

Ewan glanced downwards. He immediately saw the source of the sound and let out a loud gasp.

"What?" Ashley said behind him.

"Jesus."

There were piles of bodies on top of each other, limbs, torsos and heads stacked haphazardly together. A thick swarm of flies were buzzing around, feasting on the bodies.

"Let's get out of here," Ewan said.

"Why, what is it?"

"You don't want to. . ." Just as Ewan was speaking, he realized the bodies below him weren't human. They were Creatures in different levels of composition. Some of the bodies were just skeletons; some still had flesh on them which was shrivelled up like raisins.

Some of the bodies were disfigured with an extra nose or no mouth. The smell made Ewan feel like puking. His throat was dry and sore. He closed his eyes and took several deep breaths, trying to slow down his rapid heart rate.

"This isn't real. This can't be happening," Ewan said.

"For God sake's, Ewan," Ashley said. "What is it?"

Ewan reluctantly shifted his legs so they were dangling off the side of the tunnel. He then used his hands to push himself off onto the ground. He landed on several limbs, almost falling over. There was a dry crunch as if he had landed on dead Fall leaves. He tried to find solid footing but there were so many bodies littering the room it was impossible for his feet to find the floor.

He then looked back at Ashley as she peered into the room. She had much the same reaction as Ewan had.

"What the hell?. . ."

The curious scientist kicked in and Ewan bent down to examine the closest body. It was decomposing, yet not as a normal human being would have decomposed. Ewan poked it with his finger and found the carcass soft and jelly-like. In parts, the flesh had either rotted away or had been eaten away and exposed white bone

Ashley crouched beside Ewan. "What do you think happened here?" she asked.

"This is absolutely fascinating," Ewan said. He had gotten over his initial fear and the biologist in him took over. "I've never seen a decomposing Creature before."

"Maybe it's some sort of Creature burial . . . I'm not sure."

Ewan spotted something half buried in the corner. It was pink and fleshy. Ewan carefully made his way across the room, swatting away the flies, and bent to examine the object. He cleared away a couple of bones and cloth to expose the object. It looked to be a human hand and Ewan was reminded of when Timmy had found a hand in the garden. Was it possible a human had managed to die down here? Ewan cleared away more bones from the hand and found it was a hand, but not exactly human. It was long and narrow with refined, delicate fingers. Each finger had seven phalanges instead of the normal four – Ewan counted them –and there appeared to be two thumbs on opposite sides of the hand.

"What is it?" Ashley asked.

Ewan tried to pull the hand away from the lump of bodies but it seemed to be attached to something larger.

"Fascinating," Ewan said.

"What is?"

Ewan frowned. "Don't you see this hand?"

Ashley bent down. "It's not human."

"Not only is it not human but it's physiologically more advanced than a human hand. Notice it has two thumbs which could be used for better grip and see the smaller bones that make up the fingers? That would mean the hand would be more flexible than a normal human hand."

"What does that mean?"

Ewan started to dig with his hands to uncover the rest of the body. "Help me with this," he said. Together they managed to pull off the other body parts until they uncovered the rest of the body. Its face was narrower, its eyes smaller and its neck was rounder and longer.

"What is this?" Ashley asked.

Ewan shrugged. It looked like a bastard child of a Creature and human.

"Let's get out of here," Ashley said. "I'm liking this place less and less."

Ewan put his hands up to his temple. "Albert knew about this place. How?"

Ashley shook her head. "He must have been down here before."

"There's something he's not telling us," he said, then paused to think about it. "It almost looks like this thing. . . was used for genetic testing."

Suddenly Ewan heard a noise come from the tunnel. The footsteps were soft and cautious, like those of humans. Ewan took his knives out.

"Shit," Ashley whispered. "I think that's the search party."

"I have an idea," Ewan said. He started to jump up and down. The noise of his feet crushing bone echoed through the room and down the tunnel.

"What are you doing?"

"We're going to ambush them," he said. "Quick bury yourself under the bodies."

"You're out of your fucking mind," Ashley said.

Ewan could hear voices and the sound of the search party shuffling through the tunnel.

"Keep your voice down."

Ewan dug himself under the corpses. The stench became almost unbearable and he closed his eyes trying to ignore the flies that were on his face and in his nostrils. He hoped Ashley had hidden herself from view as well.

After awhile he heard the sound of the search party. "My God, what is this place?" Ewan heard a voice say.

"It's a fucking concentration camp," another said.

Ewan forced himself to be still. He thought of Timmy running and climbing on the train.

Wait, Timmy, wait! Ewan banged on the glass but the subway train was already in motion.

Ewan and Sophie got on the next train and sat at the front of the cart. Sophie wasn't pleased about it.

We have to find Timmy.

Why?

Because he's family and family look out for each other. I would do the same if you were lost.

But in the end Ewan hadn't; Sophie had been murdered by the Creatures and he had been powerless to stop it.

Do you think Tim would look for me if I were lost? Sophie asked.

I'm certain he would.

The mechanical female voice announced the next stop. The subway train slowed, the brakes made a high-pitched squeak as they came into the next station.

Tim was standing there on the platform with a big grin on his face. Ewan and Sophie got off and walked up to him. Ewan felt like wrapping his hands around Tim's small neck but instead he shoved them deep into his pocket and exhaled a long breath.

The sound of footsteps crunching on bones made Ewan focus on the present.

"You sure they're here?"

"I heard something."

"Let's go back and just tell the chief that they're dead."

"Not until we see their bodies. Besides, I'm hungry."

"The Creatures got them."

The voices were getting closer. He waited until they were next to him before he pushed himself upwards. He had the element of surprise and the cannibals were slow to react.

Ewan slashed at the closest cannibal's leg, next to the knee. He felt the knife go deep and hit bone. The cannibal screamed and fell backwards. The man standing next to him stabbed downwards with his spear but Ewan was able to roll sideways. Ashley killed the cannibal next to her and came up behind him and sliced his throat. Blood sprayed all over Ewan's face and body but he hardly noticed as he leapt to his feet, stabbing a surprised cannibal in the throat.

The fourth man took an arrow from his backpack. He tried to string it on his bow but he was too slow and Ewan was on him, slicing his chest open. He dropped his bow and clutched his wound, his eyes wide with shock.

Ewan watched as he fell to his knees, blood pouring onto the dead Creatures and then collapsed completely.

Ewan then turned to the last man with the gouge in his leg. He looked from Ashley to Ewan and raised his hands

"I surrender, please don't hurt me."

Ewan took a step forward and raised his blood soaked knife.

"Wait!" Ashley said.

Ewan hesitated and then lowered his knife. Ashley bent down and cut away the pant leg to look at the wound; it expanded across the entire skin.

"Give me your coat," Ashley said.

The cannibal seemed dazed and confused.

"I need to stop the blood. Give me your coat."

The cannibal managed to wiggle out of his coat and give it to Ashley who took her knife and cut a strip off of the sleeve and tied it around the cannibal's knee.

"Who are you?" Ashley asked.

"We are the First People's tribe, dedicated to rebuilding civilization," the man said.

"You're cannibals — that's what you are!"

"Only by necessity," the man said. His voice was low and pitiful. He was breathing heavily, straining from the pain. "There's no food. No more animals left."

"You were going to eat my babies," Ashley said.

"Like I said, only by necessity. We're trying to rebuild humanity."

"You people are stupid" Ewan said. "Eating meat is not a must to survive. Most root vegetables have more protein than meat. That we need meat to live is a myth."

Ewan was surprised as he felt Amy's lectures on foods, enzymes and vitamins shine through.

The Cannibals looked at Ewan with slight smiles on their lips.

"Who is this White Chief anyway?" Ewan asked.

"He is our leader. He's the one who organized us in the beginning and gave us hope."

"And I heard a mention of a samurai. Who is he?"

"He's evil. Everybody is afraid of him."

"Including the White Chief?"

"No, he's never afraid of anything."

"Does this samurai have a name?" Ewan asked.

"He only has a white man's name. Stuart . . . I think but people call him Stu. He's not a part of the tribe."

"If he's not part of the tribe why haven't you killed him?"

"Because he knows how to build at Perpetuum generator."

Ewan raised his eyebrows. "He must be lying. Even if he knew how, there are not enough working parts for the generator. Trust me, I've checked."

"His friend helps him. He used to work at Perpetuum Industries."

Ashley turned to the cannibal. "Can you walk?"

The cannibal shook his head.

"Come on, you have to try," Ashley said, holding out her hand. "What's your name?"

"I'm called Turtle."

The cannibal took Ashley's hand and tried to lift his body up from the ground but as he did so, Ashley stabbed him in the chest with her knife, digging the blade in deep.

Turtle looked up in surprise, his body quivering and then Ashley let go of his hand and his body slumped back to the ground.

Ewan opened his mouth to say something but nothing came out.

Ashley looked over at him. "What?" she asked. "He would never be able to get back to the surface."

They crawled back through the tunnel and back into the subway system. There was no sign of either Albert or the twins.

"They must have hidden somewhere when they heard the search party," Ashley said.

"Okay, but where?"

They decided Albert and the boys must have kept walking eastward, away from the search party so that was the way they went. But there was still no sign of them when they arrived at the next station.

"What do you want to do?" Ewan asked. "They would probably have gone up, back to the city."

But Ashley shook her head. "I don't think so."

"Why not? That's what any logical person would have done."

"Albert knew there were no Creatures down here. He wanted us to see something."

"But what?"

"We will only find out if we keep going."

Ewan stared up at the sign that pointed to the stairwell. "Don't you think they would have waited for us here?"

"You think the Creatures got him."

"Or whatever that mutation was."

Ashley didn't reply but instead looked up at the stairwell.

"I'm going to at least check it out. Maybe they're waiting for us up there."

Ashley nodded, but didn't move so Ewan hopped over the tracks and climbed up onto the platform and up the stairs. He felt the light hit his eyes and he blinked.

It was a beautiful, clear morning, the ocean-blue sky spilled out between the glass skyscrapers. The wind was still. Ewan felt the city's eerie silence again. The buzz from the lights and the car's motor was still in his auditory memory.

No sign of either Albert or the twins.

Ewan walked several paces, hoping to catch a glimpse of them, or anything — movement of some kind. But there was nothing. The city remained as silent and as dead as ever.

Ewan used to hate the city — the cars, the people, the loud noises, the bright advertisements. He hated how in the winter the snow would turn a blackened colour from the pollution and how trash would stay half-buried until spring.

Ewan sighed, thinking of the past.

In the morning light, Ewan checked his wound. He peeled back the crusted-blood that had concealed his skin with cloth and undid the belt that he had placed over the wound. It had stopped bleeding which was a good sign, although it was still painful.

Ewan bent down and packed some snow and applied it gingerly to the wound. Ewan gasped at the coldness of the snow as it met his raw skin but he kept the pressure and watched as the snow turned to water and ran down his leg.

He hoped the snow would prevent infection although perhaps he could find some hydrogen dioxide but maybe that was wishful thinking. He reapplied the belt across the wound and, reluctantly, turned around and walked back to the subway station, descending back into the darkness.

He found Ashley sitting on the edge of the station. She looked up at him as he approached. Her face was a mixture of sadness, apprehension and something else that Ewan didn't fully understand.

Ewan held out his hand and Ashley took it. She had taken off her gloves and her soft, sweaty palm was warm to the touch. He pulled her upwards.

Ashley gazed into Ewan's eyes. "So?"

"I guess we continue on."

They continued along the subway track for thirty minutes, moving cautiously and carefully. Neither Ashley nor Ewan said anything to each other. Ewan listened to the soft scuffling of their soles on the gravel. The track continued in a straight path, never deviating. They passed a couple of stations with exits but they didn't stop.

Ewan kept a lookout for any sign of Creatures but he found none. They came across another subway car stalled in the middle of the track but unlike the first one Ewan had seen, this one was empty.

Ewan was unsure of what they were looking for or where Albert and the twins could have possibly have gone. There was no way they could have gotten this far. The twins would never have walked this far.

Ewan turned towards Ashley to tell her but before Ewan could say anything she held out her hand, indicating Ewan to stop.

"Ash—"

"Quiet!" she said.

Ewan stopped moving, turning towards Ashley questionably but he could only see a vague outline of her in the darkness.

"Do you hear that?" she asked.

"Hear what?" Ewan listened. Was it the twins? Creatures? Something else? Whatever it was, Ewan couldn't hear it. Everything was silent.

"What is it?"

Ashley didn't say anything for some time and just was Ewan thought she wasn't going to answer him, she said, "it's a low hum."

"A hum?"

"Yes. Don't you hear it?"

Ewan listened more intently but he couldn't hear anything. Not even the wind.

Ashley continued to walk and Ewan followed her.

"Ashley?" Ewan said.

"I think I see something up ahead."

Ewan peered into the darkness but couldn't see anything. "I think we should turn around."

"Just wait a moment."

Ashley quickened her pace and Ewan was forced to follow. Ewan rubbed his dry eyes and when he opened them he saw what Ashley had seen: it was something metallic and white and seemed to be blocking the passage.

As they got close, Ewan finally could hear the hum. It was low, almost inaudible but somewhat familiar. He had heard that hum before.

"Where are we?" Ewan asked, looking around for a sign to indicate where the closest metro station was but he couldn't see anything.

"I don't know."

As they got closer the hum quickly grew in intensity and Ewan saw the metallic object in greater detail. It was some type of machine with wires and circuit boards seemingly put together in random fashion.

"What do you think it is?' Ewan asked.

The machine was pulsing with energy and Ewan could definitely tell the hum was coming from the machine.

Ashley, who was several feet a head of Ewan, tripped and fell in the darkness. He could hear her hitting the gravel ground.

"Ashley?" Ewan yelled.

He ran forward but lost his footing and skidded down what seemed to be a long gravel ramp.

He clutched around him and came up with a fabric of some kind. He felt it between his fingers and realized it was a jacket, but not just any jacket.

"Timmy!" he exclaimed.

Ewan stood up, brushing the gravel off of his clothes and turned to Ashley who was doing the same.

"It's Timmy's" he said. "I think Tim is down here."

"This appears to be an entrance of some kind."

Ewan glanced around him and saw they had fallen down a ramp.

"Somebody dug this," Ewan said. "And it wasn't the Toronto transit authority."

"You think there are more cannibals down here?"

Ewan shook his head. "No. Whatever is down there. . . the Creatures know to stay away from."

The Council

Stu stood up in front of the seven council members and looked around. He had freshly washed his kimono for the occasion. It smelled of unscented soap – although Stu was horrified to think of where the soap had come from: the fat of some unsuspecting person, no doubt.

The council members were all in their mid-forties; Stu supposed this was now old age. The old had been the first to die after the Outbreak. The White Chief seemed to be the lone exception to that rule.

The council consisted of a various degree of races – Asians, Caucasians, and one Native American.

They stared back at Stu: some with looks of curiosity, but most with pure hatred in their eyes.

Stu knew nothing about them. Otakay had not said anything about them or what they were like, but from Stu's observations they were very ordinary people. Perhaps before the Outbreak they had been longshoremen or car salesmen or receptionists or dentists or any number of normal jobs. But now they made up the seat of the new government. Stu wondered if the Native American was somehow related to the White Chief.

Otakay had driven Stu back to the shopping center where the council convened every morning. Otakay had not spoken a single word on their trip which had given Stu time to think about how he wanted to approach them.

"Will you be in the room, also?" Stu asked Otakay.

"No, I am not a council member."

"Can you listen through the door?"

Otakay frowned. "Why would I do that?"

"Because I think it's important you hear what I have to say."

Otakay didn't answer and Stu didn't press it, instead he listened to the sputtering rattle of the motor.

"Members of the esteemed council," Stu started. "I have come to you because I fear that the White Chief is no longer the best or most able person to lead you."

The Asian woman leaned forward. "You feel you are a better candidate?"

They were in a large room with a long oak desk set up. Large candles burned on the table giving off the only light in the room. The council members sat on one side and Stu sat on the other. It had probably once been a storage space.

"No certainly not," Stu replied. "But I think Otakay has proven himself worthy in battle and also as a politician. I think he should take over as the White Chief."

"Otakay?" the Asian woman spit out the name as if it was poisonous. "He's not even a member of the council."

"That may be true but nevertheless I feel he has all the qualifications. The people respect him and we need someone with fighting experience to defeat the Creatures."

"Otakay is not mature enough to become leader. He is too rash and quick tempered to ever lead the tribe."

The Asian woman stood up, and leaned forward on the table. She was wearing a simple loose-fitting t-shirt and an old pair of jeans. Her hair was short, thin and wavy.

"I believe I was right to deny you a hearing and if it wasn't for my colleagues here I wouldn't have granted you permission. I don't think I even need to put it to a vote. Good day Mr. Baillie."

Stu stood up slowly. "Can you put it to a vote? You know, just humour me."

The Asian woman sighed and turned slightly to look at the council members beside her. "All in favour of replacing the White Chief with Otakay raise your hands."

Nobody raised their hands.

The Asian woman turned back to Stu. "There you have it, Mr. Baillie."

Stu shook his head and clucked his tongue against the top of his mouth. "That's not very democratic. Shouldn't you have a secret vote?"

Stu opened his kimono slightly and took out a knife he had been hiding. He took several large steps and leapt up onto the counter and with one quick slash he sliced open the Asian woman's throat. Blood sprayed across the room and onto Stu's freshly washed kimono.

The woman raised her hands slightly. Her eyes went wide with surprise. Her mouth dropped open as if she wanted to say something.

Stu grinned back at her as she fell backwards, crashing into her chair.

The council members scattered, fleeing for the door. Stu did not chase them. Instead he watched as the blood quickly drained from the woman, dripping onto the floor. It wasn't the same as watching the Creatures tear somebody apart but it was close enough.

He smiled, dropped his knife and sat down cross-legged on the desk. He didn't have to wait long before half a dozen armed men came into the room. They quickly surrounded him and grabbed him. He didn't resist.

Someone slammed his face against the desk. Pain shot through his face as his nose made a loud crunch like the snapping of dry twigs in a fire. Someone else punched him in the stomach and he gasped for breath.

"No wait," he heard Otakay say. His voice seemed to be very distant and muffled. "Let's take him to the White Chief."

"Execute him now and get it over with."

"No, the White Chief must pass judgement."

Stu was dizzy from the pain but out of the corner of his eye he could see the large black shape of Otakay. He laughed.

"What's so funny?" somebody said.

"If we don't give him a trial we are as bad as he is."

"Trial? What for? A trial is exactly what he wants. We have five eyewitnesses."

"Nevertheless we need to treat everybody fairly."

Stu felt the blade cut deeper into his neck. "He's not even part of the tribe. He's an outsider. He doesn't have any rights."

"I am the head hunter. Do as I say," Otakay yelled.

The knife rescinded from Stu's throat and he was forced to stand upwards. He was dizzy but he managed to stabilize himself. Otakay took a step forward and head-butted Stu. His skull made a sickening crunch sound and he collapsed into unconsciousness.

Nothingness . . . Blackness . . .

Then Stu was in a familiar room with old worn furniture. The room smelled musty and airless. He was standing on a shag rug with bits of food still stuck in it. A small hanging light was the only illumination.

It was his aunt's old house — her living room to be exact. Stu knew it well. He had spent most of his childhood in this house.

But what was he doing back here?

Stu turned and saw his two cousins just as he remembered them, identical broad shoulders and short-cropped blonde hair. They were about sixteen years old, only three years older than Stu but it might have been thirty years older. Their muscles had developed while Stu was still short and scrawny.

"I'm just minding my own business," Stu said.

"You gotta learn to take a beating, Stuart."

"Please . . . no."

"Come on, Stuart!"

The two cousins rushed him. Stu turned to run but he was too late. They grabbed him by the collar and pulled him backwards. He lost his footing and fell hard onto his tailbone.

"Don't do it!" Stu squealed, but the cousins' fists were already in motion. They were untrained blows and they hit Stu awkwardly on the shoulder and neck.

"We're doin' ya a favour!"

The cousins laughed and kept punching Stu.

"You better not rat us out."

Then a blow caught him on the side of the temple and he once again collapsed into darkness.

Stu stirred in a black room. He rubbed his eyes and tried to focus. Somebody had removed his kimono so he was naked. The floor was cold and he realized he was shivering slightly. His head was pounding as if somebody was taking a large hammer to it. He lifted his head and looked around. Through his blurred vision he saw a linoleum counter in the darkness and a toilet. He was in a bathroom.

He touched his fingertips first to his nose and then his forehead.

"There goes your chance to be Mrs. Universe," a familiar voice said from the darkness.

"Graham? What are you doing here?"

Graham took a step forward so Stu could see him more clearly. Graham looked tired and worn and he smelled of sweat.

"I don't know, truthfully."

"How bad is it?"

Graham pointed to the cracked mirror. "Look for yourself."

Stu pushed himself to his feet and walked unsteadily towards the mirror. He could barely see anything in the shards of glass but what he did see was awful. His face was covered in blood, both of his eyes were purple and swollen.

"Why did you do it?" Graham asked.

"Do what?" Stu asked. He turned the taps to see if any water came out but of course they were dry. "I'm innocent of all charges. They are conspiring against me."

"You really expect me to believe that?" Graham asked.

"You believe a bunch of savages over me?"

"There were five eye witnesses."

"Yes and they all have a motive to get rid of me."

"So they killed one of the council members just to frame you?"

"They were going to eat those two little boys and that old man. You really don't think they are capable of anything?"

"They will execute you, Stuart. I can't protect you from that."

"Don't call me that!"

Graham frowned, puzzled. "What's the end game here? You're smart. I know you wouldn't have done something so stupid without a plan."

"I'm adding a spark to the powder keg."

The Cell

Ewan and Ashley continued down the steep ramp clumsily. The pathway was relatively smooth and continued at a consistent angle. Whatever this ramp way was, it was machine made. No way humans could have dug so perfectly.

Ewan was uncertain of how far they descended but he estimated they walked for twenty or so minutes.

Up ahead, Ewan saw a light. It was dim at first but it grew brighter and larger as Ewan walked. Ewan picked up his pace so he didn't notice when he kicked something soft with his toe.

Ewan bent down to examine the object and found it was an old, dirty shoe but he recognized it immediately. It belonged to Tim.

"Timmy!" Ewan yelled. He wasn't able to contain himself any longer. "Timmy?" he repeated. "Tim?"

Ewan felt his strength return to him and he started to run towards the light. Ashley caught up with him and grabbed his jacket and spun him around.

"Ewan, wait! I think it's a trap."

"Don't touch me!" Ewan yelled.

"I'm not going to let you get killed."

Ewan tried to get away but Ashley's grip was surprisingly strong. "Don't you understand? Timmy is alive!"

"No, he's not. . . At least not the way you think of being alive."

Ewan frowned. "What do you mean?"

"I mean he's been infected."

"You don't know that."

"Yes I do. . . I'm sorry. . ." Ashley glanced down at her feet. "I saw him at the hospital. He was midway through transition."

Ewan pressed his hands against his temple. "No, no, that can't be possible."

"He didn't want you to see him like that."

Ewan shoved Ashley in the darkness. She stumbled and fell backwards.

"How could you do that to me?" Ewan yelled.

321

Ashley didn't reply. She didn't move. She just lay there motionless, her lanky body silhouetted against the yellow light. For awhile Ewan listened to her heavy breathing as it echoed through the small tunnel, not trusting himself to speak or to move.

Then in a fit of anger he jumped on Ashley and wrapped his hands around her slender throat. Ashley didn't protest, instead just stared up at him with her soft brown eyes, her hands limp by her side. Tears started to slide down her cheeks but still Ewan pressed his hands harder against her skin. Her face went red as the air was choked out from her.

Ewan felt rage like he had never felt before, not even when Amy had been killed or Sophie had been taken. Amy had never lied to him, never kept things from him.

I'm going to kill her, Ewan thought. Then he suddenly felt his energy drain from his body, like a gigantic floodgate had been released and he released his hold on Ashley's neck.

Ashley gasped and then coughed, sucking the life back into her.

Ewan pressed his hands against his nose and sat there for a long time, listening to Ashley slowly regain her breath.

Eventually Ewan got up and turned and continued on towards the light. He expected Ashley to call out, to make a move of some kind but all Ewan ever heard was her slow, rhythmic breathing.

Ewan walked on. His mind felt strangely empty. He only had one goal and that was to find Tim.

As he drew closer, he could see the light came from a wide open room, the size of a gymnasium. Long, overhead light gave the room an eerie glow. Light concrete was one of the human's latest inventions before the outbreak. It's regular concrete laced with carbon fibre transistors glowing in any color desired. The walls seemed to be built with granite like stone and there were large glowing light concrete columns that rose up to support the weight of the roof. This kind of construction was cutting edge, previously only reserved to places like Switzerland or Dubai. Ewan saw it once on television but that he would stand in the middle of one of those amazing constructions, he'd never dreamed.

On either side of Ewan were smaller rooms with doors made of a material similar looking to carbon fibre yet more organic. It looked like someone assembled fallen tree leaves into a perfectly shaped carbon-fibre-looking flat door. It took a moment for Ewan to realize they were actually cells and the room seemed to be a prison of some kind, designed to keep captives –whether it was human or Creature, Ewan didn't know – but it was empty, seemingly abandoned long ago.

Ewan took out his knives and holding them in front of him, forced himself to walk through the room. Adrenaline was keeping his weary body moving forward. He scanned his eyes right to left, looking for threats as his soft footsteps echoed through the hallway.

He got to the very end of the hallway before he heard a sound of ruffling metal. Ewan turned towards the sound and saw a small, diminished figure behind a set of bars.

Ewan took a hesitant step forward and the figure raised his head into the light.

Ewan's heart seemed to fall into his stomach and his throat went dry. He dropped the knives and ran towards the cell.

"Timmy?" Ewan said, softly. "It's me. It's your dad!"

Tim's eyes adjusted to the light. "Is that you?"

Ewan reached through the bars, trying to touch his son but Tim was too far. In the light he could see Tim's skin had turned a pale yellow-green and was shrivelling. He hardly looked like Tim anymore. But it didn't matter. Ewan would find a way to reverse the effect. The old man probably knew a way.

"Don't worry, Timmy. I found you."

Ewan found tears were rolling down his cheeks, first just a trickle and then they started to stream until they poured down his face.

"Dad, you have to listen to me."

"Okay, Timmy — okay."

"You have to get out of here. There's no saving me but you can go."

"I can't . . . I've lost your mom, your sister. I can't lose you."

"You don't understand anything, do you?"

Ewan pressed his face up against the bars, causing Tim to shrink back into the darkness at the back of the cell.

"What don't I understand?"

"What's happening? What is this place?"

Ewan examined the lock on the bars. It was a rusty old padlock. He pulled on it but it wouldn't budge.

"Who put you here? Was it the cannibals?"

"What cannibals? No . . . not cannibals."

Ewan looked around for something he could use to break open the lock but he didn't see anything useful. He ran to the wall, looking for a loose stone. Eventually he managed to pry a fist-sized one loose from the cement which he used to hit against the lock but to no avail.

Ewan leaned against the bars, panting heavily. "Who put you in here?" Ewan asked again.

"There's no time to explain. You've got to get out of here."

Ewan wedged his body against the bars and stuck his hand in. He could almost reach Tim, almost touch Tim if only Tim would reach out as well. But Tim didn't move. He didn't even look up at his father.

Ewan knew what he must do and as much as he didn't like it, it would be the only way to save Tim.

"Look, I'll be back for you, okay?"

"No, Dad. They will find you and lock you up just the same as with me."

"I'll find something to break you out."

Tim lifted his head and looked at Ewan. His eyes were larger than before, darker. "I'm sorry for being a bad son."

Ewan was about to say something but then he heard heavy footsteps drawing nearer. They weren't the soft, dragging footsteps of the Creatures or the footsteps of a human being. They were something else. But what?

"It's coming," Tim whispered. "It's already too late."

"What is?"

But Tim didn't answer. Instead he covered his face with his scaly hands.

With what seemed like superhuman effort, Ewan turned away from Timmy and ran away from the footsteps, back the way he had come. He didn't look back. If he did, he didn't think he would be able to keep going.

He found himself half climbing, half crawling back up the ramp. He passed the spot that Ashley had been and found she was gone. With any luck, she would be back at the surface by now.

Ewan turned to look at the thing that was chasing him. In the reflected light he could just make out what seemed like a gigantic half-breed of human and Creature. It had a long head with an elongated neck. Its arms and legs were also long and thin.

Somehow Ewan reached the top of the ramp. He reached for the humming machine and tried to tip it onto the hole but it wouldn't budge. He ran around and pushed it from the other side and this time it did tip over.

The machine crashed onto the ground, breaking into pieces, stopping the hum. Ewan could hear the thing that was following him cry out. It was a high-pitched tone, almost ultrasonic.

Ewan turned and started to run. He wondered where the nearest station was. Not more than ten minutes he figured.

Ewan ran as fast as he could for as long as he could. He stumbled once, got himself balanced again by placing a hand on the ground and kept running. But a few minutes later he stumbled again and this time he crashed to the ground, his chin hit the gravel. He forced himself up. He was breathing heavily and he forced himself forward.

He decided to glance backwards in the darkness, but couldn't see anything. It seemed the machine had impeded the thing's way. He was glad because he didn't think he could have out run it. Whatever it was. It certainly wasn't a Creature. It didn't seem effected by light like the Creatures.

Ewan turned and again started towards the subway station but this time he walked instead of ran. He was about fifty paces away before he heard a loud rumble.

He tilted his head to one side, trying to decipher the sound. It was coming from straight ahead and sounded almost like an Earthquake.

Ewan stopped walking and just stared. In the distance he could see dust kicked up, black flecks of gravel.

Ewan began to back up slowly. Whatever it was, it wasn't good. A few seconds later a group of Creatures appeared. They were running straight towards him. Ewan turned and fled. He ran about fifty paces when he saw another maintenance tunnel to his left.

He ran over and turned the lever. It was stiff at first and Ewan put his whole body weight into it, finally getting it open.

He ran inside and swung it shut. He could hear the Creatures crashing into the door but luckily the door was made of heavy steel and Ewan doubted even the force of hundreds of Creatures could get through it.

Ewan turned and crawled along the maintenance tunnel until he got to a ladder which he climbed up. He finally got to the top and pushed the door open. Cold, bitter air and bright sunlight seeped in, hitting Ewan in the face. He pulled himself up and fell into the deep snow.

He knew it was dangerous to lie in the snow but at this point he didn't care.

Finally, he managed to regain his strength and sit upright. He looked at his surroundings but didn't recognize anything. In front of him might have been the 401 or the Don Valley Parkway. He wasn't sure. To his left were tall oak trees, dusted with ice and snow.

Ewan started walking aimlessly, half expecting to bump into Ashley or Albert but he didn't see anybody.

He stopped and rested on a bus bench. The sun gleamed through the glass. Even the cut on his stomach didn't hurt so badly. He closed his eyes and leaned his head back, half hoping sleep would take him. But he knew if he fell asleep he would likely freeze to death.

It wouldn't be a bad thing, Ewan thought. *It would be an easy death.*

What had Hamlet said about death? Ewan tried to remember but couldn't. It made him wish Ashley was next to him, cuddling up next to him, holding his hand as he slowly drifted off to sleep, to death.

No, I need to help Timmy, Ewan thought. *He's been locked up.*

A loud crash startled Ewan and he opened his eyes. Two half-humans – although they bore little resemblance to anything human – were walking slowly towards him.

In the daylight he could see them clearly as they moved in gigantic strides. They stood about eight or nine feet tall and had greyish-green skin that seemed to shimmer and change depending what light hit them. It would have almost made them invisible if it wasn't for the fact that their bodies were covered in sort of cloth or clothing. Their necks were thick and tall and pivoted their large head. The eyes were oval with large slits and sat far apart.

Then the two half-humans stopped and stared straight at Ewan. He swore he could see a small smile on one of their faces. Its teeth were big and bright.

Ewan forced himself to move. He ran out of the bus shelter and away from the half-humans. The half-humans took off after him. On the open road the half-humans were incredibly fast. Ewan turned and ran as fast as he could but he could hear the half-humans quickly catching up to him.

He needed another plan. He desperately looked around and saw a Jeep Wrangler with its door open. Ewan jumped inside and slammed the door shut. There were chunks of dried blood mixed with pink matter on the windshield and on the seat.

Luckily the keys were still in the ignition. Ewan turned them and pressed down on the gas but the engine sputtered and coughed.

"No, please no," Ewan said. He looked in the rear view mirror and saw the half-humans were almost on him.

He turned the keys again but again nothing.

He heard a loud bang and the car shook on its suspension. Ewan looked behind him and saw one of the half-humans had landed on the trunk.

Ewan turned the key a third time and this try the Wrangler sputtered and then came to life. Ewan released the break and threw it in reverse, hitting the gas pedal. The Jeep spun in the snow but didn't move.

"Dear, Jesus," Ewan muttered. His heart was pounding fast. He could feel it in his stomach.

The half-human broke the back window with a loud crack and reached in with a long slender hand. Ewan put the car in drive and slammed on the gas. Again the Jeep went nowhere. The half-human clamped down on Ewan's shoulder with an incredibly strong grasp. Ewan stared at the long fingers and couldn't help but note the half-human had the same number of phalanges as the corpse he had seen in the subway.

Ewan swivelled his head and bit down on the hand as hard as he could. The half-human made the same weird ultrasonic noise as before but didn't let go.

Ewan opened the Jeep's door and tried to make a run for it but the hand held him in place. Ewan struggled against the hand but it was useless. The other half-human came around the side and grabbed the door handle and tore it off.

These things have ant-like strength, Ewan thought.

Almost without warning the Wrangler lurked forward. Ewan felt the hand on his shoulder slide off as he grasped the steering wheel and tried to control the Wrangler without taking his foot off the pedal.

He turned the steering wheel hard and skidded, nearly missing a snow-covered fire hydrant before reaching sixty miles an hour.

Ewan dared to glance in the mirror and saw the half-humans were running behind him, their massive strides propelled them forward. They weren't losing any ground on the Jeep, that was for sure.

Ewan focused back on the road. He hit the break and swung the steering wheel hard right but the Jeep didn't cooperate. He skidded and heard the awful sound of rubber sliding on snow. The Jeep hit a snow bank and he tumbled over. The world spun around and around and then crashed back down. His body was thrown forward out of the car and his face hit the snow.

Timmy, you weren't a bad son. You were perfect. Perfect, Ewan thought, before his mind closed in darkness.

Trial and Execution

Stu was pushed down a long, dark hallway. His hands were tied together and he was breathing hard. The four guards walked quietly behind him.

If they had plans to kill him quietly this would be where they would do it. Right here, without any witnesses.

They could say he tried to escape. Nobody would know differently. It was too dark to see more than a couple of feet in front.

But nobody made a move. Nobody said anything.

Soon they turned a corner and walked down another long hallway but in this one Stu could hear the sound of the crowd that had gathered. He figured as long as there were people he would be safe.

Stu made sure he entered the auditorium with his head held high. He stared all the people in the face. He figured there were about a hundred people all staring at him. Their eyes were wide and their mouths open in curiosity.

They will soon know what I'm made of, Stu thought to himself as he walked slowly down the center isle towards the stage.

The guards directed Stu to stage right and he was motioned to stand still which he did. Stu looked out at the crowd again. There was a fire in the center of the stage which was the only light in the room so it made it difficult to see much of anything except a swaying mass of undefined objects.

Then the crowd quietened and Stu could feel movement towards his right. He looked over and the White Chief had appeared in full uniform. He moved slowly, quiet as a panther towards the fire. He stared down at the flames as they bounced and flickered, drawing elongated shadows onto the floor.

"Stuart Baillie, you stand accused of the most heinous crime: murder . . ." The White Chief paused for effect before looking over at Stu.

Stu held his gaze. The White Chief seemed even older than when he had last seen him, if that was possible. His deeply creased face was chalked with white powder. His eyes were sunken and hollow.

"How do you plead?"

"Not guilty."

The White Chief nodded and sat down in front of the fire, cross-legged. "Very well. Let's call our first witness."

The first witness was a black man who Stu recognized as one of the council members. His head was shaved and he wore a brown leather jacket. Stu guessed him to be in his mid-forties, although he looked significantly older.

Stu barely listened as he told about Stu's appearance before the council. The crowd hissed and booed when the black man testified how Stu was plotting to overthrow the White Chief. Stu studied the White Chief carefully for any emotion, but he just sat there as the black man gave his evidence.

When the man was done, the White Chief didn't ask any questions. Instead he just bowed his head and thanked the man. Next another council member appeared, a Chinese man.

He gave very similar testimony to the first council member. Again Stu looked over at the White Chief who was listening passively. After the Asian man was done, the White Chief thanked the man and the man bowed and turned and walked back behind the curtains.

This was repeated until all the council members had testified, each saying almost the same thing.

By the time they were done, Stu could sense the crowd was getting restless but the White Chief held up his hand for silence.

"This must be done properly," he spoke to the crowd. "Otherwise it is meaningless."

Next Otakay walked out from behind the curtains. He walked slowly, his head bowed.

Otakay told the crowd that Stu wanted to speak before the council but wouldn't say what it was about.

Stu grinned at this. *Liar,* he thought.

After Otakay had finished speaking, the White Chief asked his first question. "Do you want to be leader one day, Otakay?"

Otakay bowed his head. "I am guided by my visions. They show me my destiny."

"You didn't answer my question, child."

"No, great leader. You're the only man able to lead us."

"But I'm an old man, Otakay," the White Chief said, kindly. "I will not live forever. Somebody will have to take my place."

"The council will decide and I'm sure they'll make a very wise choice."

"Who do you think should lead us?"

Otakay raised his head very slightly and glanced at the crowd. "I do not know, great leader but I'm sure that person will present himself when the time comes. But hopefully not for a long while yet."

The White Chief smiled. "Thank you Otakay. You've done well."

Otakay bowed and disappeared behind the curtain.

The White Chief watched Otakay leave the stage before turning to Stu. "You have heard the evidence against you. It is time for you to defend yourself. Please call any witnesses you might have for your defence."

Stu smiled at the White Chief. "I have none."

The White Chief nodded. "Do you have anything to say in your defence?"

Stu turned to the crowd which had fallen silent. He tried to make out faces. He imagined Chenoa among them. Krista too.

"Ladies and gentlemen," he started formally. "We used to live in a world of pleasure and ease. But no more. You bonded together because you had no other place to go. Your families had been killed either by the Outbreak or by the Creatures. No doubt you thought you would be safer together than separately and while that is true, you still live in fear of the Creatures. You stay huddled up in this shopping mall, afraid to venture out. The White Chief hasn't brought you the life you deserve. What has he done to defeat your enemies? Our enemies? You deserve better than this. You deserve to rule the land like you used to."

Stu paused to see if he would get any reaction from the crowd. There was a quiet whisper.

"You are starving, forced to eat human flesh like an uncivilized, ancient race. I am here to tell you that you deserve better. You deserve somebody who will lead you against the Creatures. The White Chief is a peace time leader. What you now need is a war time leader."

As Stu spoke he was aware of a disturbance from the crowd. A young man jumped up onto the stage and started to run towards Stu as he spoke. Stu, who still had his hands tied together, stopped talking abruptly and stared at the young man. He could have been no more than eighteen or nineteen. He had long curly black hair and black intense eyes. Although Stu didn't see a weapon, the look in the young man's eyes told him he wanted to kill Stu. With his bare hands if he had to. Stu who was defenceless, turned to run.

Two guards grabbed Stu and held him tight. Stu elbowed the guard to his left and bit down hard on the fingers that held his arm. The two guards screamed and released him. Stu ran for his life.

Stu heard a cry of "Kill him!"

He looked back and saw complete chaos. The savages had swarmed the stage, overwhelming the guards who had forgotten all about Stu and were desperately trying to hold them back.

Stu parted the curtains and ran towards the back entrance where he ran into Otakay who had found a spear.

"Cut me loose," Stu pleaded.

"Not on your life."

"They're going to kill me," Stu shouted. The shouting was getting closer, slowly getting louder.

"You deserve to die." Otakay pushed Stu aside and walked out onto the stage.

Stu turned and ran down the hallway until he got to the lobby where there was a slow, steady stream of people running away. Luckily they paid no attention to Stu who hopped over the counter and found a pair of scissors in one of the drawers and used it to cut the rope.

He savoured the sounds of yelling and fighting as they echoed off the lobby walls. It brought a smile to Stu's lips. He only wished he had some music to go with it and then he would be in heaven.

The first stage of his plan had gone even better than he had anticipated. Now he could only hope that the second stage would be equally as successful.

Stu took the scissors and walked up the ramp, pushing the doors to the auditorium open. People were throwing punches, shoving each other. He was reminded of when he would get drunk at a bar while watching the football match and he would instigate a fight with a supporter of one of the teams –it didn't matter which one.

Stu walked through the crowd, making his way back towards the stage. He had to find the White Chief before the guards got things under control. He stayed alert and when he was about halfway there somebody growled and flung himself at Stu. Stu dodged easily and stabbed the man in the eye with the scissors. The man screamed and Stu dug the scissors in further until he was sure that he had reached the brain. He then pulled the scissors out and continued to fumble through the bodies, pushing people aside until he reached the stage.

He scanned the mangle of fighting bodies for the White Chief but he couldn't see the man.

He decided instead of lifting himself up and exposing himself he would walk around to the stairs at the end. A guard spotted him and jumped off the stage, attacking him with his spear. Stu dropped the scissors, rolled forward, and grabbed the spear. Then with a swift kick he broke the guard's right knee cap and then broke his jaw with an elbow.

The guard screamed and Stu pulled the spear easily away from the guard's grip and stabbed him with it. The guard let out a loud exhale of air and then coughed up blood before collapsing to the floor.

Stu ran up the stairs. He saw Otakay fighting with two savages, trying to push them backwards without really hurting them.

"Where's the White Chief?" Stu yelled at Otakay but the big black man couldn't hear him.

Stu made his way to the middle of the fire which had all but burnt out. There he found the White Chief on the ground, his limbs sprawled outwards. Two of his guards were crouched over him.

"What happened?" Stu asked, stepping forward.

The White Chief was clutching the side of his stomach. Dark blood was seeping out through his wispy fingers.

The guards shook their head. "He wouldn't leave."

"Who did this to him?"

Again the guards shook their heads.

Stu knelt down real close to the White Chief. "Who did this?"

"You've . . . won," the White Chief said.

Stu looked up at the guards. "He says Otakay."

The guards looked at each other, a silent signal passed between them.

Stu turned to the White Chief but his eyes had rolled into the back of his head and he had stopped breathing.

Captive

Ewan was sitting in his living room, marking his student's term papers. Amy was cooking in the kitchen; the smell of food was wafting through into the living room and Ewan could hear the sound of the sizzling stove and the crescendo of water boiling.

Ewan flipped the page and sighed. He wasn't even halfway through yet. Most of his students weren't interested in biology and would usually guess at the correct answers. It pained him to think of the apathy he dealt with every day, especially since he found biology so interesting. He couldn't understand why none of his students wanted to learn about the world around them and how it was always changing.

Tim and Sophie were sitting across from him, watching television. Sophie was stroking her doll's curly hair when she looked over at her dad. "Tell us how you and Mom first met."

Ewan looked up from his papers at Sophie. She was six or seven and looked like Amy. Same dark features, and thick dark hair. "Why on Earth would you want to know about that?"

Sophie just shrugged. "Just curious."

"We met at school . . . University. We were in the biology club together."

Sophie smiled. "Biology is what you teach."

"Yes . . . The study of living things."

"I know what biology is, Dad!" She whined.

Ewan laughed and held up his hands. "I'm sorry. I keep forgetting how smart you are."

"Why did Mom choose you of all her friends?"

Ewan laughed, harder this time. "I'm not sure. You'll have to ask her that."

Ewan opened his eyes. He felt numb. Timmy. . . Sophie . . . He thought he was in the living room. He was lying on something hard and cold. No, his family didn't exist anymore. Sophie and Amy were dead and Timmy was rotting in a cell.

Where was Ashley? Ley-ley, he remembered Timmy calling her. Ewan thought that was a silly nickname and he didn't think Ashley particularly liked it.

How long have I been out for? Ewan wondered.

He was still lying on the road. His head hurt. He was cold. Dirt and dust and ash were sprinkled into the white snow.

He looked around and saw the two half-humans going through the wrecked Jeep. They were making funny high-pitched clicking sounds as if they were talking to each other.

They must have heard Ewan move because they looked over at him. They leapt over the Jeep and landed in front of Ewan, their long, wide feet making surprisingly little imprints on the snow.

Ewan looked up at them, for the first time he saw them in full light. They were large, over seven feet tall. Their skin was a dull greenish colour and seemed rubbish and hard. They had loose-fitting clothes and seemed almost to blend into their skin.

On the half-human that was closest to Ewan there was a patch on its right breast that read 'Rain'.

Was Rain the thing's name?

Rain took a step closer, its head tilted forward as if curious.

Ewan felt too much pain to feel afraid.

"What are you?" Ewan gasped, between gritted teeth.

Rain didn't say anything.

Ewan looked at the other half-human. Its shirt said 'Dune.'

"I just want my son back."

Rain opened its mouth and made the strange clicking sounds but then stopped. It looked at Dune who just stared back with large black eyes.

"I . . . click . . . click . . . click. . . have . . . click. . . not . . . click . . . spoken Homo. . . sapien . . . click in a . . . click . . . long time. . . The . . . click, one they call Ewan . . . Hello."

Rain took another step forward to Ewan, holding out its long slender hands.

"That's far enough," Ewan said.

"I am the one called Rain."

"What are you?"

"Six hundred thousand years ago a group called the Denisovans split off from the Homo sapiens and the Neanderthals."

336

"Yes, I know all about the Denisovans. You're talking to a biology teacher. Get to the point."

"The Denisovans became extinct, whether they were wiped out by the Homo sapiens or something else, nobody knows. What we do know is that the Denisovans left some of their DNA behind . . . of — what do you call it?"

"Genomes?"

Rain nodded. "Yes — exactly." He pronounced the word slowly. "Genomes. It is responsible for a new mutation into a new species. Homo stripes. Post Human."

Ewan frowned. He wasn't sure if he had heard correctly through his pain. "Post Human?"

"The virus you call the Magnetar caused a mutation in the Homo sapien."

"We know that already. It was the virus that turned everybody into those Creatures."

"Click – yes. But for those who have the special Denisovan genome it changed us into Post Humans."

Ewan opened his mouth and then closed it. It was all too much. "But it takes thousands of years to mutate."

Rain shook its head. "Such primitive thinking . . ."

"It was a disease."

"No, the Homo sapien was the disease. You nearly destroyed the planet. The Magnetar is the cure. We are the cure."

Ewan tried to get up but the pain became immense and nauseated, he fell back towards the snow-covered pavement.

Rain turned to Dune and made some high-pitch clicking sounds. Dune took several quick strides and picked Ewan up and cradled him in its arms as if he was a baby.

"No . . . it doesn't make sense," Ewan said. "The Denisovans were from Siberia, from East Asia."

"Click . . . You . . . know click, click, click your biology . . . click . . . but not your history?" Dune spoke for the first time.

Ewan tried to look up at Dune. "What do you mean?"

"The . . . click, click. First people here were . . . click."

"You mean the aboriginals?"

"Click . . .click . . . not. . . click, familiar. . ."

"The Denisovan genome was in the aboriginals?"

"Yes."

337

"How do you know that? You can't possibly know that."

"We did . . . some . . . click, click, experimenting."

Ewan fell silent and neither of the Post-Humans spoke. They ran, seemingly effortlessly, across the city; leaping over cars in a single bound, over fallen debris, past fallen telephone wires over mailboxes.

The sun was fading behind cotton-like colourless clouds.

The wind blew in Ewan's face and prevented him from seeing where they were going exactly, but after about ten or so minutes they ducked into a subway station and went down the stairs, deep into the darkness.

The Post Humans ran along the tracks, fast and sure-footed in the darkness which made Ewan wonder if they saw equally as well in the dark as in the light. Their large dark eyes might be perfect.

In fact, Ewan could not see a single flaw these Post Humans had, except perhaps a vertebra, which compared to the exoskeleton of a bug.

"Why aren't the Creatures here?" Ewan asked Dune, but the Post Human either didn't hear him or chose not to reply.

They stopped at the hole Ewan and Ashley had first stumbled upon. A Post Human was working on the machine Ewan had tipped over, its long delicate fingers working at the wires.

Dune looked down at Ewan. "Click . . . this . . . click . . . what . . .click. . . stops . . . click. . . the high frequency."

"It's the high frequency?"

Dune nodded. "Hurts the sensitive ears."

They proceeded down the slope until they got to the big room.

"Timmy?" Ewan yelled, his voice echoing off the stone walls. "What are you doing with us?"

They ran past Timmy's cell into another long passageway and then came to another large stone walled room. It was dimly lit with overhead lighting that cast long, deep shadows preventing Ewan from seeing the corners of the room.

"What is this place?"

The Post Humans finally slowed their pace as they entered the room. They took Ewan into the darkness where he saw that there was a large cell with iron bars built into the stone.

Rain took out a key from his pocket and inserted it into the large padlock; it opened with a click.

Dune laid Ewan gently on his feet but he couldn't stand. His whole body jolted in pain and he collapsed forward and fell into unconsciousness.

Ewan woke up in the darkness. The darkness swallowed him, sucked his body in. Ewan blinked and tried to focus. His whole body was in pain but at least he wasn't afraid of the darkness. He had been conditioned for so long to fear the darkness that brought the Creatures but somehow wherever he was, he felt safe.

"Tim, oh, God . . . What have I done?"

"Who's Tim?"

Ewan tried to focus on the source of the voice but he only saw dark shapes and bits of shattered light.

"Who's there?"

His voice echoed in the darkness.

Then a figure stepped forward into a harsh overhead light. Ewan propped himself up onto his elbow.

"Sorry, I didn't mean to scare you. We didn't think you'd make it. Even with the drugs those freaks gave you."

Ewan leaned back and looked up at the ceiling. "How long was I out?"

"I dunno. A couple of days we figure."

"We?" Ewan's eyes were slowly adjusting to the darkness and for the first time he could tell there were other human shapes around him. "Who are you?"

"We're all captives," the man explained, twisting his body and spreading out his arms, palms upward to indicate everybody. Ewan couldn't estimate how many people were in the cell but he counted at least a dozen huddling close together.

"What's your name?" Ewan asked.

"Christian Boeving," the man explained. He was about six feet tall and had a long, shaggy beard and thin short hair. His jaw was narrow and defined and his face was dark and muddy with deep brown eyes.

"Why do the Post Humans keep us here?"

Christian looked back at the group of captives. "I'll tell you later."

He heard a familiar shout and the twins ran appearing from the darkness and gave him a hug.

Ewan gave a grunt, partly from pain and partly from surprise. They had always been timid and not prone to affection. "Boys? What are you doing here?"

"We got caught by those big ugly monsters," Justin said and Anthony nodded vigorously. Ewan stared into their tiny, round eyes, looking for the innocence he had remembered being there. But all he saw was something slightly primal that was all-too familiar.

"Does that mean the crazy, old scientist is here with you?" Ewan asked.

"I may be crazy but I'm not old," Albert said, stepping close to Ewan.

If Ewan had been able to stand he might have tried to strangle the old man. Or hugged him – he didn't know which. "You knew all about the Post Humans, yet you said nothing!"

Albert shrugged. "I only deduced it, chap. I figured the virus had produced something other than the Creatures, something more advanced and that was what killed them in the graveyard."

"Why didn't you say anything? Warn us?"

"I was leading up to it."

"Well you should have led up to it faster," Ewan snapped. He was beyond angry now.

"Please, keep your voice down," Christian said. "You're scaring everybody else."

"So they should be scared," Ewan said. "We're trapped."

"It's really beautiful if you think about it," Albert said. "What we learned from the experiments, but which was never released to the public was that the Magnetar virus attacked the upper brain functions and shut them down. Not destroyed them, mind you. No. Just sort of changed them. A rewiring of sorts."

"Billions of people are dead. Beautiful is the last word that comes to mind."

Albert flinched. "I'm sorry. My apologies. But for evolution to continue there needs to be extinction. It's the way things work.

"Tim is down here."

"Whose Tim?" Albert asked, frowning.

340

"He's my son? Don't you remember?"

Albert smiled embarrassed. "Sorry, I don't remember things like I used to."

"Yet you know all sorts of things about the Magnetar virus!"

Albert frowned. "Yes, it is funny how the brain works sometimes."

Ewan closed his eyes. All the anger had made him exhausted. He thought of Timmy alone in his cage. Why had they separated him from the rest of the humans?

"Is there any way out?' Ewan asked. "Any weakness in these cells? Did the Post Humans build these?"

"I can only surmise they did," Christian said. "And believe me there isn't a way to escape. We've tried everything."

"What if we dig past these walls?"

"With what?"

"With our hands if we need to. If we don't, we're going to die or be turned into one of those Creatures."

But Christian shook his head. "It's pure stone. We'd need a pick axe to get past it; we don't have."

"Sick and twisted bastards."

"From what we gather, Rain is the really sick and twisted one," Christian said. "They fashion themselves as saviours of the Earth or some such nonsense."

Ewan looked at Christian. "Yeah, I got the monologue already."

Ewan stared up at the ceiling as if searching for a way out. "How long have you been in here, Christian?"

Christian was silent for a long time. "I don't know. I haven't counted but a couple of months maybe."

"What did you do before the Outbreak?"

"I was an electrical engineer. Worked for Perpetuum for six years."

At the mention of Perpetuum Albert jumped up and ran over to Christian. "Those dirty rotten scoundrels," he said. "I oughta shove their generator where the sun don't shine."

Christian was confused by the outburst and looked over at Ewan. "What's his problem?"

Ewan let out a weak smile. "He just rambles incoherently. I wouldn't pay much attention to anything he says."

Albert stared over at Ewan. "Walder, I wouldn't spread misinformation if I were you. You know what happens to misinformers?"

"Let me guess: They get locked up in cages, waiting to be transformed or to be killed by the Post Humans?"

Albert opened his mouth to speak but then stopped, looking at Ewan in surprise. "How did you know?"

Ewan let out a low chuckle. Despite everything he was glad to have Albert by his side.

When Albert turned and disappeared into the back of the cell, Christian said, "You keep interesting company."

Ewan shrugged. The pain seemed to have dissipated. "When you're the last ones on Earth I suppose you can't be too picky."

Ewan heard footsteps from down the corridor and for a moment he thought they were about to be saved but then a group of about six Post Humans appeared. Their large bodies moved fluidly, hardly making a sound on the compact ground. They had large saw-like instruments in their hands.

The people around Ewan started to go crazy, screaming and breaking down into tears.

"What's going on?' Ewan asked.

"Kill day," Christian said, grimly.

The Post Humans walked past the cell and down the hallway. Ewan thought he recognized Rain in the group. They seemed to be clicking away in their strange language.

The captives quieted down but some were still sobbing and yelling. Ewan felt his blood quicken and a sharp spike in adrenaline.

Then they heard what sounded like chain saws and hideous screams from down the hallway. Several of the captives closed their eyes and covered their ears. Christian just grabbed the bars and looked into the distance sadly.

"One day our turn will come," he said.

"What's happening?" Ewan asked.

"The Post Humans kill anybody who hasn't mutated within the first two weeks of captivity."

"That's insane," Ewan replied, because he couldn't think of anything else to say.

After a while the screaming stopped and there was only the sound of a baby crying and the mother trying to comfort it.

Christian slid to the floor and turned to face Ewan, resting his chin on his knees. He suddenly looked tired and worn away. "I hope our day comes soon. I'm tired of this shit."

Ewan sat down beside Christian. The baby's wail seemed to pierce through the cell.

Neither said anything for a long time. The twins came and sat next to them. They looked scared, although they hid it well.

"Is Ashley dead?" Anthony asked.

"No, she's alright," Ewan said, putting his arm around Anthony, trying to comfort him.

"Where is she then?"

"She's back home. Safe and sound."

"Will she come save us?" Justin asked.

"I'm sure she will."

Again they heard footsteps as the Post Humans returned, walking past the cage. They were covered in bits of gore, bone and blood. They all continued past the cage except Rain who stopped and stared down at Ewan, Christian and the twins. She was surprisingly clean, as if she had just stood and watched as the others had completed their tasks.

"Click, click, who . . . is click the one they call, click, click Ashley?"

Ewan slowly stood up. Even at full height he was almost two feet shorter than Rain. "I will enjoy watching you die."

Rain laughed. "Until now, click, click . . . I had forgotten the grandeur of the Homo sapien language."

"What is the point of nursing me back to health if you're only going to kill us?"

"I have click, click, click, what you Homo sapiens call a, click, click, intuition? You're something special."

"But I don't have any of the genome in me. My ancestors are from Germany."

Rain smiled. "I wouldn't be so sure of that, click, click. You might just evolve to witness the end of this difficult chapter in Homo sapien history."

"You mean the part where you kill innocent people?"

"Please, click, click. Homo sapiens are anything but innocent. How many species have you eradicated? If you consult your own history, click, click, I believe it's more than sixty in the past couple of hundred years. And that's not including the sub species of Homo Sapiens. What do you call them? Jews, I believe?"

"That's completely different."

"You and your pitiful society does not speak on what the Earth needs."

"Who told you that the Earth needs saving?"

Rain shook her head and laughed. "Then you haven't been paying very close attention, Homo sapien. Look at your levels of pollution, your history of war."

"And you decide for yourself?"

Rain frowned. "You cannot deny these things."

"No, but for Christ's sake, we were moving past all that."

"I heard one Homo sapien say it's like making an omelette without breaking some eggs. What do you think of that logic, Magnetar?"

From down the dark hallway, a small Post Human immerged into the light. It was no more than five feet and looked like a baby compared to Rain. It had wavy brown hair and familiar eyes.

No, Ewan thought. *It couldn't be!*

"Timmy?"

The smaller Post Human made some unsure clicking sounds, as if it was first learning the language.

"He said you're . . . click, click idiot."

Ewan moved closer to the bars. He couldn't believe his eyes. In front of him was the likeness of his son, yet not his son. His pinkish skin had peeled off and underneath was a darker tone of rough scales that replaced it and his hair had mostly fallen out but there was no doubt he was his son by his large round brown eyes that penetrated through him.

"Timmy? Is that you? You're alive?"

Timmy didn't respond but just stared at Ewan.

"What did you do to him?" Ewan screamed.

"No, this one is called Magnetar. And the question is what did you do to him?"

The War Begins

Stu was back in the council room, again sitting across from the council members. A single candle was on the long wooden desk, casting its bleak light onto the corners of the room.

Stu was wearing his kimono, washed once again, and on his head he had the White Chief's headdress. He supposed he looked a little ridiculous but nobody dared to say anything.

He stared at each one individually but nobody dared to meet his gaze. The Caucasian men, the black guy and the Indian all sat there like meek idiots.

Good, Stu thought.

"I'm here to disband the council. I thank you for your loyal service."

"Yes, White Chief," they said in unison, still not looking up.

"You are dismissed."

The council didn't have to be told twice. They all got up and shuffled quickly out the door, leaving Stu alone.

Once they were gone, Stu took off the headdress and laid it on the counter when he heard a knock on the door. He closed his eyes, remembering the morning with a smile.

Otakay had screamed for mercy but Stu hadn't given it. Not yet anyways. He would get mercy at the rally tonight.

He heard a sound from the hallway and turned around and saw Graham leaning against the door. He looked gaunter than before.

"What do you want?"

"Don't expect me to call you White Chief," Graham said, pulling up a chair.

Stu laughed. "You look like shit. You should take a break. We have the generator at the museum."

Graham ran his hands through his grey hair. "Did I ever tell you how Perpetuum Industries started?"

Stu sighed. "What relevance does that have?"

"It was started by a man named Albert Winkler. A scientist. A genius, really. He was the one who created the generator, who built it."

"You want to prove you can build one too?"

Graham glanced downward. "I don't know — I suppose. I took his company away from him. It had to be done. He was no leader. If it had been up to him he would have given the technology away for free."

"When do you think you'll have the second generator up and working?"

"It's impossible to say. It could be a matter of weeks or a matter of years."

"Let me be clear with you on something, Graham. The generator is a nice perk but it doesn't hold sway over me like it did with the White Chief."

Graham nodded. "I know. I'm not stupid."

Stu studied Graham for a long time. They had spent many hours, days together and Stu thought he could read him pretty well, but he had to be sure.

As if Graham could read his mind, he said, "Stuart, I'm backing you a hundred percent. Haven't I always? My only goal right now is to build another generator."

Stu walked through the long, dark corridor until he came to a small room guarded by two savages. They stiffened a little when they saw Stu and glanced away, unable to hold eye contact.

He nodded to them and they opened the door. Stu stepped in and the savages closed the door behind him. Stu stood still, allowing for his eyes to adjust to the darkness.

Chenoa was crumpled on the hard floor in the corner. She propped herself up on her elbows and stared out at Stu, her eyes unfocused and unsure.

"I'm sorry things had to end this way," Stu said.

"Oh, it's you," she said, bitterness in her voice. She sat up and crossed her legs. She seemed as beautiful as ever — maybe more so in her helpless state. "What have you done with my husband?"

"Where is Otakay?"

...way from harm. Many people want to see him...
...lieves he killed the White Chief."
...People knew he was ambitious. He wanted to be ...hief."
...shook her head. "No. Not like that."
...emember when we first met? You said you had a ...change humanity."
...n't have to talk to you about my vision."
...hat was your real name? Before Chenoa?"
...am only Chenoa. There is no before, no after. Only now."
...The White Chief is dead. There is no need for this charade ...e."

...Chenoa looked up at Stu, the whites in her eyes seemed to ...n in the darkness. "I liked how things were before you came ...g."

"But now we can work towards going back to the way things ...ere, before the Outbreak."

"The world was broken. That was why the virus destroyed ...us. To punish us. We cannot, should not go back."

Stu rubbed his elbows. He didn't want to go back to being a lowly paramedic either but he knew like most great visionaries he had to sell the tribe a vision.

"No, we won't go back. We'll do things right this time around."

"And you're the person to do it?" Chenoa scoffed. "You'll do anything to become the next White Chief."

"All I was doing was protecting myself. The White Chief would have killed Graham and me eventually. Graham was just too short-sighted to see it."

"No the White Chief was a good man. He was just."

"You eat the flesh of your victims. Of people who you raid and attack."

"We starve otherwise. Nothing grows in this winter."

"We're going to change that."

"How?"

Stu smiled. He could see the vision of his new civilization so clearly, he felt he could reach out and touch it. "We're going to systematically kill every Creature in this city. Take the city back"

Chenoa stared incredulously at Stu. "You can't do that way."

"Why not? All it takes is the manpower, which now we . I am going to extinguish them as they tried to extinguish us."

On the Run

Ashley ran towards Albert's funhouse. It was the only place she could think of that would be safe. Her heart was pounding in her chest, trying to keep up with her limbs. She didn't look around, she didn't look back. She didn't think of anything but reaching the funhouse.

She had collapsed as soon as she got to the lab. She wasn't sure if she had passed out or not but eventually she regained her strength and sat up.

I will be safe here, she thought.

But what were those things?

She had seen them chasing Ewan. She had wanted to help him but she had no weapons, nothing to use against them. They weren't Creatures. They weren't afraid of the light and they were bigger than the Creatures.

She tried to understand what had happened but her head was pounding and she felt lightheaded from exhaustion.

Was it possible the virus had created something other than the Creatures? Something almost superhuman?

She stood up and looked around the lab. It was just as she remembered it with Albert's flasks and potions scattered across the table. Old, broken computer monitors were shoved in the corner, collecting dust.

She realized she had hoped the boys and Albert had somehow made it back here but they were nowhere to be seen. The funhouse was empty and quiet.

She sat down on one of Albert's broken chairs and closed her eyes. In the darkness, in her peripheral vision she could see Ewan clearly standing in front of her. His dirty, ripped sweater; his thinning, greyish hair, his sly, uncertain smile.

Why hadn't she told him the truth when she had first seen Timmy? Why had she kept it a secret for so long? Ewan had been right to be angry at her. She was a coward. She had tried to remain so strong for so long that she had eventually lost her strength.

She felt the tears swell up in the edges of her eyes and fought to stop them. Even alone in the dark she wouldn't allow herself to be weak. If she was going to ever see Ewan again she was going to have to remain strong, not allow any emotion to creep in.

Eventually she stood up and looked around for something to eat and found some canned baby food in the cupboard. Next she searched for a can opener and a spoon which she found in a drawer. She opened the can and quickly spooned the food into her mouth.

Before she was finished she heard a crashing sound come from the corner of the room. She stopped eating and spun towards the sound but saw nothing.

Her heart was beating rapidly. She could feel it in her chest.

She stood still not moving, not making a sound. In the corner there was a pile of junk where something could be hiding. Could one of the Creatures have made it through Albert's maze?

She took a deep breath and forced herself to move towards the junk pile. There was a sudden movement and something came out of the pile and towards her.

Ashley looked around for something to protect herself. She grabbed an empty beaker from the table and raised it. But the Creature stopped about ten feet away from Ashley.

"Click . . . Click . . . Please . . . click . . . click. Don't," it said.

Ashley was too stunned to move. The Creature was about her size, its head and neck were large. It had brownish-grey skin that looked thick and tough but yet flexible. The Creature's arms and legs were long and powerful. It was unlike the Creatures in body and shape, yet it had certain features that reminded Ashley of the Creatures.

"What are you?" Ashley asked, gripping the beaker tightly.

"We . . . click. . .are click . . click, called click, click, in your language, click, clicckk, in your language, Post Humans."

"Post Humans?"

"Evolved . . . from . . . homo sapiens."

"You evolved from us?"

"Click . . . click. Rain tells us."

"What is Rain?"

"The. . . leader of Post Humans."

"What are you doing here?"

"I followed you."

"Why?"

The Post Human didn't answer right away and Ashley thought she saw a change in its emotions, although the Post Human's face was so foreign to her, she couldn't tell for sure.

"I was click . . . click curious about humans."

"What will you do with my friend?"

"We . . .click . . . click need to save him."

"Save him from what?"

"From . . . evolution . . . or death."

Ashley shook her head. "I don't understand. You mean if he doesn't evolve he'll die?"

The Post Human reached out its hand. "Please, I click . . . click know a way."

Ashley put the beaker back on the table and reached for the Post Human's hand. It had long slender fingers and was surprisingly soft to touch. It felt almost human.

"Do you have a name?"

The Post Human turned and looked directly at Ashley. "I am the one they call Dawn."

"How old are you?"

"I am not sure. I do not remember anything before . . . click, click, click, transformation."

Ashley shook her head. Was she still awake? Was this really happening?

"Transformation from Creatures to Post Humans."

"How does that happen?"

Dawn frowned and let out a series of clicks but then stopped abruptly as if she realized Ashley couldn't understand. "Do not know exactly."

"Why are you here??"

"I was, click, how do you say? Curious?"

"Curious? Curious about what?"

"Rain says homo sapiens are virus. Kill everything that lives."

Ashley sighed. She needed to sit down again and grasped her way in the low-light until she found her chair again. "Maybe he's right. We do tend to kill everything, including each other."

"You seem, click, click, nice. Not dangerous."

"Of course some are more dangerous than others."

351

"Rain is, click, click, is dangerous too."

"He has Ewan, and the boys and Albert, doesn't he?"

Dawn didn't say anything for awhile but then she nodded. "Rain is a she, not click, click a him. She exterminates homo sapiens because she thinks they are a virus."

"Can you take me there? To Ewan."

"No it's too dangerous for a homo sapien."

"Dawn, do you have a family?"

"What is a family?"

"It's a core group of people who you love the most. They're called a family."

"I don't know what that is."

"Well they are my family. I would rather die than live without them."

Dawn didn't say anything for a long time. Ashley watched it closely.

"I know I'm probably putting you in jeopardy by asking this," Ashley said. "But I think you came here because you were more than curious. You wanted to know if this . . . Rain person is lying to you."

Dawn nodded. "If homo sapiens are a virus then aren't we a virus too?"

"I don't know, Dawn. I can't answer that. All I can tell you is it's not right to kill anything just for the pleasure of it."

"I will take you."

Ashley smiled and tried to hug Dawn but it managed to quickly dodge underneath Ashley's outstretched arms.

"Click. Click. Click . . . What are you doing?" Dawn asked, sounding alarmed.

"Relax I was just trying to hug you."

"Hug?"

"It's a gesture between two friends."

"We're friends?" Dawn asked.

"If you want to be."

Dawn made a couple of clicking sounds. "I would like that very much."

Ashley woke up early and found Dawn in the lab room, staring at the wall.

"You okay?" Ashley asked.

"We don't sleep, click, click in the same, click humans and Creatures."

"So you've just been staring at the wall this entire time?"

Dawn didn't answer. It just stared back at her.

"We have to leave soon. You hungry?"

Ashley packed some baby food and some bottled water and anything she could see that she thought would be useful.

The coldness seemed to have dissipated and the sky was a clear, cloudless blue. They walked along Bloor Street. Dawn seemed to effortlessly glide along the top of the snow with her long, powerful strides but it was slow going for Ashley who was also cautious of the savages that might be out searching for them.

They saw nobody, however. The beautiful city was dead and silent.

"Will anybody realize you're gone?" Ashley asked.

Dawn scanned the horizon. "Maybe but, click, it's doubtful."

"Don't you have parents?"

"Is that the same as family?"

"Yes."

"We don't have the same social hierarchy as homo sapiens."

"But you must have some sort of social structure. This Rain is obviously the leader."

"Rain assigns certain positions to Post Humans based on the skills they exhibit."

They continued their journey until they reached a subway station and there they paused.

Dawn looked at Ashley with its large dark eyes with large pupils. As Ashley stared back, she thought she almost looked human. The way she stared was so unique, so off base that Ashley didn't quite know how to feel.

"You sure you want to do this?" Dawn asked. Ashley wasn't sure if it was her imagination or something else but the tone in her voice seemed to have changed into something different entirely.

Ashley didn't trust herself to speak. Didn't trust herself to move. Dawn's look and her voice had created a stirring sensation in the deepest pit of her stomach. And then all of a sudden out of the corner of her eye she thought she saw Ewan standing there again. But when she glanced in her direction he was gone.

Dawn went into the subway station first. It was damp and musky and the smell of rotting flesh choked Ashley and made her eyes water.

"Stay close to me," Dawn whispered.

They descended to the bottom of the stairs and soon as Dawn stepped onto the floor several Creatures appeared from the darkness. Dawn pivoted quickly – faster than Ashley had ever seen anything move – and snapped the first Creature's neck. There was a loud popping sound as the Creature fell. Dawn head butted the second Creature so hard it was like a hammer had crushed its skull.

The third Creature hesitated. It was the first time Ashley saw a Creature uncertain of what to do. The hesitation didn't last long as Dawn jumped on it and sunk its teeth into the Creature's neck. Black bile spouted from the wound, hitting the wall.

The Creature struggled uselessly for a couple of seconds but then lay there lifeless.

Dawn stood up and looked at Ashley who couldn't help but gasp at the sight of Dawn, its face shrouded in darkness, black blood running down its mouth.

"What's wrong?" Dawn asked. "You're safe now."

Ashley took a deep breath, trying to quell her impulse to turn and run. "Nothing, let's keep going."

"Sometimes death is necessary."

Ashley was confused but then she remembered what she had said about killing.

"I don't think of those Creatures as alive."

"We'll be moving quickly. Can you keep up?"

"I'll try."

Dawn turned and started off at a pace that for a normal human being would be a run. Ashley jogged after it, trying not to lose the Post Human in the darkness.

They travelled along the tracks for a couple of minutes before Dawn stopped at a large hole that looked like it had been caused by an earthquake or a stick of dynamite. It was only about six feet in diameter and looked unstable, as if it might cave in at any moment.

"This leads to the prison cells."

"I can't keep up this pace. We need to go slower."

"If we go any slower Rain will find us."

"We're going to have to try."

Dawn nodded and stepped into the hole in the wall and Ashley followed.

Ashley didn't think it could get any darker but somehow the darkness grew even thicker as they descended into the depths of the Earth.

The ground below Ashley's feet was broken and sharp. A couple of times Ashley stumbled, almost twisting her ankle. It was slow going and when Ashley stopped to listen she couldn't hear Dawn in front of her.

For the first time, Ashley wondered if she was stepping into a trap. But for what purpose?

Ashley saw what Dawn had done with the Creatures. Dawn could have easily knocked her out and taken her to the Post Human city.

Is that what it is, Ashley wondered. *An underworld city?*

How many Post Humans were there? Ashley shuttered to think about it. However many there were, even one could kill her without hesitation.

Ashley wanted to call out to Dawn but she was afraid of who might hear. If they had such great speed and eyesight they probably had amazing hearing as well.

Ashley didn't know how long she spent in the tunnel. It seemed to gradually grow smaller and smaller until she had to stoop to keep going.

She wondered how Dawn fit through the passageway. There was no way a full-grown Post Human could be able to use the tunnels which made her wonder what they were for.

Ventilation perhaps. Even the Post Humans had to breath, Ashley supposed.

Eventually a small yellowish dot appeared in front of her. She grew excited and quickened her pace but her toe hit a large rock and she stumbled, falling onto her hands and knees.

She got back to her feet dusting off her jeans. Her palms were grazed and bleeding but she was otherwise uninjured.

She focused back on the dot and made her way towards it. The dot gradually grew larger until it filled her vision. When she came closer, she realized it was some type of light coming from a larger room.

She stopped to listen and for the first time she heard low voices mumbling to each other. She couldn't hear what they were saying but they were human voices - she was sure of it. Many of them. She hadn't heard such an array of talking for such a long time. Their soft treble sounds were comforting. She wanted to run towards them, to embrace them but she forced herself to move slowly.

She got to the entrance of the room and stopped. From her vantage point she couldn't see anything — just a rock wall but she now could make out what the voices were saying.

"It's tiny compared to the others," one man said.

"Why do you think it's here?" another man asked.

"I don't think it's here to kill us," a woman said.

They must be talking about Dawn, Ashley said.

But still Ashley didn't move. She felt safe in the darkness of the tunnel. To take a step out into the open was to expose herself. She thought of how brave she had been, how she had saved Ewan's life.

She inhaled deeply and thought about how everything that mattered to her was right before her, only a couple of steps away. She had to choose to move forward. There was no going back, not without Ewan, the boys, and Albert.

Ashley shielded her eyes from the light and walked out into the room.

There was a loud gasp as she looked around. On either side of her were large prison cells filled with humans. The ceiling and walls of the room were glowing in a dark purple tone. There were pillars holding up the ceiling and the room reminded her of a cathedral. She had never seen something this beautiful and yet so scary. She almost didn't realize that she was standing the middle of the room and she was totally exposed. Everybody was staring at her, wide-eyed.

"Is there an Ewan here? Two boys?"

"Ashley?" came the familiar voice.

The sea of people parted and Ewan appeared. He looked thin and weary but he was still alive.

A rush of adrenaline hit her and Ashley ran to him and before she could understand what was going on she was kissing him through the bars. His dry, crispy lips on hers. She vaguely heard the mass of humans but it was like a ripple coming from under the water. At that moment all she could think about was Ewan.

It was Dawn's voice that snapped her back to reality.

"What are click, click, you, click doing?" she asked.

"Nothing," Ashley said, growing shy all of a sudden, and stepping away from the bars. She turned to Ewan. "Are the boys here?"

Ewan nodded. "Yeah, they're here."

"How about Timmy?"

Ewan swallowed hard. "He's turned, into . . . one of them," he indicated Dawn.

"You should kill it!" someone screamed. There was a mummer of agreement.

"No," Ashley said, raising her hands. "Dawn is on our side."

"The only good Post Human is a dead Post Human!"

"You want me to let you rot in here?" Ashley said.

"The one they call Ashley, we must hide," Dawn said. "I hear Forest coming."

"Forest? You mean trees?"

Dawn grabbed Ashley and with incredible strength dragged her back to the tunnel.

They got there just as Ashley heard quick footsteps approach and then a deep, angry voice.

"Homo sapiens, stop making noise or we'll exterminate you."

The voice was loud and terrifying but it didn't seem too interested in finding out what the commotion was about and soon Ashley could hear the Post Human turn and walk away.

"We call that one Forest in Homo sapien," Dawn said. "He is the . . . click, click, in charge of the hunters."

Ashley nodded. "How do we get everybody out?"

"We need to get the key."

"And where is it?"

"It's one level down in the control room."

"Jesus," Ashley said. "How do we get into the control room?"

Dawn's mouth opened in what Ashley thought was a smile — but she wasn't completely sure.

"You don't but I can get it easily."

"Okay.

Dawn turned and walked towards the larger entrance, that Forest had disappeared into.

"She's going to warn them," somebody cried out.

"Be quiet," somebody else said.

Once Dawn was gone, Ashley ran towards Ewan again who was leaning against the bars.

"How are you holding up?" Ashley asked.

"As well as can be, I suppose."

"Can we get Timmy away from them?"

Ewan shrugged. "That's all I've been thinking about."

"Ashley!" came two tiny voices.

Ashley glanced to her left and saw Justin and Anthony running towards them. Their clothes were ripped and torn so they were practically half naked. Mud and dirt covered their faces, hair and hands.

"Boys!" Ashley cried out. She bent down and reached through the bars and took hold of them.

"I'm sorry I lost you. It'll never happen again. I promise."

The two boys, who had been so brave, burst into tears.

"It'll be okay. We'll get you out of here."

"How did you meet that Post Human?" Ewan asked.

"Her name is Dawn," Ashley said. "And it was the one who found me."

Ashley gave a quick explanation of all the events that had transpired over the last day.

It didn't take long for Dawn to return. She was holding a large object which she gave to Ashley. It was a copper-like rod with a starfish shaped tip. Ashley realized it was a key.

Ashley took the key and quickly inserted it into a matching form on the wall next to the door and undid the locks. The people started to stream out and headed towards the exit.

"Not that way," Dawn said. "Back to the, click, tunnel."

But nobody listened or heard because they kept running. Someone running by Dawn even tried to punch the Post Human who ducked just in time.

"Nobody hurt Dawn," Ashley yelled, amidst the loud thundering of feet.

Ashley turned to Dawn. "I'm so sorry."

"Anger is to be expected," Dawn said, simply.

Ashley watched helplessly as more and more people continued to the exit.

"Hello there lass!"

Ashley turned to the familiar voice and saw Albert smiling at her. Ashley hugged him tightly; she could feel his white beard scratch against her neck. "I'm so happy to see you."

"Well I'm still breathing," Albert said.

People continued to push past them towards the exit.

"How do we stop them?" Ashley asked. She yelled at Ewan who was several paces away. "You need to do something."

Ewan nodded.

"Dawn is right," Ewan yelled, running towards the entrance. He waved his hands and got people's attention, forcing them to stop running.

"We need to organize. Listen to what Dawn has to say."

"They'll be here any moment," someone screamed.

"Which is why we need to be quick and do exactly what Dawn says."

Dawn didn't say anything but instead motioned everybody to follow. Ewan was the first to run after Dawn, Ashley followed and soon everybody streamed towards the tunnel.

Ewan stopped at the tunnel entrance. "Okay, everybody form a line. We need to do this quickly."

Again people hesitated, and several pushed and shoved but Ewan yelled at them to stop and eventually they listened. Soon a line was formed and people quickly moved into the tunnel. It was an efficient process but there were too many people.

Ashley whispered to Ewan. "We're never going to get everybody through before they come back."

Ewan nodded and turned to Dawn. "How long before the Post Humans returns?"

"I don't know."

"Could you distract them?"

Dawn nodded. "I will try."

Dawn turned and walked to the entrance.

"I hope Dawn's okay," Ashley said. "I would hate anything to happen to her."

Ewan put an arm on Ashley's shoulder. "Her?"

"Well Dawn is a female name."

"You really care for her don't you?"

"She is risking a lot for what she believes in, turning against her own kind. That takes guts."

The man who had been standing beside Ewan approached.

"Ashley I want you to meet Christian Boeving."

Christian shook Ashley's hand. He had a firm handshake and a concentrated gaze. He looked like a man who had suffered greatly. "Pleased to meet you," he said politely.

Christian turned to Ewan. "She's very pretty."

Ewan smiled faintly, embarrassed. "Christian, you should get in line,"

"I'm not going up until everyone is safe."

Ewan leaned in, speaking in just a whisper. "The Post Humans will be back soon and those on top will need a leader. Somebody they can trust."

"Then you should go," Christian said. "Take your pretty girlfriend."

"I'm not exactly his girlfriend," Ashley said, feeling herself going red in the face.

Both Christian and Ewan turned and frowned at her.

What a stupid thing to say, she thought. *Why did I have to say that?*

"I just thought-" Ashley said. "Never mind."

"Let's just hope Dawn manages to distract them long enough," Ewan said.

They waited around for nearly an hour. For Ashley, the waiting was agony. She began to pace around the prison cell. There weren't many people left. Was it possible this was going to work? That everybody was going to get away alive?

Ewan approached Ashley. He seemed to have become a different person since he had first stumbled down the tunnel and had been caught by the Post Humans. Perhaps it was meeting the other humans, trapped and helpless. Or perhaps it was the final realization that Timmy, was gone and, even though there was a live, a part of him would be lost forever. Whatever it was he had become more serious, less carefree.

"I want you to get in line."

Ashley shook her head. "I'm not leaving without you."

"What about Anthony and Justin? Think of them. You said you would never lose them again."

Ashley looked towards the tunnel. The line was beginning to shorten. "Okay. But if you're captured again or killed I'll never forgive you."

Ewan smiled, leaned towards Ashley and kissed her. "It's a deal," he whispered.

Ashley climbed up from the tunnel and into the subway station. She saw several dead Creatures, their skulls bashed in. Beside them were dead men and women, their sides split open, fresh blood was still pouring out from their bodies.

Ashley looked away. Was it her fault? She had led them this way.

It is a chance we took, she thought.

She picked up a rock and moved slowly, quietly along the tracks. She could hear footsteps in front of her and behind them but didn't see a sign of the Creatures.

Unable to contain herself, she ran up the steps towards street level.

When the light hit her eyes she began to feel lightheaded and had to steady herself on a lamp post.

She was surprised by how much time had passed since the morning. She looked up at the sun and estimated it was midday.

Many dishevelled people were milling around, looking at each other, uncertain of what to do next. There were all types of people of all different ethnic backgrounds. The oldest was probably in the mid-forties and the youngest was probably around Justin and Anthony's age.

Ashley estimated there were probably several hundred people in the streets. Whatever they did, they would have to decide fast. Soon dusk would be on them and the Creatures would be out.

What were they going to do? Where would they stay that would be safe from the Creatures and from the new threat of the Post Humans?

"You want something to eat?"

Ashley turned and saw Christian standing beside her. In his hand he was holding out some mushrooms. Ashley hadn't realized how hungry she was.

"Has everybody else had something?" she asked.

She realized no matter how hungry she was, she had probably eaten before everybody else had.

"Yeah, we've been searching the area, waiting for everybody else," Christian said. "We managed to find some stuff."

"I'll have one," Ashley said.

"How long have you known Ewan?" Christian asked.

It seemed an awkward question and Ashley didn't know if it was some half-hearted attempt to make conversation or if there was an alternative motive for the question.

"I don't know. Couple of months I suppose."

"He seems like a good man," Christian said casually. There was that same glint of pain that Ashley had first seen, a hopelessness that hadn't changed since their escape.

"How long were you down there for?" Ashley asked, swallowing the last of the mushroom. She wished she could have some more but she didn't want to be greedy.

Christian shrugged. "I don't know. It seemed like an eternity."

"Is he going to be okay?"

Christian nodded. "Yeah, he's tough."

"Who are these Post Humans?"

"I was hoping you would know more about them than me since you seemed to have befriended one."

"I already told you that Dawn is on our side."

"So she seems."

"What possible reason would she have for freeing us unless she wanted to help us?"

"I'm not sure but I don't trust her. They don't have any feelings. I saw them kill us without a moment's hesitation."

"I'm sorry what you experienced down there, Christian. I can't begin to know what it felt like."

Christian didn't say anything after that. He looked past Ashley at something that seemed far off in the distance. He finally spoke, saying, "We need to figure out what we're going to do now."

"I have no idea." Ashley said.

"Do you think Ewan will have a plan?"

"I think you overestimate him."

Christian shook his head. "No, I think you underestimate him."

Ashley smiled.

"One of the guys said before the Post Humans exterminated him that the army, just after the outbreak, had stockpiled weapons on Toronto Island."

"You think he was telling the truth? You don't think somebody would have found them already?"

Christian shrugged. "If there still are some weapons, perhaps we can use them against the Post Humans."

Ashley nodded but before she could say anything more, there was a loud rumbling from below. The Post Humans had discovered their disappearance.

Extinction

Otakay was standing on the stage. His eyes seemed fixated upon the ground.

He was completely naked except for a large piece of rope tied around his wrists. He was breathing heavily, and large droplets of sweat were pouring down his large muscular body, leaving a tiny pool of perspiration on the worn carpet.

The tribe had slowly shuffled into the theater to watch Otakay's execution and was now pulsating with a vibrant energy. They yelled and swore at him. Threw things at him.

Otakay didn't move, didn't look up, seemingly oblivious to the events that were going on around him.

A brawl broke out in the crowd which momentarily brought a greater source of entertainment for the crowd.

But when Stu climbed onto the stage and stood next to Otakay the fighting stopped, the talking stopped, everybody stood absolutely.

Stu looked around thinking about how it hadn't been long ago that he had been in Otakay's place.

Stu looked around the room as he spoke. "The council has voted to condemn Otakay to death for his crimes against the tribe but before we proceed, he would like to say a few words."

For the first time, Otakay stirred, lifting is large head and stared into the crowd.

"I admit to the crime," he said. "I killed the White Chief out of pure jealousy. Because I thought I could do a better job of leading."

The crowd erupted again into commotion as he spoke but Stu raised his hands for silence.

"The traitor has confessed. We will give him a quick painless death but first we must flush out his accomplice."

"What are you doing?" Otakay yelled to Stu but only Stu could have heard him over the crowd, as it again was deafeningly loud.

364

Two savages brought Chenoa in through the main doors of the theater. Like Otakay she was naked except for the rope that tied her hands. Unlike Otakay who stood unabashedly, Chenoa was unsuccessfully trying to cover herself from the many peering eyes.

Stu looked around and saw the crowd absolutely loved it. They roared in approval as Chenoa was hulled up on stage. Her long red hair was no longer beautifully braided and was a tangled mess around her shoulders.

"We had a deal," Otakay was saying, but nobody was listening.

Stu turned to Otakay and smiled. "I changed my mind."

Predictably Otakay launched himself at Stu but several guards wrapped their hands around his body, preventing him from going anywhere. He screamed and cursed, his large veins popping from his muscles.

Stu drew his sword and ran it along Chenoa's bare skin. It made this soft scraping sound like that of a razor blade against a cheek. Chenoa was pale and frightened but it only made her that much more beautiful.

"Kneel," he commanded and Chenoa reluctantly sunk to her knees. Her breath grew shallow and desperate.

Stu circled her, savouring every moment. She quivered uncontrollably.

"Head straight, shoulders back, and this won't hurt a bit," Stu said.

Chenoa did as she was told and Stu parted her hair to expose a thin protruding neck. He put his sword so it rested on her neck. He turned to look at Otakay who was still struggling to get free. Stu couldn't help but smile back at him; this resulted in him struggling harder but to no avail.

Stu felt the loud thumping of adrenaline in his ears. This was better than ever. Better than feeding all those poor people to the Creatures. He now had an audience that was cheering him on.

Chenoa was still quivering when Stu turned his attention back to her.

"Relax it's almost over," Stu said. "Soon you'll meet the White Chief again."

Stu changed his grip on the sword, widened his stance on the carpet and pulled his sword back over his head and with a gentle smoothness brought it back down. It cut through Chenoa's neck with a loud 'thwack' sound, almost like punching a pillow. Chenoa's body immediately collapsed to the ground. Her head did a couple of summersaults before it stayed still.

Otakay let out a loud, animalistic howl then broke free of his captives. He ran towards Chenoa, bent down to her body.

Stu turned to the crowd which was still cheering. "Traitors cannot be tolerated," Stu said.

Stu turned, gripped his sword with both hands, did a small stutter step towards Otakay and swung his sword. This blow wasn't as clean as his first and caught Otakay, who shifted his weight slightly, on the shoulder, cutting deep, squirting blood everywhere. Otakay swayed backwards and Stu took another swing, this time slicing him in the neck. The wound was deep but didn't cut all the way through. Otakay's arms, still bound together, rose towards his neck but then he collapsed next to Chenoa.

Stu stepped over him and stared down. Stu's sword was dripping blood.

It took an incredibly long time for Otakay to die. Blood poured out of his nose. He coughed and spat up large chunks of blood before his whole body quivered and he died.

Stu turned to the tribe. He could feel the blood slope around his feet. "We will dine well tonight!"

This got the largest cheer of them all.

Stu watched as Kimi appeared from the building and walked through the deep snow over to his car.

Kimi was a broad-shouldered man, tall, with a thick scraggily beard. He walked slowly, deliberately. His lumbering pace angered Stu who wished he would move a little faster.

Kimi was Stu's choice to take over Otakay as leader of the hunters. He wasn't as big or as strong as Otakay but he would serve the purpose, at least for now.

Kimi leaned down and Stu rolled down his window so they could speak, letting in a gust of cold air that made Stu shiver.

"The building has been sterilized, White Chief," Kimi said.

"For God's sake, don't call me that," Stu said. "How many times have I told you?"

Kimi shrank from Stu. "Sorry sir. It won't happen again."

Stu paused, letting his anger subside. "Any loss of life?"

"No sir."

"That's good, let's move on then."

Kimi nodded and hustled back to the building where he would collect his hunters.

Stu was annoyed that most of the tribe refused to go back to their real names, instead most of them elected to stay with the ones the White Chief had given them.

Stu shook his head at the tribe's superstition that the virus had been some kind of cleansing and this was their chance to make a new society and adopt a new life.

The hunting party, which consisted of fifty men, slowly made their way out of the building and went into the adjacent one.

Stu waited in the warmth of his car. There was nothing to do but wait. He supposed he could have joined the hunting party but the truth was he was afraid of assassination in the darkness more than the Creatures. It would be too easy for an errant knife to find its way into his back.

So Stu waited, supervising from a safe distance. A couple of hours later Kimi came back with the same report. One of the hunters had suffered a cut across his arm but nothing serious.

"You've done very well," Stu said.

"I'm only doing my duty," Kimi said.

"How are your men? Are they tired? Need some food?"

"I think we can do another building."

"Very good. I have a few matters to attend to back home. I expect a full status report when you get back."

"Yes sir."

Kimi nodded and turned back towards the building. Stu tapped his driver on the shoulder and he pulled the Lincoln Town Car out onto the road, avoiding all the debris and garbage that littered the street.

Stu watched the city out the window, lost in thought so he didn't notice when the Town Car hit something on the ground and the front tire popped and let out a loud hiss. The car swerved before coming to a stop.

"What did you run over, you idiot?" Stu said.

The driver jumped out of the car and rushed to inspect the damage.

"I'm very sorry sir," he stammered.

Stu lifted the door handle and stepped out into the freezing weather and walked up next to the driver.

"Do you know how to change a tire?" Stu asked.

"Yes. . . I think so."

"But you've never done it before, have you," Stu said, icily.

"I'm sure it's not that hard. It won't take a moment."

"Forget it. What I want you to do is kneel."

The blood drained from the driver's face as he realized his fate. His eyes went from left to right as if he was looking for an escape.

"I'm sorry sir. I'll fix it soon I promise."

"If you don't want me to hurt your family as well, I suggest you do as I tell you."

The driver began to cry and sob.

Stu just watched with delight, a slight smile crossed his face. It reminded him of the simpler times when he would chain people to the fence and watch the Creatures devour them, bit by bit.

"I promise you it won't hurt a bit."

The driver slowly sank to his knees, tears still rolling down his cheek.

Stu took out his sword and placed it against the driver's neck who recoiled at the blade.

"Ssshhhhh," he said, letting out a puff of steam from his lips. "You need to extend your neck so I don't miss."

"Please, don't . . ." the driver whimpered.

"Yes I know you have a wife named Tiponi and she's with child."

The driver stopped crying and for the first time looked directly into Stu's eyes. "Then how can you-"

But the driver never got to finish the sentence as Stu pulled his hands back and then with one elegant motion cut the driver's head off. Blood spurted upwards like a fountain and splattered the car, the white snow and Stu's kimono.

Stu wiped the blade on the snow and then went to get the spare tire from the trunk. He whistled a tune he remembered from childhood as he lifted the car with the jack, and loosened the bolts.

Only when he finished changing the tire, did he think to check what had caused the tire to pop. He stood up and backtracked several paces. In the snow, he found what looked like to be a bone snapped almost completely in half. Bits of greenish flesh still clung to it.

The flesh looks unlike the flesh of either human or Teki, Stu thought. The jagged part from the break had obviously been what had caused the puncture.

Stu examined the bone, curiously and on a whim decided to throw it in the back of the car.

Graham examined the bone closely, using a microscope he had found in one of the office rooms, amidst piles of paperwork.

"So," Stu said, impatiently. "What is it?"

"I'm no expert but I would guess it's a humerus — part of the arm."

"Is it from some kind of animal?"

Graham shook his head. "Animals this size have been extinct for years."

"So it's from a Teki?"

"That is the most likely explanation," Graham said, putting the bone back on the table.

Stu noted a hesitation in Graham's voice. "But you're unconvinced?"

"I don't know."

"If you were to guess?"

"I would say it must be something new, something different. Perhaps the virus has mutated some people into something different than a Teki."

"Like what?"

"I can't possibly know until I have more evidence. I heard rumors long ago, but never really thought much of them at the time."

"You think something else is out there?"

"Remember that life is always evolving, nothing is ever stagnate so whatever it is, it is probably better equipped than the Teki."

Stu crossed his arms and leaned back against the wall. "After we destroy the Creatures we should find out what this thing is."

"It may be best if we just leave it be," Graham said. "It may not be a threat to us."

"Everything is a threat to us! Look around us!"

"The biggest dinosaurs were actually vegetarians," Graham pointed out.

"Whatever it is, we're going to have to find out and discover for ourselves. I don't like unknowns."

"What do you propose to do?"

"Smoke it out."

"How? You don't even know its habitat."

"Sun Tzu said if you know your enemy, you do not need to fear a hundred battles. I told the tribe we shouldn't live in fear and I mean to keep that promise."

Graham took a deep breath. He seemed suddenly old. His hair greyer and his face more wrinkled. "Let's assume that it also has to hide from the Teki."

"Where would it go?"

"No idea, somewhere light, I suppose."

"True but if it was drawn to light then we probably would have encountered it before," Stu said.

Graham folded his hands together and stared into the distance. "Unless the Teki had to hide from this new entity. Look at how large this bone is. I would estimate, if this is normal size, the new entity would stand between seven and eight feet tall."

"So maybe it's not scared of the Teki but it would certainly have its own space."

Graham picked up the bone and stared at it thoughtfully. "I always wonder why the Teki decide to sleep in the buildings."

"What do you mean?"

"Their natural instinct would be to hide, right? Self-preservation is engrained in the genetics of any species. They need to hide from humans yet they pick office buildings and houses. The very places humans are likely to look for them. So if you were a Teki where would the most likely spot be to hide?"

Stu frowned. He wasn't sure what Graham was getting at. "I don't know, the darkest spot I guess — furthest to get to but easy enough access to be able to hunt at night."

"Exactly and where is that?"

Stu thought for a moment. "Underground."

"Yet they don't. I wonder if that's because something higher up in the food chain is always occupying it?"

Stu crossed his legs and closed his eyes. The snow bit into his bare legs but he ignored the numb pain that crept up his body. He heard the slow whistle of the wind as it bounced from building to building.

Empty your mind, think of nothing.

Usually Stu didn't have any trouble meditating but this time strange thoughts crept in. He thought about his aunt and her two sons. They were large, chubby kids with identical crew cuts. Stu was no match for even one of them.

Stuart, you're a fucking idiot.
Where's my He-man, Stuart?

Stu tried to push the thoughts out of his mind. He had a difficult task ahead of him but once he completed it then the tribe would be his. They would worship him like the White Chief. Revere him.

Stu managed to settle his mind but he wasn't able to get into his usual deep trance. After awhile he gave up and opened his eyes.

He focused on the buildings around him. The colours seemed more poignant, the sounds of Graham's slow breathing behind him seemed as loud as a steam engine.

Stu turned and looked at Graham. He was wearing a large isolated coat.

"You sure you want to do this?"

Stu nodded. "You are scared. It's only natural."

Graham looked down at the dry snow. "Why are you never scared?"

"I lived my entire life in fear, up until I was fifteen which was when I first learned to control it and then shut it out."

"Krista is here."

"Where? What does she want?" Stu hadn't spoken to her since he had learned of her miscarriage. He had no use for her and didn't want to see her.

"I'm not sure," Graham said.

Graham turned and waved to a group of hunters that were standing about twenty paces away, waiting respectively. They parted and Krista walked tentatively forward, her eyes held steadily on the street before her. She was wearing a tie-dyed shirt and an old pair of jeans. Her hair had grown longer and was tied back into a ponytail.

"What do you want, Krista?" Stu asked, impatiently.

Finally Krista looked up at Stu. Her lucid eyes seemed stronger than before.

"My name is Makawee," she said.

Stu glared at Graham who only stared mildly back. They still rebelled quietly against him despite everything he did for them.

"I don't have time for this," Stu said.

Krista reached out her fingers and touched Stu on the shoulder. "I envy you. You still haven't had your vision."

"Is that everything?"

"You're going to be purified by the Earth and when you return you will see things as we do. A whole new world will open up to you."

Normally Stu would have gotten angry at her for calling him Stuart but he was too puzzled to be angry. What was she talking about purifying?

He decided she had spent too much time with the savages.

Stu looked at Graham who was still silent so Stu turned and walked towards the subway entrance but before he got there Graham called out. "What happens if you don't return?"

Stu stopped and looked at Graham. "Don't worry. I'll be back."

Stu took out his Samurai sword - he had just sharpened it - and started to descend into the darkness.

As the blackness hit him, he thought of something strange. He remembered a video game he used to play that somebody told him used to be based on an old book. He couldn't remember the name of the video game but it was about this Italian soldier who went into the depths of hell to rescue his girlfriend.

He had no girlfriend but he kind of felt like he was going to the depths of hell to fight the demons that the Italian fought.

Three Teki came at him but he shifted and sliced them apart easily. He was pleased with how easily his blade cut their skin.

He advanced down the station and hopped onto the tracks. He saw no more signs of the Teki which meant Graham's hypothesis

372

was proving correct. He tried to keep his mind sharp but it kept wandering back to that stupid video game he used to play.

He remembered there were several levels that had been taken from the book. He remembered seven – or was it eight levels? He wished he could remember what it had been called.

Stu stopped and took a sip of water before resuming his journey.

I'm taking a journey to the depths of hell, he thought. *Where no man has ever gone before.*

He sensed something was wrong. He couldn't hear anything so it wasn't a Teki. It was something different. He closed his eyes, took several deep breaths, calming his pulse that was beginning to escalate.

When he opened his eyes again and looked out into the darkness he saw what his senses had tried to alert him to. Before him the track had disappeared into a large crevasse that sunk into the Earth below.

I really am going to hell, he thought.

Stu sheathed his sword and examined the gaping hole. It was a steep drop but no means vertical. It was possible to climb down if he was careful.

He turned around and crouched, holding the edge of the cement and lowered his right foot first until he found a stable rock. Shifting his weight, he lowered his other foot.

He repeated the process until he was deep into the hole. He didn't know how long he continued to climb or how far down he went. Eventually the hole levelled out and he no longer had to climb down backwards.

He paused and had another drink of water.

He looked around but still the blackness was complete. He couldn't see more than two feet in front of him. He took out his sword and held it out in front of him; if anything came his way, it would be greeted by the point of steel.

Stu wondered what these Oni – as he had named them in his mind – looked like and how dangerous they would be. Graham said they would be tall and strong. Would they be intelligent as well, or would they be as stupid as the Teki?

Stu continued on in the tunnel. The ground had become smoother as if the tunnel had been made there on purpose and perhaps it had – maybe some sort of access tunnel for the subway system.

Stu walked faster, anticipating meeting the Oni. He would enjoy doing battle with somebody who was worthy for a change. It had been too long since he had a real challenge.

"Oni, come and get me," Stu shouted. His voice echoed off the walls but he got not reply.

It was getting warmer the further he went. Would he end up at the molten core of the Earth? Were the Oni some sort of shape-shifters formed from the lava?

Stu paused. He thought he saw something up ahead. Yes, there was definitely something there. It was a light source of some kind, a little orange dot. Stu tightened his grip on his sword and charged. He ran until he was out of breath. The dot continued to grow but seemed to taunt him.

"You scared of me Oni?" Stu said. "You don't want to fight me?"

Stu slowed down and worked on slowing his pulse again. It was stupid to rush into danger. He had to control his body, his mind and spirit, be patient and let things unfold at their proper pace.

After he decided to walk, the orange dot seemed to come towards him.

"Yes, come to me, Oni. Show your face."

Suddenly, out of nowhere, the name of the computer game came to him: Dante's Inferno. He vaguely remembered it had been a famous book about descending into hell. Someone, a teacher probably, had talked about it in one of his classes. How appropriate he would remember it now.

The orange dot expanded into a dull glow until it halfway filled Stu's vision. He started to hear a low humming that sounded very much like a Perpetuum generator.

Stu didn't rush or hurry. He kept on at an even pace until he stepped out from the tunnel. He found himself in a big room with large stone pillars that reached towards the ceiling. The room looked empty and Stu didn't hear anything except the humming from the lights.

Stu walked around the perimeter of the room, taking everything in. The floor was made from large stone and filled in with glowing cement. The room could have been newly made or it could have been made by aliens . . . it was impossible to tell.

There was an unused water fountain in the middle of the room with ornately carved cherubs along the edges. Next to it was a bust of some important figure or other – it might have been Abraham Lincoln for all Stu knew – with a long, white face and a thick beard. Its empty eyes stared back at Stu. Stu walked up to it and looked down at it. The bust's stare seemed to move with him, glaring at him every which way he went, judging him.

Stu picked the bust up and smashed it against the stone floor, shattering the plaster into pieces.

On the walls were rows and rows of paintings in various styles. They looked very old and Stu wondered where they had all come from. Had the Oni taken them from the museums? Could the Oni appreciate art?

Stu saw a doorway leading to another room and he walked towards it. It had a large double wooden door that seemed to belong in a giant castle.

Stu opened the doors and found himself in a wide, long, well-lit passage way. He walked down it until he came to a fork in the road. There he hesitated and for the first time considered what would happen if he got lost in the Oni's underworld but Stu quickly dismissed the thought. Whatever his fate was, it wouldn't be to die of hunger and thirst in the pits of hell.

Stu chose the left tunnel and found himself descending steeply. He continued for several minutes until he heard a familiar humming sound.

I must be on the right path, Stu thought.

The humming grew louder until it sounded like an angry hornet's nest. As he walked on he found it harder to concentrate. Things, memories jumped into his mind and then quickly disappeared. The humming grew almost unbearable and Stu had to cover his ears to keep from the sound hurting them.

Stu wanted to stop for some more water but the humming became maddening and he felt if he stopped moving forward he wouldn't be able to continue.

Stu eventually saw an oval door ahead. It had a simple oval handle in the middle.

Stu grasped the handle and pulled. The door was heavier than he imagined but with his strength he swung the door open and found himself covering his eyes from the sudden intense light that filled the room.

Stu struggled to adjust but it burned his eye sockets. The humming and the white light were almost too much.

Where was the light coming from?

Eventually his eyes adjusted and he saw that, unlike the previous room, this room was fairly standard in size, and it had at least a dozen Perpetuum generators about twice the size of the one that Graham had been working on at the ROM. They were tall rectangles with a single cord that threaded together and disappeared beneath the floor. The rectangles pulsated in hundreds of different colors like a heartbeat.

Stu tried to grapple with how much power was in this one room. From what Graham had told him, there was enough energy to power the entire North American continent. If he could somehow take the generators back to the surface he was sure he could make some sort of weapon that would keep the tribe and anyone else who opposed him under control.

He wondered why the Oni needed that much power and if they had a weapon of their own to use on humans.

Stu was still standing there when he noticed a sliding door opened on the other side of the room and a huge Oni appeared. It was in roughly a humanoid form with arms and legs but it was even larger than Stu imagined. It didn't seem to have an outline but seem to move like a waterfall in every which way. He couldn't tell what colour it was either. It seemed to shift in dark palettes from grey to green to black to blue.

The only thing Stu could fixate on were its large dark eyes.

Stu smiled, feeling calm and collected, just as he had been taught to do. "We finally meet, Oni."

The Oni let out a series of clicks that seemed to resonate across the entire spectrum of sound.

Stu crouched, raising his sword above his head and waited.

It didn't take long for the Oni to run across the room, passing through the Perpetuum generators.

Stu barely had time to register the quickness of the Oni's movements before it was upon him. The Oni swiped with one large hand which Stu sidestepped and simultaneously cut downward with his blade. He felt the steel meet flesh and the Oni let out a loud roar. Black blood sprayed across the room.

"Not so easy, is it, Oni."

Stu ran between the generators. There wasn't much room to maneuver which gave him, the smaller target, an advantage.

The Oni hesitated this time, staring at Stu with those big black eyes. The Oni circled Stu but he was careful to keep the generator between him and the Oni. He sensed the Oni probably wanted to keep the generators intact.

Stu kept moving until he saw his time to strike. He jumped, swinging his sword, digging the blade into the Oni's shoulder but before Stu could withdraw the blade the Oni grabbed the sword with its big claw-like hands and ripped it out of Stu's grasp. The Oni examined this strange weapon before he threw it across the room.

Stu took out his shorter skaku knife and crouched back into his attack position. The Oni leapt at Stu who fell back behind another generator. The Oni swiped but missed and hit the generator. The generator crumpled like it had been hit by a sledgehammer and sent a shockwave that threw Stu back.

Stu felt himself crush against a generator and then spin and fall onto his face.

Stu forced himself onto his feet. His vision was blurry but he managed to look around for the Oni and saw it lying on the ground motionless.

Stu saw his sword in the corner. He limped towards it, grabbed it and approached the Oni. The Oni still didn't move. Stu raised his sword and sliced its neck. Its skin was tough however and it took several blows. It had been ages since Stu had needed more than one stroke to cut off a head.

He took the head, collected his skaku knife and limped towards the doorway.

He entered another large room and the first thing he realized was there was a thick musty stench of rot. It was dark except for a single flame that burned in the center and flickered and danced to some unknown beat.

In rows, equal distance apart there were big wooden boxes.

Stu stepped into the room and found his feet hitting something hard and uneven. When he examined the floor he found he was stepping on decayed bones. He bent down and collected the bones. Unlike the one that had punctured the car, these were smaller and thinner. They could have been human or Teki. There was no way to know.

Stu didn't want to walk across the bones but he needed to get away from the humming and so he made his way unevenly towards the center flame.

When he reached the center he stopped and looked around. Except for the bones and the strange boxes, the room was plain and ordinary. He put the Oni's severed head down and went over to the closest box to examine it. The wood looked fairly new and well-constructed and appeared to be held together by some sort of white glue. He looked for a latch or a handle but found none that would indicate the box's use; he decided to dig his knife into a weak spot in the wood and pry it open.

Once he had wedged a little hole big enough to stick his hand out of, he managed to pry one plank loose.

He almost stumbled back, tripping on the bones. Inside was a human face but its eyes were open and black, its iris long and cat-like.

Stu expected the half-Oni to jump out of the box and attack him but it didn't move. Stu regained his composure and examined it again. It didn't appear either dead or alive. It wasn't breathing — or at least it didn't appear to be breathing but yet there seemed no sign of decay, no smell wafting from the body.

Perhaps it is in some sort of stasis, Stu thought.

Stu didn't want to wait to find out. He turned, collected the severed Oni head and walked across to the exit.

He found himself in another series of tunnels with several passageways splitting off. Stu didn't think too much of which way to go and chose the first choice that came to him. He eventually found himself in a much larger tunnel, about thirty feet in diameter and with lights that came on with his movement. This tunnel seemed to be a major artery as it had several side doors but Stu decided to go straight.

There was no sense sending a message unless he did it directly.

At the end of the tunnel he saw a large, wooden castle-like door, much like the first one he encountered.

He drew his sword and pulled the heavy door open. He was surprised to find himself in a room that looked like his old apartment building. The room was a couple hundred square-feet wide and had a white sofa in the middle and a television in one corner. Across the room from the television was a work desk with a laptop computer and a notepad and writing utensils.

What is this place, Stu wondered.

It looked almost human. There was even wallpaper and a Persian carpet in the middle.

Stu heard a soft thumping noise and an Oni appeared from the passageway opposite Stu. In the orange light, the Oni looked very much like the first one. Its large head sat upon a long thin neck and its eyes staring back at Stu.

Stu tossed the severed head at the Oni. It landed perfectly and rolled towards the Oni's feet.

The Oni let out a series of piercing clicks and jumped at Stu.

Even though Stu was ready, the speed at which the Oni crossed the room was staggering and Stu barely had time to lift his sword. The Oni didn't stop and hit Stu with a strong blow from its right hand that knocked him to the floor.

Stu's sword went flying and he rolled just in time to prevent himself from being crushed by the Oni which again was on him. Stu kneeled and drew his skaku blade and held it at the ready.

The Oni attacked him predictably. This time Stu was able to get under the blow and dig his knife into the Oni. The skin was tough and the thrust that would have dug deep into a human's organs was only superficial on the Oni.

Stu looked up into the Oni's large, black eyes. He could smell its fierce hot breath on his face.

The Oni seemed to smile at Stu – although Stu wasn't sure if he imagined it or not.

Stu jumped and pulled his head back and with all his strength head-butted the Oni which seemed to stun it. The Oni stumbled backwards, giving Stu time to dive and grab his sword. The Oni quickly recovered and lunged at Stu who managed to cut the Oni's hand, causing black blood to splatter onto the furniture.

The Oni stepped back and let out a shriek of pain.

Stu crouched in wait. The Oni circled Stu, wearier now. Stu shuffled on the balls of his feet. His eyes fixed on the Oni. Even in the light, it was hard to track the Oni's movements as its skin seemed to reflect an array of colours.

"Come on Oni, I'm waiting."

"You're. . . click. . . click a single strange homo sapien."

Stu frowned. Had the Oni just spoken?

The Oni used Stu's moment of confusion and lashed out, grabbing Stu's sword hand, easily twisting the sword out of his hand. It then grabbed Stu's neck and slammed him down on the ground. Stu took his skaku blade out of the belt but the Oni wrenched Stu's arm once again. Stu heard a loud snap of his bones breaking. Stu stifled a scream.

The Oni leaned over Stu as pain flooded up Stu's body and he struggled to remain conscious. "You can speak?"

"I learned homo sapien," the Oni said, circling Stu.

Stu didn't move. He waited for what the Oni was going to do next but it kept circling.

"What are you waiting for?" Stu asked

"For Forest."

Stu sat up, prodding his broken arm with his fingertips. He would never have foreseen his years as an ambulance driver would be useful to diagnose his own injuries. The Oni's movements had been so fast and powerful it had produced a fairly clean break and would probably heal alright. If he was allowed to live that long.

"What is Forest?"

Stu glanced over at his sword. It was lying about ten feet away. Would he get it before the Oni stopped him?

As if realizing what Stu was thinking, the Oni grabbed Stu by his kimono and held him down. It let out a series of clicks.

"Is that some kind of language?"

But before the Oni could answer, there was a slow rumble and several Oni appeared from both sides of the room. Stu looked around. He was surrounded by about six or seven Oni.

What was he going to do now?

Little Big Horn

They had been walking for what seemed like a long time, although Ewan could tell by the sun it had only been a couple of hours.

Ewan glanced back at the slow march.

I would be faster if I was alone with Ashley, Ewan thought.

But he pushed the thought out of his mind. He looked around at the people walking beside him and behind them. There was probably an equal mixture of men and women. Most were thin, boney, and wore rags for clothes. These people, who were possibly the last people on the Earth, needed his help. Ewan couldn't abandon them, even if he wanted to.

Ewan saw Albert making his way through the group of people.

Ewan turned and walked faster, hoping to avoid Albert, but the old man was quick when he wanted to be.

"Sonny, sonny," he said. "Somebody stole all my baby food," he said.

Ewan glanced at Albert. "Nobody stole anything. You distributed it all."

"Oh, yes, of course. I meant to say I don't have enough. I wasn't expecting to feed an entire village."

Ewan stopped walking. "Maybe we'll find some food along the way. The sun is going down so we should probably look for shelter.

Ewan looked around the city for the hundredth time wondering how they were going to hide hundreds of people from the Creatures who would be waking soon.

Should they split up? In some ways it seemed the most logical thing to do, but there was also safety in numbers.

"Have you heard the rumour about Toronto Island?" Ewan asked.

Albert shook his head. "No. I suspect any weapons there are long gone by now."

Ewan let out a sigh. He was afraid this rumour was nothing but false hope and if there weren't any weapons on the island then they would be easy prey for the Creatures or the Post Humans.

He had been against the idea but Christian and Ashley had talked him into making the island their destination. He had wanted to get out of the city, away from the Post Humans and the Cannibals but he knew equal danger waited for them outside the city as in it and so he relented.

"What do you think we should do?" Ewan asked. "Are we walking into a trap?"

But Albert only shrugged.

Ewan looked behind him and spotted Dawn. She was easy to spot since she was about a foot taller than anybody else around her.

Dawn quickly scuttled up next to Ewan. "I can go find some food."

Ewan had seen how close it had become with Ashley. She rarely left Dawn's side and so he had tried to warm up to the Post Human but he found it unsettling being close to Dawn. He wasn't sure if it was his experience with Rain and Forest or if it was the fact that Dawn was supposed to be the evolution of humans. There was something else too, something about her that seemed strange — perhaps she was sent as a spy to teach the other Post Humans about people's habits. "We should stick together," he said.

But Dawn didn't listen and turned and disappeared down an alleyway.

"Dawn, wait!"

"Leave her," Christian said.

But despite all his misgivings he didn't want Dawn running off and leaving them exposed. It was the only reason they had escaped and the only reason they were alive.

Ewan ignored Christian and ran after Dawn. He reached the end of the alleyway and saw Dawn in the distance. She was obviously only walking at about half speed but even so Ewan had trouble keeping pace.

He paused when he reached the shadows, wondering if there were any Creatures hiding and waiting for him. But the more he hesitated the further Dawn got ahead of him.

Ewan ran, following Dawn as she turned a corner. After several blocks, Dawn stopped and turned into a store. Ewan followed her in. The shelves, like most other stores, were empty and everything of any use was gone.

"Dawn? Ewan called out. "Where are you?"

Ewan saw something move in the darkness and instinctively knew it was a Creature. He had obviously disturbed its slumber.

Ewan groped for a weapon and found a mop handle lying on the floor. He squatted down and picked it up.

"Dawn? Where are you? Creatures are in here."

Ewan backed away from the Creature. The Creature ran towards him. Ewan waited then bent the handle back and swung. He timed it well and connected full-force with the Creature's cheek. The Creature's head snapped back but it kept coming. It collided with Ewan, knocking him to the floor. The Creature tumbled also, skidding just beyond Ewan.

Ewan rolled, picked up the mop handle and brought it down on the Creature's face. He smacked it again and again until it was nothing but a bloody pulp.

Ewan looked up to see Dawn running towards him. A Creature climbed over the shelving and jumped onto Dawn's back, sinking its teeth into Dawn's neck.

Dawn tried to shake it off but it latched onto her with its claws. Ewan got up and hit the Creature with the mop handle. The Creature toppled over and before Ewan could raise his stick again, Dawn had jumped on the Creature, grabbed its head and bashed it against the floor until there was a loud cracking sound and it lay still.

"Come on" Ewan said, holding out his hand to Dawn. Dawn hesitated and then got up.

"You saved me," Dawn said. "Why?"

"Do you know what a guardian angel is?"

Dawn shook her head. "No."

"How long have you been watching us, Dawn?"

"Does it matter?"

"I think you've been watching me for a long time, staying out of sight. You saved my son and I from the Creatures back near the ROM, didn't you? Back when they attacked us."

Dawn nodded slowly. "I found you Homo sapiens. . . interesting. I wanted to help."

"Well that makes you my guardian angel and I'm only happy to return the favour and save you."

Dawn seemed to process this. "It was one of us. Disfigured but still. . ."

Ewan examined Dawn's neck wound. It looked superficial but it was still bleeding heavily. "Now you're disfigured."

This made Dawn burst into tears. Ewan realized he had said something stupid but he was surprised by her reaction. What was a Post Human doing crying anyway? He didn't even realize they were capable of tears.

"You're really different from Forest or Rain or the others," Ewan said, eventually.

"Maybe it's being around homo sapiens."

Ewan forced a smile. "Maybe it's my electric personality."

"Electric? I don't understand."

Ewan just shook his head. "Never mind — stupid joke. We should find some food quickly and return to the others."

Together they found a couple of cans of beans beneath a broken shelf.

"You think this will suffice?" Ewan asked.

"It will have to do for now."

They started to walk out to the street but something stopped Dawn.

"Dawn, we should go."

But she didn't answer. Instead she bent down and scooped something up from the floor. It was a wooden pendent. Ewan's stomach lurched and at first he thought it was the same one Sophie had worn but even in the darkness he could see the shape was wrong.

"That's a pretty pendent."

"It's nothing special. It's not even gold," Dawn observed.

Ewan suddenly felt lightheaded and he put his hand out against a shelf to steady himself. Those words resonated deep inside his chest and made it hard to breath. Was it even possible? Sophie?

"Just because it doesn't sparkle, doesn't mean it's not special," Ewan mumbled, but even to him he felt the words were far away, lost to him.

Ewan leaned harder against the shelf.

"What's wrong?" Dawn asked, looking at him quizzically.

"Sophie?" Ewan muttered. It brought up a volcano of pain and suffering, memories that he had long tried to forget. Of Timmy, of Amy, of them just being together in their house.

"Are you Sophie?"

"I don't understand."

"Why did you say those words?"

"I don't know. I just thought of them."

"My daughter said that to me once."

"I don't understand your system of reproducing. What is a daughter?"

"My child, her name was Sophie," Ewan struggled with the words. Then he said, "I think you're her."

"Sophie?" Dawn said, testing the syllables on her tongue. "Sophie?"

"Yes Sophie."

Dawn and Ewan got back to the group of escapees and distributed the food among them. Ewan had expected fights to start but everyone seemed docile, perhaps too tired and weak to put up much of a fight.

They rested and then walked on for another couple of hours before they decided they needed to find a place to stop for the night. Everybody was tired and scared and so they decided to rest while Christian, Ewan and Dawn went scouting. Ashley elected to stay with the boys. They had been more clingy ever since they had been reunited with Ashley.

They got to a clearing where there were few tall buildings and saw a grassy hill in the distance.

"Let's go check it out," Christian suggested.

They followed a road up as it wound up to the middle of the Park.

"I think this is High Park," Christian said, as they passed an old brick building that looked like it had once been a school.

As they continued to walk they came upon a frozen over swimming pool surrounded by a chain link fence. There was a yellow slide that had probably once brought a lot of pleasure to young boys and girls. Beyond that there was what looked like a tennis court.

Christian walked over and looked. Christian wiped away a patch of snow on a brick wall. Underneath it read in block writing, "High Park Swimming Pool."

"My father used to bring me here," Christian said, putting his hands on his hips and surveying the surrounding area. "In the summer we would go once every couple of weeks."

"We should keep moving," Ewan suggested.

But Christian didn't look like he had heard Ewan.

"We would watch the baseball over there," Christian said pointing to a field with an even higher fence surrounding it. "It was only minor leagues but we still enjoyed it."

Christian started to make his way over to the baseball field.

"Christian, what are you doing?" Ashley asked. "We need to stay together on the road."

But again Christian ignored her and continued to wander off.

Ashley looked at Ewan who just shrugged and followed Christian.

"Who wants to play some ball?" Christian asked once they reached the field. Christian scooped up some snow with his bare hands and made a snowball. He playfully tossed it at Dawn who dodged.

"No, you're supposed to catch it," Christian said, sounding annoyed.

Dawn looked questionably at Ewan.

"Don't worry about it Dawn," Ewan said. He then turned to Christian. "We have the group waiting for us and it's getting dark."

"I just want to play some ball for a little while," he said. "Just a couple of minutes. I used to be good at it," Christian said, scooping up some more snow and packing it into a ball.

"Christian, if you don't come right now, we're leaving you here."

Christian threw the snowball down on the ground and walked back to the street without saying a word. The rest of the group followed.

At the top of the hill they came to what had once been a building but now was no more than a structure.

"This used to be a restaurant," Christian said. "After I played in the pool and watched baseball, Dad would treat me to an ice cream here."

Ewan didn't say anything. He didn't know what to say.

Finally they decided that High Park gave them a good vantage point of the city and a defence system against the Creatures.

386

The three scouts went back and reported what they had found to the rest of the group.

The escapees spent an hour tearing down what was left of the restaurant and collecting firewood from the surrounding trees and bushes to start a perimeter of bonfires which Ewan hoped would last the night and would keep the Creatures away.

Ewan knew the bonfires would probably advertise their position to the Post Humans but he also knew that once night hit, they would be defenceless against the Creatures.

Ashley went out with Ewan. She had managed to convince the boys they would be safe if they stayed with the rest of the group.

They walked aimlessly for ten minutes, covering the destroyed streets. Once in awhile they would stop and listen for any signs of Creatures or the Post Humans but they didn't hear anything, not even the wind.

They came to a park which had a couple of trees and a steep bushy incline. Ewan wished they had some decent tool, however they snapped off as many branches as they could and sorted the ones dry enough to use for a fire.

Ewan remained mostly silent during the search. He could feel Ashley glancing in his direction every so often and watching him closely but he pretended not to notice.

"Something's changed," Ashley said, once they had found a good stack of wood.

"No, it's nothing. I'm just thinking about Timmy."

Ashley remained silent for a while as they walked. "No, something happened when you ran off with Dawn. She's different too."

"How can you tell? You've known her less than twenty-four hours," Ewan snapped.

"Maybe so but I know you."

"And maybe that was a mistake," said, but no sooner had the words left his mouth did he regret them.

Ashley opened her mouth but she was too stunned to say anything. Her face was a mixture of anger, hurt and surprise.

"How many times have I saved your life?" She asked.

"Look, Ashley, I just need some space right now. Somehow I have the lives of hundreds of people in my hands and I don't know how to handle it."

Ashley frowned and scratched at her palms; they were exposed to the cold because she had taken off her gloves so she could break the branches. Her palms had turned an inexplicitly swollen red.

"What happened to your hands?" Ewan asked.

Ashley looked at her hands as if realizing her condition for the first time. "I don't know," she said, startled. "What do you think it is?"

"It's okay. It just looks like you've had a brush with poison ivy."

"Damn it," Ashley said. "That's the last thing I need right now."

"You're not allergic to it or anything, are you?"

"No, I don't think so."

"Leave the firewood. We need to pick all the poison ivy."

"Why?"

"I'm going to extract the urushiol from the leaves. I think we can use it against the Creatures."

"How? What's urushiol?"

"Urushiol is a fluid in the poison ivy's sap. If we use a concentrated amount it might be effective against the Creatures."

"But you're not sure?"

Ewan shrugged. "I don't know. It depends on whether the Creatures get allergic reactions or not."

They took an extra thirty minutes collecting all the poison ivy they could find. On their way back to camp, Ewan went searching for some red plastic cups, the type you serve beer in at large parties. He found them at a dollar store and took as many as they had.

"What are the cups for?" Ashley asked.

"You'll soon find out," he said.

By the time they arrived back at the camp it was almost dark.

Ewan found they had a good pile of wood. He figured it was enough to last them through the night if they were careful.

Ewan and a group of the men built the protective pit around them and tossed the wood in while the women collected the urushiol into a bucket somebody had found.

Once the men were done building the moat – as Ewan thought of it – they decided to take turns stoking the fire and keeping watch for any unusual Creature activity.

Ewan elected to keep the first watch. He decided he probably wouldn't get much sleep anyway.

Christian had found some butcher knives and Ewan took one to patrol the fiery perimeter.

The sky darkened and the fires brightened. Ewan would tend the fires, poke at the ash and expose fresh log to the burning.

In the distance he could see the Creatures moving restlessly back and forth, congregating. Ewan estimated there were at least a couple of hundred of them, just beyond the light, staring at the fire as if hypnotised.

Strangely he thought of living in the museum with Tim. At the time he would have welcomed death. He had no hope. No chance of a future.

Yet . . . now that he wasn't there with Timmy beside him, he missed it: his shallow breathing, his small warmth. In fact, he would have given anything to be back there with him. At the ROM he had been closer to Timmy than he ever had been and now ever would be.

Before the virus he had been immersed in work and other tribulations of everyday life. He hadn't spent nearly as much time with the kids as he would have liked.

Even now that there was a small glimmering hope for humanity, he wished he was back at the ROM with just him and Timmy.

There was a rustle behind Ewan and he pointed his knife at the sound. From the darkness Christian appeared. His beard and shaggy hair seemed wilder in the camp light.

"Sorry about your kid."

For a moment Ewan was going to ask which kid but then Christian didn't know about Sophie – or Dawn - and he wasn't sure Christian would understand.

Christian walked up next to Ewan and stared into the abyss of darkness beyond the fires.

"Is it your turn already?" Ewan asked.

Christian shook his head. "No, couldn't sleep."

Christian picked up a piece of wood and started to sharpen it with a knife he pulled from his pocket. "Never liked the darkness, not even before the virus. I guess I never outgrew that kid phobia."

Christian wasn't looking at Ewan, but his eyes shifted sideways and Ewan had the feeling Christian was studying him intently.

"Nyctophobia."

"Huh?"

"It's fear of the dark," Ewan said, again thinking of Tim. He seemed to be all around him at this moment. "Some psychologists think it's a manifestation of separation anxiety disorder which is when you have acute anxiety when you're away from home or the feeling of being from home."

"No shit Sherlock."

Ewan smiled weakly. "Sorry . . . Sometimes I get carried away."

Neither Christian nor Ewan said anything for a long time.

"Do you think we'll make it?" Christian asked, finally.

"I don't know," Ewan replied honestly. "I think we can deal with the Creatures . . . maybe if we got somewhere there wasn't any Post Humans. . ."

"I lost most of my family early in the virus. Sometimes I think it's a blessing," Christian said. "But to think one of those things out there once was my wife or my dad or my mother, well, it can drive a person crazy."

"I think you need to get some rest."

For a moment, Ewan thought Christian was going to resist, but instead he finished sharping his stick and turned back into the darkness.

Again Ewan was alone and his thoughts drifted back to Tim. He thought of Amy beside him, sleeping softly. She was wearing her pink pajamas, her hair fresh, wet and smelling of vanilla shampoo.

Ewan continued his patrol of the perimeter, adding logs to the fire if the flames were getting low.

He could hear the Creatures out beyond the hill. They reminded Ewan of wild dogs, snapping and snarling in the distance.

Ewan suddenly felt exhausted. He hadn't had much to eat and they had travelled far in a short time. He wanted to close his eyes and go to sleep but he knew he couldn't until somebody came to take over his watch.

Ewan felt a thump that was coming from to his right. He looked around and saw he was back in his old house.

"What was that?" Amy asked, sleepily, turning over to face Ewan. Her pajamas were falling loosely off her narrow frame.

Ewan put a hand on Amy's head. "Just the kids goofing around."

"They're supposed to be in bed — asleep."

"I know. It's fine."

Amy frowned and sat up, wrapping her arms around her chest. She looked over her shoulder at Ewan. "You okay?"

"Why didn't you tell me about Dawn?"

Amy walked around the bed to Ewan's side. She bent down and put a finger on Ewan's lips. "Remember to protect the children."

Ewan shook his head. "I tried and failed. "

Amy straightened up, putting her hands on her knees. "You know what to do, Ewan."

"Dawn and Timmy," Ewan said. "Timmy!"

Ewan awoke to Dawn's gentle touch on his shoulder.

"Dawn — I didn't hear you there."

"You were asleep."

"I'm okay."

Dawn looked at Ewan strangely.

"What is it?" Ewan asked.

"Do you really think I'm your daughter?"

"I don't know. Do you remember anything before. . . before your transition?

"If I really concentrate I can see homo sapiens, lots of them walking around. I see what do you call them, click, click, big, metal things that move around?"

"Cars."

"Cars," Dawn repeated.

Ewan turned his shoulders so he was facing Dawn squarely and for the first time he noticed all her features. Her wide nose, her large black eyes, her defined cheek bones and high forehead. She didn't look at all like Sophie, but then how would he know how a human turned into a Post Human? Dawn was slightly taller than he was but she somehow seemed physically smaller and although he had no way of telling Dawn's age, he felt she was younger too.

"Father?' Dawn said, as if she was testing out the word, just as she had said car.

Ewan felt his throat tighten and his chest sink. For a moment Dawn sounded like Sophie had. But was it just a trick of imagination? Wishful thinking?

"Yes?" Ewan said, feeling as if his lips weren't his own.

"I remember you."

Ewan almost stumbled backwards. If he had fallen he would have landed in the fire but luckily Dawn caught him.

Ewan felt groggy as if all of his brain receptors misfired at once.

"No, that's not possible," Ewan said.

"I do. I do remember. I remember you."

"Do you remember your mom? Your brother?"

Dawn looked down at the ground. "No. I only have a picture of you. You're sitting in the living room, reading. There's a light by the chair."

"Dawn," Ewan said, gently. "We didn't have a light by the chair — not in the living room."

"But I remember it," Dawn insisted. "Maybe it was from a different house. I don't know."

Ewan shook his head. "No, we moved into that house when Amy was pregnant with you."

Dawn stared at Ewan and then turned and walked away.

"Dawn, wait," Ewan called out. But Dawn didn't stop. Ewan wanted to run after her, but he didn't want to leave his post, not until somebody was there to relieve him.

Ewan waited, hoping Dawn would return but when she didn't, Ewan noticed something else. The Creatures had suddenly stopped making any noises. When Ewan turned to face them they seemed to be frozen in place. Their small, shrunken eyes fixated on him. Ewan walked up and down the camp until he was certain all the Creatures were behaving the same: they were all standing perfectly still staring at the camp as if they were an army awaiting orders.

Were they waiting for something? The fire to go out? Something else?

Ewan quickly walked the perimeter of the camp, looking for any holes in his defence but the fire was burning beautifully.

Ewan waited but he couldn't shake the feeling that the Creatures were waiting for something.

Ewan turned and yelled, "Christian! Come here!"

392

Ewan had to yell a few more times before Christian came running towards him, holding his knife and stake in front of him.

"What? What is it?"

Ewan pointed to the Creatures. "I don't like it."

Christian frowned, puzzled.

Then something came at them through the dark. The large object landed about ten paces from them and Ewan had just enough time to register that it was a fire extinguisher before it exploded into a cloud of thick white smoke.

Several more fire extinguishers fell and exploded, covering the bonfires with smoke.

"Quick!" Christian said, running towards the dying fires. Ewan followed him, shouting over his shoulder for Dawn to raise everybody.

It didn't take much for the people to realize they were under attack and those that were up helped with stoking the fire. But adding fresh wood to the fire wasn't working. He looked down to see why and realize the wood was covered in some sort of sticky liquid — no doubt an anti-flammable chemical of some sort.

As Ewan stood there, examining the fire that was quickly becoming extinguished he realized the Creatures didn't have the sophistication for this sort of attack.

The Post Humans must be behind it, Ewan thought.

Ewan straightened up and looked down the hill. The Creatures were quickly swarming up towards them.

God, there are so many of them, Ewan thought. Thousands of them, maybe ten thousand...

It seemed as if all the Creatures in the entire city were descending upon them.

As he watched, he felt something turn painfully in his stomach. He wished he had taken Ashley and the boys and sneaked off from the group. Alone they could survive, but against thousands of Creatures...

Ewan took a deep breath and the painful knot in his stomach loosened. He had faced hard situations before and he was still alive. If he could organize the humans so they fought together, they might just have a chance.

The Seventh Circle

The Oni didn't kill Stu, at least not right away. They closed in on him, all the while communicating in that disgusting language that sounded like a train crossing railroad tracks.

Eventually the Oni seized Stu and dragged him across the room, down a dark corridor and tossed him into a small, dark room. Stu got up and searched his surroundings. It was no bigger than six feet by four and only had the single steel locked door.

He felt very much like he was in jail. He felt a sense of helplessness creep into the recesses of his brain. He tried the handle on the door but it was of course locked. He pounded on it.

"Anybody there?"

He felt along the cracks of the door for some flaw he could exploit but there was nothing. He took a deep breath.

Stay calm Stu. You'll be fine, he told himself.

He sat down cross-legged and began to meditate. It didn't take long to fall into a deep trance, all the emotions left him and he felt, once again calm and in control.

Stu wasn't sure how long he was in there. It could have been a couple of hours, it could have been a couple of days. He had trouble concentrating at first but after awhile he controlled his breathing and he was able to empty his mind of all thoughts.

He was interrupted by a sound in the corner of the cell. He opened his eyes, expecting to find mice or rats but when he didn't see anything he slid until he was in the dark corner.

"Now it's your turn to die," a familiar voice said behind him.

Stu turned and saw Otakay sitting, cross-legged, his palms resting on his knees. Beside him sat a huge white tiger.

"What are you doing here?" Stu asked. "I killed you."

Otakay nodded. "I met my ancestors and they told me my work on this Earth wasn't done. That the tribe still needed me."

Stu shook his head. "You've been replaced. I ate your heart and shat it out the next day. It was delicious."

Otakay laughed. "You think I'm a vision."

"Yes."

"Then that means you're truly one of the tribe. We are the pure, the ones who survived the virus."

"I'm not a savage."

"It's sad that you don't see it."

"You're not real," Stu said, suddenly feeling panicky. *What is happening to me?* Stu wondered. *Am I losing my mind?*

"You're afraid," Otakay said. "Just like when you were a little boy."

"Don't talk about that," Stu yelled.

Otakay chuckled in the darkness and reached over to pet the white tiger. "Don't talk about your cousins that beat you mercilessly? That made your life hell? Shouldn't you thank them? After all you would have not survived if it wasn't for them."

"That's not true."

Otakay tilted his head slightly. "Isn't it? You think you would have survived the chaos after the virus if it wasn't for their cruelty? Wasn't it them who made you learn martial arts and sword fighting?"

Stu close his eyes and covered his ears. "You're dead. You can't speak to me."

"The dead don't have any mouths? The dead don't have any voices?"

Otakay suddenly stopped talking and when Stu opened his eyes again he found himself back in his aunt's house. He could tell by the yellowish stain on the carpets from all the cigarette smoke.

Stu slowly walked down the hallway towards the television room. He could hear the sound of his aunt's favourite soap opera blaring from the room. The dim colours from the television danced on the white walls.

Stu walked slowly down the hallway, towards the noise. He felt like he was being summoned like when he was a kid and he had broken a vase or a dish while cleaning. Stu turned into the room and stepped on the shag carpet, careful to avoid the Doritos that had been ground into the floor.

But it wasn't his aunt who was sitting in her old, cracked leather chair but the White Chief.

"Welcome white man, welcome," he said, in his deep gravelly voice that was so mesmerizing to listen to.

"You're in my seat," Stu said.

"Am I now?" The White Chief said. "You white men are always the same, stealing and taking whatever you want."

"This is my aunt's house!" Stu yelled.

"But once it was nothing but a grassy field and belonged to nobody. My ancestors roamed the land hunting freely."

"And before that it belonged to the dinosaurs. I'm the tribe leader now. That's all that matters."

"No, white man. What matters is evolution. The Oni will take over. It is inevitable as it was that humans took over from the dinosaurs. We are facing the sixth extinction."

"What are the Oni? Where did they come from?"

"They evolved from us. They will be the ones who explore the universe, not us. They will colonize the solar system."

Stu shook his head. "Not if I can help it."

"It's too late. I have foreseen it in my visions."

"Your visions are wrong."

Stu heard a loud noise that came from behind. He turned quickly but saw only darkness. Then a door opened and a puddle of light spilt into the room. It was so bright he had to shield his eyes.

A big Oni ducked into the room. It was by far the largest one Stu had seen so far and it appeared to be wearing some kind of green uniform. Its large form blocked out most of the light.

"In homo sapien, click, click, I am called Forest," the large Oni said.

"Are you the leader?"

"What do you mean, click, click?"

"I need to speak with the one who is in charge."

"Why did you come here?"

"To speak with the one in charge."

"Speak."

"You're a lackey. I have no time for lackeys."

"The one called Rain is exterminating your kind as we speak. Soon you'll be the only homo sapien left."

"What are you going to do with me?" Stu asked.

"We wait to see if you transform."

Stu stood up and walked towards Forest until they were no more than a couple of feet apart. They stared at each other until Forest said, "you're a curious homo sapien. What do they call you?"

"They call me the White Chief."

"I've never known any homo sapien with that kind of name before."

"How many humans do you know?"

"We have captured thousands. Some have transformed. . . some have been exterminated."

"Transform into Oni?"

"Oni. What is that?"

"Okay Forest. I think we can help each other out."

This seemed to take Forest aback. "How?"

"We both want the same thing. Total domination."

Escape

Ewan smashed into a group of Creatures without slowing down. He swung his knife around, cutting several Creatures. He turned and stabbed another one in the neck. Out of his peripheral, he saw a Creature leap at him. He was too slow to bring his knife around but before the Creature landed on him, Dawn slammed into it, knocking it to the ground. Dawn quickly recovered, regained her balance and reached down to snap the Creature's neck.

Ewan stared at Dawn in surprise. "I could have taken it — I mean if you hadn't stepped in."

Dawn smiled and looked down at the Creature. "It was a woman."

"These things have sexes?" Ewan had always thought of the Creatures as just things, not hes or shes.

The Creatures were coming at them in waves. The humans were trying to beat them back with the wood and stones but they weren't having much effect. One human threw a burning stick into the center of Creatures. One burst into flame, snarling horribly until it fell forward into the snow.

"We need to fall back," Ewan said, motioning everybody back into the center of the camp. But nobody seemed to pay much attention to him.

Christian ran up to Ewan. "What are you doing? We need to hold the line."

A Creature attacked them. Christian crouched and hacked at it with his knife until it fell down.

Ewan grabbed Christian by the shoulders. "We need to grab the sap and form a protective circle. We can't have the Creatures flank us."

"But-" Christian started.

"Just trust me," Ewan said.

Christian nodded and started to yell at everybody to fall back. People seemed to listen to Christian and they started to run back up hill to the center.

Without anybody to defend the fires, the Creatures quickly burst through the holes and into the camp. The Creatures caught the slower humans and quickly devoured them. Ewan could hear their awful yelps but he didn't look back.

Ewan ran to where he had left the big pot of urushiol. He took the red cups and started to pass out the urushiol around.

"Throw this on the Creatures," he said.

I hope this works, he thought as the people started to clammier around his pot. The Creatures quickly approach and Ewan stood up to watch as the humans ran to meet them holding their cups. If Ewan wasn't so afraid and terrified, it might have been funny to watch.

When the Creatures and the humans met, the humans tossed the urushiol onto the Creatures. The urushiol started to smoke horribly, burning the Creatures. The Creatures gave hideous screams, clawing at their skin.

Ewan smiled and started to pass out the urushiol quicker until there was nothing left. The Humans pushed the Creatures back towards the fire. The Creatures began to scramble, trying to get away from the urushiol, pushing and shoving other Creatures into the fire.

But soon the Creatures realized the humans had run out of urushiol and they quickly counterattacked.

Ewan looked up at the sky which was a dark purple. Morning was still at thirty minutes away and he wondered if they could hold out for that long.

The humans were tiring quickly, unable to fend off the Creatures for much longer. Ewan saw a middle-aged man swing a log, completely missing a Creature allowing it to leap onto him, burying its teeth into the man's face. The man screamed, dropped his log and tried to push the Creature off of him but the Creature was too strong.

Ewan ran towards the man but before he took two steps it was too late as the Creatures had pulled him a part.

Ewan looked around for Ashley. She was nowhere in sight. He saw Dawn and Albert together by a pathway and fought his way towards them.

He turned to Albert. "Have you seen Ashley?"

"Who's Ashley?" he asked.

"The young woman with the two boys."

"Oh her. Lovely lass," he said.
"Where is she?"
"No, idea, sonny."
Ewan turned to Dawn. "I want you to run."
"I'm not leaving you, Father."
Ewan felt his throat involuntarily tighten as Dawn spoke. "You have a future. You just need to get back to the other Post Humans."
Dawn shook her head. "No, they know I helped you. My only home is with you."
Before Ewan could reply, Dawn ran ahead and started to attack the Creatures. Her movements were fast and furious as she dodged and struck with the finesse of a ballet dancer.
Ewan and Albert fought their way to the front line. Two Creatures ran out of a tall bush and attacked Albert. Albert beat one back with his stick but the other slipped in behind his defences and sunk its teeth into Albert's shoulder. Ewan shuffled sideways and stabbed the Creature right through the eye. Albert beat the other Creature until it stopped moving. Albert turned around and looked at Ewan. His chest was heaving heavily. He touched his shoulder and looked at his blood and then back up at Ewan.
"I've been shot," he said, and then collapsed. Ewan stumbled forward and managed to catch him before he fell.
Albert reached up and touched Ewan's cheek.
"Farewell, fair cruelty," Albert said.
"Oh come off it," Ewan said, pressing his left hand against Albert's wound. "You're not dying."
"Walder, you've been very helpful. Tell that husband of yours he's lucky to have you."
"Amy?" Ewan said. He could feel the tears swell up in his eyes.
"Take my squirt gun," Albert whispered and then closed his eyes. "It has my special soda in it."
"Special soda?" Ewan said, shaking his head.
"Use . . . against . . .Post Humans," Albert said, his hand fell away from Ewan's face.
Ewan laid Albert down gently and picked up the knife again.
Dawn appeared by Ewan. "You'll have to leave him."
"But he'll die."

"Perhaps but if you don't we'll all die."

Ewan wiped away the tears from his face and dug into Albert's pocket and took the water gun out.

Ewan looked up just in time to hear a low buzzing. It sounded like a swarm of bees approaching but when the noise came closer, Ewan saw it was an army of Post Humans. He could see about fifty of them, Rain was leading the charge.

Ewan watched as they leapt over the dying flames and attacked the Creatures. The Creatures scrambled but were trapped between the humans and Post Humans. Once the Post Humans had killed the Creatures they advanced onto the humans. The humans dropped their weapons and ran but they had nowhere to run either and the Post Humans savagely started to snap necks or trounce the humans.

Albert had told Ewan to use his special soda against the Post Humans. Ewan examined the liquid in the gun. It was a clear, bubbly liquid. It looked like it was no more than water mixed with a touch of soap.

Nevertheless, it was Ewan's last chance. He ran towards Rain who snarled triumphantly when she recognized Ewan.

"The one they call Ewan," Rain said. "It's time for you to die."

"Not yet, it isn't," he said, raising the squirt gun and pressing the trigger. The liquid squirted out and hit Rain in the chest. Nothing happened at first but then the liquid started to burn away Rain's skin just as the urushiol had against the Creatures and Rain ripped at her flesh.

"What did you do to me, homo sapien?" Rain roared.

Ewan stepped forward and sprayed Rain again, this time hitting her in the face melting it. Ewan pressed the trigger again and again, feeling a cool sense of satisfaction as Rain squirmed in pain and then collapsed.

Ewan bent over the Post Human's body but Rain was dead.

Soon a loud clicking sound spread through the ranks of the Post Humans and they turned and fled, leaving the humans alone.

Ewan surveyed the damage. It looked like one of those old Civil War photographs with bodies thrown about everywhere.

Again Ewan desperately looked around for Ashley. He eventually found her with Justin and Anthony.

Ewan ran over, wrapped his arms around her and kissed her.
"I'm so glad you're safe," Ashley said.
"Come, the old man needs us."
They ran back to Albert who was still lying where Ewan had laid him down. At first Ewan thought he was dead but when they approached, Albert coughed and opened his eyes and stared up at Ewan.
"Leave me here, good chap. I'm useless to you."
"And miss out on hours of entertainment?" Ewan said.
"Hardly."
They checked on the other wounded. Ewan told Ashley to go find bandages and chemicals.
"Take somebody with you?" he said.
"No, I'll be fine," she said, and ran towards the nearest houses.
The most common were bites which didn't seem so bad. By the fire pit, Ewan discovered one woman who had been disembowelled but was surprisingly still alive. She was thin and lanky. Her body was twitching from the pain. Her long dark hair was matted against her forehead and cheeks.
Ewan knelt on one knee to examine her.
"Kill me," she whispered, looking up at Ewan with large, brown eyes. Ewan tried to remember if he had seen her before but she looked unfamiliar.
Ewan creased his lips and nodded.
"Christian, give me your knife."
Christian silently obeyed. The handle suddenly seemed cold and heavy in his hand. He stared at the woman's eyes, trying to understand what she was thinking.
Perhaps it's best not to know, Ewan thought.
Ewan brought the knife down on her neck and she lay still.
Ewan wiped the blade on the snow and gave it back to Christian. Ewan didn't say anything else until Ashley returned with supplies. She didn't find any bandages but she did manage to find some bed sheets; she had cut them into strips.
Ewan wrapped the pieces of sheet around wounds.
Ewan returned to Albert. He knelt down, cleaning the wound with the snow and then wrapping it up.
"You'll live," Ewan said, helping Albert to his feet.

"Unfortunately," Albert grumbled.

"When did you get so sour?"

Albert just looked away.

"What was in that soda anyway?"

"It's something I've been working on for years, a special compound that reacts to the Magnetar Virus. I can't remember exactly what I put in it. I tried so many different combinations."

"Well you better try," Ewan said. "We're going to need more of that stuff."

Plea Bargain

The door opened to the cell with a loud squeaking clang. Stu expected Forest to enter, but instead a different Oni stepped in. This one was slightly smaller but still tall and thick-shouldered.

"What do you want?" Stu asked.

But the Oni didn't reply but instead grabbed Stu by the neck and dragged him out of the cell. Stu fought the Oni but it was too strong.

The Oni dragged Stu down the corridor past a couple of doorways and into an open hallway. There he tossed Stu into the middle as if he was light as a baseball. Stu tried to roll but instead landed hard onto the stone.

Refusing to show pain, he forced himself to his feet and looked around. The room he was in was well lit. It had several long desks and on the walls were old movie posters.

Forest sat in a large chair in front of Stu. He seemed to be looking down at Stu with contempt.

"We have reconsidered your proposal," Forest said.

Stu wandered the perimeter of the room, not saying anything. He needed time to think and stall. What had changed since their last meeting? He stared at the wooden desks and the chairs too small to seat any Oni. The room looked like it could be in any office building or school, yet everything was a little bit off, as if some high-end decorator had placed things in a certain way after a long night of heavy drinking.

"Where is your leader?"

"I told you, we don't have any leader."

"Did you kill him?"

The Oni let out a high-pitched snarl. "We do not commit killings of our own, like your species."

"Tell me, if you hate humans so much why do you have movie posters up on the wall?" Stu asked.

Forest made several clicking sounds as if it didn't understand. "It is just decoration but soon we will fill these walls with our own artwork and our own inventions and not have to rely on homo sapiens."

Stu sat down at one of the desks. The legs creaked below his weight.

"Did your leader die in battle? Did those pesky homo sapiens kill him?"

Forest didn't say anything but just sat there, gripping onto the arms of the chair.

"I can't help you if you don't tell me anything," Stu said.

"We had some captives who escaped. Rain took a group of Post Humans to exterminate them."

Stu laughed. "Post Humans? That's what you call yourself?"

"In homo sapien, that is the translation."

"Okay, how did they escape?"

"That's not important," Forest said. "They did and somehow got this chemical that eats away at the skin. That's how they killed Rain."

"You want me to kill them for you?"

"Yes."

"And in return I get my freedom."

"Yes," Forest said, again.

"Also you leave my tribe alone."

"What's a tribe?"

"My people — my homo sapiens."

"I can't, click, click, promise you that."

"Then you'll have to take your chances. I won't be able to kill your captives without my tribe's help and for that I'll need their guaranteed safety."

Forest didn't say anything for a long time. Finally he spoke, "If they don't transform and they stay away from us then I promise not to interfere with your tribe."

Stu emerged from the subway system to find Kimi waiting for him in the Town Car. Stu took a deep breath of fresh, cold air. He never thought he would enjoy the smell of air so much before. He sucked in a deep breath, feeling the coldness fill his lungs and then let it out in a puff of smoke.

Kimi turned on the car and drove towards Stu. He got out and opened the backdoor, giving Stu a small bow.

"It's good to see you, sir," he said, giving no indication of pleasure.

"It's the White Chief, you idiot."

"But sir, you said-"

I know what I said," Stu said. "Please don't make me repeat myself."

"Of course, White Chief."

Stu smiled at this and put one arm on Kimi's shoulder. Kimi frowned, looking concerned.

"We're going to be alright," he said.

"What happened down there, Chief?"

"I made a deal with the devil."

The ride back to the museum was a quiet one with only the sound of the sputtering motor to keep him company. Stu tightened his grip around his sword and watched as the world passed him by. The sky seemed especially bright today, reflecting the pure whiteness of the snow.

Stu was overcome with a feeling of beautifulness. He had never seen the city as beautiful before but that was before his vision. The Oni would rule the world one day, and perhaps the universe but that didn't mean they couldn't live together in relative peacefulness.

After all, Sun Tzu said, *the person who knows when to fight and when not to will be victorious.*

To fight the Oni would be crazy. At least until they stole the poison from the captives. Stu instinctively knew the captives were the same people who had inhabited the ROM and that made him want to kill them and eat them even more. They had escaped once and now it was only fate that would make them intercede again.

He thought of Krista, or Makawee as he should call her and how she said he would have his vision beneath the ground and she had been right.

Stu found Graham in the basement working on the Perpetuum generator as per usual. Graham stood up and smiled when Stu walked in.

"I think you need a new name," Stu said.

Graham frowned. "What happened to you down there?"

"I had my vision, just as Makawee said I would."

Graham frowned. "Who's Makawee?"

"The one formally known as Krista."

"Okay . . .What happened exactly?"

Stu told Graham everything since they had last seen each other.

"The Oni just let you walk away after you killed one of them?"

"They want the humans to kill each other. Prevents them from having to do it themselves and risking their own lives."

Graham crossed his arms. "It also reinforces the stereotype that we do nothing but kill each other. It might be a good propaganda tool."

"What are you talking about?"

Graham shrugged. "Just that perhaps some of these Oni have doubts about killing off humans — we are related, if what you say is correct, the Oni transformed from the Teki. This might persuade some of the Oni that humans are a disease that needs to be eradicated."

"Doesn't matter to me what they think. As long as they keep their bargain."

"How can we trust them?"

"We find out about this poison that killed their leader. If we have that we'll at least have a tool that will keep them honest."

Graham shook his head. "It must be something very intricate. Maybe something that was left over from before the outbreak that can't be duplicated."

"Whatever it is, I want you to find out what it is."

"Me?" Graham said, raising his eyebrows. "I'm already working full time on the generator. I don't know the first thing about chemistry."

Stu shook his head. "No, you misunderstand me. You're going to infiltrate their ranks and steal it."

"You want me to spy for you?"

"In Art of War Sun Tzu placed great importance on knowing the enemy and sabotage."

407

Graham stared at Stu and for a moment Stu thought Graham was going to refuse but instead he just nodded. "Okay, I can do that."

Stu went up to bed and collapsed. He hadn't been able to sleep while he had been in the cell and so he found his mattress inviting. He thought he would dream of Otakay or the White Chief but instead his sleep was uninterrupted.

He woke first thing in the morning feeling refreshed and reenergized.

Forest hadn't told him specifics about the captives, only that they probably numbered in a couple of hundred at most. The Oni had said they had suffered severe casualties in the night raid but Forest couldn't tell him specifically how many captives there were still left — or indeed how many had even escaped.

It didn't matter. His tribe was well trained and battle-hardened from fighting the Teki. The captives were unarmed and unsuspecting. Stu would hit them with a daytime raid when they would be most vulnerable.

The trick would be to catch them. They had over a full day's head start on them and Stu had no idea where they were going. The Oni had said they didn't have a destination, that they were just running blindly away. Stu thought Forest was probably right, but the Oni had misjudged the captives once and Stu didn't want to make the same mistake.

Stu meditated for several minutes and then ate some roots for breakfast. He talked over his strategy with Graham. He would take the Town Car so he could make contact faster, giving him time to find out more about the enemy and find the poison.

"Just make sure they don't see or hear you driving," Stu warned. "We don't want them to get suspicious."

Graham nodded.

Stu assembled fifty of his best men and after they had collected enough supplies to last them a day or two they set out.

Stu watched as Graham climbed into the Lincoln. "Good luck," he said, shutting the door.

He watched as Stu turned the corner onto Saint George's Street before his attack party set off after him.

"We need to move fast," Stu told the savages. "If you can't keep up, we'll leave you behind. Understood?"

Everybody nodded.

Stu turned and set the pace. They marched quickly through Queen's Park, clearing the Teki as they went. It was a good warm up for what was hopefully to come. The attack party didn't even suffer a single casualty; this pleased Stu.

They marched down Younge Street, moving quickly through the dilapidated buildings that were made up of shattered glass.

It didn't take them long to reach High Park. The escaped people were nowhere to be seen of course. They climbed the hill slowly just in case, making their way through the Spruce trees.

"Jesus Christ," Kimi said, when he saw the top of the hill where the battle had taken place.

Stu had never seen such carnage before. The stench of rotten flesh was heavy in the air and the buzzing of black flies made a horrible sound. The snow was soiled with black bile and crimson red blood. In places it was mixed so thickly, Stu couldn't tell that underneath there was snow. Stu estimated that there were about a hundred dead humans and at least five times that many Tekis scattered around.

"Alright we're going to rest here," Stu said. "In half an hour we're going to search the dead, see if we can find any clues of where they could have gone."

Stu thought one of the savages would ask if they could cook the flesh of the dead but even they seemed repulsed by the idea.

Once they had rested, the savages searched the dead but didn't find anything useful. The ground had been so badly trampled that it was hard to find a clear path but once they did they followed it out of the park and followed the tracks south along Parkside Drive.

Once on Parkside, the hundreds of feet became clearer. On their right they passed what had once been a beautiful garden with hanging baskets and terraces but years of neglect left only a shadow of its former self. They passed a playground that had been built to look like a medieval castle.

They walked until they reached the expressway; Stu remembered it had once been one of the busiest expressways he had experienced. It had always seemed gridlocked, no matter what hour of the day it was.

More than once, as an ambulance driver, he had gotten stuck on it. They made their way through the wrecked cars as quickly as they could but it was slower than Stu would have liked. They got off the expressway onto Lakeshore Boulevard. To their right was the great lake and to the left stretched tall buildings seemingly endlessly into the distance. He could see the Perpetuum building rising above the rest. He could even make out the sign, long burned out. PERPETUUM INDUSTRIES: THE FUTURE IS NOW!

About thirty minutes later, Stu stopped to examine the tracks. They were fresh, no more than a couple of hours old.

"We're almost upon them," Stu told Kimi who nodded.

"What do you want to do Chief?"

"We will proceed with caution."

"Where do you think they're going?"

Stu stared out to the lake. "I think there is only one play they can be doing. Toronto Island. They think they will be safe if they put some water in between them and the Teki."

Stu grinned. It was almost too easy. They would never be able to cross the water and he could trap them and crush them against the port.

"We're going to find somewhere to camp. We can't light a fire, otherwise they'll know we're coming."

"What do you suggest?"

Stu looked around at the towers. It was still fairly light out and they had at least another four hours of sunlight but there was no point moving on until Graham reported back.

"Let's find the top floor of some building and barricade ourselves in. We should be relatively safe."

Toronto Island

'Join the Navy, See the World,' the sign said.

Ewan stopped to stare at it. The words were in bold black ink against a blue background. It seemed strange the sign was still there, standing as if somebody would walk into the adjacent building and enthusiastically join.

But of course there was no Navy, no Army, no world. Just an odd reminder of how strange the human race had been.

"What is it?" Ashley asked.

Ewan bowed his head and continued to walk. "It's nothing."

Ewan had a distant cousin that had joined the Navy. He didn't think he saw much of the world.

I wonder what ever happened to him? Ewan thought.

Had he been called back to Toronto to defend the city against the Creatures? There were so many people Ewan wondered about - how they had died. He supposed he would never know. He wasn't sure he wanted to know.

They walked past the naval division and towards the main ferry terminal. The group stopped there while Ewan and Christian went to examine the ferry. They found the actual ferry had been destroyed and was now sitting halfway in the water. There was no way they were going to make it across in that thing.

"What do we do now?" Ewan asked.

"There are a couple of marinas around here. I'm sure one of them still has a boat we can use."

"Don't count on it," Ewan said. "What happens if we don't find a working boat before nightfall?"

"Then we swim," Christian said.

Ewan shook his head. "Not all of us could make it across. What about the children?"

Christian shrugged. "We can't survive another attack by the Creatures or the Post Humans. We need those weapons."

"If they exist."

"They have to exist or we're fucked."

Ewan didn't say anything. He knew Christian was right.

411

When they got back to the group Ewan said, "Okay, listen up everybody. We need to find a boat that will take us across to the island. There are two marinas. We passed one and another one a little further down. We need to split up and search them as quickly as possible."

Ewan and Christian quickly organized everyone into two groups and they broke up and started the search.

Ashley decided to go with Ewan who was in charge of the group that was taking the marina to the east.

"I'm sure somebody thought of this before," Ashley said. "I'm sure all the boats are gone."

Ewan shrugged. "As soon as I come up with a better plan, I'll be sure to tell you."

Ewan thought Ashley was going to scold him for being snarky but she didn't say anything, which, Ewan thought was perhaps worse.

They arrived at the marina and Ewan quickly organized the search. Ewan and Ashley took the northeast side. All the most expensive boats had been vandalized and torched. There was a sailboat in relatively good condition but was halfway submerged in the water.

"You think it's fixable?" Ewan asked.

They climbed aboard and looked below deck. The cabin was filled with about three feet of water. Pots and pans were floating in the water.

"I don't know," Ashley said. "We can try pumping out the water to see where the damage is but my guess: it'll never make it across."

Next they came across a speed boat without its engine. It seemed seaworthy if only they could find a couple of oars.

"It would take forever to get everybody across in this," Ewan said.

"Perhaps, but it's an option. Let's keep looking and see what else we find."

They searched for another ten minutes and then reconvened with the rest of the group. It was determined that the small speed boat was their best option even though nobody had found any oars. The oars had probably been taken as either weapons or as firewood.

"What about the house boat?" someone asked.

There was a house boat in the middle of the marina but it was attached to the dock.

"No, it's welded to the dock. It's not going anywhere," someone else said.

Ewan walked towards the houseboat. It looked like at some point it had sustained some fire damage but otherwise seemed in good condition. Somebody had probably lived there and had made it his last stand.

Ewan turned towards the man who had examined the houseboat. "Did you look inside?"

The man shrugged. "Once I saw it was welded to the dock I just glanced in. It's pretty disgusting."

Ewan stepped aboard. Ashley followed closely behind him. The smell of iron and stale meat hung heavily in the air. He glanced backwards at Ashley who stood with her face full of resolve and determination. It was that look that gave Ewan the courage to turn the steel handle and open the door.

There was a figure stretched out on a table. Ewan couldn't tell if it had been a man or a woman. It had no face and most of its flesh was gone. Dried blood was splashed across the room. It was on the walls, on the floor and even on the ceiling. The corpse was missing an arm and a leg and seemed like most of its insides had been eaten by the Creatures.

Ewan covered his mouth and nose with the sleeve of his shirt but it did little good as the stench was overwhelming.

Ewan backed out of the cabin and went along the back of the house boat. Ashley followed him. He opened the board that covered the engine. It was old and rusted but looked intact.

Ewan bent down and realized there was still gas in the tank.

"I can't believe it," Ewan said, showing Ashley.

"Don't get too carried away, it's probably broken down and gummed up the engine," Ashley said.

Ewan returned to the cabin and went into the helm of the boat. He turned the keys which were still in the ignition. The engine sputtered, coughed and then died. Ewan looked at Ashley who seemed to give him a look that said, *I told you so*.

Ewan tried several more times but each time the engine would start and then die away.

413

"Even if we do get this thing started," Ashley said. "This thing isn't going anywhere. Perhaps it's best if we just syphon the fuel and use it on another boat."

Ewan looked up through the window. He could see the group of people staring at him. Nobody was talking; each person looked as if they were silently willing him to succeed, pleading with him.

At that point he knew he couldn't let them down. He had to succeed. He grabbed the key again and turned. This time the engine rumbled, shuttered and then started to run.

Ewan pumped his fist in the air. Ashley gave a little jump and hugged him.

"Okay, how can we detach this thing from the dock?" Ashley asked.

In the end it didn't prove that hard. The weld that fused the dock with the house boat proved too strong but the dock surrounding the house boat was rotten in several places. Ashley used her knife to surgically cut away the rotten part of the dock until the ramp and the rotten portion fell into the water.

Cheers went up as the house boat was now free of its shackles.

Christian was designated captain of the house boat and he quickly organized people into different groups. He calculated even at full capacity, it would take three trips to ferry everybody over onto the island. Ewan, Ashley, Dawn and the two boys were on the first trip over to the island. Ewan thought the first ones to explore the island were in the most danger and subsequently didn't want to bring the two boys but Ashley didn't want to be separated from them, even for thirty minutes.

They landed at the airport and the first thing Ewan noticed were the F-35 Fighter jets that lined the runway. He counted twenty-five of them all together.

"You think any of them still work?"

Ashley let out a rare laugh. "You're going to go bomb the Post Humans? You're more likely to crash and kill yourself."

"I'm a pilot," a man said, stepping forward.

"What's your name?" Ewan asked.

"It's Hudson."

"What do you fly?"

"I just flew recreation. Cessnas mostly."

"Nothing military?"

"No, but I'm sure I can understand the basics."

They went over to examine the planes. They were covered with snow. There were no weapons on their wings and when Ewan wiped away the snow, he found most of the cockpits were cracked and frozen over.

"We need to find shelter before anything else," Ashley reminded them. "There's probably Creatures on the island, even a few can cause us trouble."

Ewan nodded. "You're right. We'll come back to the planes. They'll be there tomorrow."

They decided they would search the control tower first. That would be the best place to make camp for the night but first they had to make sure there were no Creatures to bother them.

There were a few Creatures in the tower but the group of humans easily killed them.

Once they had finished searching the tower, they came out and were surprised to find a figure standing there in the center of the airport. He looked to be wet and was shivering cold.

"Don't move," Ewan said cautiously. He raised his knife and advanced on the man. The man was maybe in his mid-sixties. Thin but strong looking. He had light silvery hair with a strong cheek and jaw.

The man raised his arms when Ewan was about ten paces away. "I'm unarmed," he said.

"Who are you?" Ewan asked.

"The name's Graham."

"Where did you come from?"

"I live on the island."

"How come you're wet?"

"I just came from the other island. I swam across when I heard your boat."

Ewan looked back at Ashley and the others but they didn't seem to show any indication of what he should do.

Ewan took a deep breath and lowered the knife. The man didn't seem to be harmful in any way, although he did seem strangely confident. Perhaps he was just curious.

"Do you mind if I search you?" Ewan asked. "Just in case."

Graham shrugged. "If you must."

It did seem like a ridiculous idea since there was very little to search. The dampness had made his clothes stick to his body and so there were very few places he could conceal a weapon. Ewan patted him down like he had seen in movies. He checked Graham's pockets and his belt but there was nothing there.

"You must be freezing," Ewan said. "We should start a fire."

They went over to the forested area and managed to snap off a few dry branches and after they had dug out the snow they started a fire.

Graham sat close, warming himself up. Ewan stayed away from the fire but watched the flames as they slowly flickered and strutted along the logs.

"Where did you come from?" Graham asked.

"It's a long story," Ewan said. "We should save it for another time."

Ewan didn't want to talk about escaping from the Post Humans. He didn't know if Graham had encountered the Post Humans yet and he didn't want to alarm him.

"I would prefer to hear it now," Graham said, now distrust was creeping into his voice.

So Ewan told Graham everything from when he had lived at the ROM with Tim, to meeting Ashley to getting captured by the Post Humans.

Graham seemed most interested in the Post Humans. He asked what they looked like, how they acted, about their strange language.

"You say you're a biologist," Graham said. "How did they evolve so quickly and into such superhuman beings?"

Ewan shrugged. "I'm not sure but there is still a lot about evolution that baffles us. Mammals have evolved in some profound ways. There was some evidence that elephants used to evolve by developing shorter tusks to avoid poachers. My guess it was somehow triggered by the virus in ways nobody comprehended."

There was silence for awhile. Graham stared into the fire and Ewan took the time to watch him. He certainly seemed intelligent and now that he had dried off somewhat he seemed familiar too.

Had he seen him somewhere? Perhaps he had been a teacher at the university.

"How long have you been here?" Ewan asked.

"I'm not sure," Graham replied. "I've been living on the island of a couple of years now. There are still Creatures here but a lot less than on the mainland and we tend to live somewhat harmoniously."

"Have you discovered any weapons here? Perhaps in an undercover bunker?"

Graham looked up at Ewan confused. "An undercover bunker? No I haven't, but then again I haven't really looked, so it's possible."

Ewan frowned. It seemed strange that Graham wouldn't explore the entire island but then he remembered not all the islands were interconnected and travelling from one island to another wasn't very easy.

"Somebody said there was a rumour that the military stored some weapons here, bombs, missiles, and guns."

Graham frowned deeply and Ewan wondered what he was thinking. Perhaps he was cursing himself for not looking harder.

Eventually he shook his head. "No, I never found anything."

"How about those planes? Have you tested them?"

Graham looked over to where Ewan was pointing. He stared at the F-35s as if he was just seeing them for the first time."

"I can't fly," he said simply. "And wouldn't know how to work them if I tried."

Ewan found himself frowning again. Something wasn't right with Graham. His answers seemed a little bit strange, but he dismissed it for now. Perhaps he was just secretive because he was mistrusting. Ewan would probably have acted the same way if a group of people had suddenly descended on the ROM. He remembered the cannibals who had captured the two boys and wondered if they were still there.

The second boatload of people eventually arrived. Ewan and Ashley went out to greet them.

417

"It's getting dark," Christian said as the people hurried onto land. "I'm not sure if I have time to bring the third group over before nightfall."

"Why don't you pick them up and just stay out on the lake for the night?" Ewan said. "You should be safe from the Creatures at least."

Christian seemed to like the idea and backed the boat up again. "We need to secure the airport tower," Christian said. "We'll explore the island more in the morning."

Ewan watched the boat get smaller in the distance, the water making tiny ripples, fanning out into little dark arrows. He figured they would be the safest and he briefly regretted not getting Ashley and the boys to go with Christian but it was too late now.

Ewan guided the group of people towards the airport. They collected furniture and other objects to board up the control tower.

Although everybody was tired, the work didn't take too long and soon the control tower was secure. From the top, Ewan had a three-hundred-and-sixty degree view of the surrounding area. Even in the faded light he could see Christian's ferry reach the other side. The golden-white stars were beginning to appear in the sky. The rest of the city seemed quiet and Ewan wondered what happened to the Post Humans. He wondered if they would attack again during the night or would they send the Creatures after them again?

He figured to mount any sort of attack they would have to cross the water and Ewan would have plenty of time to prepare.

Ewan went downstairs and surveyed the barricades. Once he was satisfied that all of the doors and windows were secure, he ordered everybody to try and get some sleep. Like the previous night, Ewan took the first watch.

He went back up to the top of the control tower. The stars were out and Ewan found himself staring up in wonder. He hadn't enjoyed watching the stars since he had been back in the ROM. Looking up at the stars reminded him of Tim, Sophie and of course Amy.

He heard footsteps and when he turned he saw Ashley standing in the doorway. She seemed hesitant, unsure if she really wanted to disturb him.

"It's quiet out there," she said.

"How are the boys?"

"They're fine. They're asleep."

It was true. Ewan hadn't seen a Creature approach the control tower. Perhaps there weren't many on the island.

Ashley sat down beside Ewan. Neither said anything for awhile. Below them they could hear snoring and the occasional fart as the group of escapees slept.

"What was the poem you quoted?" Ewan asked.

"I don't remember."

"Roland something?"

"You mean Song of Roland?"

"I think so. Do you remember any more of it?"

Ashley shook her head. "No."

"Do you remember anything more? I would like you to recite something to me."

"I dunno. I don't remember much."

"Just anything. It doesn't matter."

"I think I can remember Macbeth -Tomorrow, tomorrow, tomorrow creeps on at a petty pace. . ."

"How about something not so depressing?"

Ashley smiled. "Now you're just being demanding."

Ewan laughed. "I suppose so — just forget it."

"No, it's okay," Ashley said. She started to perform bits and pieces of different Shakespeare plays, muddling them up and making sentences up but it didn't matter to Ewan.

When she was done, she sat down next to Ewan and rested her head on his shoulder.

"If you're tired, you should go to sleep," Ewan said. "We have a big day ahead of us tomorrow."

"Ewan . . ."

"Yes?"

"Do you see a future for us?"

"You mean us or the human race in general?"

"Both."

Ewan sighed. "The human race can't last forever. Maybe Rain was right. We were just parasites, using up the planet's resources . . . Hopefully the Post Humans will be more careful with resources."

"So we just accept that we lose?"

"It's more than that," Ewan said. "I think Dawn is my daughter."

"You mean Sophie?" Ashley said. "How is that possible?"

"How do you remember her name?"

"Of course I remember it. I thought she was dead."

Ewan shook his head. "I did too. The Creatures took her and I thought they killed her, but what if she transformed, just like Timmy did? What if they had the gene that turned them into Post Humans?"

Ashley smiled. "There was something about her that I liked and now I know why."

"So it's not that I think we can preserve the human race but I think we can preserve our ancestors."

Ashley raised her head and slipped her hand across Ewan's neck. "So how about making use of the time we have?"

Ewan smiled. "How would you suggest we do that?"

Ashley kissed Ewan on the shoulder. "I have a few ideas."

The Traitor

Ewan woke up in the morning, for once feeling refreshed and rejuvenated. Ashley was curled up beside him, her long hair fell across his chest.

"Good morning," Graham said.

Ewan propped himself up on his elbow to see Graham was sitting, peering down at them.

"What are you doing here?"

"I came up here to take next watch and saw you had fallen asleep."

Ewan got up, waking Ashley.

"Anything happen?"

Graham shook his head. "No, quiet night. No Teki insight."

"Teki?"

"Oh — sorry, I meant Creatures. Teki is just what I call them."

"Why?"

Graham just shrugged. "I picked it up from an old friend."

"What does it mean?"

"Have no idea. I think it's Japanese."

"Your friend was Japanese?"

Graham turned and stared out the window in a gesture that Ewan took to mean he didn't want to talk about his friend.

"I'm sorry," Ewan said. "I don't mean to pry."

"It's okay," Graham said. "The past is painful for me, as I imagine it is for everybody else."

"Yes, everybody has lost their family."

The humans spread out over the island, looking for food. While everyone else was preoccupied, Ewan and Ashley looked for somewhere the military would have kept weapons.

They knew there was nothing in the control tower so they looked for an undercover bunker but after an hour they couldn't find anything. The snow made things more difficult as the hatch could have been buried anywhere underneath.

"What are we looking for?" Ashley asked.

"I have no idea. A hatch of some kind I imagine."

"You think the weapons are underground?"

"I'm not sure there are weapons to begin with. You would have thought somebody would have found them by now."

"Perhaps they are well hidden. I'm sure the military didn't want them to fall into the wrong hands."

Nobody found any food either except for a few berries that didn't quench anybody's hunger.

"What are we going to do?" Ashley asked.

"Hope that there is enough fuel in the ferry for a trip to the mainland," Ewan said. "As safe as we are out here, I don't think we want to be stuck."

Ewan and Ashley went to meet Christian who was just bringing the boat into dock. After spending a night on the boat, his passengers were happy to be back on dry land again.

"We have no food here," Ewan told Christian. "How much fuel do you have?"

"I should have enough for several trips if the engine doesn't fall apart."

"Okay, do you want to take a couple of people and go find food? We're going to keep searching for the weapons."

"You don't think they exist, do you?"

Ewan shrugged but was saved from explaining himself again when Albert, who had just gotten off the boat, let out a loud yell. He seemed to have recovered from the battle, although he was still pale and had a bandage around his shoulder.

Ewan and Ashley rushed over to him. "How the bloody hell did Meyer get here?"

"What are you talking about?" Ewan said. "You're not making any sense."

Albert pointed to Graham who was just staring curiously at Albert. Ewan looked at Ashley who just shook her head.

"Albert, it has been a long time," Graham said, but Albert just recoiled and let out a low snarl.

"You know Albert?" Ewan said.

"We haven't spoken for many years but, yes . . . we used to be business partners."

Ewan placed his hands together, finally understanding. "You're Graham Meyer."

"He's a shadow in the night," Albert said. "Coming to take away my company."

"Your company is no more, Albert," Graham said, quietly. He spoke to Albert in a respectful manner, one that Ewan hadn't seen anybody use for the crazy old man. But it reminded Ewan that Albert Winkler had once been the top of his field, had created the greatest invention since the internet. In this world, it was an easy thing to forget.

"Okay, Albert you need to calm down."

Albert nodded but then launched himself at Graham. Graham was caught unprepared and toppled over onto the snow with Albert on top of him. Despite Albert's wounds, he started to pummel Graham with his fists but luckily his blows were ineffectual and Ewan managed to drag him off of Graham before he could do much damage.

Ewan helped Albert back to his feet, but before he could stand, he fainted. Luckily Ewan caught him and laid him on the ground.

"Albert?"

Albert opened his eyes and looked up at Ewan who was staring down at him, concerned. "Did I win?"

Ewan stared back at Graham who had also slowly stood back up. His nose was bleeding and his left eye was swollen. He bent down, packing some snow and held it on his face.

"Yes, you won, old man."

Albert propped himself up onto his elbows.

"You still angry with me, Albert?" Graham waited as if he expected an answer but Albert just growled at him.

"You think I did it because I wanted all the credit, because I wanted all the control and I wanted all the money. But the truth is, Albert, you could never have done it by yourself. You would still be tinkering away in your lab. And when I pushed you out it was for the good of the company. Your presence was stagnating progress."

Albert, seemingly reenergized, jumped back to his feet but Ewan stepped between the two men. "There's no use fighting over the past. We need to focus on finding weapons, otherwise we are all going to be dead."

"There are no weapons on this island," Graham said. "I would have found them."

"You sure about that?"

Graham nodded. "I would have found them."

"Okay, we have two of the brightest minds here," Ewan said. "We need to figure out a way to defeat the Post Humans."

"They must have a weakness," Graham said. "We figure out what that is and exploit it."

"Albert created a soda that burns them. The problem is that we don't have enough of it and no way to produce it."

"Soda?" Graham asked.

"That's just what we call it," Ewan said. "It's some sort of chemical compound."

Graham turned to Albert. "What is in it?"

"No, I'm not telling you anything, you thief!"

"Albert, please, he can help us," Ewan said.

"I can make some more in my lab if you let me."

"If you just tell me what's in the compound, I'm sure we don't need your lab," Graham said.

"No," Albert said, shaking his head adamantly. "Fool me once, shame on me, fool me twice shame on both of us."

"I don't think that's how the saying—" Graham said, but was cut off by Ewan.

"It doesn't matter. Let's keep searching for the weapons for now. If we don't find anything, tomorrow we will send a party to go back to Albert's lab."

But Albert shook his head. "There is equipment that can't be moved. I must go."

"But Albert, you're in no condition to travel anywhere."

"I must go Ewan," he said, fixating on Ewan.

Ewan smiled. "I didn't think you ever remembered my name. What happened to 'the Walder guy'?"

Albert waved his hand in the air. "I have my moments but how can I not remember you? The way Amy talked about you."

"Stop it," Ewan said, abruptly. He felt his body begin to shake. She still had power over him. "If you think this is going to get you anywhere, you're wrong."

"Where is this lab?" Graham asked.

"By the ROM museum."

"No, don't tell him," Albert said. "It's a secret lab. Let me go alone."

Ewan shook his head. "No, you'll need to take someone. How about Ashley, you trust her."

"This is ridiculous," Graham said. "From what you're telling me, you need a whole team to make enough of this soda to kill these Post Humans. And that's if Albert has enough materials to make a batch large enough."

Ewan looked at Albert who was silent.

"Well?"

Albert glanced down at the ground. "I don't know how many there are so it's impossible to say conclusively that I will be able to make enough."

"How long will it take you?"

Albert shrugged. "Probably a week with the lassie's help."

"Okay," Ewan said. "We need to regroup, find food before we do anything. Perhaps we can get those fighter jets working," Ewan said.

Everybody agreed on that. Christian took a group of twenty people back to the mainland to search for food while the rest of the group, except for Hudson who examined the warplanes, spread out on the island.

Although the island was small they searched slowly, covering every inch of the island, making sure there was no secret hatch anywhere.

After two hours they didn't discover anything except the occasional Creature, hiding in the bushes away from the sunlight.

At one point, Ewan paused. "I think we're going about this wrong."

"What do you mean?" Ashley asked.

"We are doing this blindly. If you were the military, where would you hide weapons?"

"Probably at the airport where it would be easiest to transport in and out."

"Okay, but they're not at the easiest part of the island, how about the hardest?"

Ashley looked around. Toronto Island was actually a collection of half-a-dozen small islands. There was a thick cluster of trees interspersed with buildings that seemed tranquil, untouched by the war. "I wish we had a map of the area. It would make things a lot easier."

425

Ewan called Graham over. "What is the hardest area to get to?"

Graham shrugged. "I'm not sure. Perhaps the island by the marina?"

"Where did you come from again?" Ashley asked. "I was by the other marina, on the small island."

Graham pointed to an island in the distance. "I came from over there but I move around a lot."

"And how long have you lived there?" Ewan asked, watching Graham closely.

"I already told you a couple of years. Before I was just wandering around the city," Graham said. "But to be honest with you if the government was hiding the weapons, I doubt I would have been able to find them."

Ewan felt a sinking feeling in his stomach. For awhile there he allowed himself to hope but now he was feeling more discouraged than ever. Still he tried to put on a brave face for everyone he talked to.

Ewan took a break and went back to check on Hudson who was sitting in one of the cockpits, flipping controls.

"Any progress?" Ewan asked.

Hudson shook his head. "No, none of them are working. I can't even turn them on. I think the military disabled them before they abandoned them."

"Anything we can do?"

"I'm not sure, I'll try and think of something."

Ewan nodded, disappointed. "Okay, I'm going to the control tower, if you need anything that's where I'll be."

"Sure."

Ewan climbed the stairs, his feet echoing in the cement stairwell. He thought, back when he was living in the ROM with Tim, that everything would be alright once he met other people, that the loneliness would be gone. But now he felt lonelier than ever. Tim was gone. He supposed he still had Ashley and Dawn, but it wasn't the same.

He reached the air control room and looked out. He wanted to see if he could spot the ferry. There was nothing he could do if, for some reason, Christian hadn't made it across the water, but he felt productive doing it anyway. It was better than searching for non-existent weapons.

Ewan was surprised to find Dawn sitting in the control tower. She was staring at her wooden pendulum.

"What are you doing up here?"

"Not sure," she said, slipping her necklace into her shirt. "Thought it would be quiet here. The homo sapiens, they don't like me, father."

"Dawn, why did you lie to me about remembering the house?"

Dawn didn't say anything for a long while.

Ewan stepped up to the window. He could see the ferry on the opposite side of the water. He couldn't see Christian or any of the search party anywhere. He wasn't sure if that was a good sign or not.

"I guess I just wanted you to accept me. To believe I'm your daughter."

"Oh Sophie, I believe it, but some things are just hard to accept. I know it doesn't make much sense to you but that's the best way I can explain it."

"I . . . don't understand," Dawn said.

Ewan turned towards Dawn. "I'm not sure I fully understand it myself."

Ewan walked over and gave Dawn a hug. It felt strange wrapping his hands around Dawn's rough skin. Sophie had been so small and fragile while Dawn was broad-shouldered and looked like if she was hit by a dump truck she could get up again, uninjured.

"Dawn, I want you to do something for me."

"What is it?"

"I want you to get away from us. You need to survive. The Post Humans are going to come after us and they're not going to stop until they kill us. I don't want you to be collateral damage."

"What is . . . collateral damage?"

"It's being hurt unintentionally."

"I can't leave you father."

"Think of the future. I love you. I want a legacy. You can tell your children about me and they can tell their children about me." Even as Ewan said this he knew he was being ridiculous. Dawn was

427

a Post Human and they didn't have any children. They had no family — at least not in the conventional sense.

"What about the weapons?" Dawn asked. "If you had those then you could fight the Post Humans."

"There are no weapons, Dawn. It's just a rumour to try and keep people occupied."

"I have heard homo sapiens talk about love . . . what is it?"

"It's a feeling we have. I suppose it's what makes us human."

"Do you think I'm capable of love?"

Ewan took Dawn's round, smooth head in his hands and stared into her eyes. Somewhere behind those slim pupils was his daughter.

"Yes, I think you're capable of love."

By mid-afternoon Christian and his group had come back with some plants and a couple of mice to eat.

Afterwards, Ewan felt energized but they still didn't find any weapons.

Ewan took first watch that night. The Creatures gathered around the control tower in larger numbers this time, but they couldn't find a way past the barricade.

At midnight Ashley came to replace him, but even she seemed depressed and discouraged, barely saying a word to him. Ewan went downstairs, settling on the floor to sleep.

He was woken up a little while later by a familiar noise. He sat up and realized that Graham and Albert were wrestling.

Ewan jumped up and quickly separated them.

"He stole my soda," Albert said.

"I'm sure it's safely in your bag," Ewan said.

Albert dumped out his backpack. There were little bits and pieces of wire, batteries and string. "It's not here. I caught him going through my stuff."

Ewan turned to Graham who simply shook his head. "I wanted to make peace with him but he wouldn't listen to reason. He just attacked me, same as before."

"In the middle of the night?" Ewan said. "Can I see your pockets?"

"Why do you want to see them?" Graham said. "You don't believe me?"

"You've given me no reason to."

Graham shook his head and turned to go back to his spot on the floor but Ewan put a hand on his shoulder. "Empty your pockets."

Graham turned, staring at Ewan thoughtfully. "And what if I refuse?"

"It would make me believe you have something to hide, but why you would want to steal Albert's soda, I'm not sure."

Graham sighed and dug into his pocket. He pulled out Albert's squirt gun and dangled it in the air.

Albert gave a small shout and jumped towards Graham but he expected it this time and managed to dodge backwards.

"We can't put this in the trust of Albert," Graham said.

"He's never let me down before," Ewan said.

"We need to find out what's in this and duplicate it."

"Why are you so interested in this?" Ewan said. "And you were interested in the lab."

"Because like you, I don't believe there are any weapons on this island. It's just some silly rumour. This," Graham said, waving the squirt gun in the air, "Is the only thing that can help us now. People may not realize it now but when they do, they'll figure out that you could have prevented this they will turn on you."

Ewan grabbed Graham by the collar and shoved him up against the wall. The loud thud woke people up.

"What's going on?" somebody said.

"Meyer was trying to steal my soda," Albert said, excitedly.

"I want to see where you lived," Ewan said. "I want some proof that you are telling the truth."

"You'll have to swim," Graham warned.

"If you can make it then I can."

Ewan released Graham who straightened out his shirt.

"In the meantime stay away from Albert."

The Messenger

Ewan couldn't sleep for the rest of the night. He kept dreaming that he was being chased by the samurai and when he woke he thought he heard Tim next to him, but, of course, when he looked over he only saw Ashley sleeping soundly next to him.

In the morning Ewan, Ashley, and Graham set off across the island until they reached the south most corner of the island. There they veered east through the trees. They walked slowly, looking for any signs of the Creatures but the island seemed mostly barren. They passed the lighthouse and on their left side there were a cluster of smaller islands.

"How difficult is the swim?" Ashley asked.

"Not too difficult," Graham said. "Probably fifty meters at the best."

"Why did you kick Albert out of his company?" Ewan asked.

"Is that what this is all about?"

"No," Ewan said. "Ever since you arrived there has been something wrong."

"Kicking Albert out was purely a business decision. The company had simply outgrown him and he was holding progress back. I know he feels cheated and hurt by it but I made him more money than he could possibly spend in his life time," Graham said.

"He would have made money regardless."

"Yes but not as much as he did with me at the helm."

They fell silent until they reached a spot where Graham stopped. Across from them was a small island covered in trees.

"This is it?" Ewan asked, skeptically.

Graham nodded. "There are no Creatures over there. I promise."

"Alright," Ewan said. "Ashley will go first, Graham after and then I'll go last."

"Sounds like a plan."

Ewan and Graham watched as Ashley dove into the water. Ewan was skeptical that she would be able to make it across but she swam effortlessly, reaching the other side in about five minutes.

Ewan turned to Graham. "Your turn."

Graham nodded and dove into the water with equal gracefulness as Ashley.

Ewan waited only a few seconds before he dived in after Graham. Once over, he didn't want to give Graham a chance to escape.

Ewan was by far the weakest swimmer of the three and despite jumping in after Graham, he felt himself falling behind.

He didn't look up but concentrated on moving his arms and legs, keeping his body still. He tired quickly, feeling the oxygen seep from his body like a faulty tire. But he forced himself to continue. It took only another minute before he felt his arms and legs go heavy and it took every ounce of strength to continue.

Eventually he felt the water getting shallower and he allowed himself to relax slightly and look up. He was only a dozen or so feet away from the island so he put his head back down and started to swim again, reenergized.

When he reached the shore he crawled up out of the water and lay on his back.

Graham came towards him. He was soaking wet and breathing heavily as well. "I should really teach you how to swim better."

Graham unbuttoned his jacket and took out a knife. Ewan had a knife of his own shoved into his waist at the small of his back but he was too exhausted to reach for it. Instead he tried to crawl away but even that proved too difficult.

Luckily Ashley reacted fast. She picked up a three-foot-long log and swung it at Graham. She moved quickly and Graham had to stumble backwards in order to avoid her swing. This gave Ewan enough time to push himself to his feet. The blood rushed away from his head and he struggled to stay conscious.

But he managed to see Graham lunge at Ashley who used her superior reach to knock the knife down.

Ewan reached around and grabbed his knife. He faked a lunge at Graham which was enough to draw his attention away from Ashley.

"It's two against one," Ewan said. "You're not going to win this fight."

Graham didn't say anything; instead he just smiled, shifting his glance from Ashley to Ewan.

He stuck his knife towards Ewan which gave Ashley an opportunity to step towards him and with a huge swing she connected with his jaw. There was a loud crunching sound and Graham dropped his knife and crumpled to the ground.

Ewan, still not completely recovered, shuffled over to where Graham lay while Ashley grabbed his knife.

"Pat him down, make sure he's not carrying any other weapons," Ashley said.

Ewan searched Graham who was beginning to groan loudly but he didn't find any more weapons.

Ashley helped Ewan prop Graham up so he could speak.

"You're going to kill me?" Graham asked.

"Why did you lie to us?" Ewan asked.

"I was sent to scout you out."

"The cannibals sent you?"

Graham nodded. "Yes."

"The White Chief is your leader?"

"Was, not anymore."

"Who is?" Ashley asked but Ewan answered. "The samurai is."

"How do you know about Stu?" Graham asked.

"That's his name? Stu?"

"Yes. How did you know about him?"

Ewan didn't want to tell Graham about the nightmares he had about the samurai, chasing him down a dark corridor. "Where is this samurai now?"

"He's waiting for my return."

"He tracked us here?"

"Yes."

"How many people does he have?"

"I don't know."

Ashley took a step back and swung the log. Graham ducked his head and raised his arms. There was another loud popping sound as the log connected with Graham's fingers. Graham screamed as they bent backwards.

"If you don't want me to break your other hand I suggest you tell us the truth."

"I think close to fifty but they are true fighters. You will never be able to defeat them."

Ewan was silent while he thought. There must be some way to stop this useless bloodshed.

"If we let you go back to them, will you tell them about the Post Humans?"

"I can do that," Graham said slowly.

"We need to work together. We can't be killing each other. That's exactly what they want . . . for us to kill each other."

"I don't know if I can swim with this hand," Graham said, holding up his mangled hand.

"We'll go back and get Christian to come get you," Ewan said.

"Okay," Graham said, nodding.

"I want you to convince them. I mean really try."

Graham nodded, more forcefully this time. "I never wanted to fight to begin with."

"Ashley and I will," Ewan said, but before he could finish the sentence Ashley took her log and swung it at Graham, who never saw the blow coming. Ashley connected with his temple. Graham went down again but this time Ashley didn't relent. She stood over him, bashing his head in with the log.

"What are you doing? Ashley?" Ewan yelled, tearing Ashley away from Graham but by that time it was too late. Graham was a bloody mess. His legs spread out across the sandy floor.

Ewan knelt down, pressed his fingers against his neck, feeling for a pulse. When he didn't find one, he looked up at Ashley. "You killed him."

"You wanted to waste precious gas on him, for what? The cannibals will never side with us."

"You don't know that," Ewan yelled. "He was the only chance of avoiding more killing."

"These are the people who were going to eat Justin and Anthony."

"So is this revenge? Is that it?"

"The only thing he would have done was alerted them that we know about them."

Ewan thought of something. "My God, what about Christian?"

Christian was going to take another hunting party to see if they could find some more food.

"We need to get back," Ashley said.

The Vision

Stu had meditated for the better part of the last few days and it had done wonders for his body and mind. He had never felt sharper, more alert. He knew he was ready for what he must do.

When he heard the sound of a dozen feet squeezing along the unpacked snow, he opened his eyes. He saw a group of people coming towards him. They wore tattered clothes and most of them had their bones jutting out from their skin as if they were survivors of a concentration camp.

They stopped about ten meters away from Stu. They gave each other worried looks. Finally a large man with a scraggily beard and short hair stepped forward.

"Who are you?"

Stu stood up. "My name is Stu Baillie. What's yours?"

"Christian Boeving. What are you doing out here in the middle of the road?"

"I might ask you the same thing."

"You don't seem too surprised to see us," Christian said.

Stu raised his eyebrows. "Should I be?"

"You're armed. I must ask you to put down your weapon."

"You're not very trusting, are you?"

When Christian didn't reply, Stu nodded, and unbuckled his sword and placed it on the ground.

Stu saw Christian relax a little. "I don't mean you any harm," Stu said.

Christian took a step forward towards Stu but before he could reach him, an arrow came out of the shadows and struck Christian in the neck. He turned, his face full of surprise. He half raised his hands but before they could get to his neck he fell to his knees. Another arrow struck him in the chest and his large body fell forward into the cement.

"But they do," Stu said.

The savages ran from their hiding places and quickly attacked the rest of the humans who tried to escape, only to realize they were surrounded and outnumbered. There were loud cries but they were quickly stifled as the savages slaughtered the humans.

The attack didn't last more than a couple of minutes and once it was over Stu surveyed the corpses. "We're going to eat well today."

"We should attack at once," Kimi said. "Once they realize their hunting party doesn't return we will have lost the element of surprise."

"They'll think they were killed by the Oni," Stu said.

"Still, I think we should attack soon."

"We wait for Graham to come back."

"And what if Graham doesn't come back, White Chief? What if they have neutralized him?"

"Then we attack at night, when they least expect it."

They spent the day stripping the meat from the corpses and since Stu still wouldn't let them build a fire they ate the meat raw. It was tough and hard to swallow but afterwards Stu felt full. It was a feeling Stu had almost forgotten existed.

They spent most of the rest of the day waiting around for Graham. The savages were beginning to get restless and a couple of fights broke out among them.

Stu went to Kimi. "You need to control the troops. I'll execute them if I have to, just to make an example of them.

"Yes, White Chief."

"I'm going to go meditate, if you need me."

Stu went off to a street corner he used to meditate. It offered the advantage of being away from the camp but gave him a good vantage point if anybody tried to assassinate him. He still didn't fully trust the savages, although they seemed to have come to respect him when he took the name of the White Chief.

This time he fell into a deep meditation. Otakay and Chenoa appeared before him. They were holding hands and smiling at him. Their happiness irritated Stu.

"Why are you smiling?"

"You don't understand there are forces bigger than us at work."

"What are you talking about?"

"We're talking about the Magnetar virus. You can't stop it. It will eventually wipe out the human race. The Post Humans will win, no matter what."

Stu smiled. "You're wrong about that. We will prevail."

"Just like the Neanderthals and the Denisovans? Homo sapiens will die out and they haven't even been around for a third of the time their ancestors homo erectus were."

"No, we will get the weapon used to kill the Oni. Graham will get it."

"Graham?" Otakay laughed. "He's not coming back to you."

Suddenly Graham appeared next to Otakay and Chenoa. At first, Stu didn't recognize him. His face was bashed in, his eye had come out of its socket.

"Otakay is right. We can win the battle, but we can't win the war. The enemy is far superior."

Stu opened his eyes, jolted back to reality. The sky was clear and bright. Perhaps it would warm up soon and the snow would melt.

He stood up, dusted the snow off of his kimono and went back to camp. Kimi greeted him formally.

"I trust your meditation proved satisfactory?"

Stu was still a little shaken and he forced himself to smile. "Yes, I have to say it was. We're going to attack tonight."

The Final Battle

Ewan woke with a start from Ashley's shaking. Despite his exhaustion, he again had difficulty falling sleep and he wondered the last time he had been able to have a decent rest.

"The ferry is coming across," she whispered, urgently.

"What time is it?" he asked, suddenly alert. When Christian hadn't come back with his hunting party he immediately feared the worse.

"You think it's Christian?" Ashley asked.

"I think we need to prepare for the worst," Ewan said. "Wake everybody who can fight and make sure they're ready."

They aroused everybody quickly. At first, the survivors looked around confused but it didn't take long for them to realize danger was closing in on them. Ewan knew they didn't have much time to prepare. The ferry would soon be across. Somewhere a child started crying.

Ewan estimated they had over a hundred people, both men and women. They had large knives and spears fashioned from tree branches as weapons. Not the most convincing army, but it would have to do.

"We need to protect the control tower," Ewan said.

"From what?" he heard Albert call out from the darkness.

"Go back to sleep old man," Ewan whispered.

When Ewan and Ashley had come back without Graham, they had to explain everything that Graham had told them. Albert had been most upset that he hadn't been the one to kill Graham, but nevertheless he had given Ashley a congratulatory hug. "Well done, lass," he had said. "I always hated that man's guts."

Albert now stared with an intense glare that Ewan had never seen before. "They're here, aren't they?" Albert asked Ewan.

"We think so," Ewan said. "Either way we need to go down to meet them."

"Then I'm coming," Albert said.

"No, you aren't," Ewan said. "You need to stay here and protect everyone."

But Albert couldn't be persuaded. "Walder, we're wasting time arguing."

Ewan let out a large sigh. "Alright but stay close to Dawn."

They slipped out the door, attacking the Creatures that were still there. The Creatures seemed weak – perhaps from lack of a food source – and were easily overwhelmed. Once all the Creatures were dead, the humans barricaded the door again. Once that was done they went down to the dock to greet the ferry.

They reached the shore just as the ferry was pulling up. Ewan tried to peer through the darkness to see who was at the helm but he couldn't see anything through the night.

Dark waves lapped against the shore, making a hard slapping sound. Ewan held his breath waiting for the inevitable to happen. Who would jump off the ferry's side? Would it be the Post Humans? Something else?

The boat didn't slow as it reached the shore and crashed into the ground, smashing the bow. The loud snapping of wood smashing against gravel and dirt echoed through the quiet night.

"Hold it," Ewan said. "Weapons at the ready."

But nothing happened. The ferry's motor kept running but it was stuck. They waited but nobody came out. Ewan scanned the boat for signs of activity but nobody seemed to be aboard. Ewan held his breath, not daring to speak. They waited for what seemed like forever.

"Okay, let's go see what happened," Ewan said.

They boarded the boat quickly and did a quick search and found, indeed, it was empty. The wheel had been jammed in place with a couple of rocks.

"It's a false alarm," Ewan said.

"Perhaps they just wanted to scare us," Ashley replied.

But before Ewan could nod he heard shouting from outside. Everybody rushed to the window. Outside, to Ewan's left he could see the cannibals running towards them, fanning out. Their bodies slick with water. Ewan realized what had happened. They must have swum across, using the ferry as a decoy and had now out flanked them.

The survivors wasted no time and charged the cannibals. A few arrows flew through the air and struck the survivors. There were screams and shouts. In less than a minute the two sides met, colliding with each other.

Ewan jumped off the boat and ran towards the battle. He could feel adrenaline crushing his chest, thumping against his skull. The sounds that were so clear and fresh suddenly became muted and distant. Ewan struggled to focus to remain sharp.

He looked around and saw Ashley and Dawn were beside him. The cannibals had better weapons than the survivors, that was evident from the moment they started to fight but Ewan was surprised to find the survivors were equally as ferocious as the cannibals. They knew they were fighting for more than their lives, but the very survival of the human race.

Ewan smashed into a line of cannibals, dodging and shifting their attacks. To his right he saw Dawn smashing the cannibals with her fists. A cannibal attacked her from the left; she dodged, grabbed the spear and snapped it into two. The cannibal's eyes went wide and he turned to run but Ashley quickly ran him down.

"We need to find Albert," Ashley yelled.

Ewan surveyed the battle field, looking for Albert but he couldn't see him through the fighting. The scrapes and clangs of spears and knives and swords reverberated across the battlefield.

A cannibal appeared with a large spear and struck at Ewan. He dodged backwards, almost losing his balance but he then rocked onto the balls of his feet and struck with his knife. The cannibal knocked the thrust away easily and elbowed Ewan in the jaw.

Ewan felt his mouth fill with blood as he lifted his hand to his mouth. But Ewan had no time to think as the cannibal jumped at him again. Ewan collapsed to one knee, the spear just missing his right shoulder and as he did, he stuck his knife upwards, hitting soft flesh. Ewan pulled the knife out of the cannibal's stomach and attacked again but this time the cannibal managed to dodge and mount an attack of his own.

Ewan backed away, feeling the cannibal was tiring as his blood was oozing from his body. The cannibal charged forward but Ewan kept shifting sideways and backwards. Eventually the cannibal made a lazy attack and Ewan pounced, grabbing the man's right wrist and then digging the blade deep into the cannibal's chest. The cannibal let out a last gurgle of air before collapsing onto the ground.

Ewan pulled the knife from the limp body and looked up. There was a large melee of flesh and muscles. Blood sprayed everywhere and soon the soft ground was soaked with it.

"We need to try and break a hole in their attack," Ewan yelled at Ashley, who was a couple of yards away finding. "I think they are weakest on the left."

Ashley killed a cannibal and then shuffled over to Ewan. "What?"

"We need to break through," Ewan repeated.

Ashley nodded in agreement and they made their way to the left of the battlefield, killing cannibals as they went.

They had reached the thinnest part of the cannibal's line when Ewan saw the samurai appear from the darkness. He seemed even more terrifying than he did in Ewan's dreams. The white kimono he wore was drenched in blood. His sword was dripping as it sliced through human flesh. The samurai seemed to move effortlessly, unafraid of anything, attacking and killing with little effort.

"We need to kill the samurai," Ashley said.

Ewan felt his throat go dry but he managed to nod. "Let's do it."

They fought their way over to the samurai but before they got to him, they bumped into Albert. He had somehow managed to grab one of the cannibal's spears and was swinging it around, using more like a sword than a spear.

"Albert, you need to fall back," Ewan said. "Go back to the boat."

"I'm not going anywhere Walder," Albert said, smiling gleefully.

But those were the last words he spoke.

The samurai appeared from out of the darkness, shuffled over and with one motion sliced off Albert's neck. It was a clean cut and Albert's head tumbled to the ground. His body stayed in the air for a moment longer as if it was unsure what had just happened but then it too fell to the ground.

Ewan didn't register what had happened right away. He couldn't believe what he had just seen. It had happened so fast.

"Albert," he said, barely above a whisper. He then fell to the ground.

He looked up at the samurai who smiled menacingly down at him. The samurai looked just like he had in his dreams.

"Sayonara," the samurai said, lifting his bloody sword.

Ewan felt too paralysed to move. He just stared up at the samurai, hoping it would end as quickly as it had for Albert.

But before the samurai could deliver his blow, Dawn smashed into him. The samurai fell to the ground but quickly tucked himself into a roll and came up standing. He had lost his sword in the collision but drew a knife from his belt.

Dawn attacked but the samurai was quick and dodged her blows. Ewan had never seen someone move so quickly. The samurai faked with a series of moves and then spun and plunged the knife into the side of Dawn. Dawn let out a loud gasp then knocked the samurai over with a backhand.

The samurai was slow to get up this time but he managed to scramble and collect his sword.

Ewan glanced at Dawn who had pulled the knife from her body and was holding the wound with her large hand.

Ewan immediately knew what he had to do. If the survivors had any hope of winning, he would have to draw the samurai away from the battle.

Ewan stepped up to the samurai, holding his large knife. He knew it was a pitiful weapon against a samurai sword but it was all he had.

"I saw you in my dreams," Ewan said. "You don't look nearly as bad in real life."

The samurai ignored the taunt and stepped towards Dawn.

I must protect her, Ewan thought. *I must protect everyone.*

He ran and blocked the samurai's path. The samurai crouched and attacked but Ewan was ready for it, each time jumping away.

"I'm the leader," Ewan said. "Come try and kill me."

"You're a coward," the samurai yelled.

"You can't touch me," Ewan said, laughing.

The samurai stepped forward but each time Ewan stepped back, away from the battle. This seemed to enrage the samurai who became emboldened with each step.

Ewan sensed the time was right and he turned and ran for his life. He ran as fast as he could towards the trees, only looking over his shoulder once to make sure the samurai was following him.

"You can't run from me," the samurai yelled.

Ewan cut through the trees, not caring if he encountered any Creatures until he found the pathway on the eastern side of the island.

He ran along the pathway until he reached the lighthouse. There he stopped and looked around him. The samurai was nowhere to be seen.

Had he double backed to the battle? Had he decided to break down the airport building? Ewan waited there for a few minutes, breathing heavily but just as he decided he would go back he saw a movement in the darkness and a glimmer of white.

Ewan cut across the ground, heading the way they had gone earlier with Graham. Ewan didn't look back this time but could hear the sound of the samurai behind him.

Ewan had no plan except to keep the samurai occupied as long as possible and away from the fighting where he could do the most damage.

On a whim, Ewan cut to the left sharply and made his way through the park with the statues of turtles. He vaguely remembered that the park was named after the children's story Franklin the Turtle.

Tim had never cared for the story about Franklin but Sophie wanted them read to her over and over again. It usually fell to Amy to read to Sophie since Ewan had disliked the stories almost as much as Tim had.

Ewan jumped the fence and passed the different statues and the overgrown gardens. He looked behind him but couldn't see the samurai. Perhaps he lost him or perhaps he had turned around.

It didn't matter now. Either way, Ewan felt he had no choice but to continue.

He found himself winding along a small pathway towards a small auditorium. He supposed that once there had been plays and shows put on for the kids. Once again he thought of Amy, Tim and Sophie.

Had they ever been to the gardens before? He couldn't remember. Why hadn't he taken them here when they had the chance?

Ewan passed the auditorium and came to a small field which he crossed. Halfway across, he tripped over something in the snow. He looked and saw there was a large lock protruding from the ground.

Ewan wiped away the snow and found a hatch. It looked newer than the surrounding area, although the lock was old and brittle, probably from the extreme cold.

Ewan dug around and quickly found a large rock that he used to hammer on the lock. It took several tries but the lock broke away and Ewan was able to lift the hatch. He peered down into the darkness but couldn't see anything. A stench of stale air wafted up from the shaft and into Ewan's nostrils and down his throat, causing him to cough loudly.

Just as he was about to descend into the hole, Ewan looked up and saw the samurai up on a hill about twenty yards away. Ewan thought about jumping out of the hatch and running for it but instead he started to climb downwards into the darkness, knowing he would be trapped and there was no way out.

Ewan didn't look up. He just kept lowering his body, rung after rung until he felt his feet touch solid ground. He blinked, trying to get his bearings but there was only darkness. He stumbled along the cement corridor, unable to see anything, his hands searching out in front of him.

He felt something strange, as if he had been there before. Then he remembered that his corridor had been the one in his dreams. The one the samurai had chased him down. He didn't have time to stop and think what it meant. He quickened his pace until he was almost jogging through the darkness.

Only once did he stop to listen. The samurai's footsteps were soft and light but even he couldn't hide their sound in the tight space.

This is not good, Ewan thought. *Not good at all.*

Ewan resumed onward. He didn't know how long he had been going forward before he came to a large room. There was a crack of light coming from somewhere above. Perhaps a shaft of light was seeping though from the surface. Wherever it came from, he could see that on the walls were racks and racks of what appeared to be bombs. He let in a gasp of air as he realized the amount of firepower contained in this room. He wondered if any of these bombs still worked.

Albert can figure it out, he thought to himself, before realizing Albert was dead. Images of Albert dying flashed through his mind and a feeling of hatred swelled up in Ewan. It felt foreign, something he had never really felt before, even towards the Creatures who had killed Amy.

Ewan quickly pushed the thought away and continued through the room. The next room contained missiles. He looked around, wondering how large this underground bunker was. He walked into the next room where he found an overhead bulb light still working. How was that possible? Where was the energy for the small bulb coming from?

But he didn't let himself linger on the problem for long because his eyes shifted and he saw racks of hundreds of machine guns lining the wall from floor to ceiling. He grabbed the nearest gun and held it in his arms. It looked old and slightly rusted around the edges. But he still felt an immediate thrill of power as he pointed it at the entrance way he had just come from.

He pulled the trigger but it wouldn't budge. Was it so rusted it wouldn't work? But then he remembered something like that happened on television before.

These things have safeties, Ewan thought. He felt around in the darkness until he came to a switch which he flicked. The trigger snapped back but nothing happened. He felt around the gun again before stupidly realizing it wasn't loaded.

Some soldier I am, Ewan thought.

He desperately looked around for ammunition but couldn't see any in the darkness. He saw there was another room at the end and he ran towards it. He felt dizzy with adrenaline. He stepped in and was happy to find it was filled with bright metallic objects, lined up on the walls.

He had no idea what sort of ammunition there was, there seemed to be all sorts of sizes but eventually he fumbled around and found some that fit into the magazine. He heard a satisfying click as he inserted the magazine back into the gun.

He turned around and raced back the way he'd come. He stopped at the first room where it narrowed into the corridor and knelt on one knee and pointed the gun.

At first, Ewan couldn't see anything but then a white shape appeared in his vision as if it was a ghost. Ewan pressed the trigger down, the gun recoiled on his shoulder but nothing happened. He pressed the trigger again and he could feel the hammer but something was jammed.

The samurai seemed to realize what was happening, gave a strange battle cry, and charged him, raising his sword. Ewan felt his blood pumping through his body as everything seemed to slow down around him. He could see every little detail on the samurai's face, the hatred in his eyes, the crease on his large forehead and the concentration on his cruel lips.

The gun suddenly felt heavy in his hands; his fingertips moist with sweat. He kept holding down the trigger. The click, click, click sound echoed throughout the chamber.

Ewan blinked and then looked down at his gun. The samurai was only a few paces away. A shell fell from the gun and suddenly there was an explosion of light and sound and Ewan was knocked backwards. The kick from the gun sprayed bullets upwards.

When he looked again, Ewan saw the samurai slumped over just a foot away from him, blood poured from his body from several bullet wounds.

Ewan stared at the body for what seemed like an eternity. He had killed the samurai.

Home

Ewan stood impatiently with Ashley and Dawn outside of the ROM. Ewan and Ashley each held a shiny machine gun in their hands. The hard metal still felt cold and awkward. It made Ewan think of ol' Bessy, Tim's small revolver, and it made him miss Tim even more.

But we will be reunited soon, Ewan thought.

It was midday, probably around mid-March, Ewan figured, although he had lost track of the seasons a long time ago. Regardless of when it was, it was turning out to be a fairly warm day. Hovering just above freezing and the sun glistened off of the museum's jutting glass panels. Soon the ice would melt, winter would be over and spring would allow plants to grow again.

Ashley turned to Ewan. "How are you feeling?"

Ewan nodded and smiled. He tried to say something but for some reason his mouth felt frozen over and he was unable to speak.

After he had killed the samurai, he had gone back to the battle. It had been a gruesome affair, blood and bodies everywhere. But the survivors had managed to escape back to one of the airport hangars where they remained barricaded up. The cannibals looked to be strategizing when Ewan stepped from the woods with his machine gun.

He fired several bullets in the air and quickly got the cannibals to surrender. Ewan was glad. There had been enough bloodshed for one day.

Through the next several days Ewan had convinced the cannibals they should work together against the Post Humans. After learning Stu Baillie had been killed, they readily agreed. There was still a lot of work to be done but Ewan felt they had made some positive steps forward.

Ewan blinked and forgot about the past when he heard the soft sound of crunching footsteps.

"Here he comes," Ashley said. "You sure you're ready for this?"

Ewan nodded again, holding his breath.

A Post Human came from around the corner, stopping halfway up the block. It was about Ewan's height with long arms and legs. Its skin was a mixture of colours, part rainbow, part chameleon, seemingly changing with every step, blending into the background.

Ewan strained his eyes to look at the Post Human. They really were magnificent, perhaps one day they would be able to work together and rebuild.

Perhaps.

"Tim?" Ewan said.

Although in Post Human form, there was no doubt it was Tim. Ewan wasn't sure how he knew — something in Tim's eyes, something that never really changed despite everything.

Ewan dropped his gun and ran towards Tim, barely hearing Ashley yelling from behind him.

"Dad," Tim said and ran towards him. They met in the middle and embraced. Ewan felt Tim's strength as he wrapped his arms around him. Tim looked at Ashley.

"Hi Ley-ley."

Ewan began to cry uncontrollably. How many nights had he dreamt of this? How many times had he replayed this moment in his mind? Perhaps it wasn't exactly how he envisioned it but he would take it. After everything that had happened, everything they had both been through, yes, he would take things as they were.

Ewan had held his emotions in when they had buried Albert Winkler on Toronto Island, nowhere near giving him the proper send-off that the genius deserved but under the circumstances it would have to do. It was more than most people got. They buried the others who had died separately.

Ewan had said some meaningless words that gave no comfort to anybody. There was a lot of sorrow but there was also something else.

Justin and Anthony had taken Albert's death particularly hard and even some of the other survivors had cried at the funeral. The survivors felt hopeful. Nobody had felt hopeful since the Outbreak. They had their freedom and now had weapons to protect themselves.

Ewan was also saddened to hear of Christian's death, although he supposed he had already known when the ferry had arrived empty. The cannibals told Ewan about the ambush but left out a lot of detail. Ewan didn't ask. He didn't want a reason to hate them.

"Does this mean they accept our terms?" Ewan said to Tim.

"Yes, Dad, I'm free."

Ewan had sent Dawn to broker peace with the Post Humans. Once the Post Humans had learned about the underground weapons, Ewan was able to negotiate a truce with them. Ewan guessed, correctly, that the Post Humans had no stomach to fight a war of nutrition, especially against a side that had suddenly gained a huge advantage. Ewan had made one of the conditions that he got Tim back.

"Tim, I would like you to see your sister," Ewan said.

"Sophie? She's alive?"

Dawn walked up shyly, her head slightly bowed. "Hi Tim."

"Sophie, is that really you?"

"Yes, brother."

Tim went over and hugged Dawn. She looked over at Ewan who nodded, *it's okay.* Dawn gave a strangely human smile before returning the hug.

Ewan laughed and looked up towards the sky. It was a brilliant blue colour — the colour of an endless, peaceful ocean.

Thank you Amy, thanks for watching over us, Ewan thought.

And for the first time Ewan felt Amy was actually looking out for them.

He thought about when she looked up at him with her large brown eyes, her life leaving her body, like water gurgling from a bathtub and his dying promise to her. He missed Amy but she could wait a little longer for him.

Then Ewan remembered the beautiful stallion they had seen walking back to the ROM. How it galloped in the snow, its neck stretched upright and mane flowing like a cape. It had been a miracle and here was another one.

Ewan looked around at the survivors and the cannibals. They were still weary of each other but he hoped in time that would change. They had a society to rebuild.

"Come on, let's go back inside," Ewan said. "We have a lot of catching up to do."

The End

About the authors:

Guido Baechler was born in Lucerne, Switzerland. At the age of 19 he married and moved to the Sunshine State Florida where he started a family with two boys. He is a filmmaker, producer and writer - https://tinyurl.com/GuidoBaechler During the past two decades he travelled the world, living on several continents and made Australia, Texas and Canada his homes. During the second decade he started developing the story you are about to read. The project was known under R(e)Evolution as an early stage movie idea, later it became registered with WGA under the working title "Cause & Effect" and finally made its book release as re.EVOLUTION. This is Guido's first book and he felt it was best to team up with Joel Mark Harris, an acclaimed writer. re.EVOLUTION is the first part of a Trilogy.

Guido is working with Jeridoo Universe www.jeridoo.ch / www.jeridoo.com to produce a 5-year limited television event of re.EVOLUTION. Twitter/Instagram @guidobaechler www.fb.com/GuidoBaechler

Joel Mark Harris graduated from journalism school in 2007. He is the author of four books. He also wrote and produced the feature-length film Neutral Territory. Joel has won countless awards as an author, screenwriter and producer, including the Pinnacle Achievement Award for Best Thriller.
He is the founder of Story Laboratory, a company that helps writers, filmmakers and other artists market their work.
He lives in Vancouver, Canada with his girlfriend. You can visit him at joelmarkharris.com or on twitter @joelmarkharris.

Made in the USA
Columbia, SC
13 April 2018